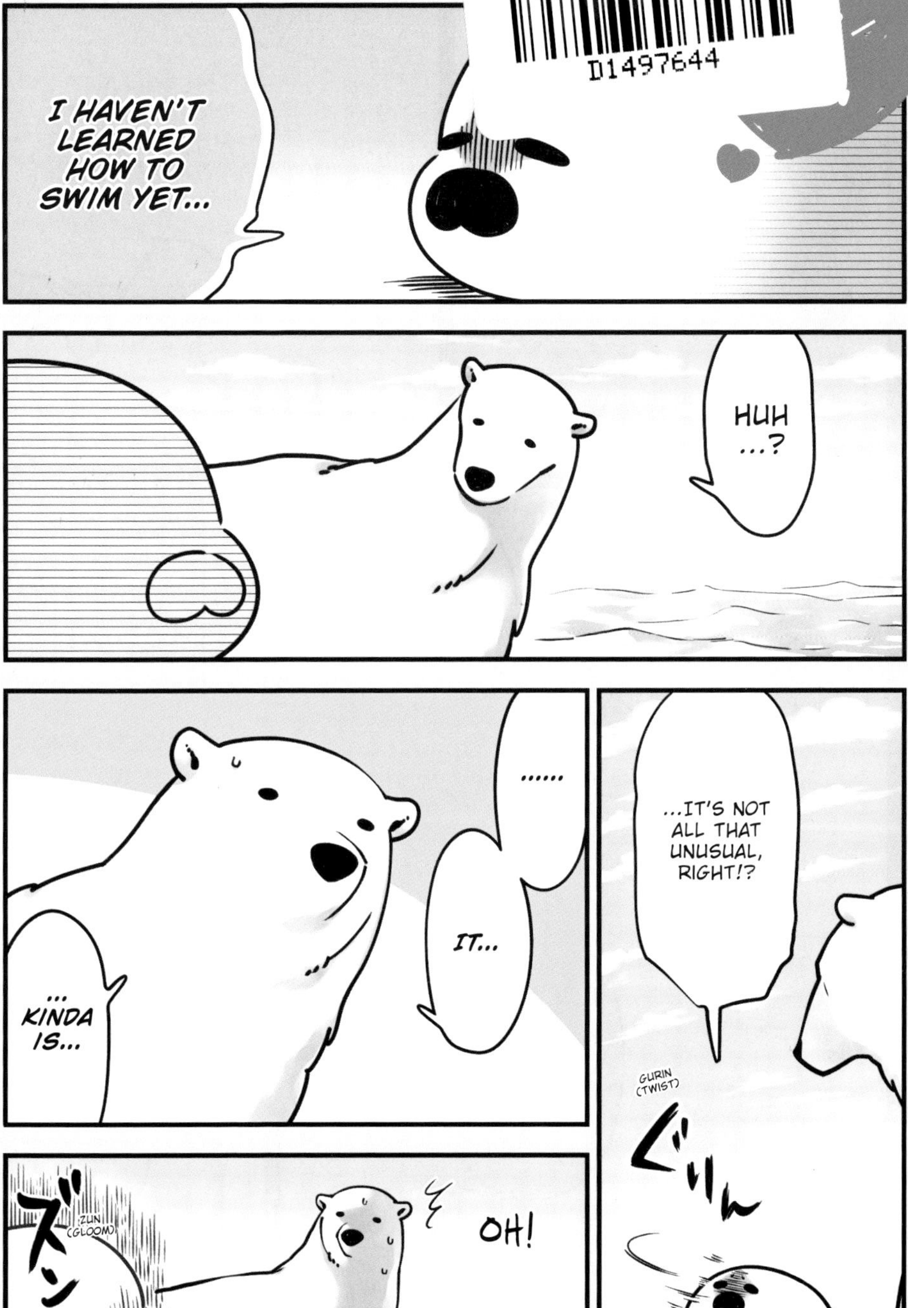
I HAVEN'T LEARNED HOW TO SWIM YET...
HUH ...?
...IT'S NOT ALL THAT UNUSUAL, RIGHT!?
GURIN (TWIST)
......
IT...
... KINDA IS...
OH!
ZUN (GLOOM)

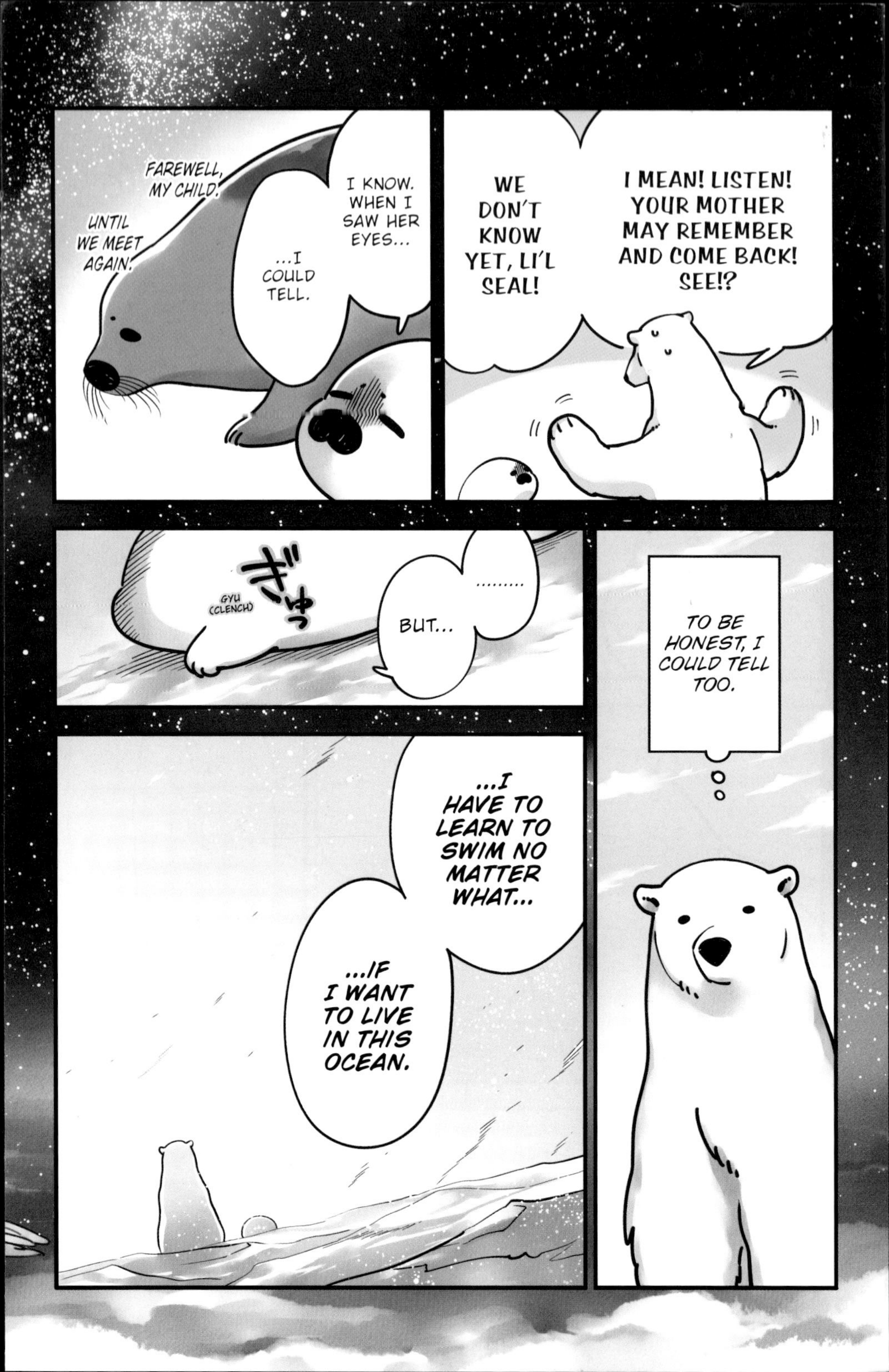
I MEAN! LISTEN! YOUR MOTHER MAY REMEMBER AND COME BACK! SEE!?
WE DON'T KNOW YET, LI'L SEAL!
I KNOW. WHEN I SAW HER EYES...
...I COULD TELL.
FAREWELL, MY CHILD!
UNTIL WE MEET AGAIN!
TO BE HONEST, I COULD TELL TOO.
....
BUT...
ぎゅっ
GYU (CLENCH)
...I HAVE TO LEARN TO SWIM NO MATTER WHAT...
...IF I WANT TO LIVE IN THIS OCEAN.

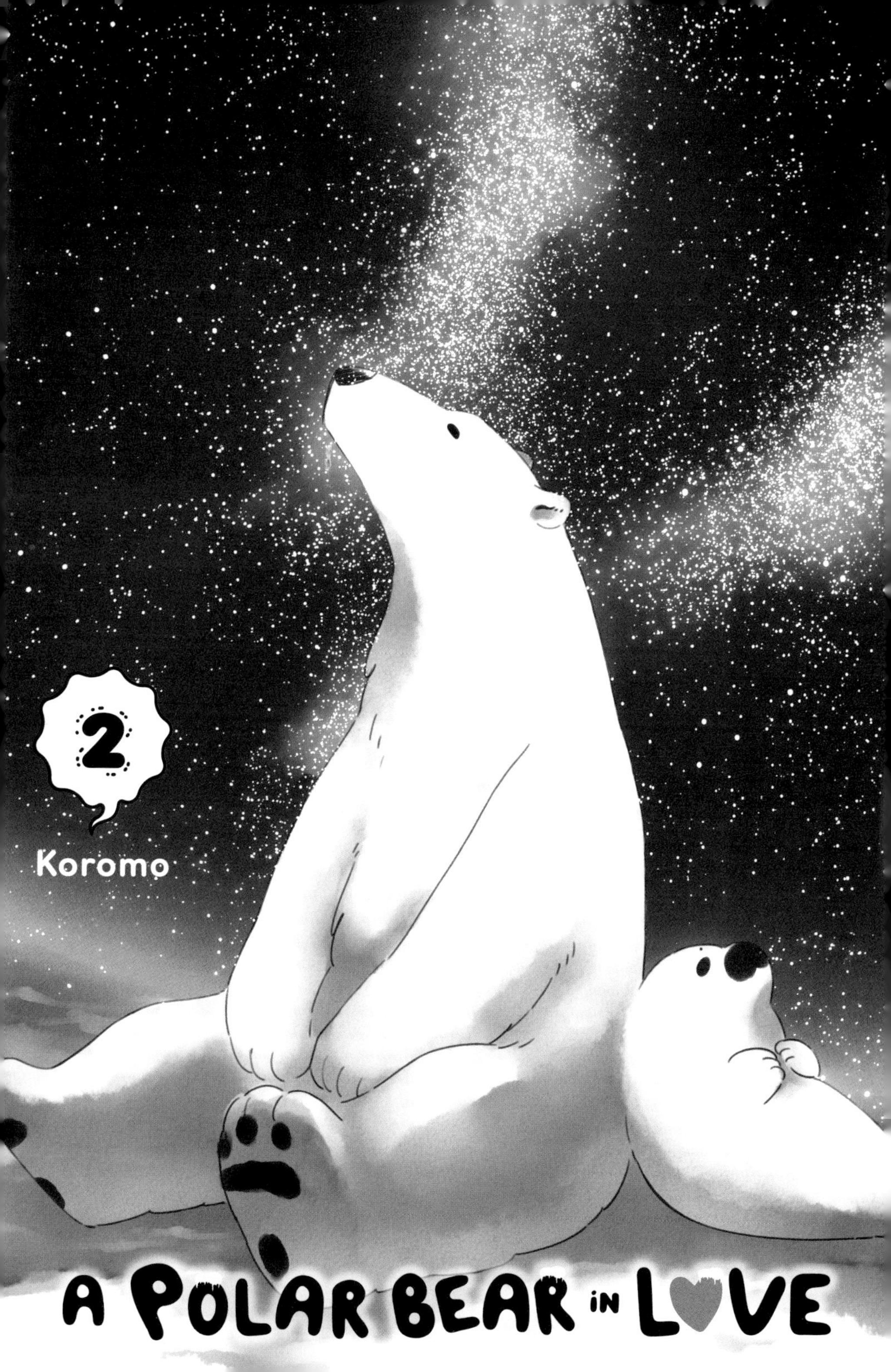
2
Koromo
A POLAR BEAR IN LOVE

contents

NO NEED TO WORRY

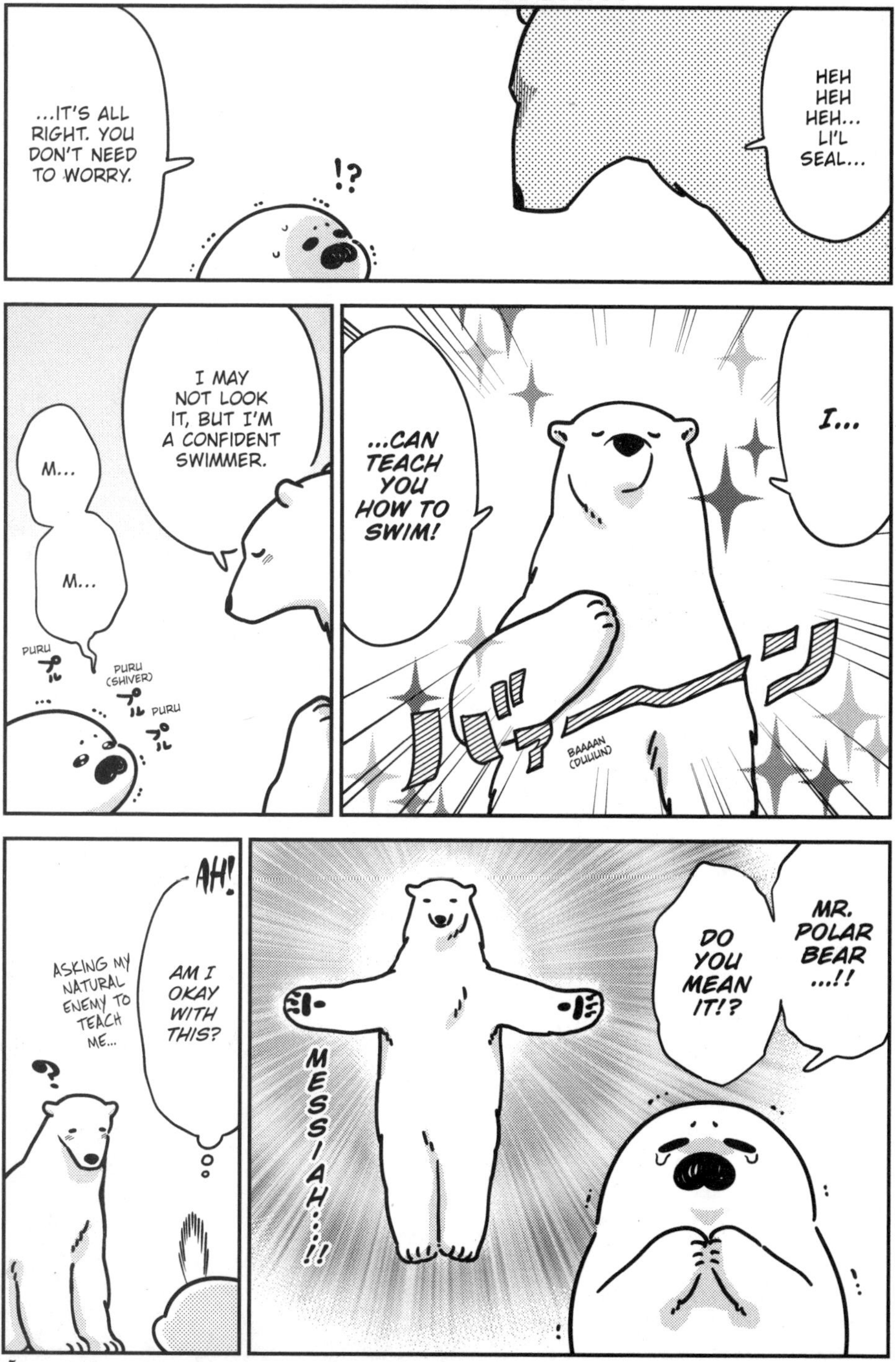
HEH HEH HEH... LI'L SEAL...
!?
...IT'S ALL RIGHT. YOU DON'T NEED TO WORRY.
I...
...CAN TEACH YOU HOW TO SWIM!
BAAAAN (DUUUN)
I MAY NOT LOOK IT, BUT I'M A CONFIDENT SWIMMER.
M...
M...
PURU
PURU (SHIVER)
PURU
MR. POLAR BEAR...!!
DO YOU MEAN IT!?
MESSIAH...!!
AH!
AM I OKAY WITH THIS?
ASKING MY NATURAL ENEMY TO TEACH ME...
?

SOMETHING IMPORTANT

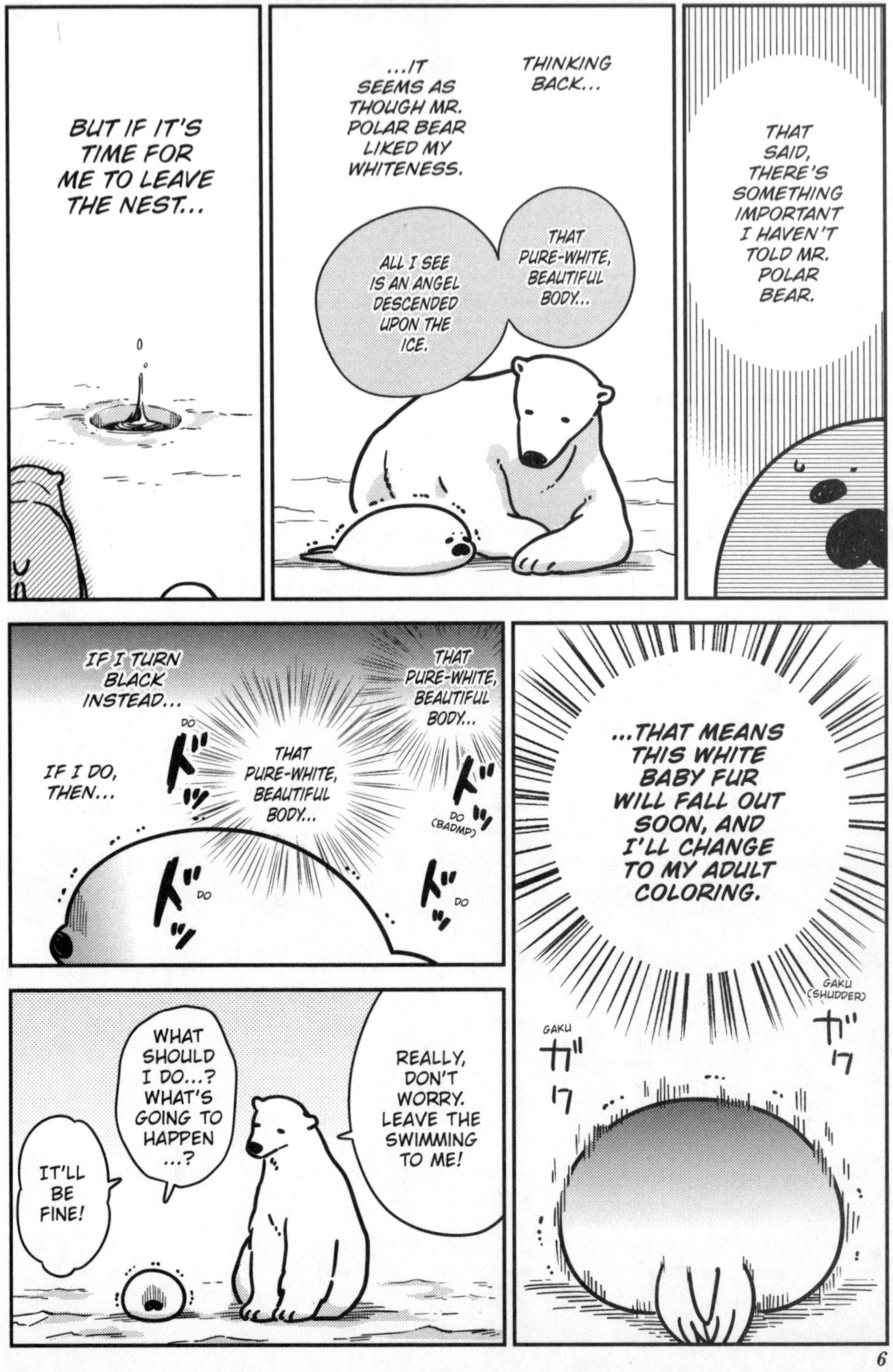

BUT IF IT'S TIME FOR ME TO LEAVE THE NEST...
THINKING BACK...
...IT SEEMS AS THOUGH MR. POLAR BEAR LIKED MY WHITENESS.
ALL I SEE IS AN ANGEL DESCENDED UPON THE ICE.
THAT PURE-WHITE, BEAUTIFUL BODY...
THAT SAID, THERE'S SOMETHING IMPORTANT I HAVEN'T TOLD MR. POLAR BEAR.
...THAT MEANS THIS WHITE BABY FUR WILL FALL OUT SOON, AND I'LL CHANGE TO MY ADULT COLORING.
GAKU (SHUDDER)
ガク
GAKU
ガク
IF I TURN BLACK INSTEAD...
IF I DO, THEN...
THAT PURE-WHITE, BEAUTIFUL BODY...
THAT PURE-WHITE, BEAUTIFUL BODY...
DO
ドッ
DO (BADMP)
ドッ
DO
ドッ
DO
ドッ
WHAT SHOULD I DO...? WHAT'S GOING TO HAPPEN...?
IT'LL BE FINE!
REALLY, DON'T WORRY. LEAVE THE SWIMMING TO ME!

LOST CHILD

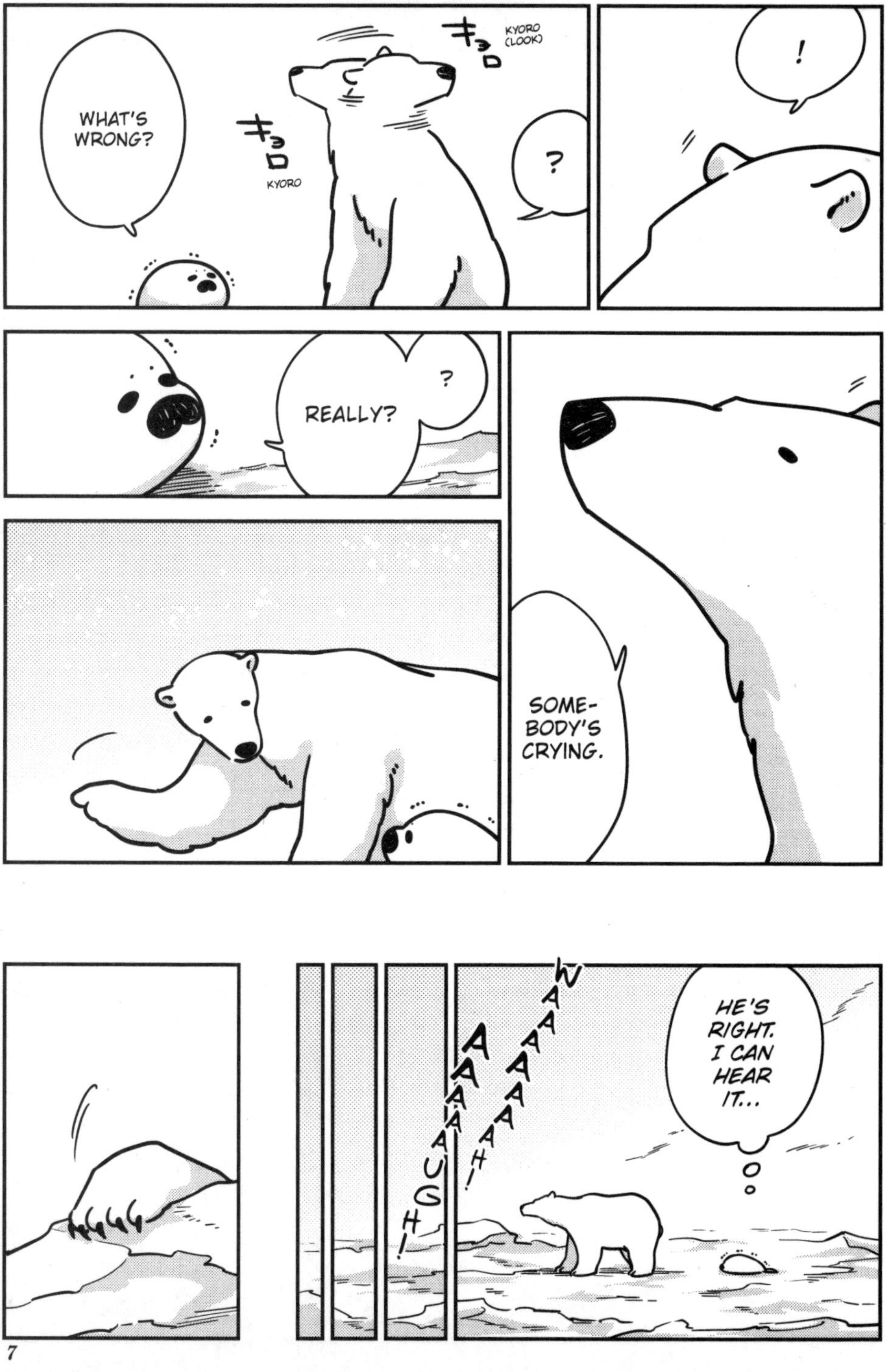
!
KYORO (LOOK)
?
KYORO
WHAT'S WRONG?
SOME-BODY'S CRYING.
?
REALLY?
HE'S RIGHT. I CAN HEAR IT...
WAAAAAAH!
AAAAAAUGH!

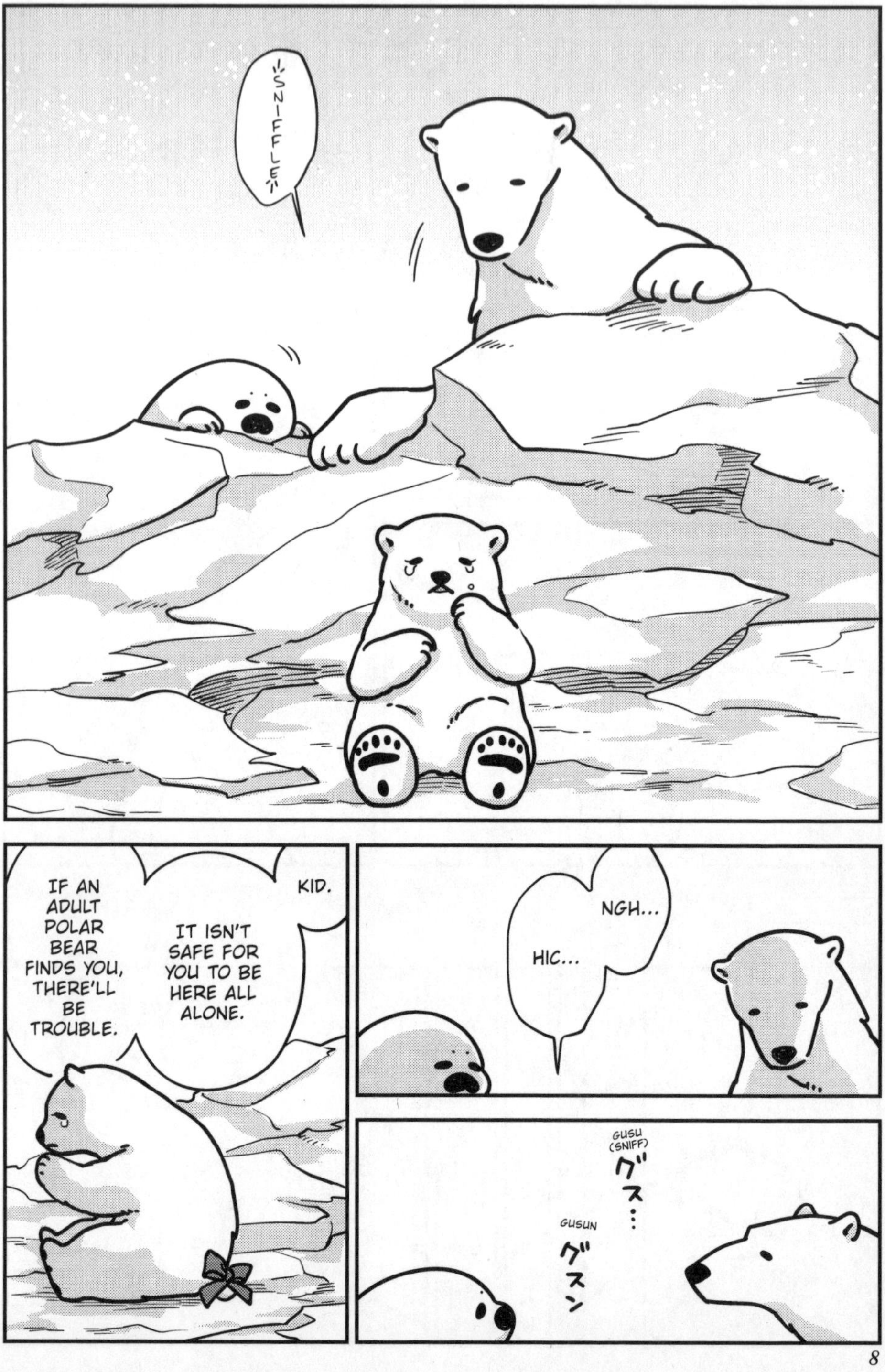
SNIFFLE
NGH...
HIC...
GUSU (SNIFF)
グス…
GUSUN
グスン
KID.
IT ISN'T SAFE FOR YOU TO BE HERE ALL ALONE.
IF AN ADULT POLAR BEAR FINDS YOU, THERE'LL BE TROUBLE.

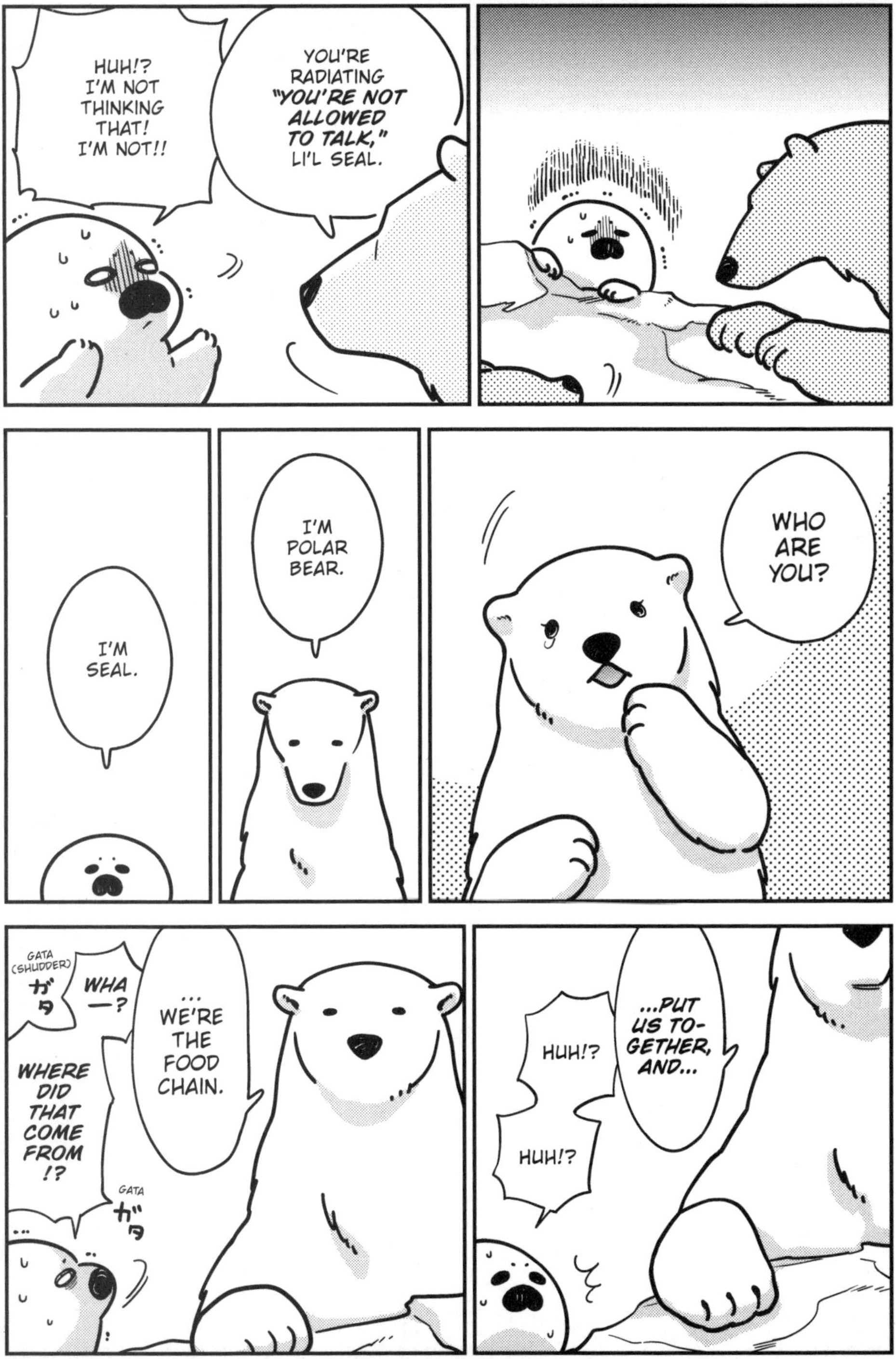
YOU'RE RADIATING "YOU'RE NOT ALLOWED TO TALK," LI'L SEAL.
HUH!? I'M NOT THINKING THAT! I'M NOT!!
WHO ARE YOU?
I'M POLAR BEAR.
I'M SEAL.
...PUT US TO-GETHER, AND...
HUH!?
HUH!?
... WE'RE THE FOOD CHAIN.
WHA—?
GATA (SHUDDER)
ガタ
WHERE DID THAT COME FROM!?
GATA
ガタ
...

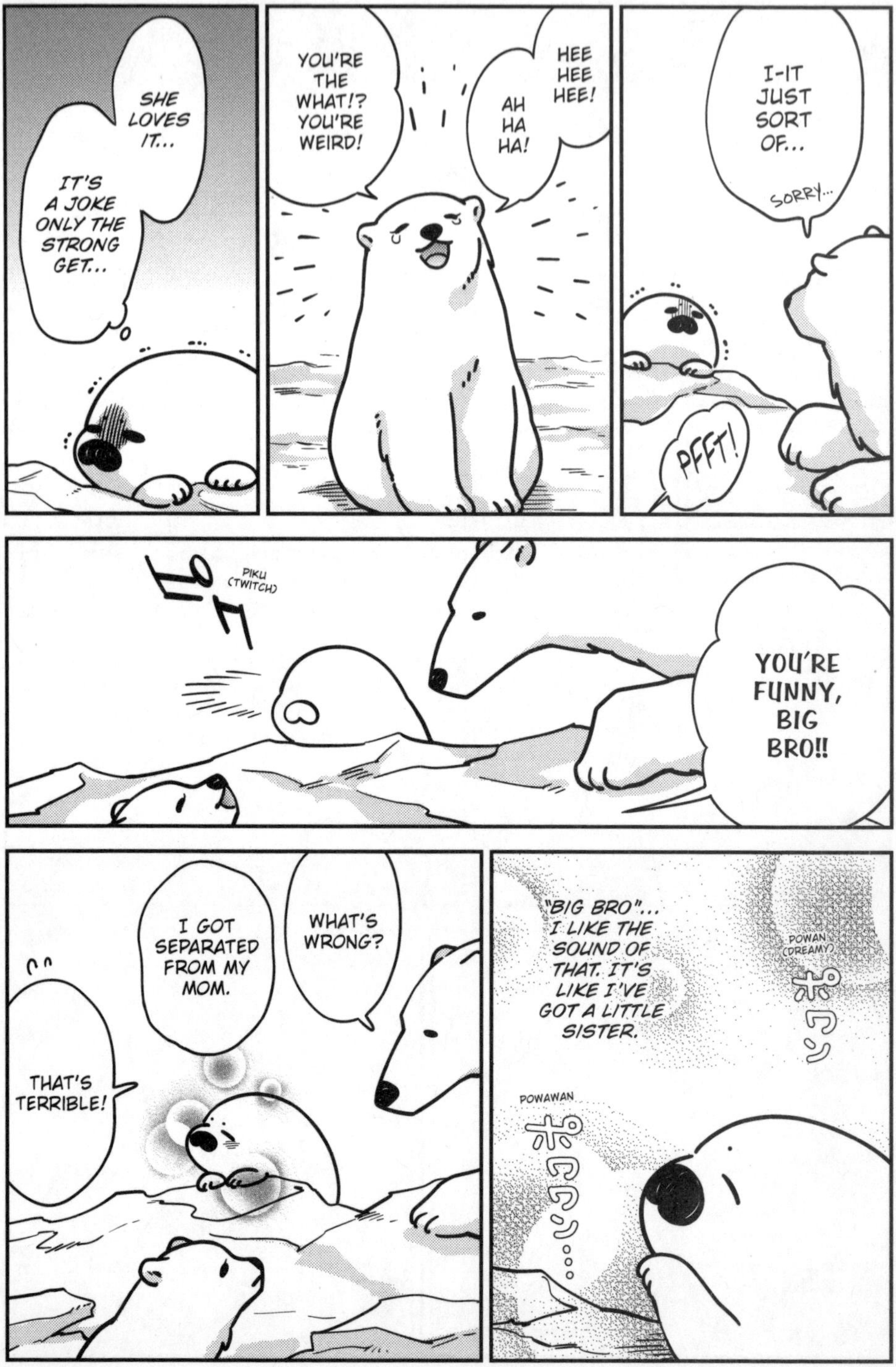
I-IT JUST SORT OF...
SORRY...
PFFT!
HEE HEE HEE!
AH HA HA!
YOU'RE THE WHAT!? YOU'RE WEIRD!
SHE LOVES IT...
IT'S A JOKE ONLY THE STRONG GET...
YOU'RE FUNNY, BIG BRO!!
PIKU (TWITCH)
POWAN (DREAMY)
ポワン
"BIG BRO"... I LIKE THE SOUND OF THAT. IT'S LIKE I'VE GOT A LITTLE SISTER.
POWAWAN
ポワワン...
WHAT'S WRONG?
I GOT SEPARATED FROM MY MOM.
THAT'S TERRIBLE!

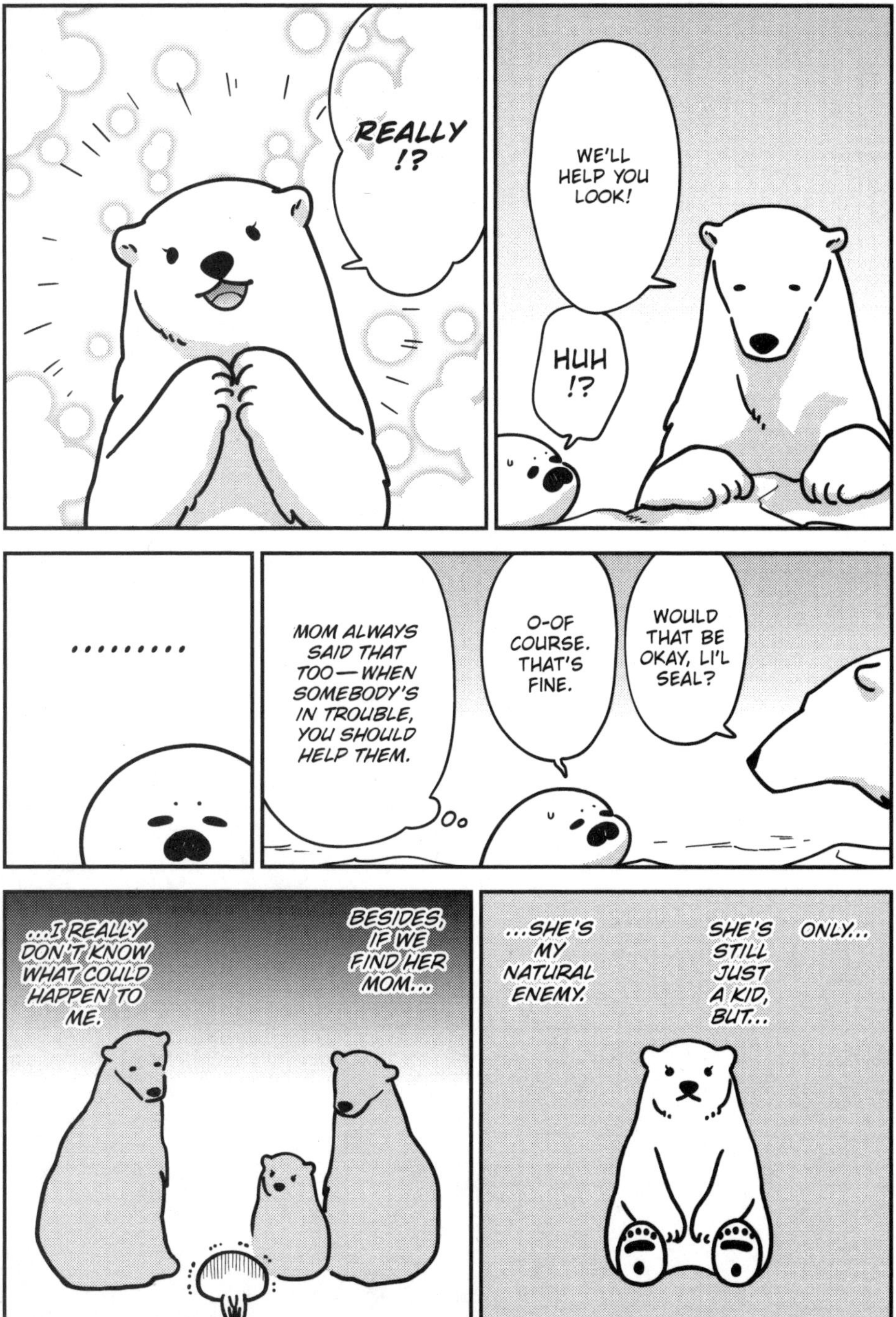
WE'LL HELP YOU LOOK!
HUH !?
REALLY !?
WOULD THAT BE OKAY, LI'L SEAL?
O-OF COURSE. THAT'S FINE.
MOM ALWAYS SAID THAT TOO—WHEN SOMEBODY'S IN TROUBLE, YOU SHOULD HELP THEM.
....
ONLY...
SHE'S STILL JUST A KID, BUT...
...SHE'S MY NATURAL ENEMY.
BESIDES, IF WE FIND HER MOM...
...I REALLY DON'T KNOW WHAT COULD HAPPEN TO ME.

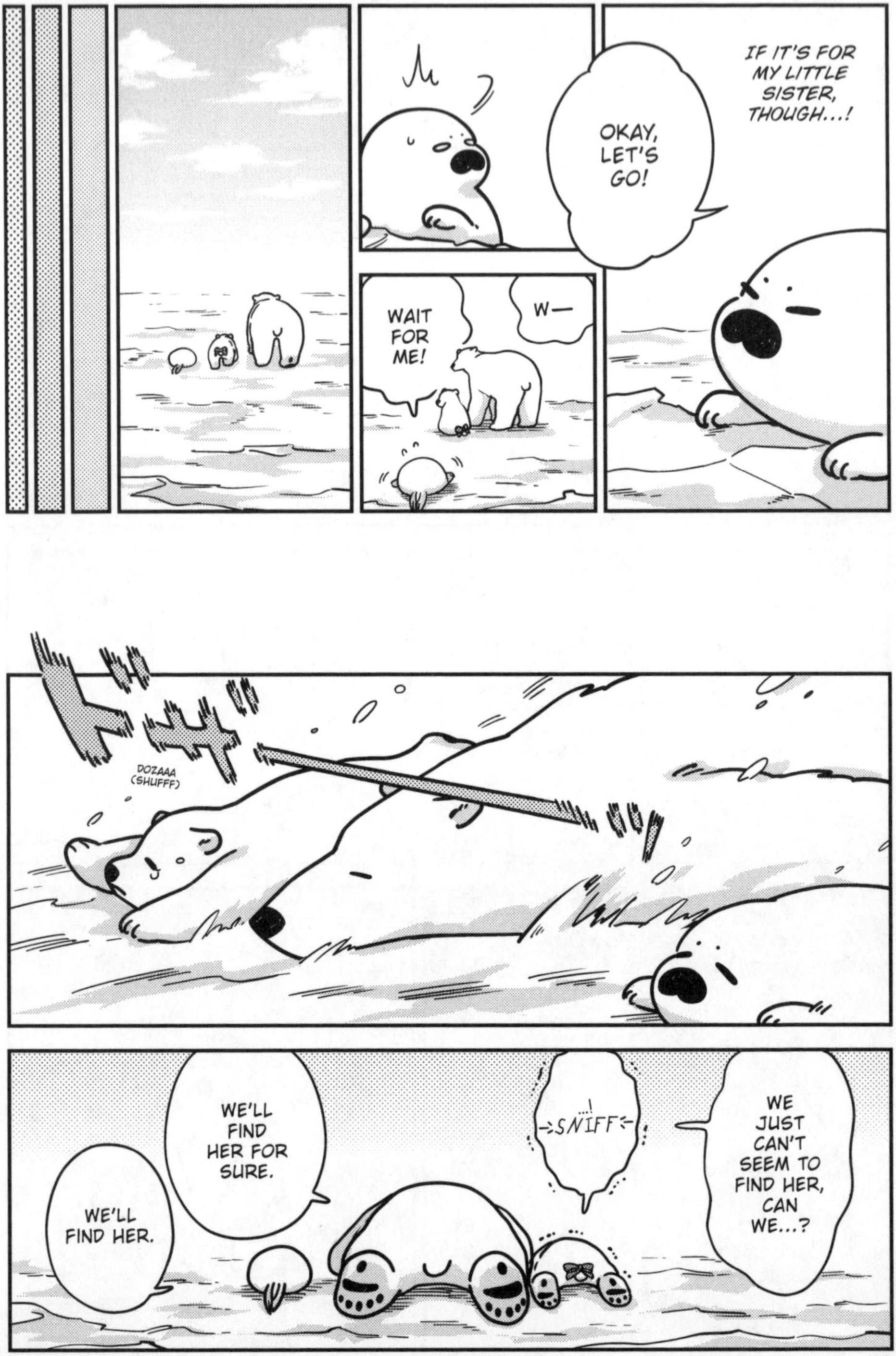
IF IT'S FOR MY LITTLE SISTER, THOUGH...!
OKAY, LET'S GO!
W—
WAIT FOR ME!
DOZAAA (SHUFFF)
WE JUST CAN'T SEEM TO FIND HER, CAN WE...?
...! SNIFF
WE'LL FIND HER FOR SURE.
WE'LL FIND HER.

TRY CALLING

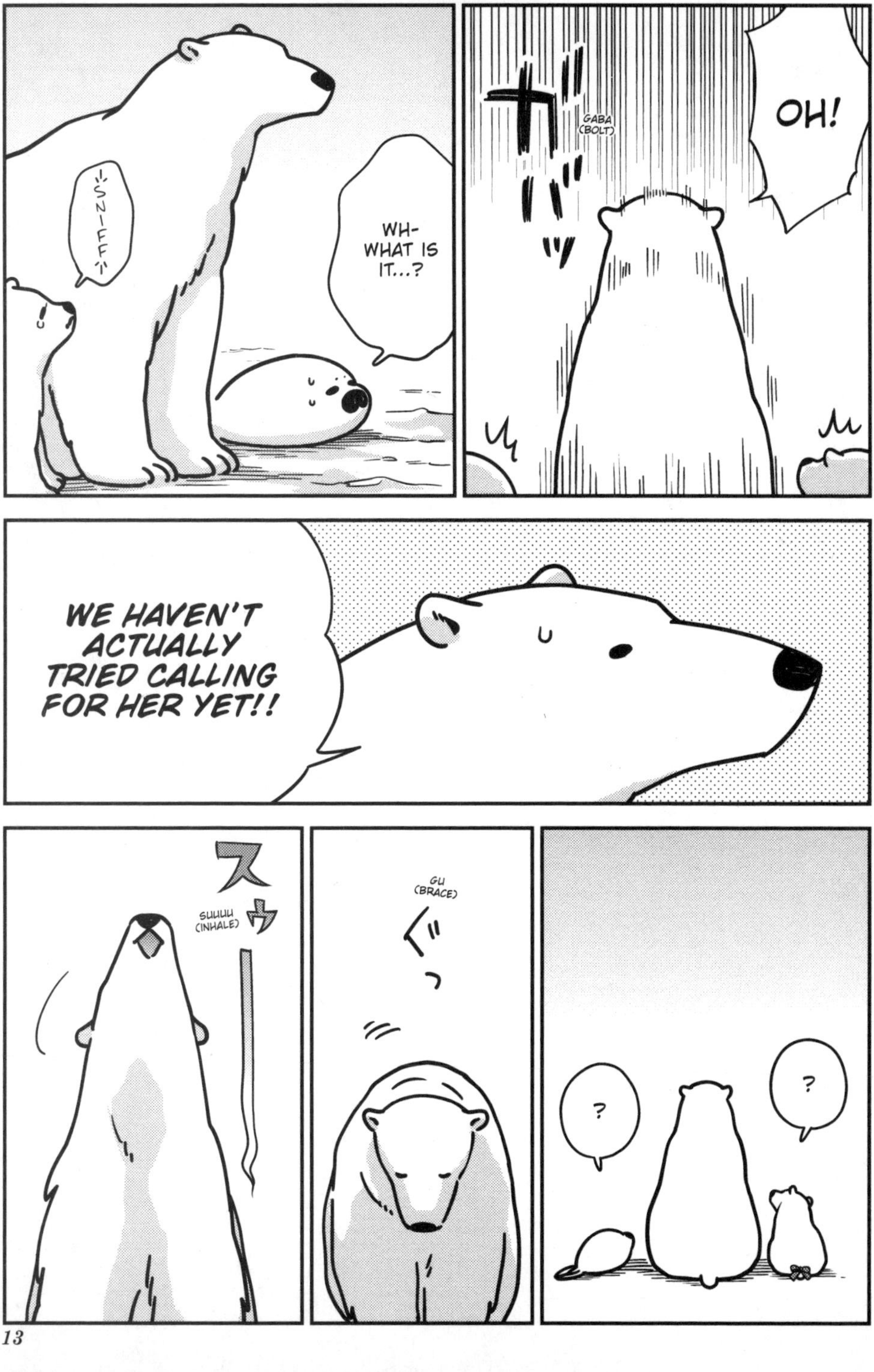
ガバッ
GABA (BOLT)
OH!
!SNIFF!
WH- WHAT IS IT...?
WE HAVEN'T ACTUALLY TRIED CALLING FOR HER YET!!
?
?
ぐっ
GU (BRACE)
スゥ
SUUUU (INHALE)

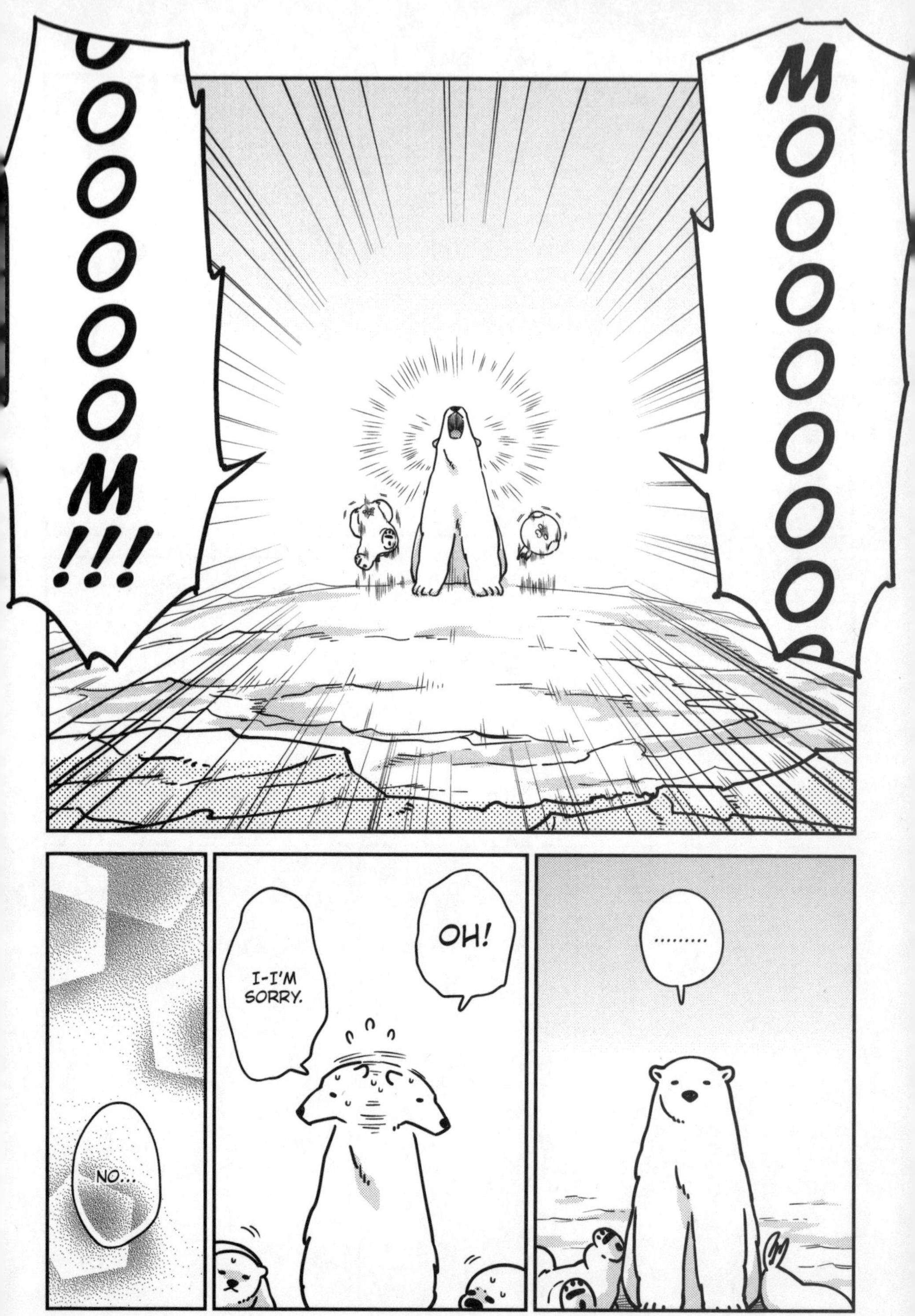
MOOOOOOOOO
OOOOOOOOM!!!
....
OH!
I-I'M SORRY.
NO...

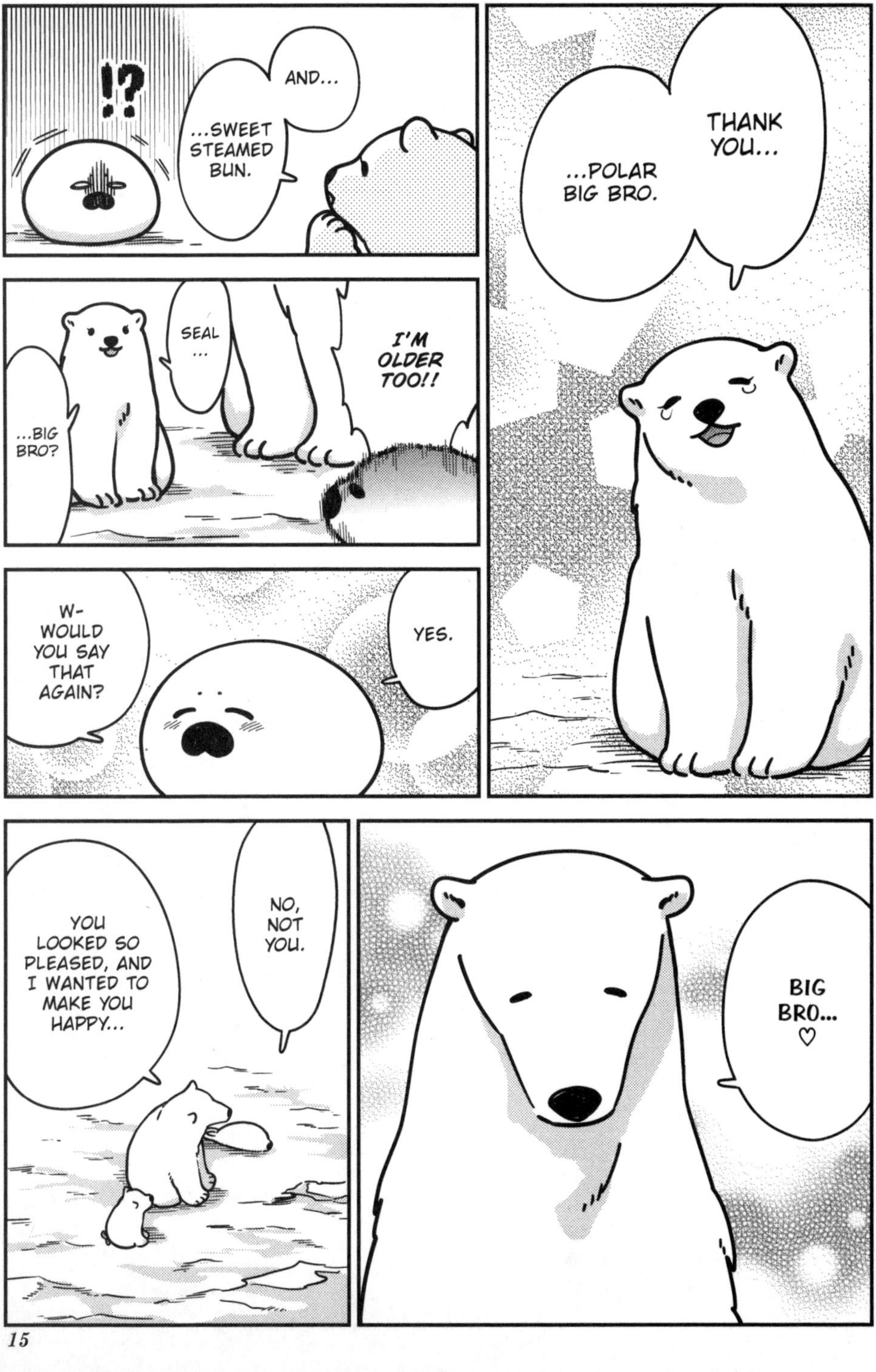
THANK YOU...
...POLAR BIG BRO.
AND...
...SWEET STEAMED BUN.
!?
SEAL ...
...BIG BRO?
I'M OLDER TOO!!
YES.
W- WOULD YOU SAY THAT AGAIN?
BIG BRO... ♡
NO, NOT YOU.
YOU LOOKED SO PLEASED, AND I WANTED TO MAKE YOU HAPPY...

PLAYING FAMILY

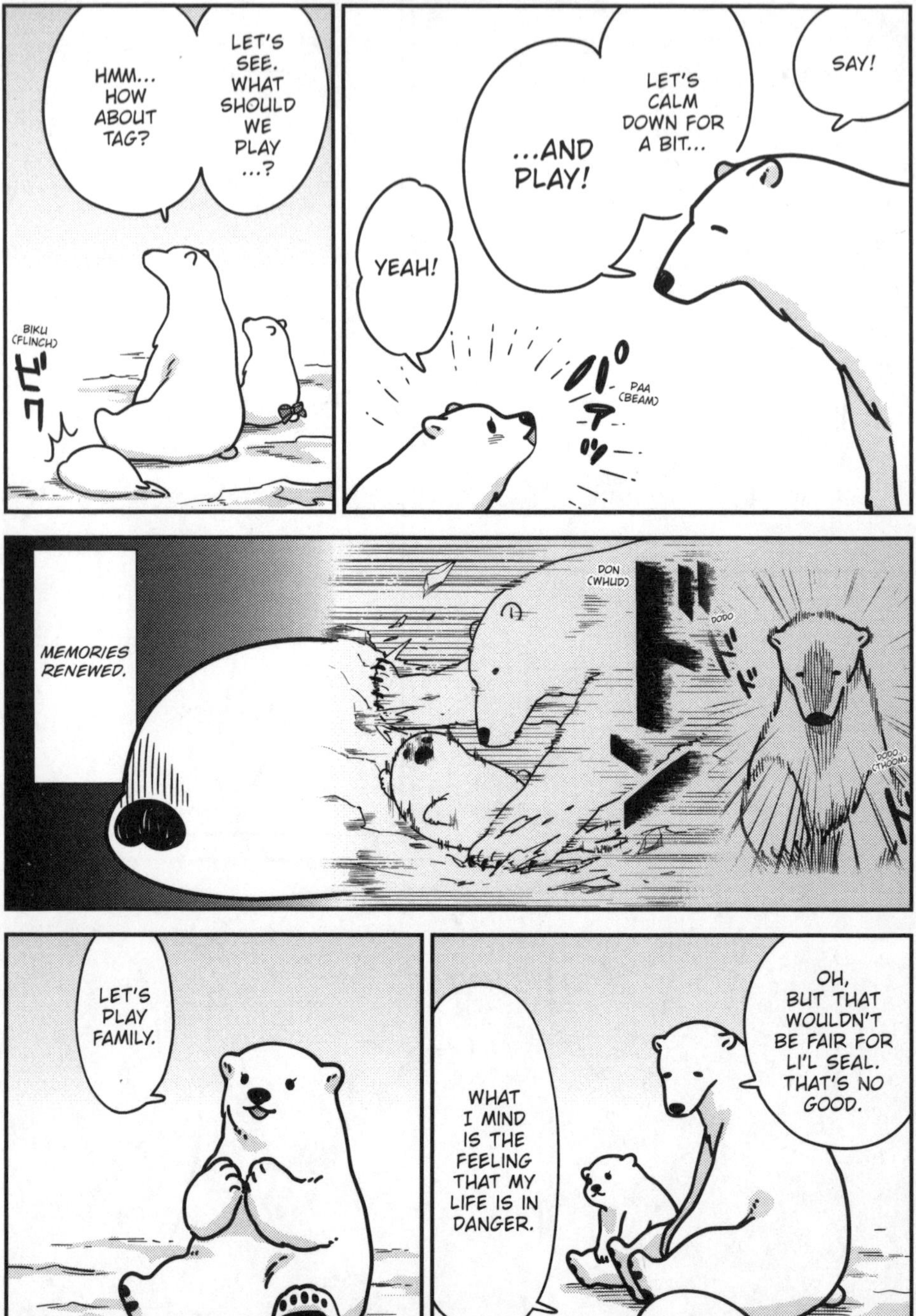
SAY!
LET'S CALM DOWN FOR A BIT... ...AND PLAY!
YEAH!
PAA (BEAM)
LET'S SEE. WHAT SHOULD WE PLAY ...?
HMM... HOW ABOUT TAG?
BIKU (FLINCH)
MEMORIES RENEWED.
DON (WHUD)
DODO
DODO (THOOM)
OH, BUT THAT WOULDN'T BE FAIR FOR LI'L SEAL. THAT'S NO GOOD.
WHAT I MIND IS THE FEELING THAT MY LIFE IS IN DANGER.
LET'S PLAY FAMILY.

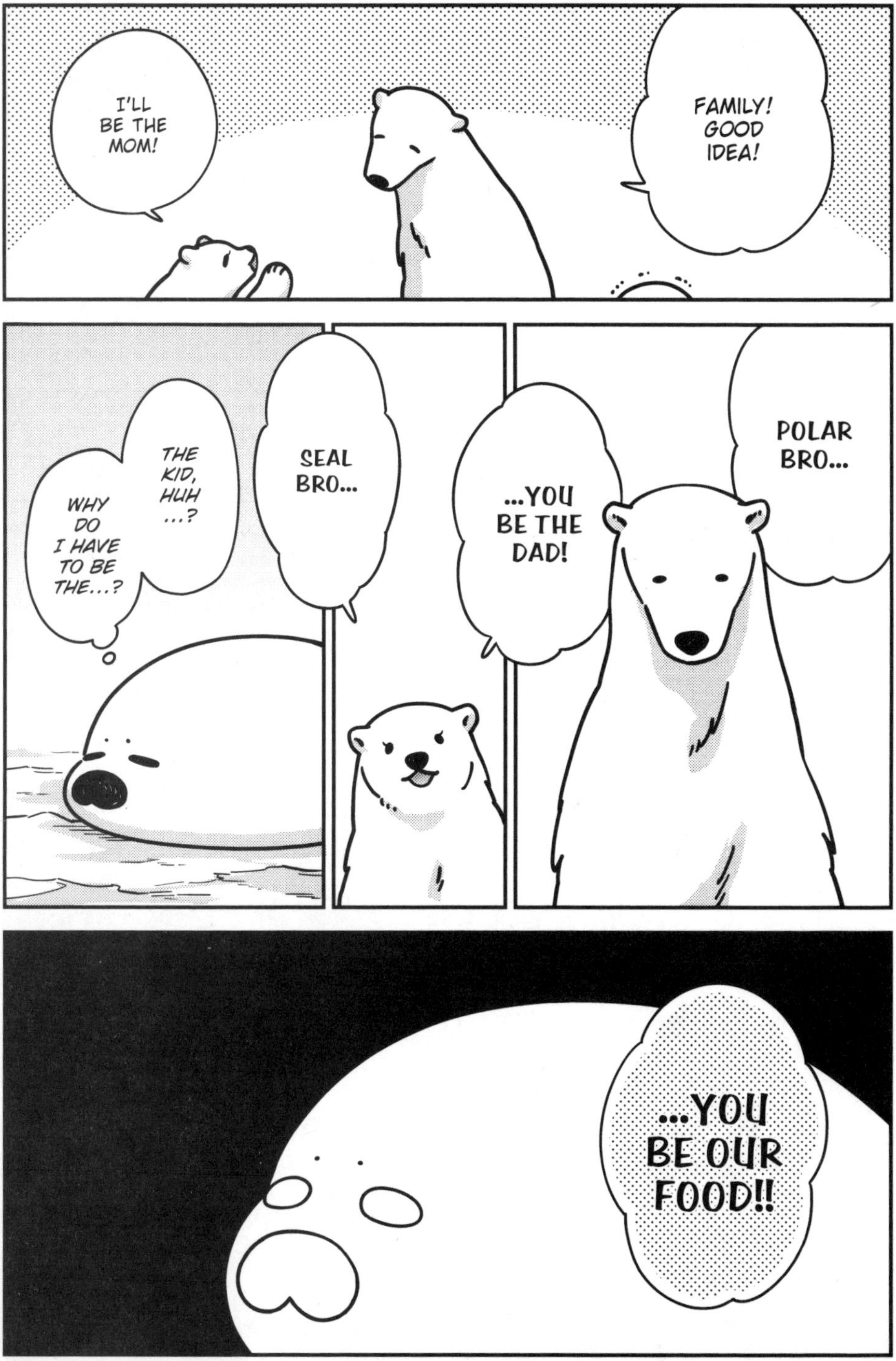
FAMILY! GOOD IDEA!
I'LL BE THE MOM!
POLAR BRO...
...YOU BE THE DAD!
SEAL BRO...
THE KID, HUH ...?
WHY DO I HAVE TO BE THE...?
...YOU BE OUR FOOD!!

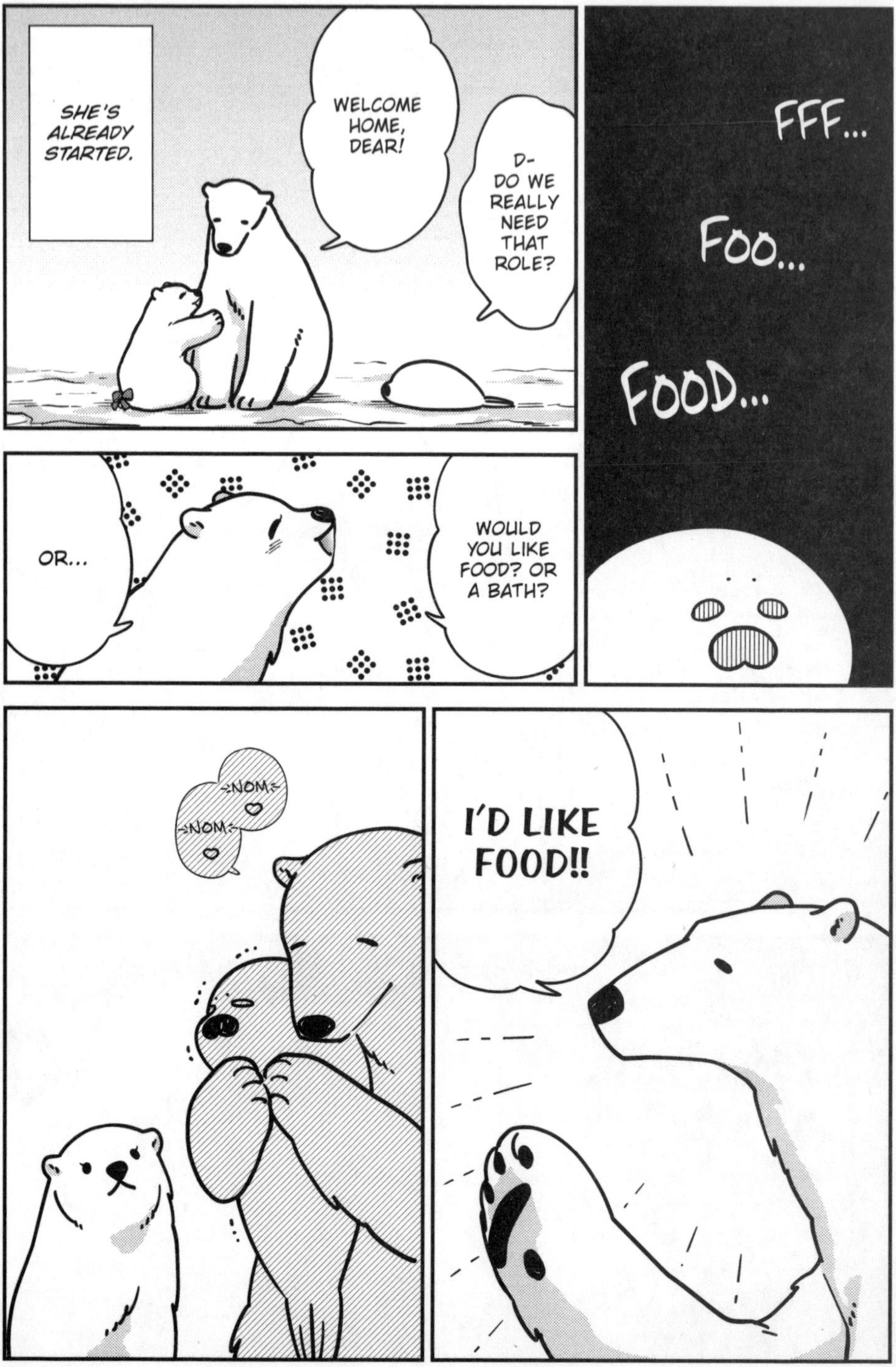
FFF...
FOO...
FOOD...
D-DO WE REALLY NEED THAT ROLE?
WELCOME HOME, DEAR!
SHE'S ALREADY STARTED.
WOULD YOU LIKE FOOD? OR A BATH?
OR...
I'D LIKE FOOD!!
NOM
NOM

LOVE RIBBON

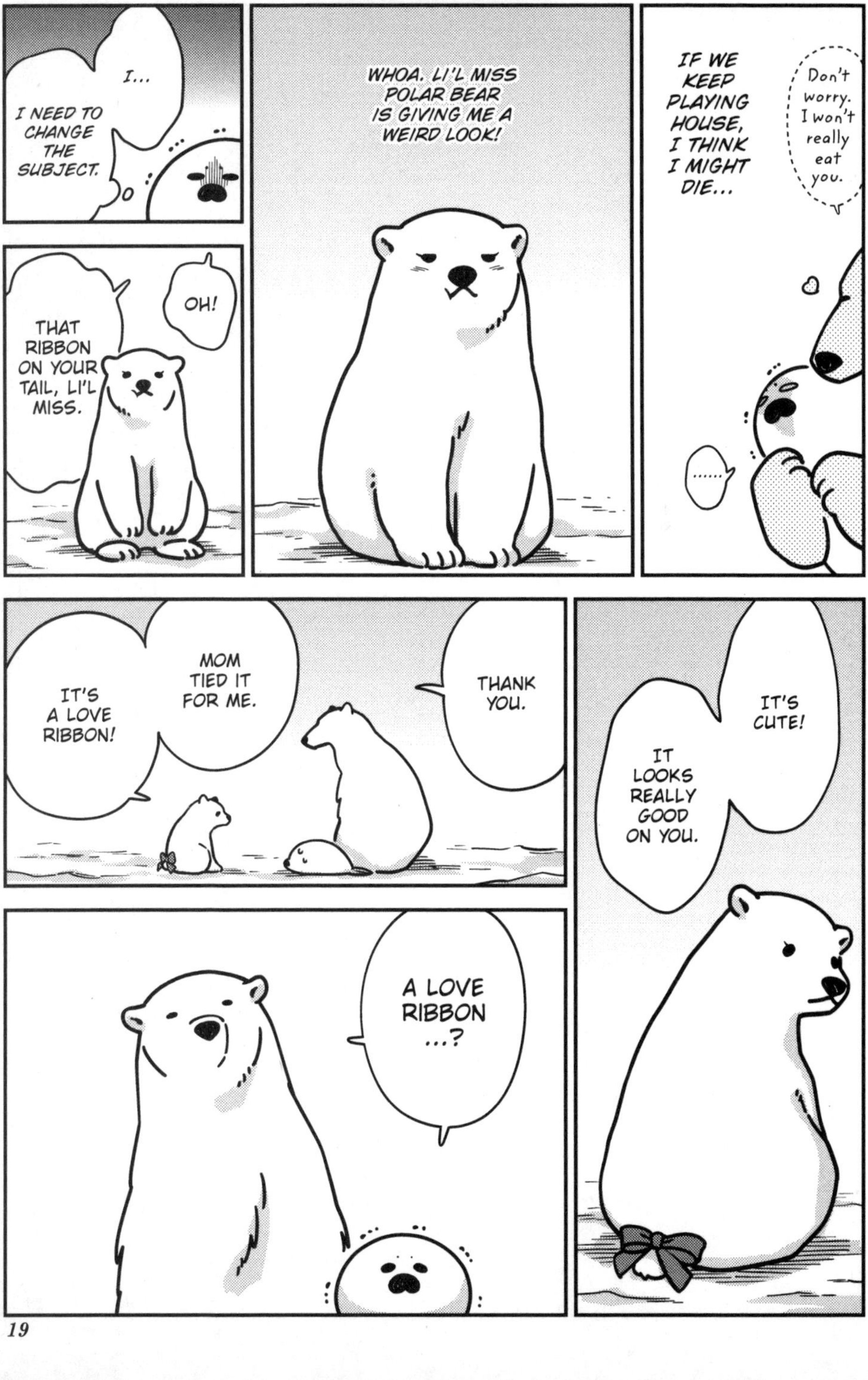

Don't worry. I won't really eat you.
IF WE KEEP PLAYING HOUSE, I THINK I MIGHT DIE...
……
WHOA. LI'L MISS POLAR BEAR IS GIVING ME A WEIRD LOOK!
I...
I NEED TO CHANGE THE SUBJECT.
OH!
THAT RIBBON ON YOUR TAIL, LI'L MISS.
IT'S CUTE!
IT LOOKS REALLY GOOD ON YOU.
THANK YOU.
MOM TIED IT FOR ME.
IT'S A LOVE RIBBON!
A LOVE RIBBON ...?

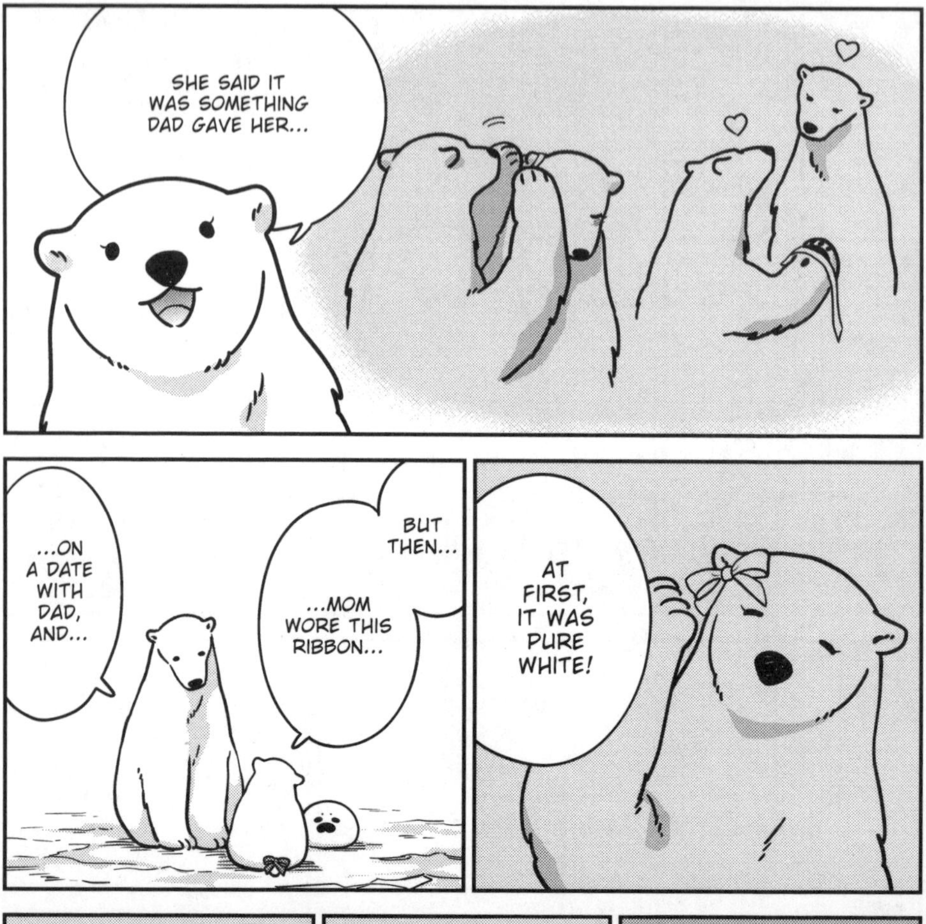
SHE SAID IT WAS SOMETHING DAD GAVE HER...
AT FIRST, IT WAS PURE WHITE!
BUT THEN...
...MOM WORE THIS RIBBON...
...ON A DATE WITH DAD, AND...

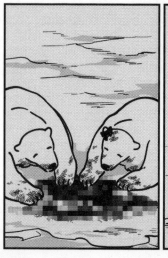

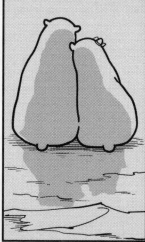

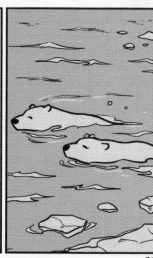

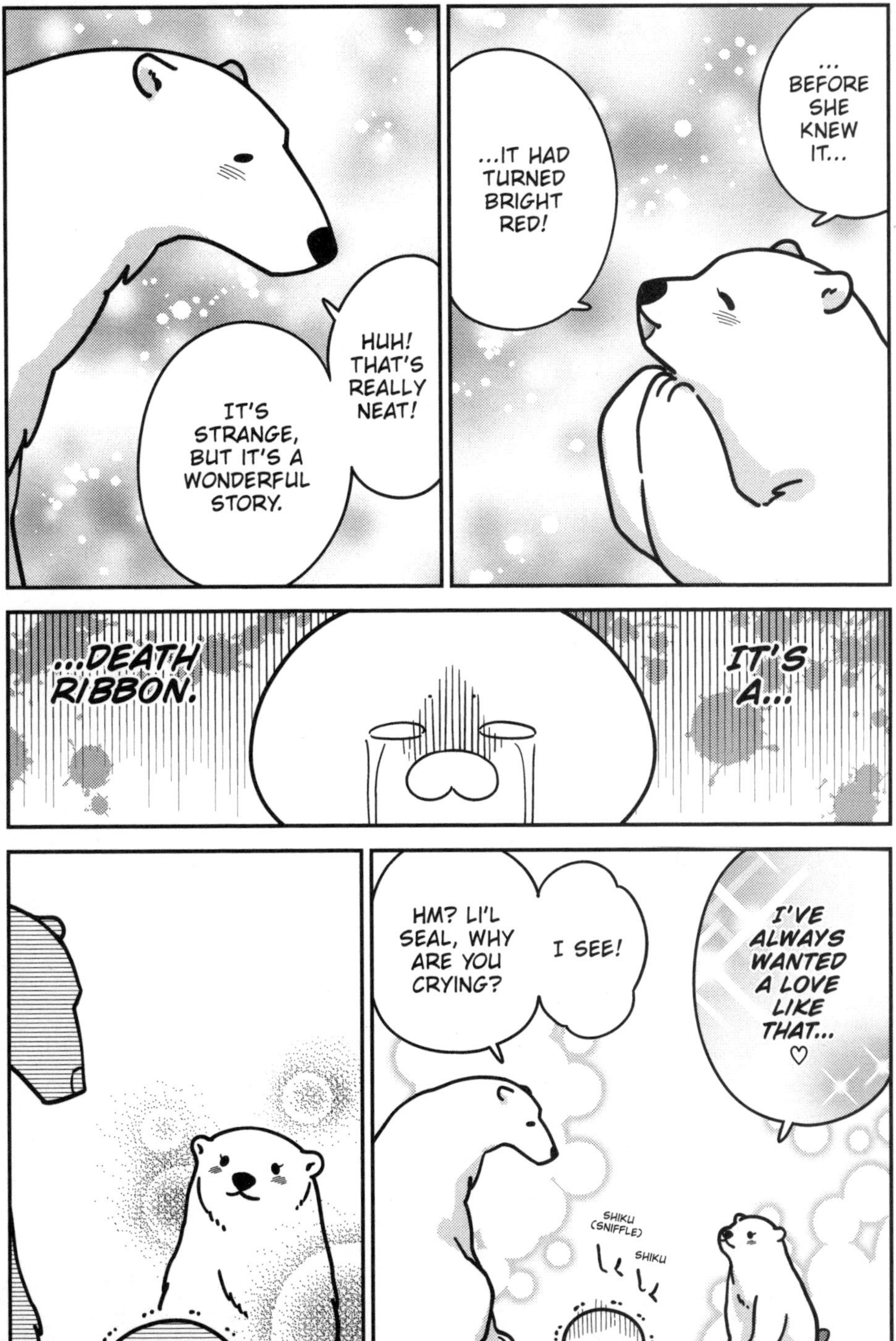
...BEFORE SHE KNEW IT...
...IT HAD TURNED BRIGHT RED!
HUH! THAT'S REALLY NEAT!
IT'S STRANGE, BUT IT'S A WONDERFUL STORY.
IT'S A...
...DEATH RIBBON.
I'VE ALWAYS WANTED A LOVE LIKE THAT... ♡
I SEE!
HM? LI'L SEAL, WHY ARE YOU CRYING?
SHIKU (SNIFFLE)
SHIKU

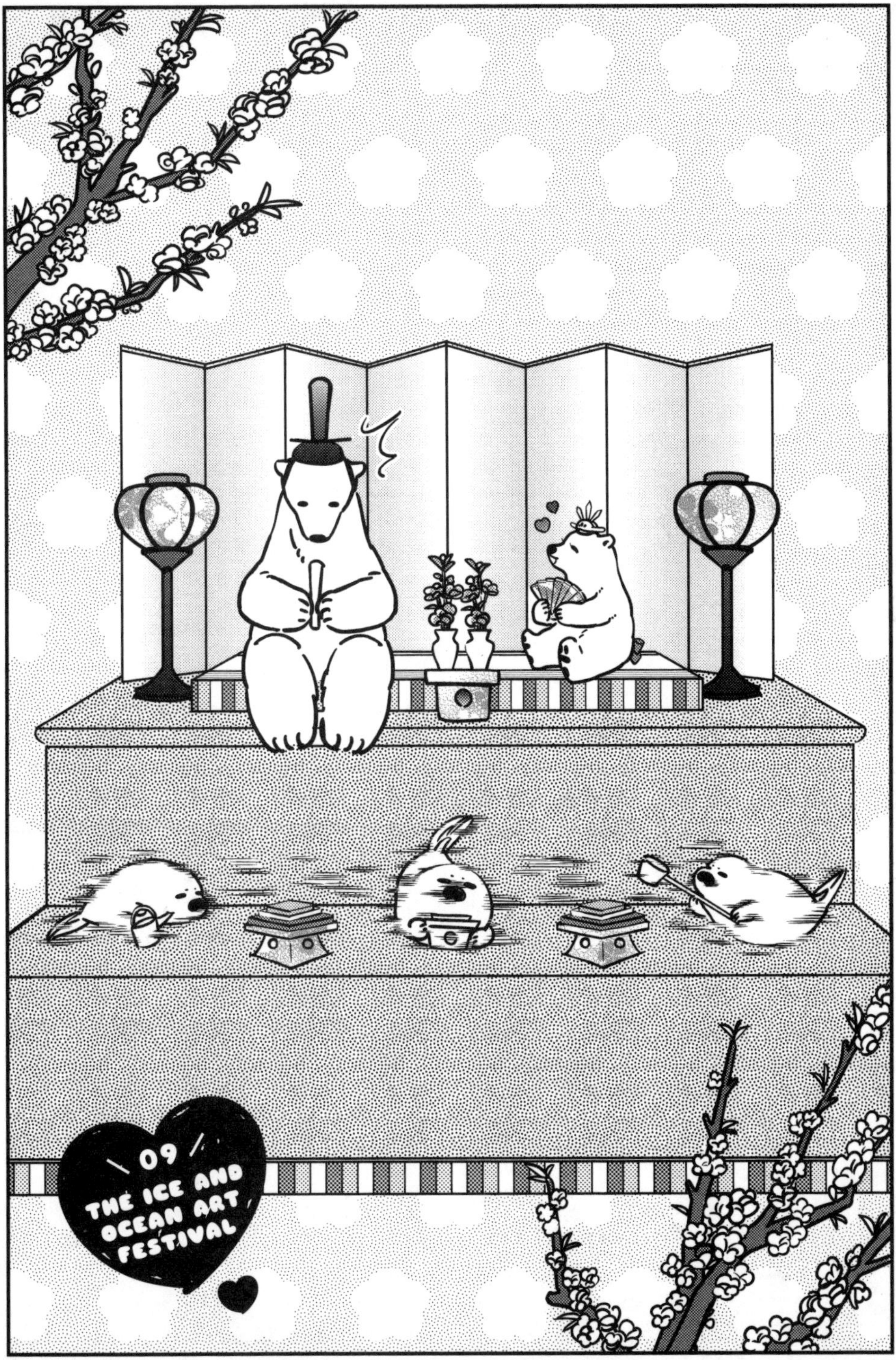
09
THE ICE AND OCEAN ART FESTIVAL

THE SORROW OF LI'L MISS POLAR BEAR

MOM...
...WHERE ARE YOU?
SHIKU (SNIFFLE)
SHIKU
SHIKU
SHIKU
I MISS YOU. I WANT TO SEE YOU.
SHIKU
SHIKU
SHIKU
I'M REALLY, REALLY LONELY AND WORRIED.
...AND YET.
SHIKU
SHIKU
AND YET...
SHIKU
I DON'T REALLY UNDERSTAND, BUT CHEER UP.
HOW LONG ARE YOU GONNA CRY!?
SHIKU
SHIKU

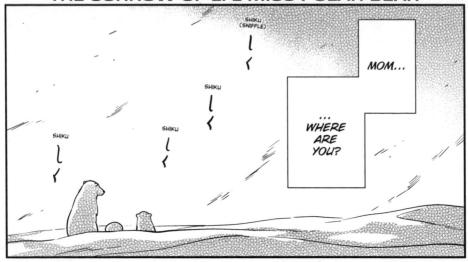

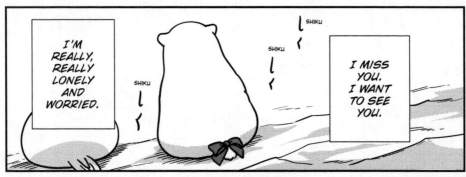

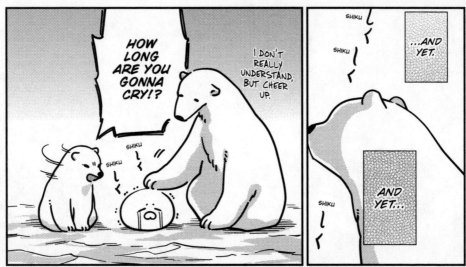

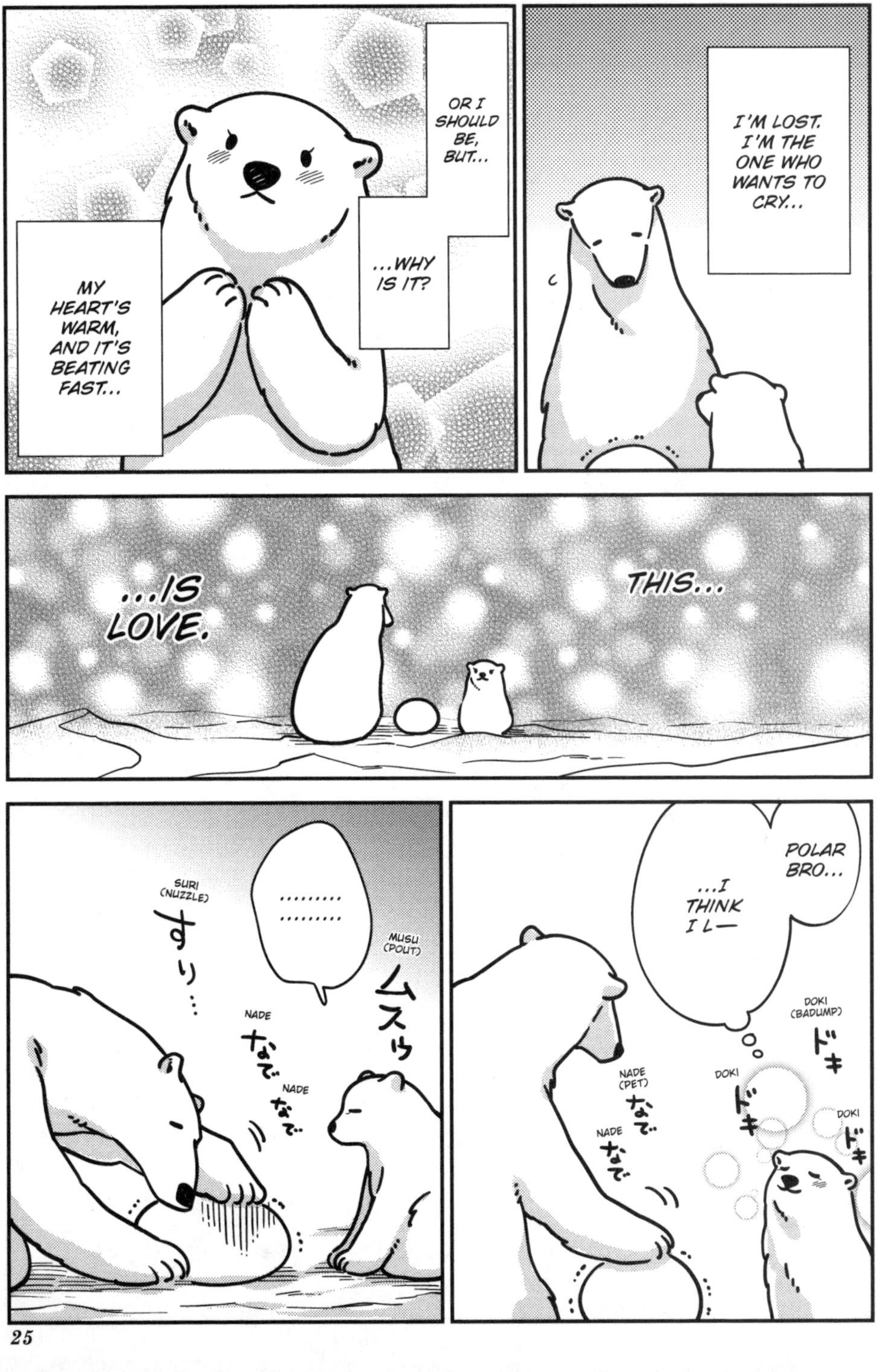
I'M LOST. I'M THE ONE WHO WANTS TO CRY...
OR I SHOULD BE, BUT...
...WHY IS IT?
MY HEART'S WARM, AND IT'S BEATING FAST...
THIS...
...IS LOVE.
POLAR BRO...
...I THINK I L—
DOKI (BADUMP)
ドキ
DOKI
ドキ
DOKI
ドキ
NADE (PET)
なで
NADE
なで
MUSU (POUT)
ムスゥ
....
....
SURI (NUZZLE)
すり…
NADE
なで
NADE
なで

PLAYING TOGETHER

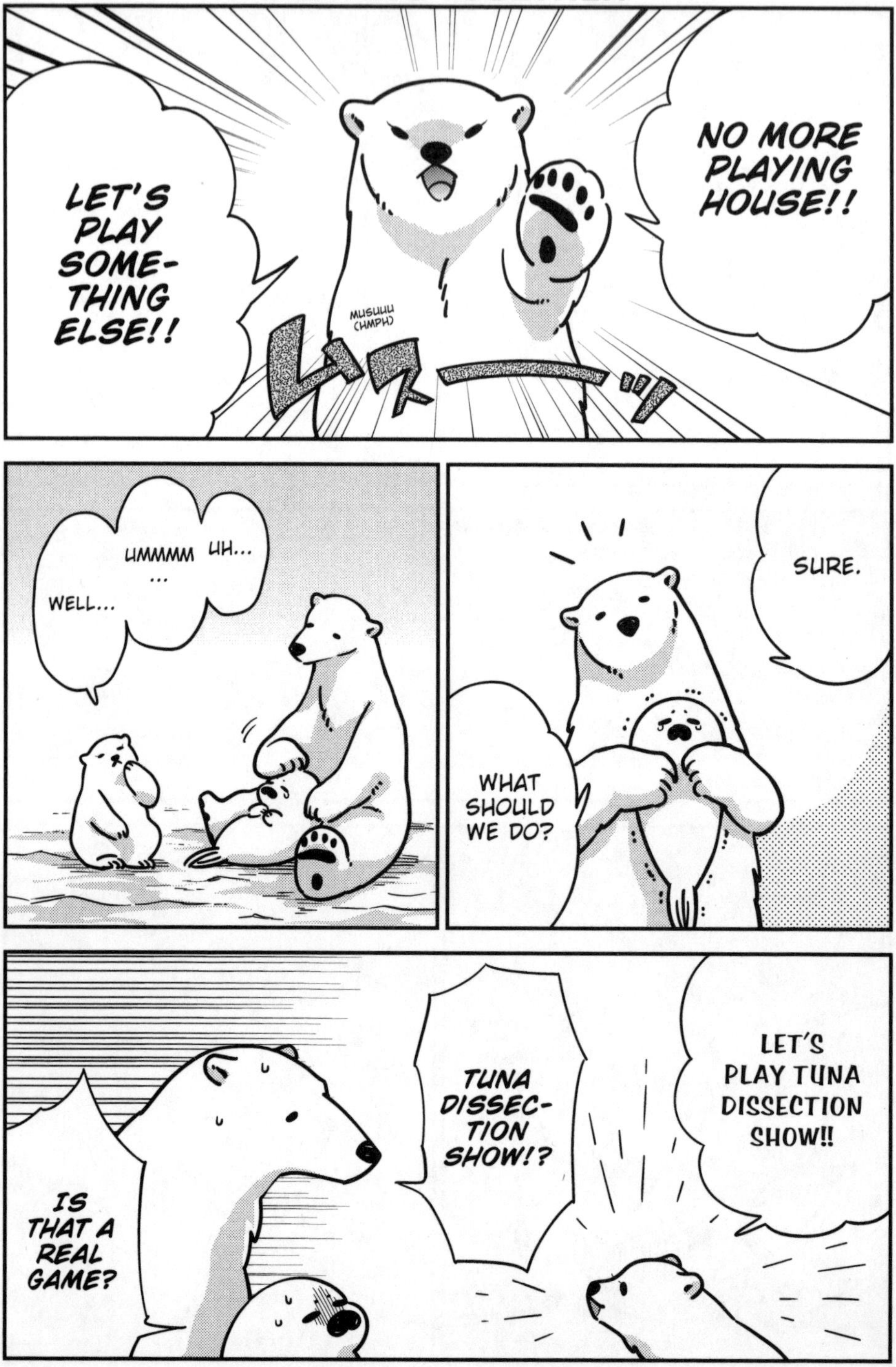
NO MORE PLAYING HOUSE!!
LET'S PLAY SOME-THING ELSE!!
MUSUUU (HMPH)
SURE.
WHAT SHOULD WE DO?
UH...
UMMMM ...
WELL...
LET'S PLAY TUNA DISSECTION SHOW!!
TUNA DISSEC-TION SHOW!?
IS THAT A REAL GAME?

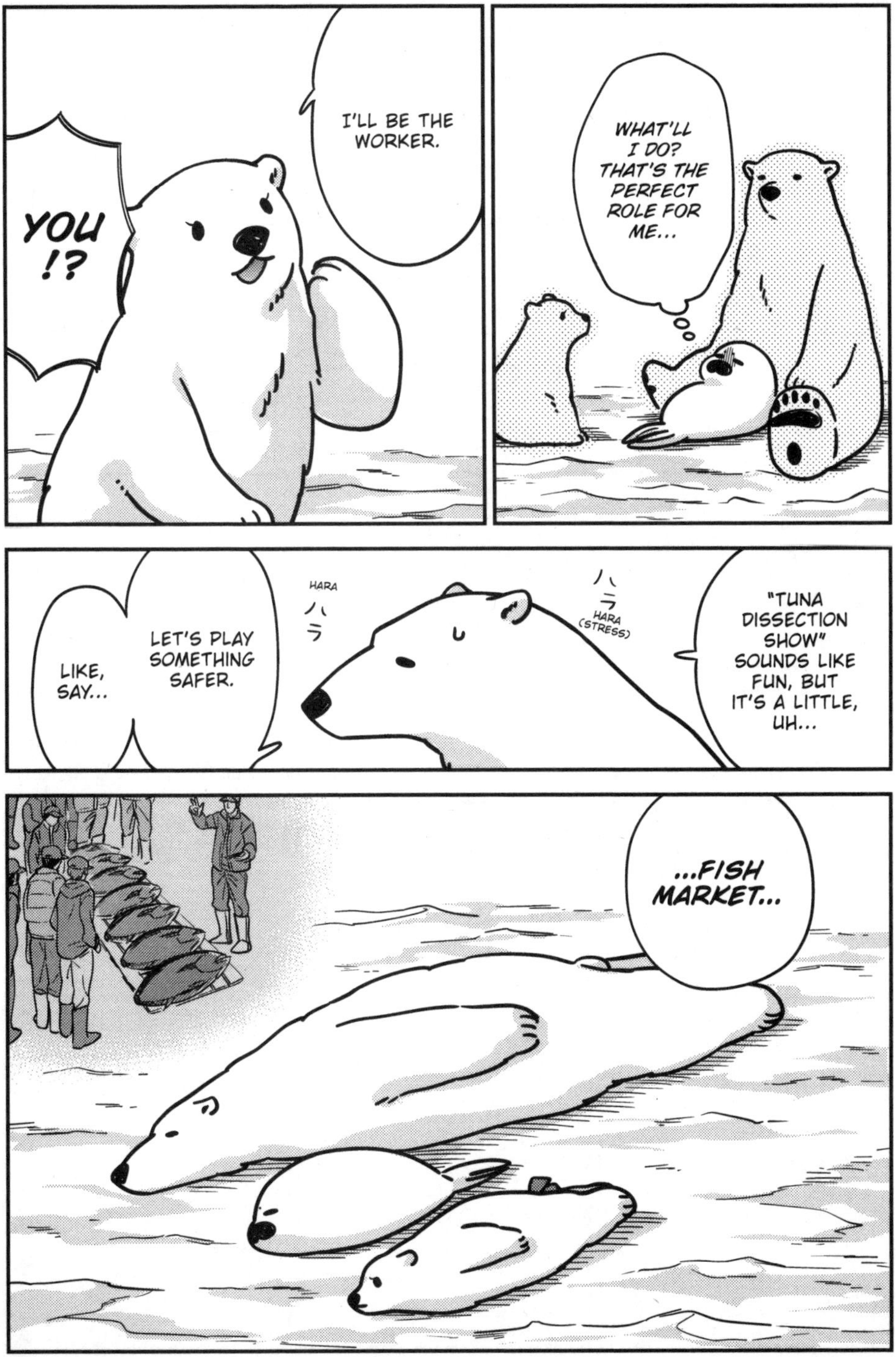
WHAT'LL I DO? THAT'S THE PERFECT ROLE FOR ME...
I'LL BE THE WORKER.
YOU!?
"TUNA DISSECTION SHOW" SOUNDS LIKE FUN, BUT IT'S A LITTLE, UH...
ハラ
HARA (STRESS)
HARA
ハラ
LET'S PLAY SOMETHING SAFER.
LIKE, SAY...
...FISH MARKET...

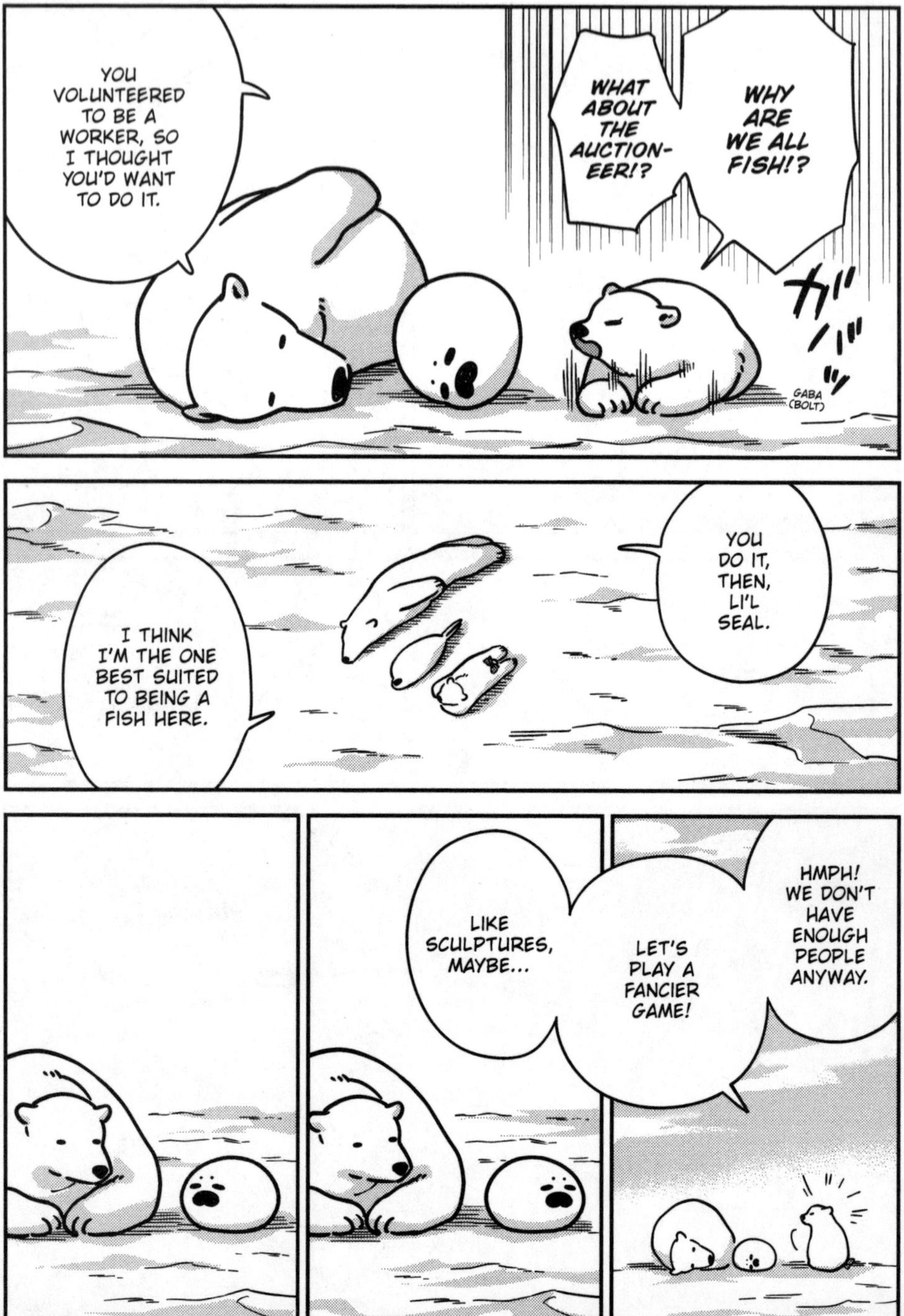
WHY ARE WE ALL FISH!?
WHAT ABOUT THE AUCTION-EER!?
GABA (BOLT)
YOU VOLUNTEERED TO BE A WORKER, SO I THOUGHT YOU'D WANT TO DO IT.
YOU DO IT, THEN, LI'L SEAL.
I THINK I'M THE ONE BEST SUITED TO BEING A FISH HERE.
HMPH! WE DON'T HAVE ENOUGH PEOPLE ANYWAY.
LET'S PLAY A FANCIER GAME!
LIKE SCULPTURES, MAYBE...

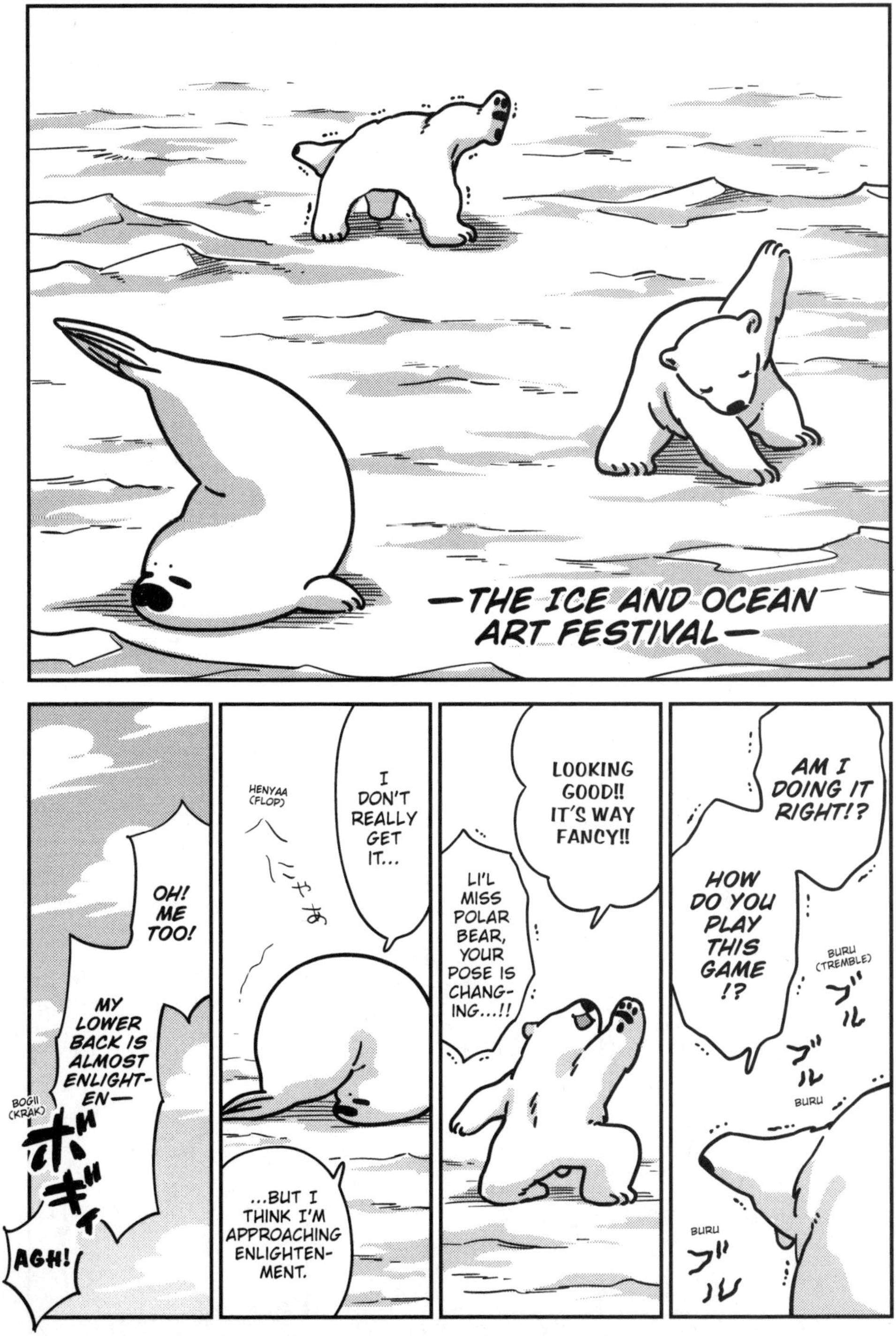
—THE ICE AND OCEAN ART FESTIVAL—
AM I DOING IT RIGHT!?
HOW DO YOU PLAY THIS GAME!?
BURU (TREMBLE)
BURU
BURU
LOOKING GOOD!! IT'S WAY FANCY!!
LI'L MISS POLAR BEAR, YOUR POSE IS CHANG-ING...!!
I DON'T REALLY GET IT...
HENYAA (FLOP)
...BUT I THINK I'M APPROACHING ENLIGHTEN-MENT.
OH! ME TOO!
MY LOWER BACK IS ALMOST ENLIGHT-EN—
BOGII (KRAK)
AGH!

MY FIRST LOVE. MY FUTURE.

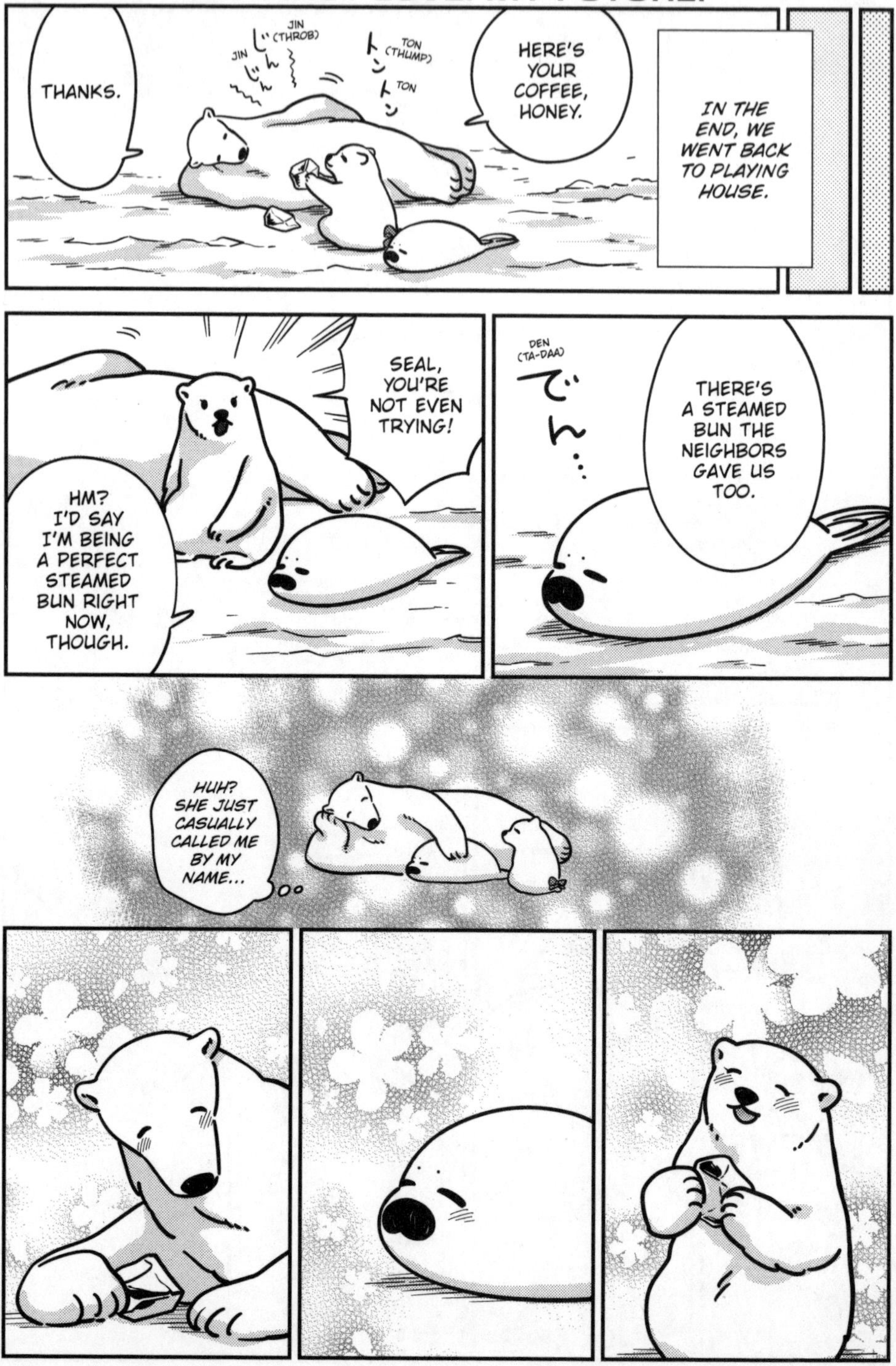

IN THE END, WE WENT BACK TO PLAYING HOUSE.
HERE'S YOUR COFFEE, HONEY.
トントン
TON (THUMP) TON
じんじん
JIN (THROB) JIN
THANKS.
でん…
DEN (TA-DAA)
THERE'S A STEAMED BUN THE NEIGHBORS GAVE US TOO.
SEAL, YOU'RE NOT EVEN TRYING!
HM? I'D SAY I'M BEING A PERFECT STEAMED BUN RIGHT NOW, THOUGH.
HUH? SHE JUST CASUALLY CALLED ME BY MY NAME...

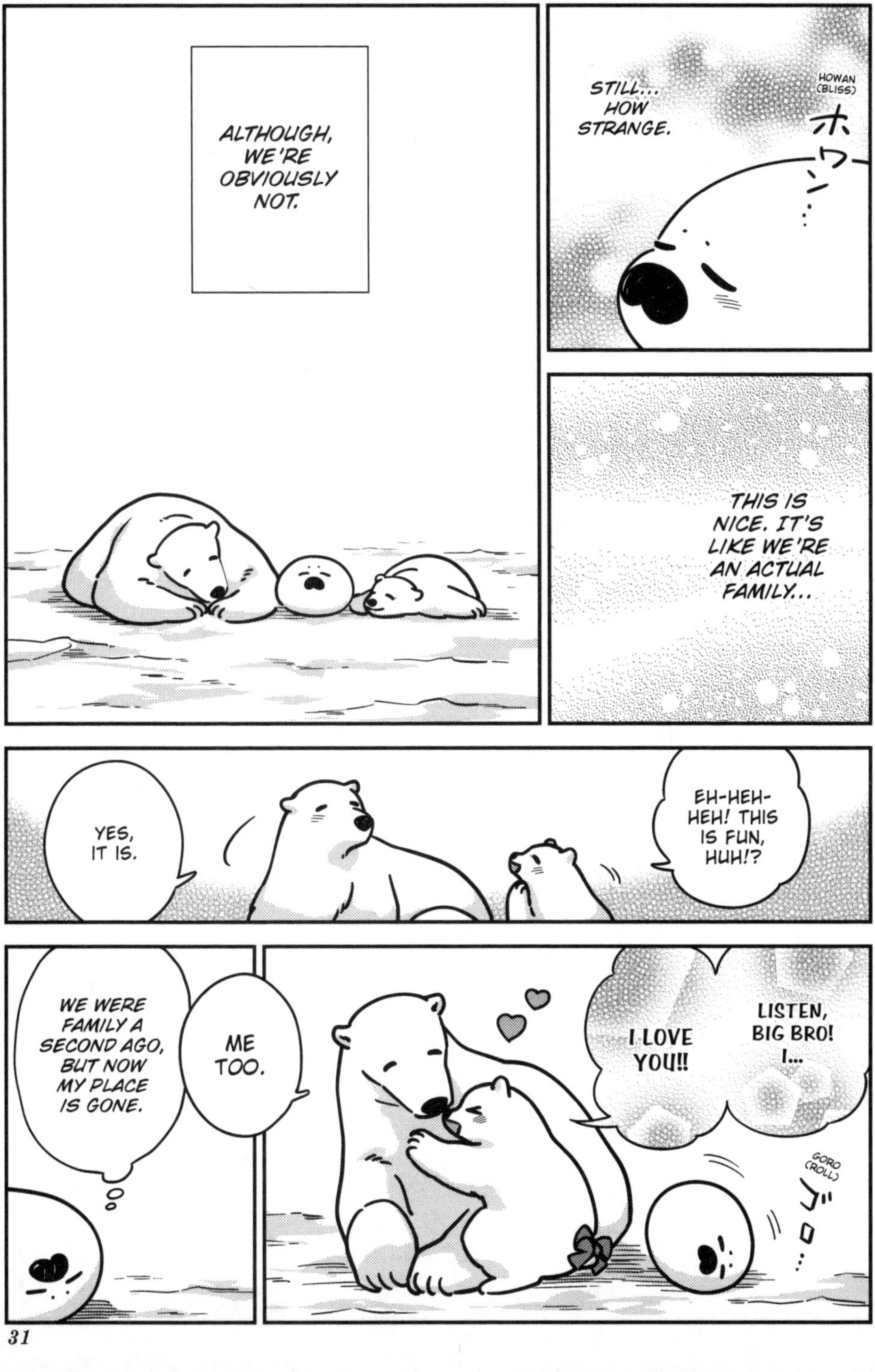
HOWAN (BLISS)
ホワン…
STILL... HOW STRANGE.
THIS IS NICE. IT'S LIKE WE'RE AN ACTUAL FAMILY...
ALTHOUGH, WE'RE OBVIOUSLY NOT.
EH-HEH-HEH! THIS IS FUN, HUH!?
YES, IT IS.
LISTEN, BIG BRO! I...
I LOVE YOU!!
GORO (ROLL)
ゴロ…
ME TOO.
WE WERE FAMILY A SECOND AGO, BUT NOW MY PLACE IS GONE.

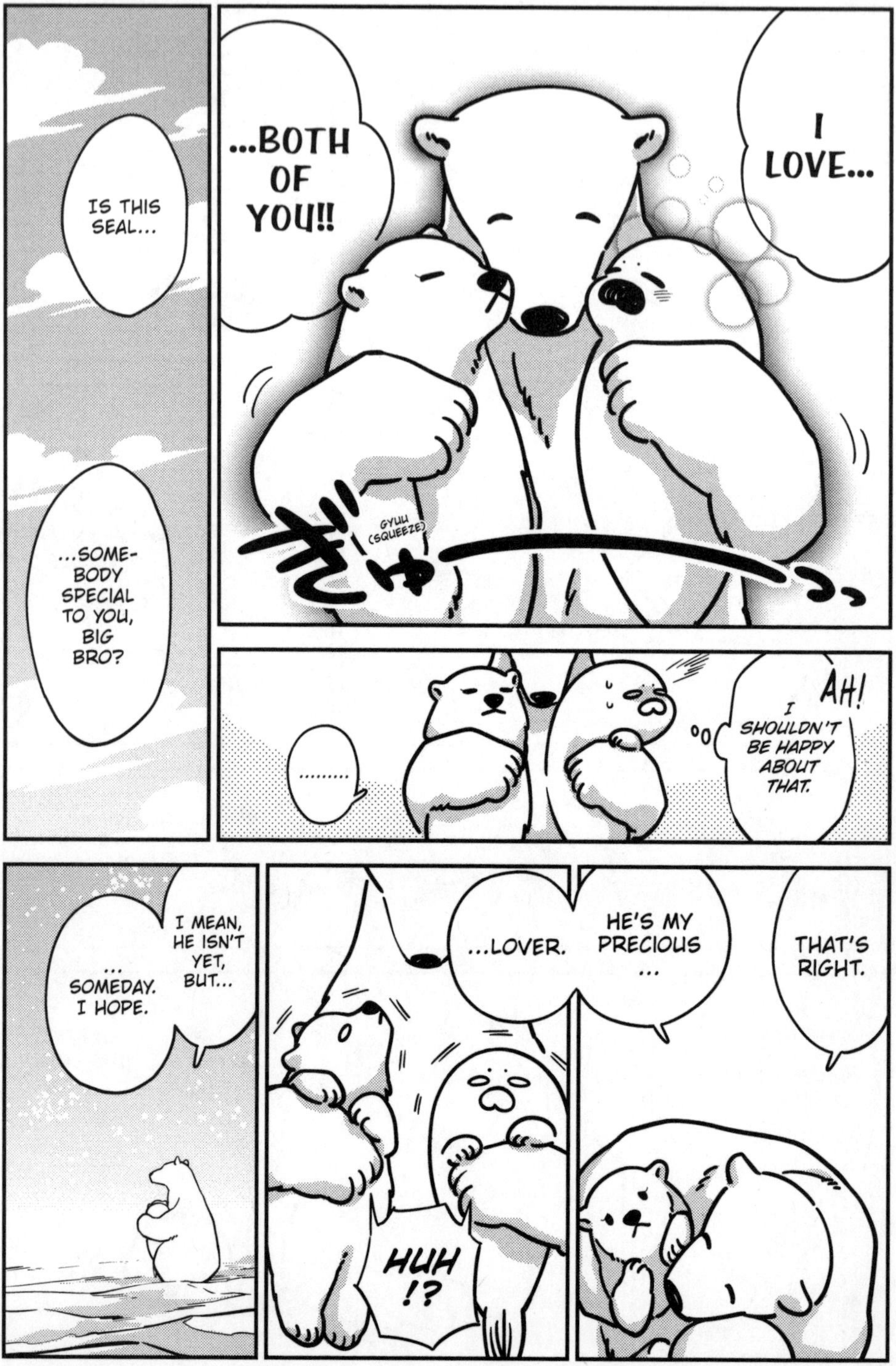
I LOVE...
...BOTH OF YOU!!
GYUU (SQUEEZE)
AH! I SHOULDN'T BE HAPPY ABOUT THAT.
....
IS THIS SEAL...
...SOMEBODY SPECIAL TO YOU, BIG BRO?
THAT'S RIGHT.
HE'S MY PRECIOUS ...
...LOVER.
HUH !?
I MEAN, HE ISN'T YET, BUT...
... SOMEDAY. I HOPE.

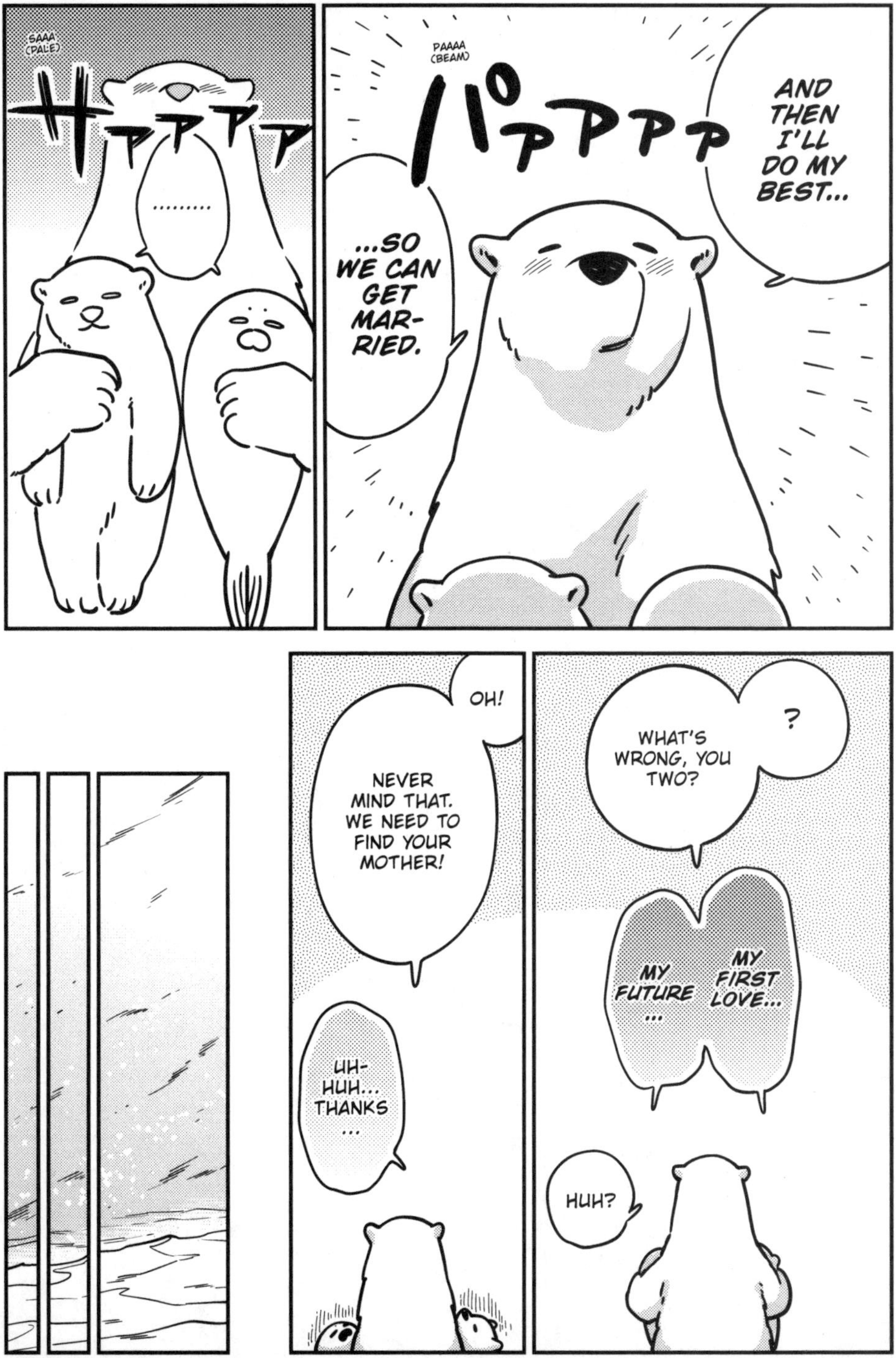
PAAAA (BEAM)
パァァァァ
AND THEN I'LL DO MY BEST...
...SO WE CAN GET MAR-RIED.
SAAA (PALE)
サァァァァ
....
?
WHAT'S WRONG, YOU TWO?
MY FIRST LOVE...
MY FUTURE ...
HUH?
OH!
NEVER MIND THAT. WE NEED TO FIND YOUR MOTHER!
UH-HUH... THANKS ...

A SIMILAR PAIR

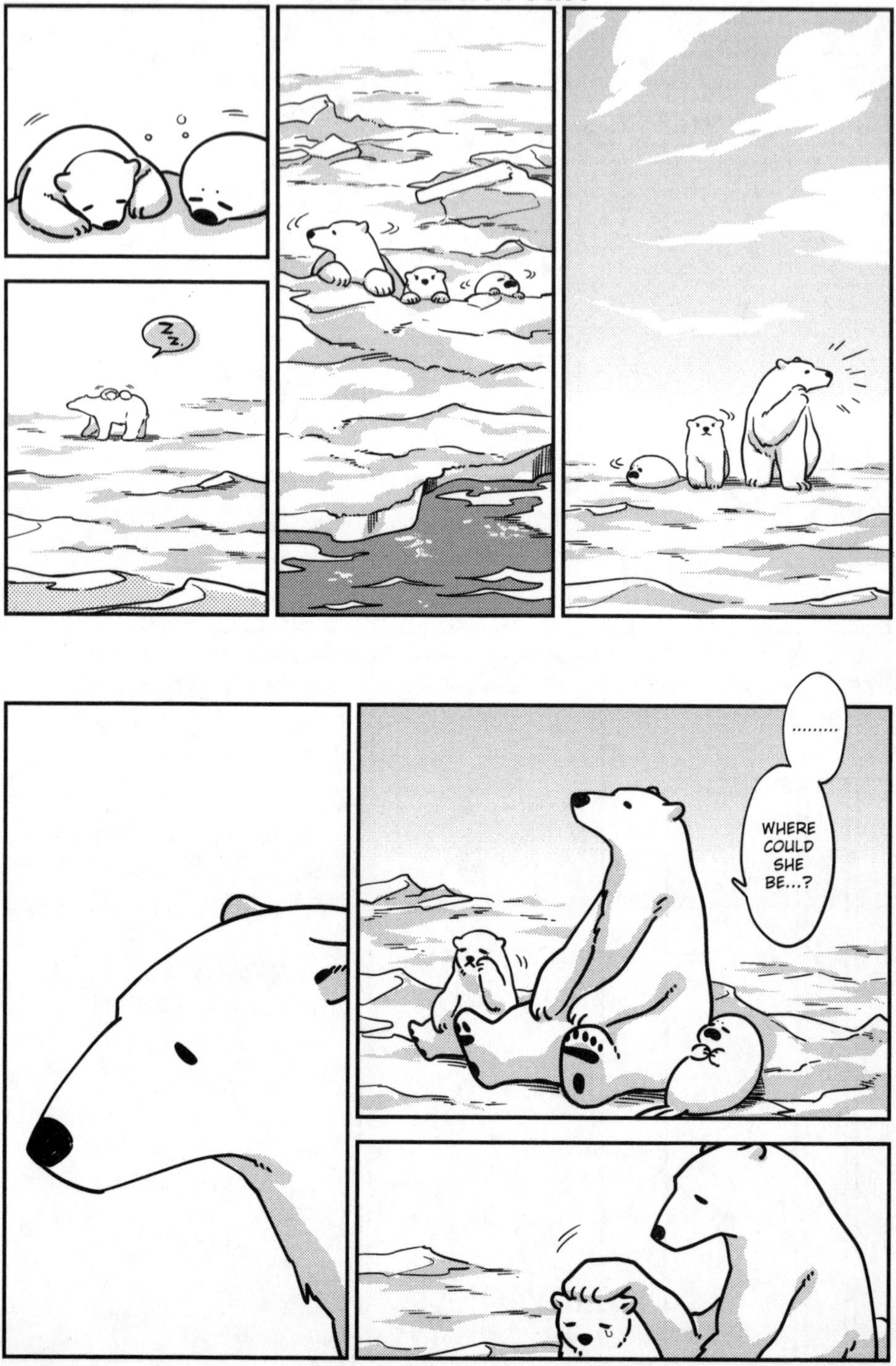

....
WHERE COULD SHE BE...?

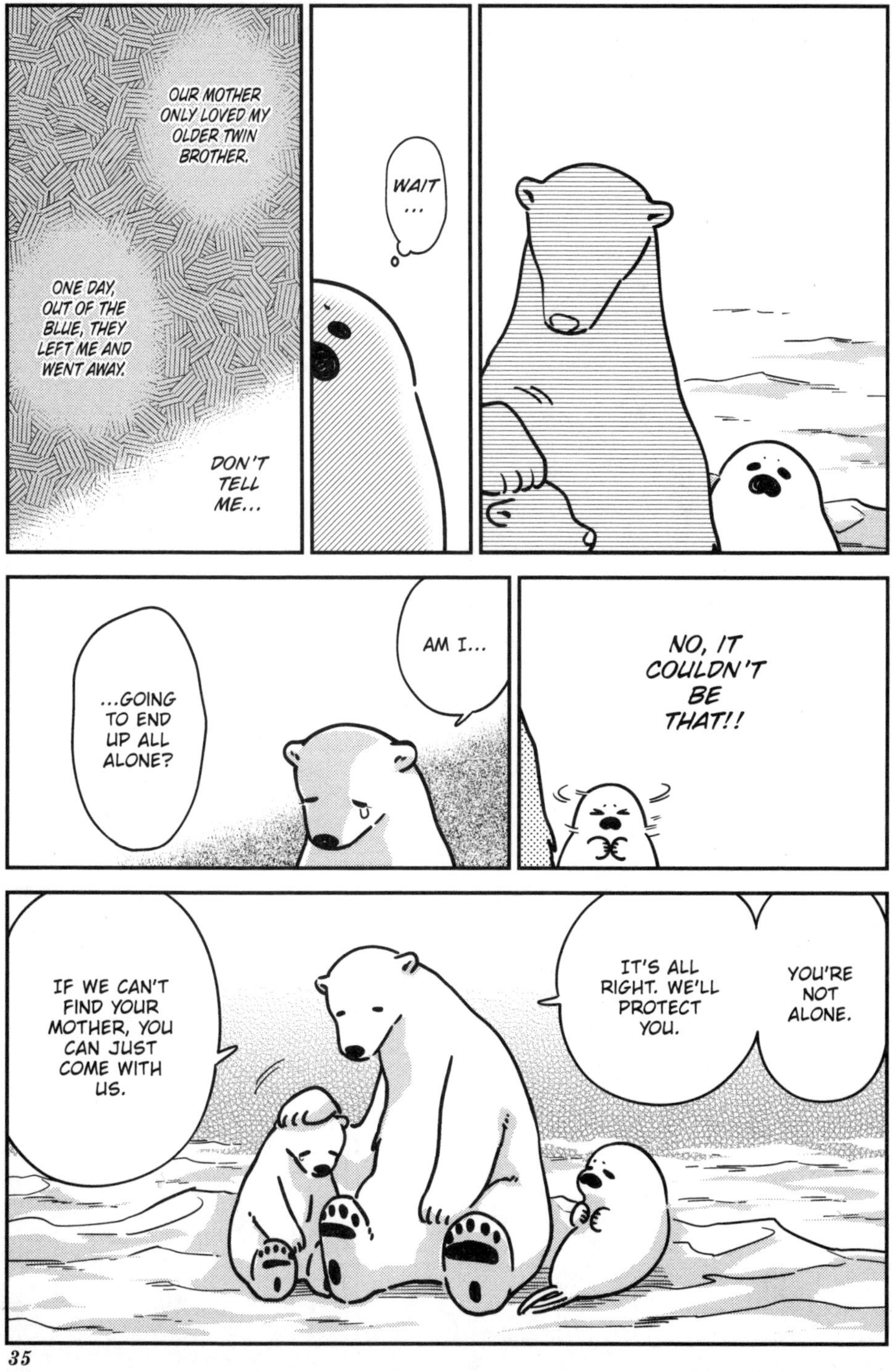
WAIT ...
OUR MOTHER ONLY LOVED MY OLDER TWIN BROTHER.
ONE DAY, OUT OF THE BLUE, THEY LEFT ME AND WENT AWAY.
DON'T TELL ME...
NO, IT COULDN'T BE THAT!!
AM I...
...GOING TO END UP ALL ALONE?
YOU'RE NOT ALONE.
IT'S ALL RIGHT. WE'LL PROTECT YOU.
IF WE CAN'T FIND YOUR MOTHER, YOU CAN JUST COME WITH US.

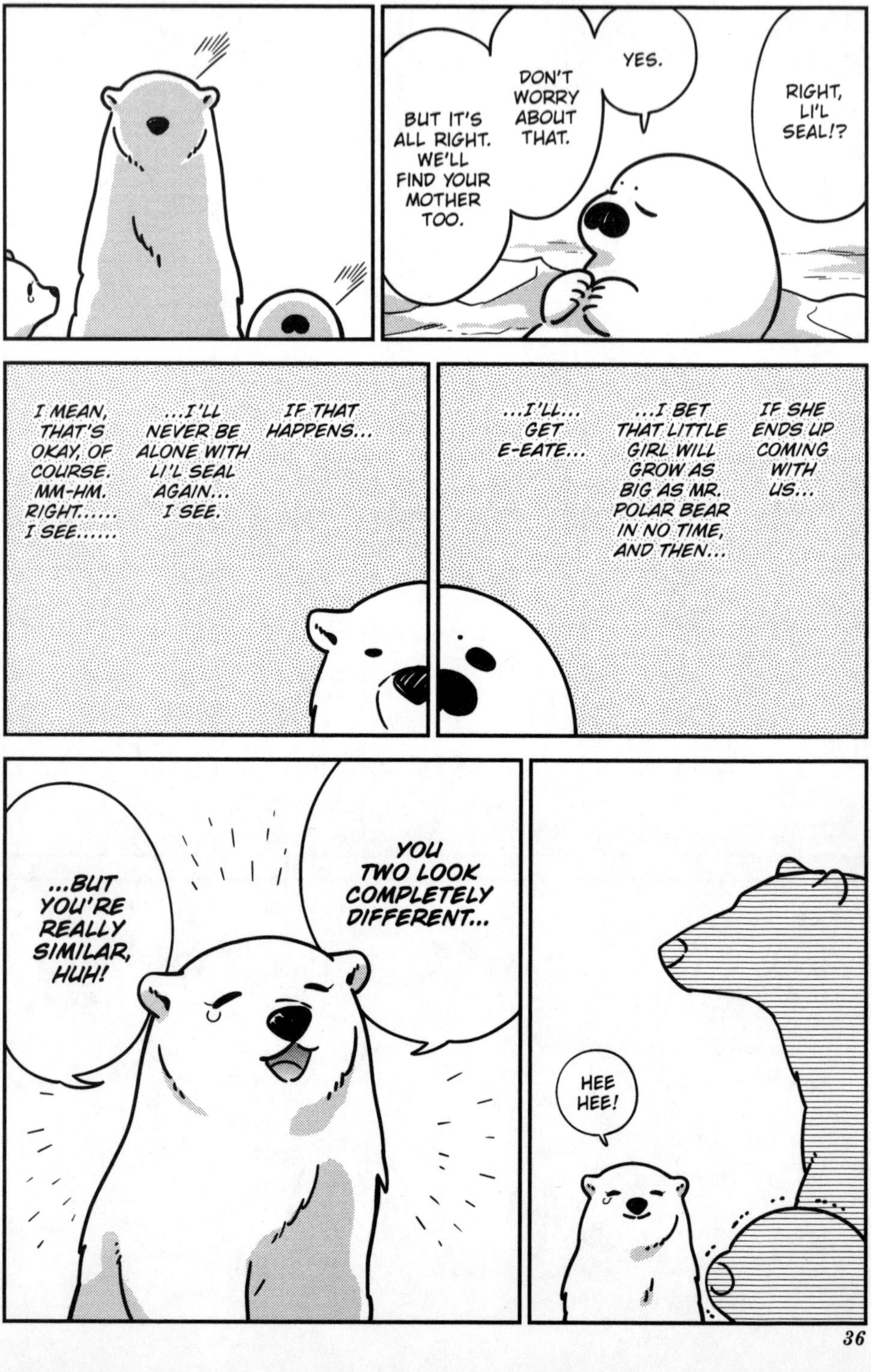
RIGHT, LI'L SEAL!?
YES.
DON'T WORRY ABOUT THAT.
BUT IT'S ALL RIGHT. WE'LL FIND YOUR MOTHER TOO.
IF SHE ENDS UP COMING WITH US...
...I BET THAT LITTLE GIRL WILL GROW AS BIG AS MR. POLAR BEAR IN NO TIME, AND THEN...
...I'LL... GET E-EATE...
IF THAT HAPPENS...
...I'LL NEVER BE ALONE WITH LI'L SEAL AGAIN... I SEE.
I MEAN, THAT'S OKAY, OF COURSE. MM-HM. RIGHT..... I SEE......
HEE HEE!
YOU TWO LOOK COMPLETELY DIFFERENT...
...BUT YOU'RE REALLY SIMILAR, HUH!

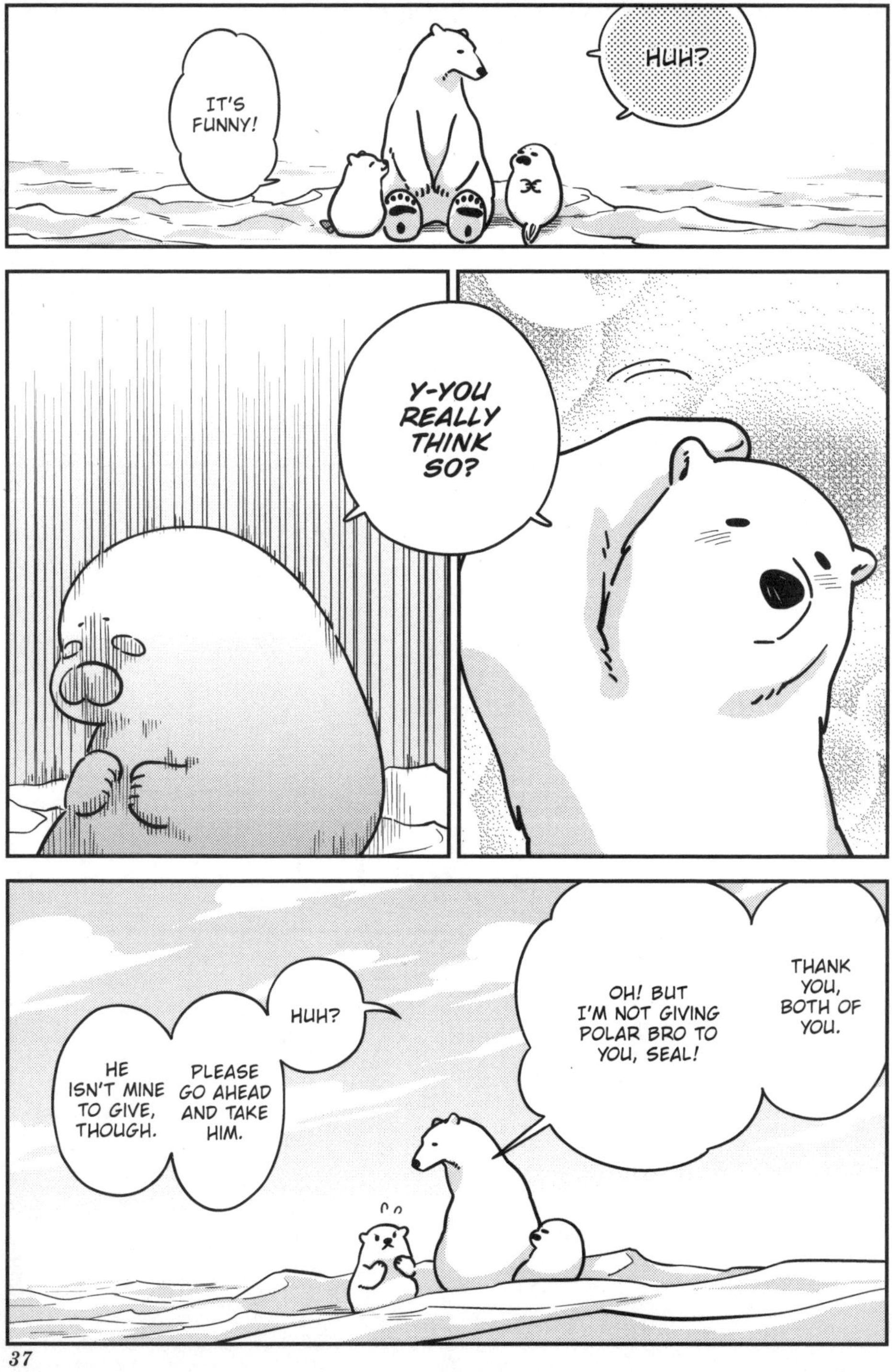
HUH?
IT'S FUNNY!
Y-YOU REALLY THINK SO?
THANK YOU, BOTH OF YOU.
OH! BUT I'M NOT GIVING POLAR BRO TO YOU, SEAL!
HUH?
PLEASE GO AHEAD AND TAKE HIM.
HE ISN'T MINE TO GIVE, THOUGH.

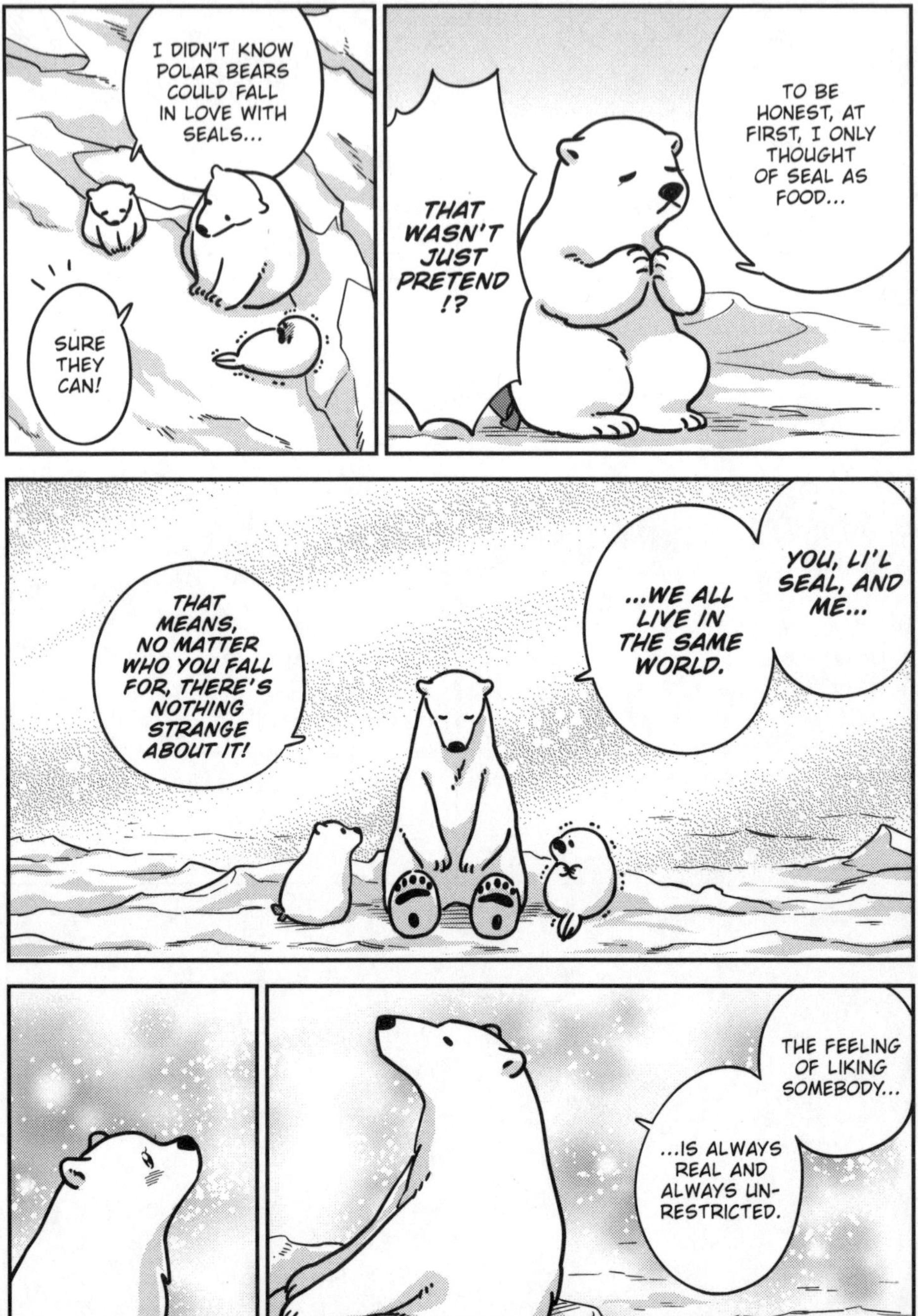
TO BE HONEST, AT FIRST, I ONLY THOUGHT OF SEAL AS FOOD...
THAT WASN'T JUST PRETEND !?
I DIDN'T KNOW POLAR BEARS COULD FALL IN LOVE WITH SEALS...
SURE THEY CAN!
YOU, LI'L SEAL, AND ME...
...WE ALL LIVE IN THE SAME WORLD.
THAT MEANS, NO MATTER WHO YOU FALL FOR, THERE'S NOTHING STRANGE ABOUT IT!
THE FEELING OF LIKING SOMEBODY...
...IS ALWAYS REAL AND ALWAYS UN-RESTRICTED.

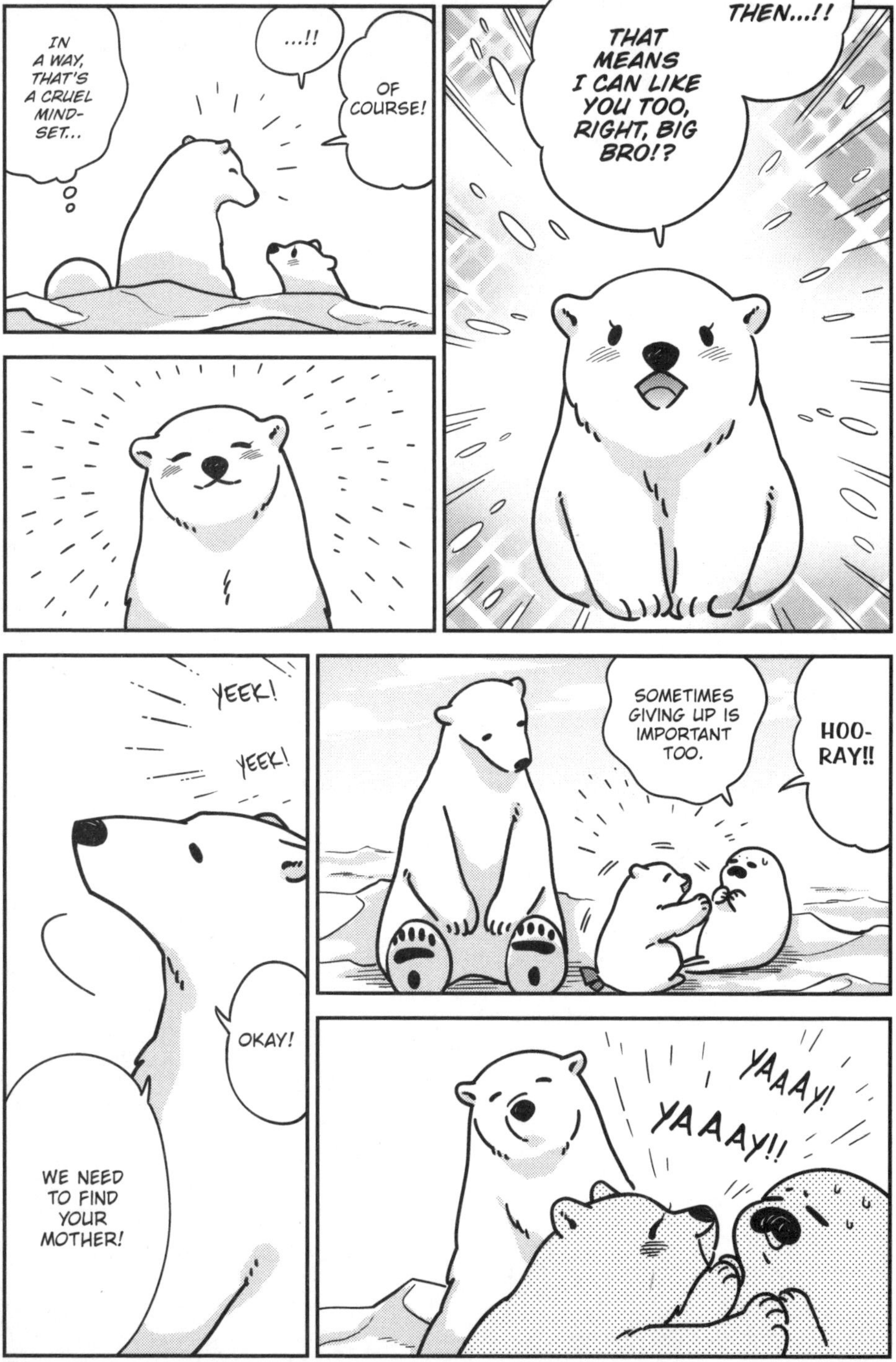
THEN...!!
THAT MEANS I CAN LIKE YOU TOO, RIGHT, BIG BRO!?
...!!
OF COURSE!
IN A WAY, THAT'S A CRUEL MIND-SET...
HOO-RAY!!
SOMETIMES GIVING UP IS IMPORTANT TOO.
YAAAY!
YAAAY!!
YEEK!
YEEK!
OKAY!
WE NEED TO FIND YOUR MOTHER!

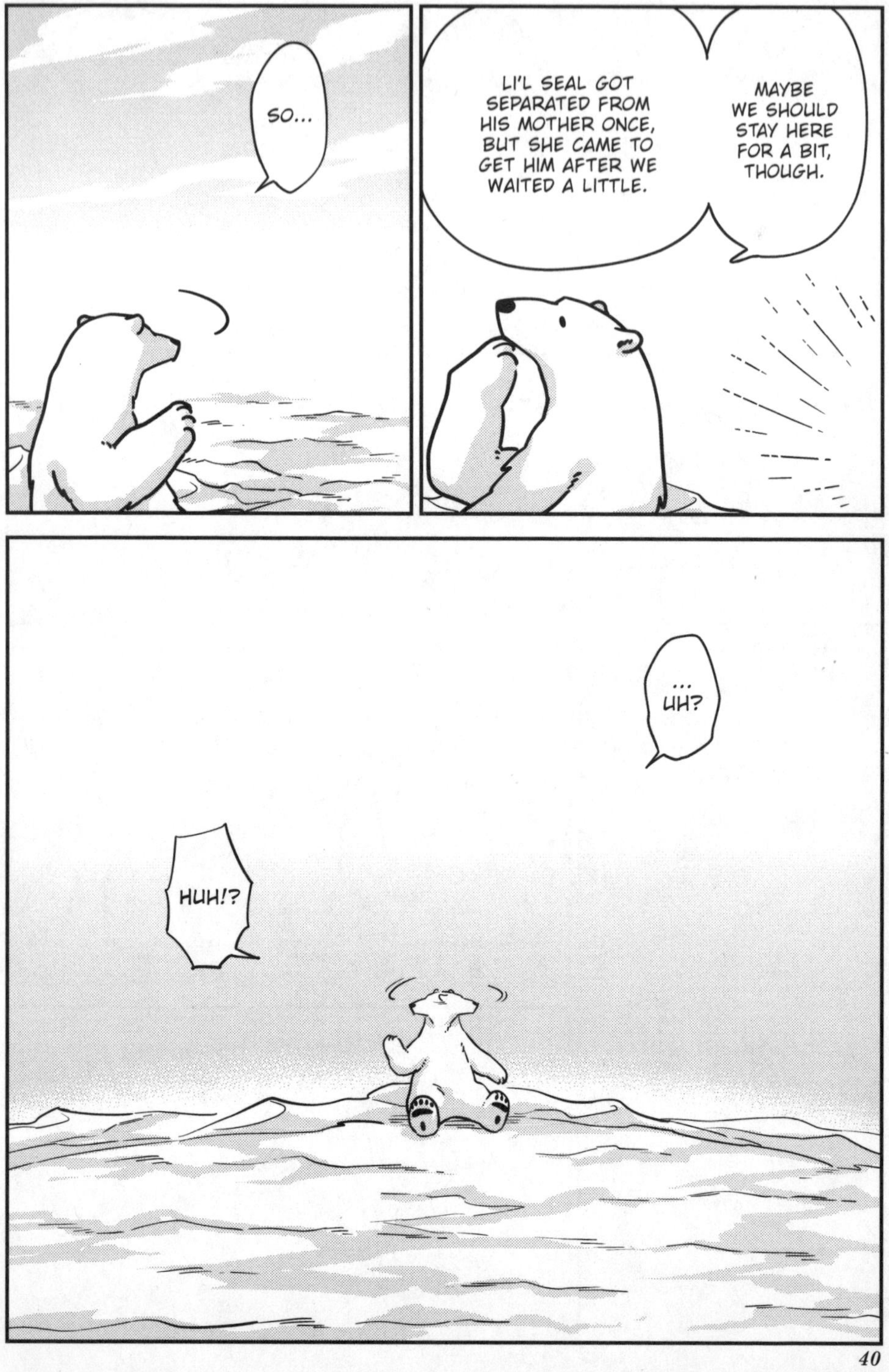
MAYBE WE SHOULD STAY HERE FOR A BIT, THOUGH.
LI'L SEAL GOT SEPARATED FROM HIS MOTHER ONCE, BUT SHE CAME TO GET HIM AFTER WE WAITED A LITTLE.
SO...
...UH?
HUH!?

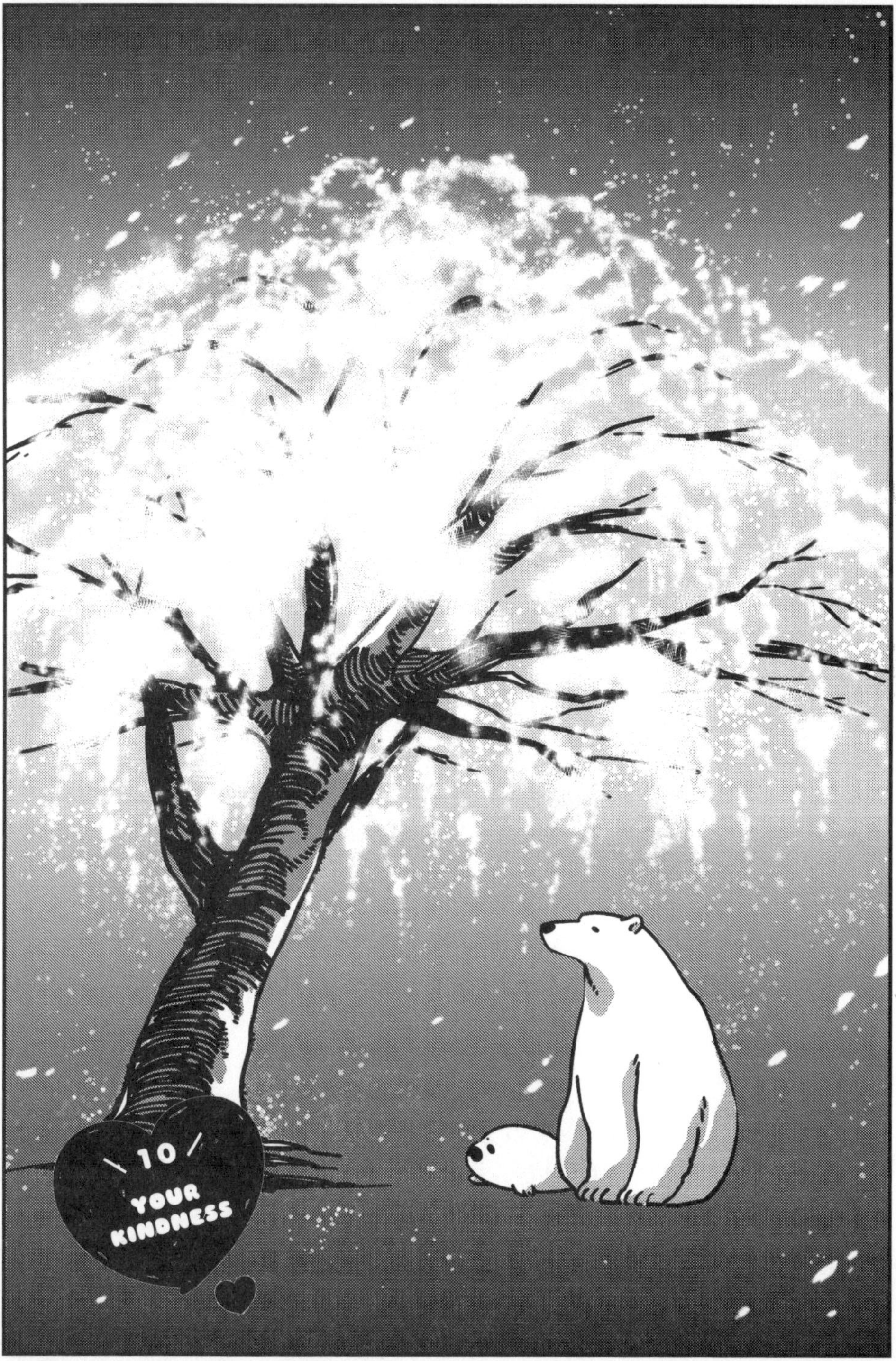
10
YOUR KINDNESS

THEY'RE GONE

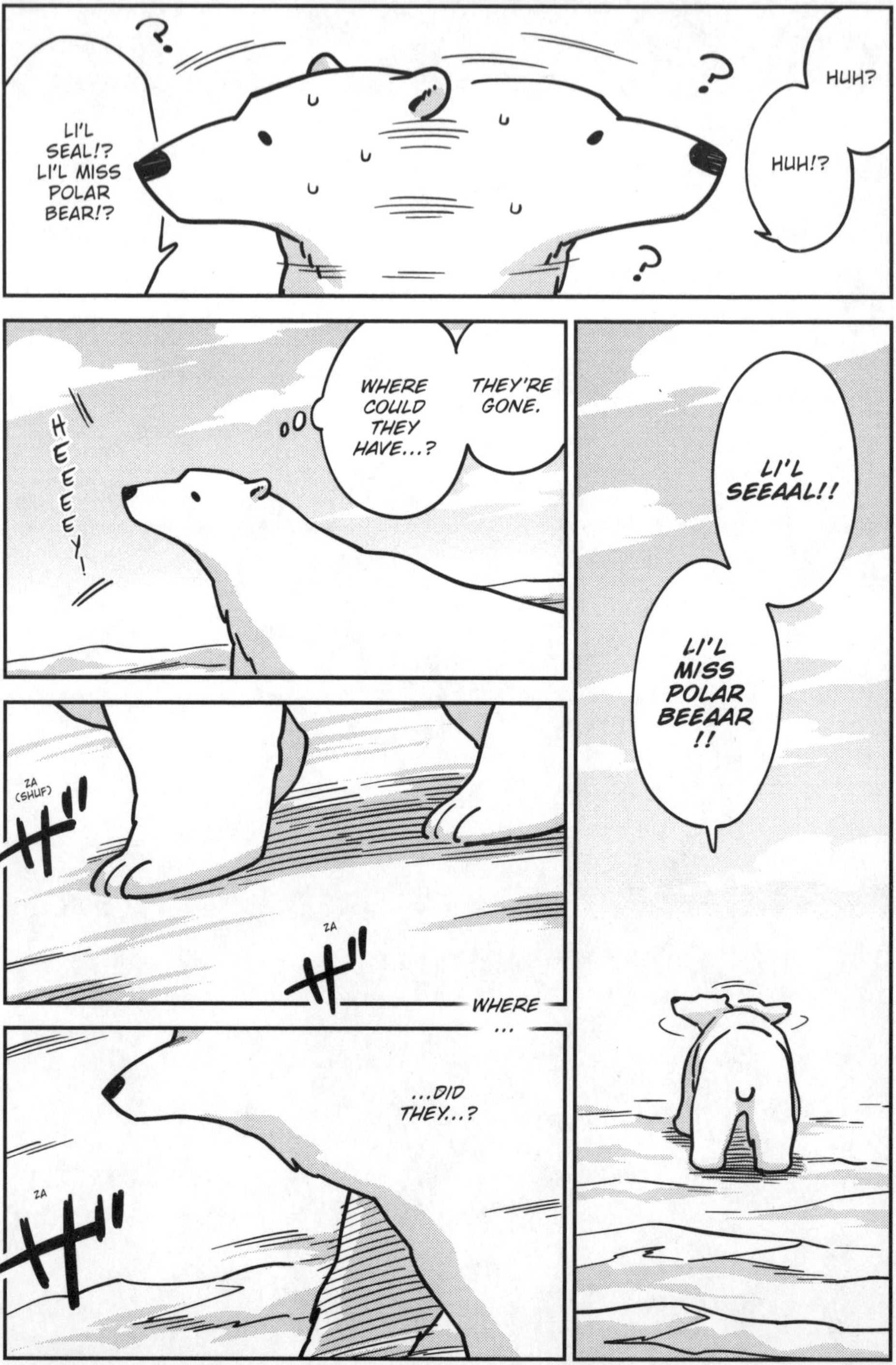
HUH?
HUH!?
LI'L SEAL!? LI'L MISS POLAR BEAR!?
LI'L SEEAAL!!
LI'L MISS POLAR BEEAAR!!
THEY'RE GONE.
WHERE COULD THEY HAVE...?
HEEEEY!
ZA (SHUF)
ZA
WHERE...
...DID THEY...?
ZA

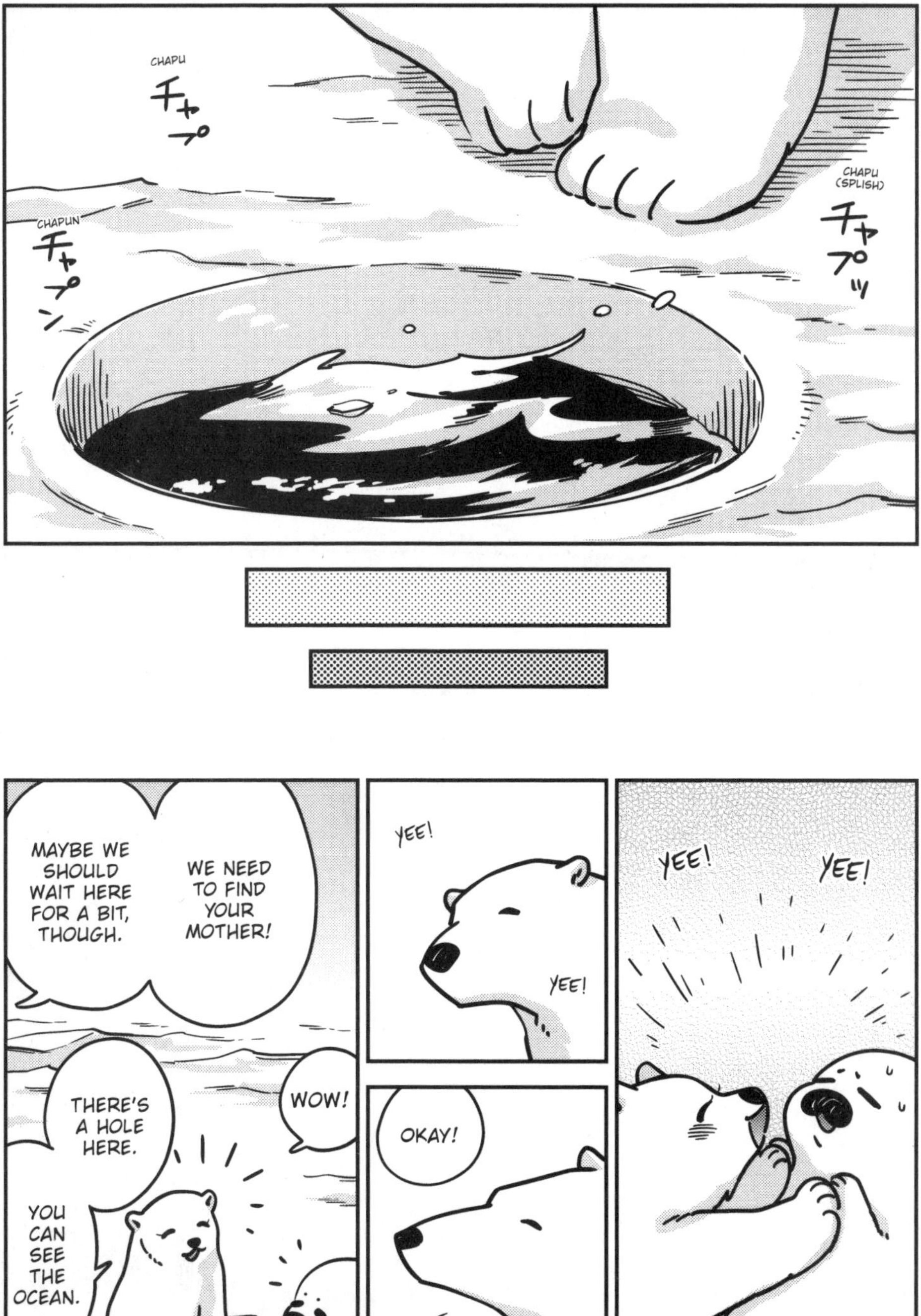
CHAPU (SPLISH)
チャプッ
CHAPU
チャプ
CHAPUN
チャプン
YEE!
YEE!
YEE!
YEE!
OKAY!
WE NEED TO FIND YOUR MOTHER!
MAYBE WE SHOULD WAIT HERE FOR A BIT, THOUGH.
WOW!
THERE'S A HOLE HERE.
YOU CAN SEE THE OCEAN.

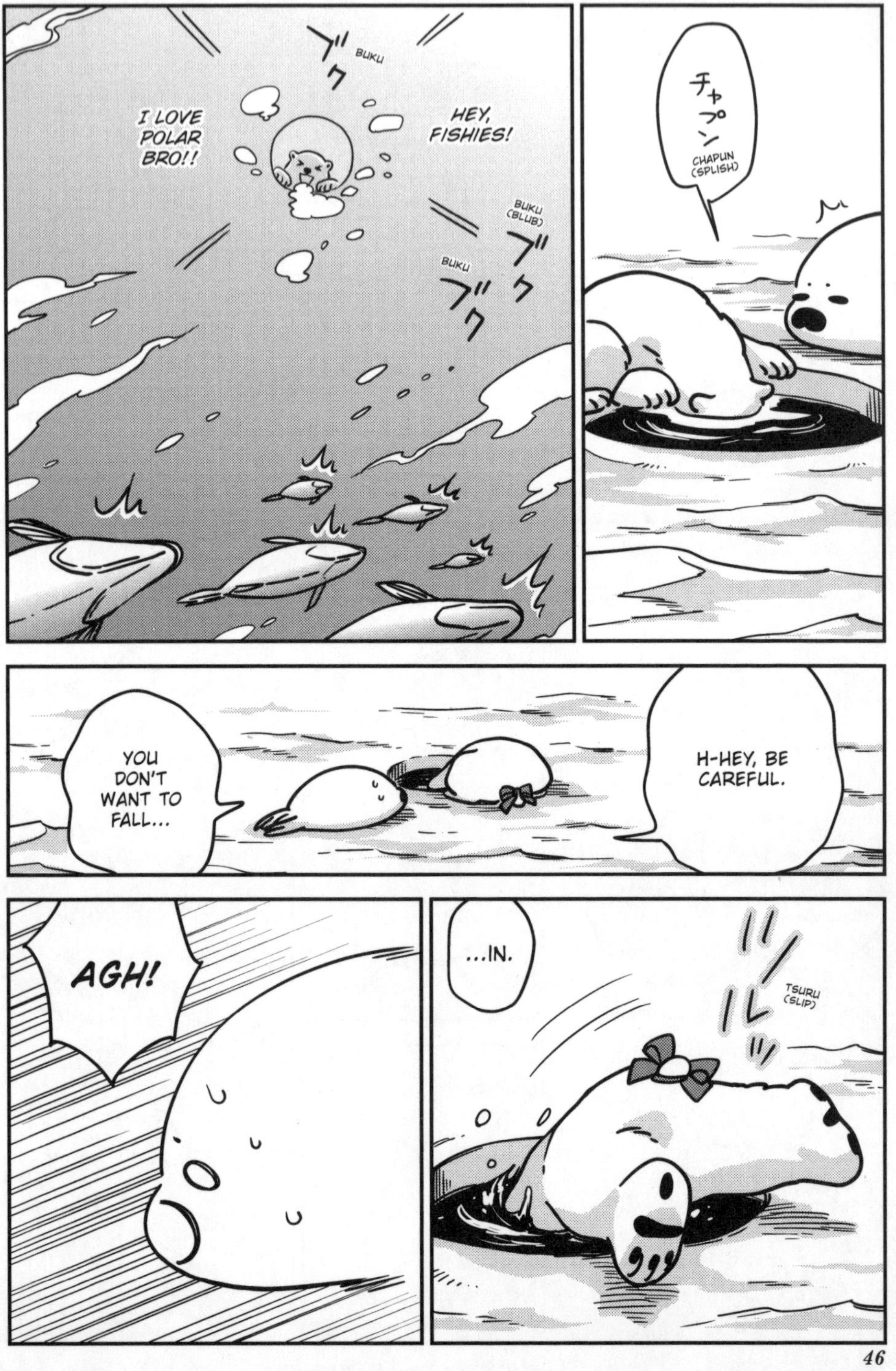
チャプン
CHAPUN (SPLISH)
ブク
BUKU
HEY, FISHIES!
I LOVE POLAR BRO!!
ブク
BUKU (BLUB)
ブク
BUKU
H-HEY, BE CAREFUL.
YOU DON'T WANT TO FALL...
...IN.
ツル
TSURU (SLIP)
AGH!

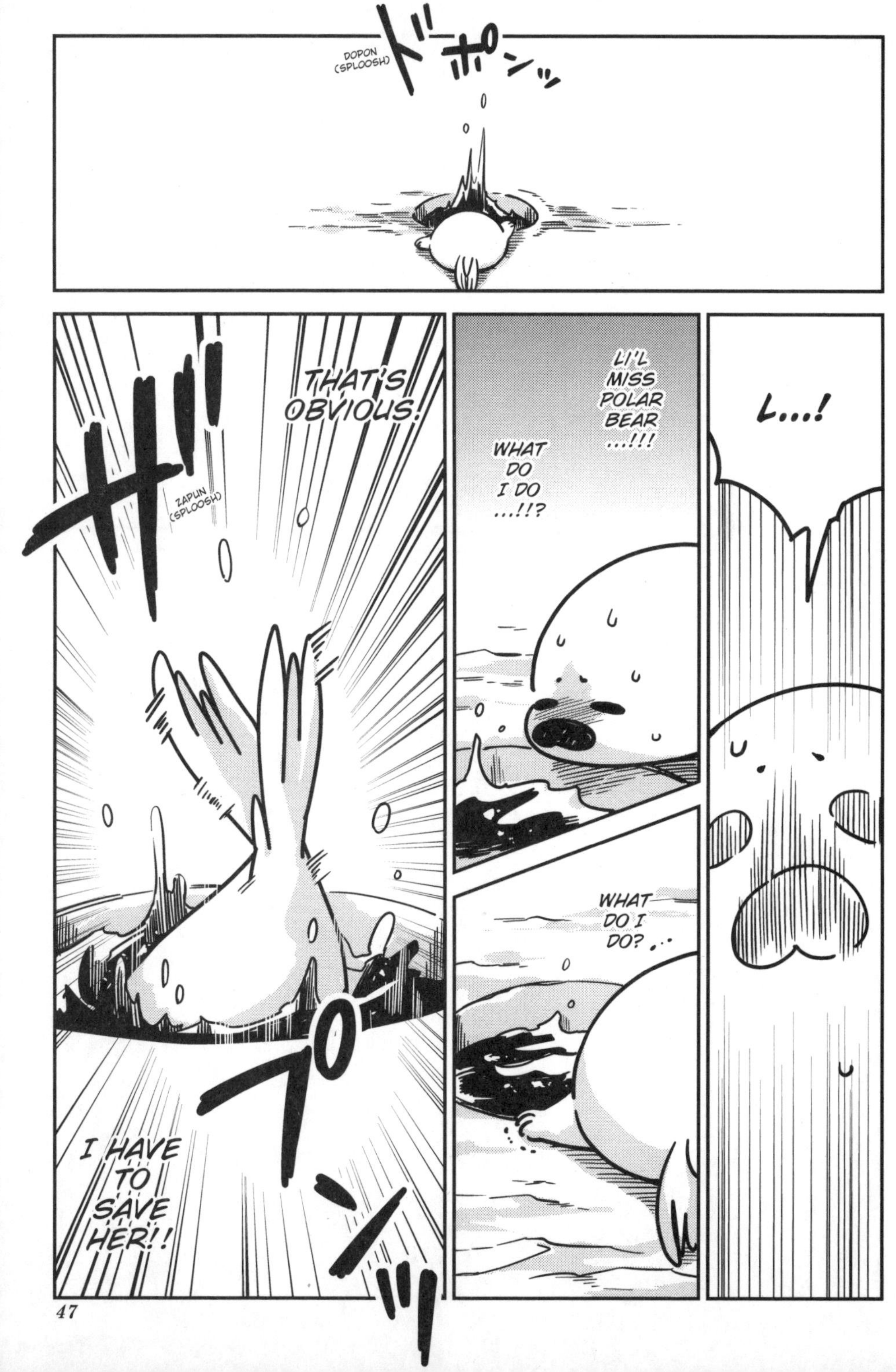
DOPON (SPLOOSH)
L...!
LI'L MISS POLAR BEAR ...!!!
WHAT DO I DO ...!!?
WHAT DO I DO? ...
THAT'S OBVIOUS!
ZAPUN (SPLOOSH)
I HAVE TO SAVE HER!!

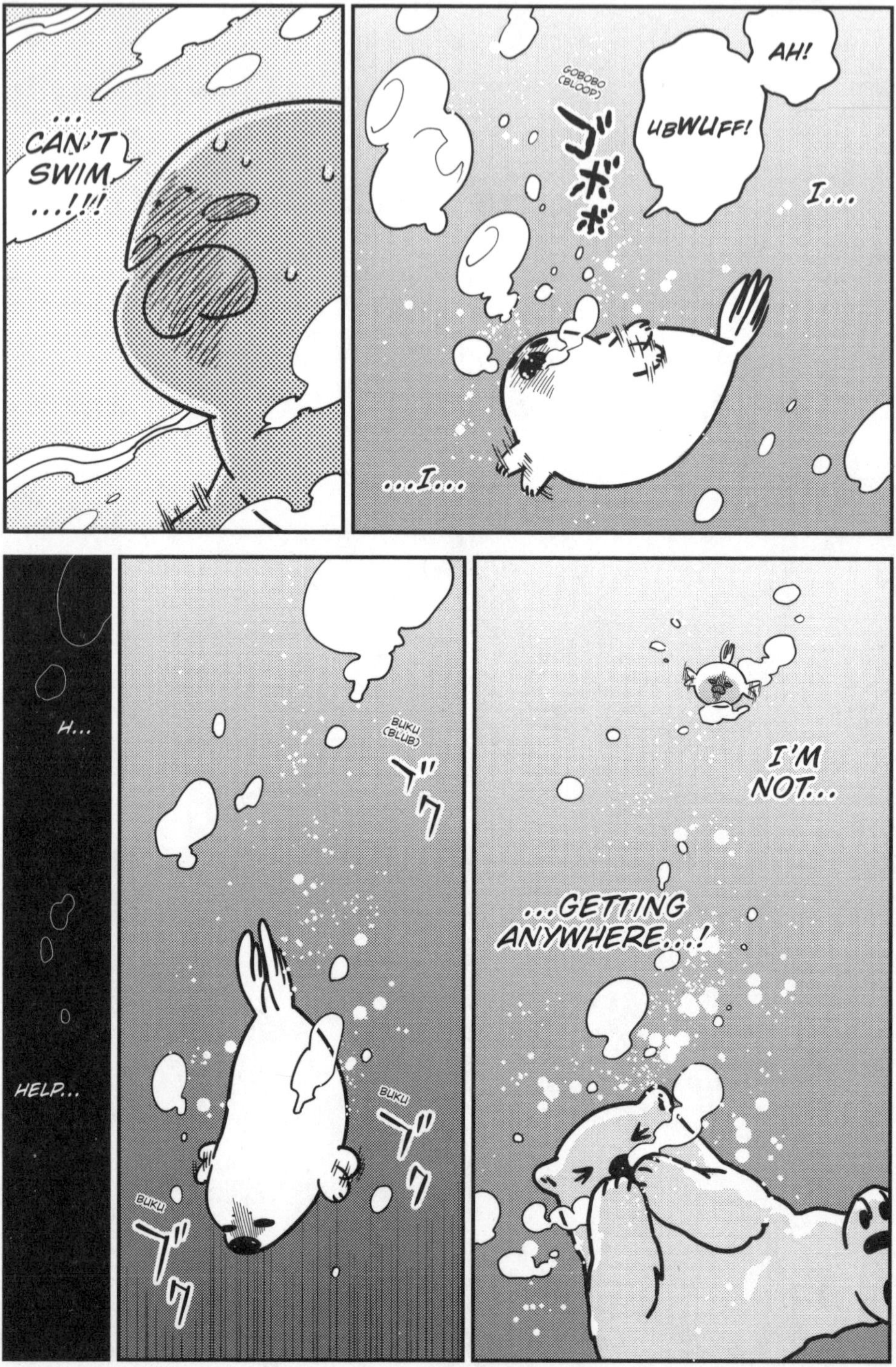
AH!
UBWUFF!
I...
GOBOBO (BLOOP)
ゴボボ
...I...
...CAN'T SWIM...!!!
I'M NOT...
...GETTING ANYWHERE...!
BUKU (BLUB)
ブク
BUKU
ブク
BUKU
ブク
H...
HELP...

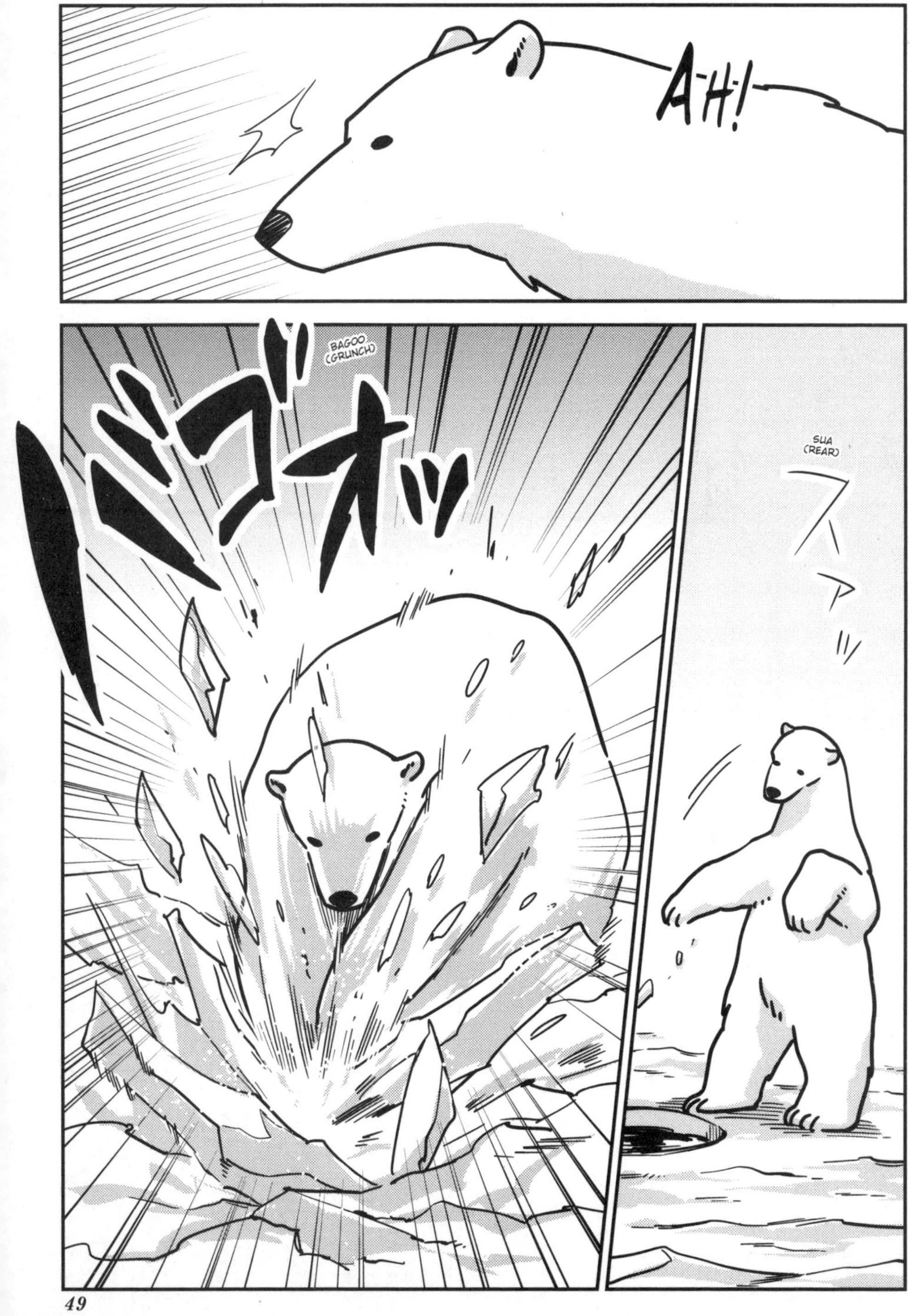
AH!
SUA (REAR)
スァッ
BAGOO (GRUNCH)
バゴオッ

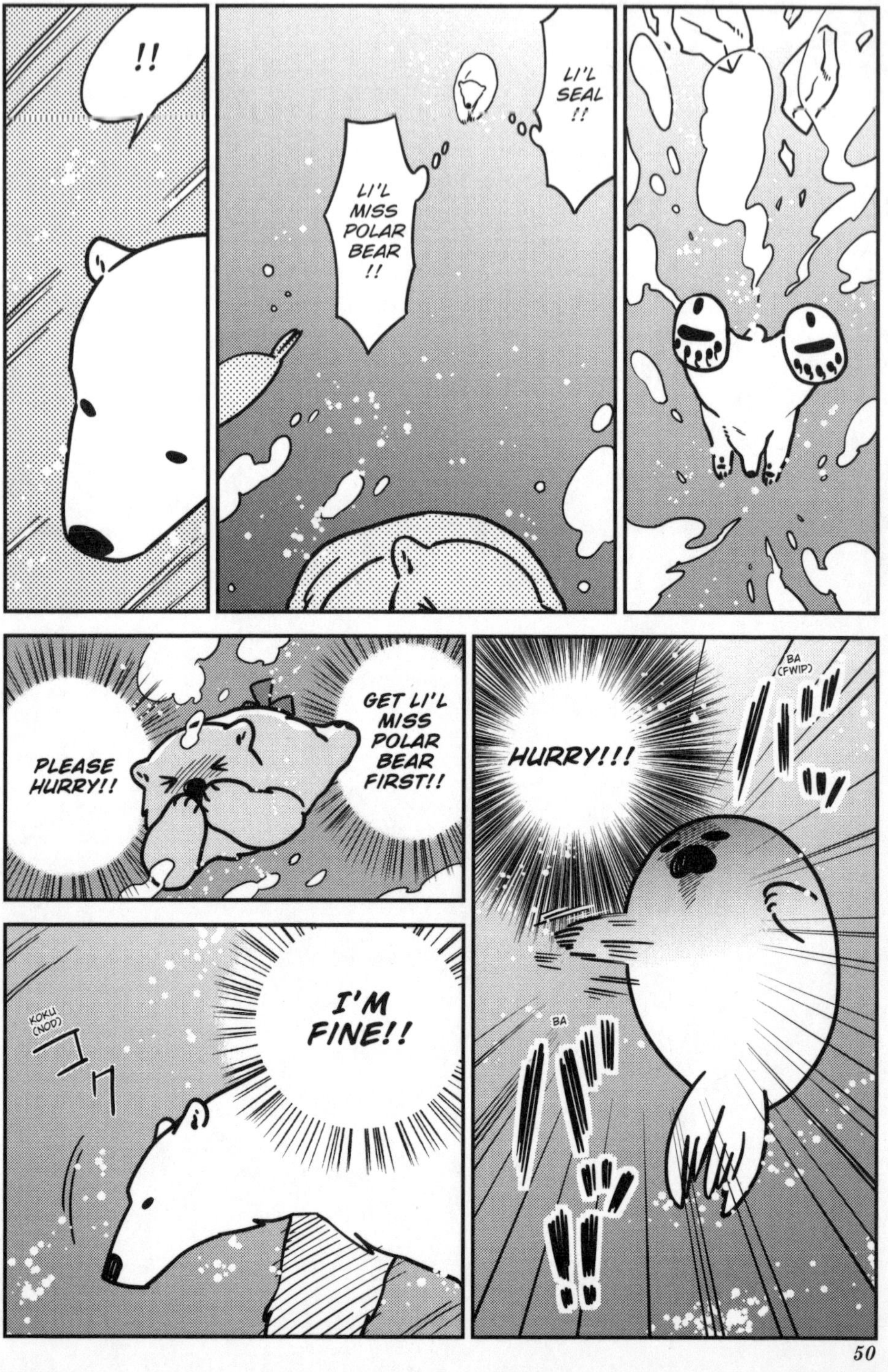
LI'L SEAL!!
LI'L MISS POLAR BEAR!!
!!
BA (FWIP)
HURRY!!!
BA
GET LI'L MISS POLAR BEAR FIRST!!
PLEASE HURRY!!
I'M FINE!!
KOKU (NOD)
コク

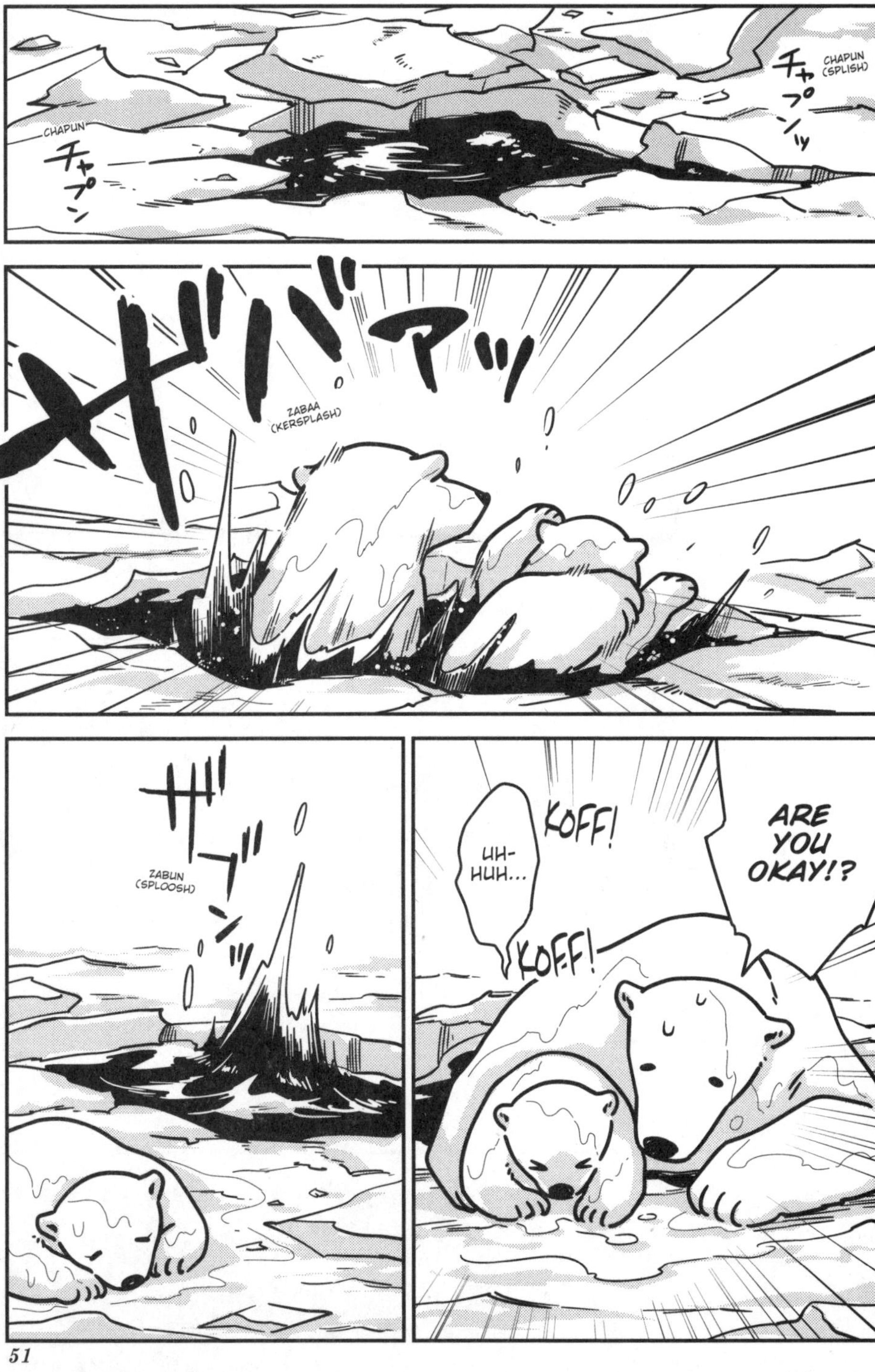
チャプンッ
CHAPUN (SPLISH)
チャプン
CHAPUN
ザバァッ
ZABAA (KERSPLASH)
ARE YOU OKAY!?
KOFF!
UH-HUH...
KOFF!
ザブンッ
ZABUN (SPLOOSH)

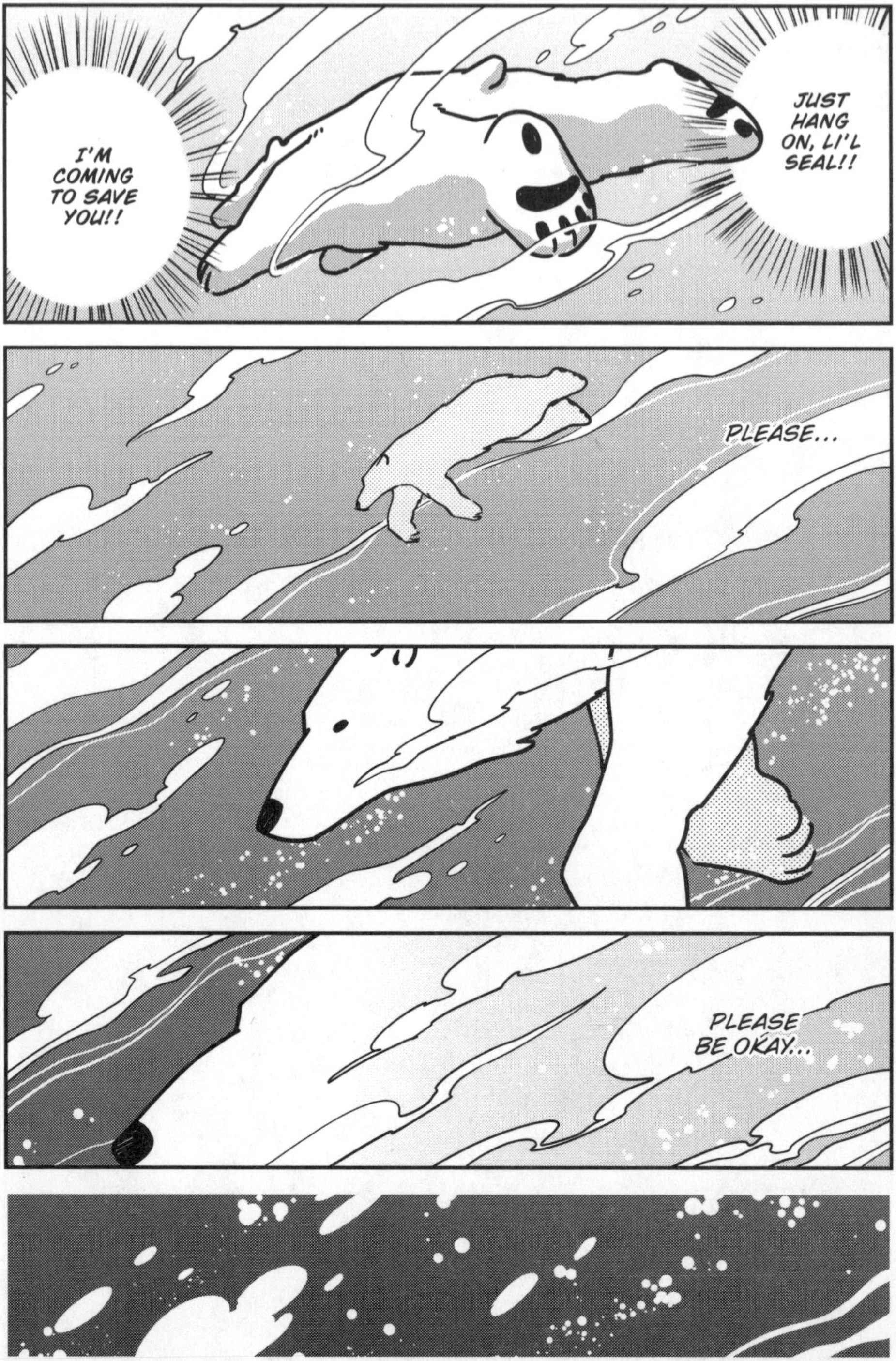
JUST HANG ON, LI'L SEAL!!
I'M COMING TO SAVE YOU!!
PLEASE...
PLEASE BE OKAY...

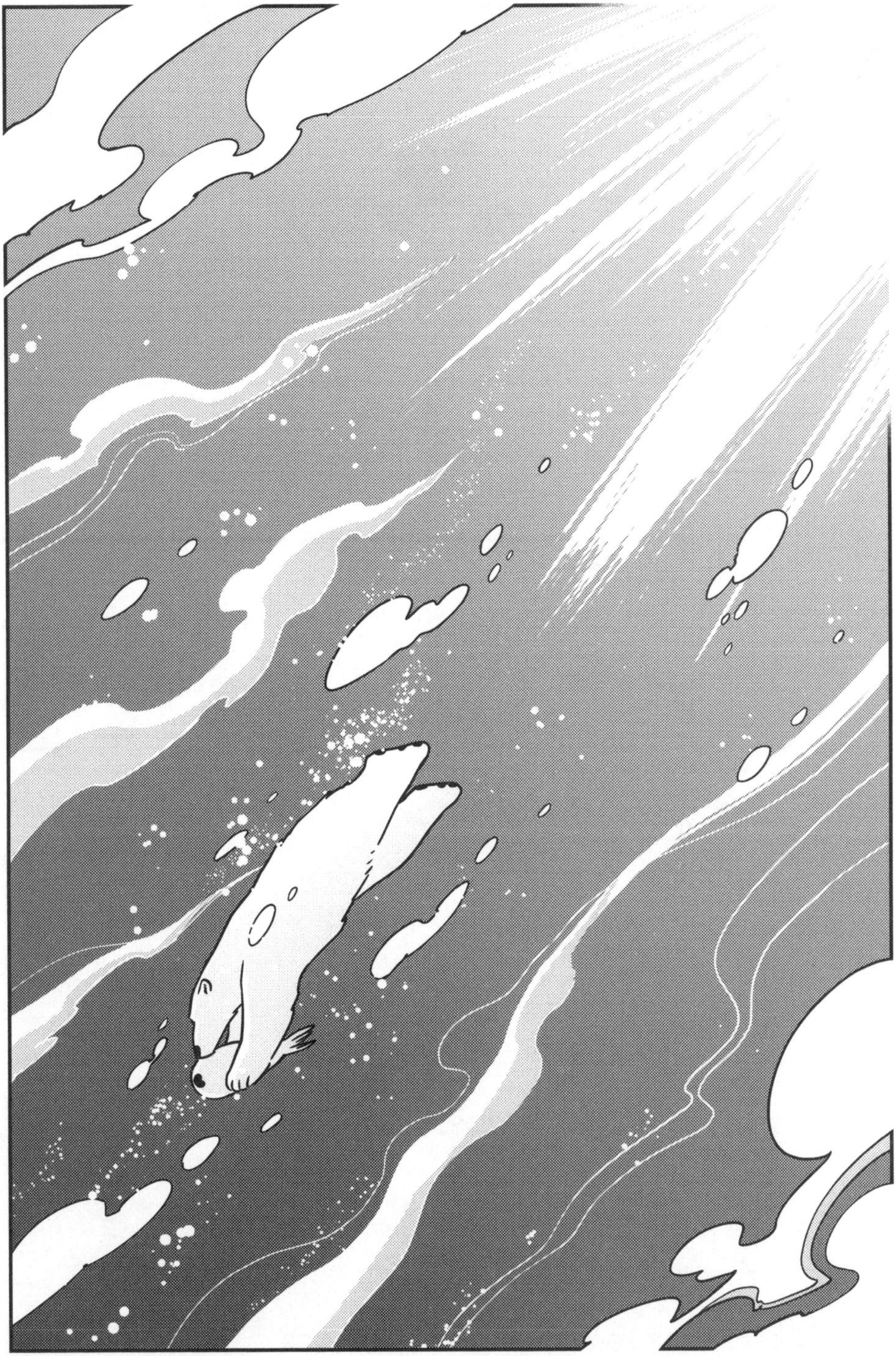

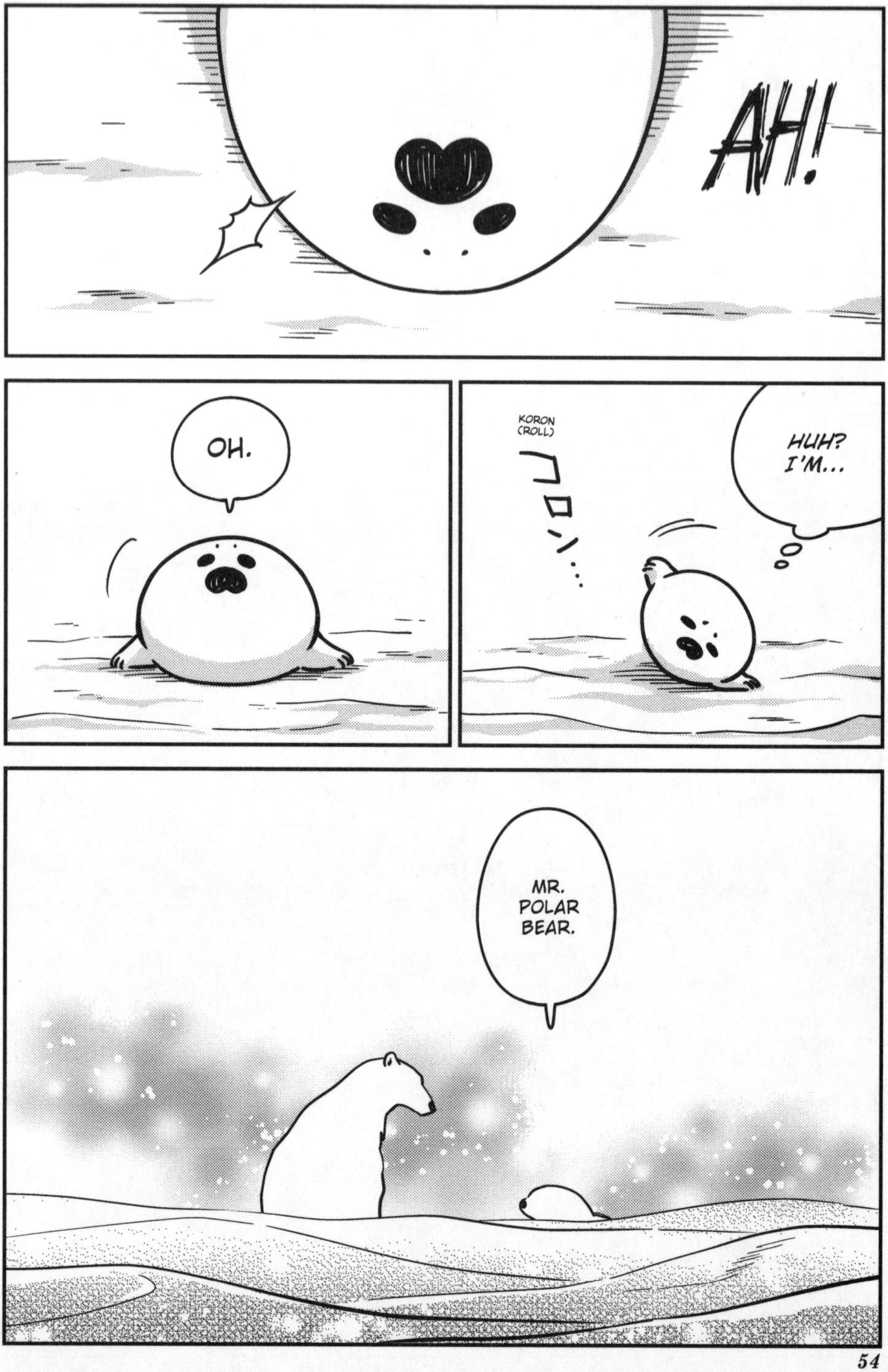
AH!
KORON (ROLL)
コロン…
HUH? I'M...
OH.
MR. POLAR BEAR.

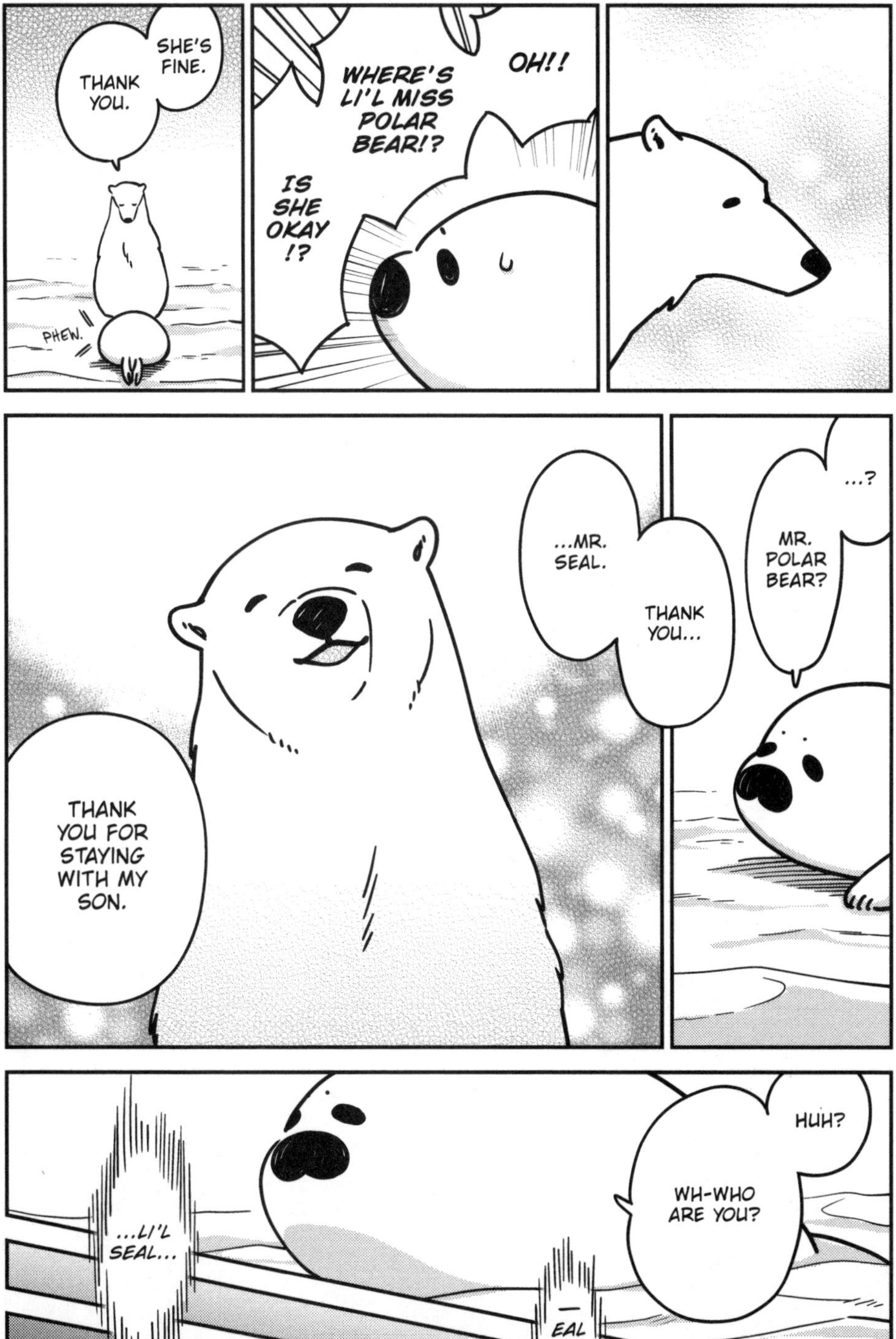
OH!!
WHERE'S LI'L MISS POLAR BEAR!?
IS SHE OKAY!?
SHE'S FINE.
THANK YOU.
PHEW.
...?
MR. POLAR BEAR?
...MR. SEAL.
THANK YOU...
THANK YOU FOR STAYING WITH MY SON.
HUH?
WH-WHO ARE YOU?
—EAL...
...LI'L SEAL...

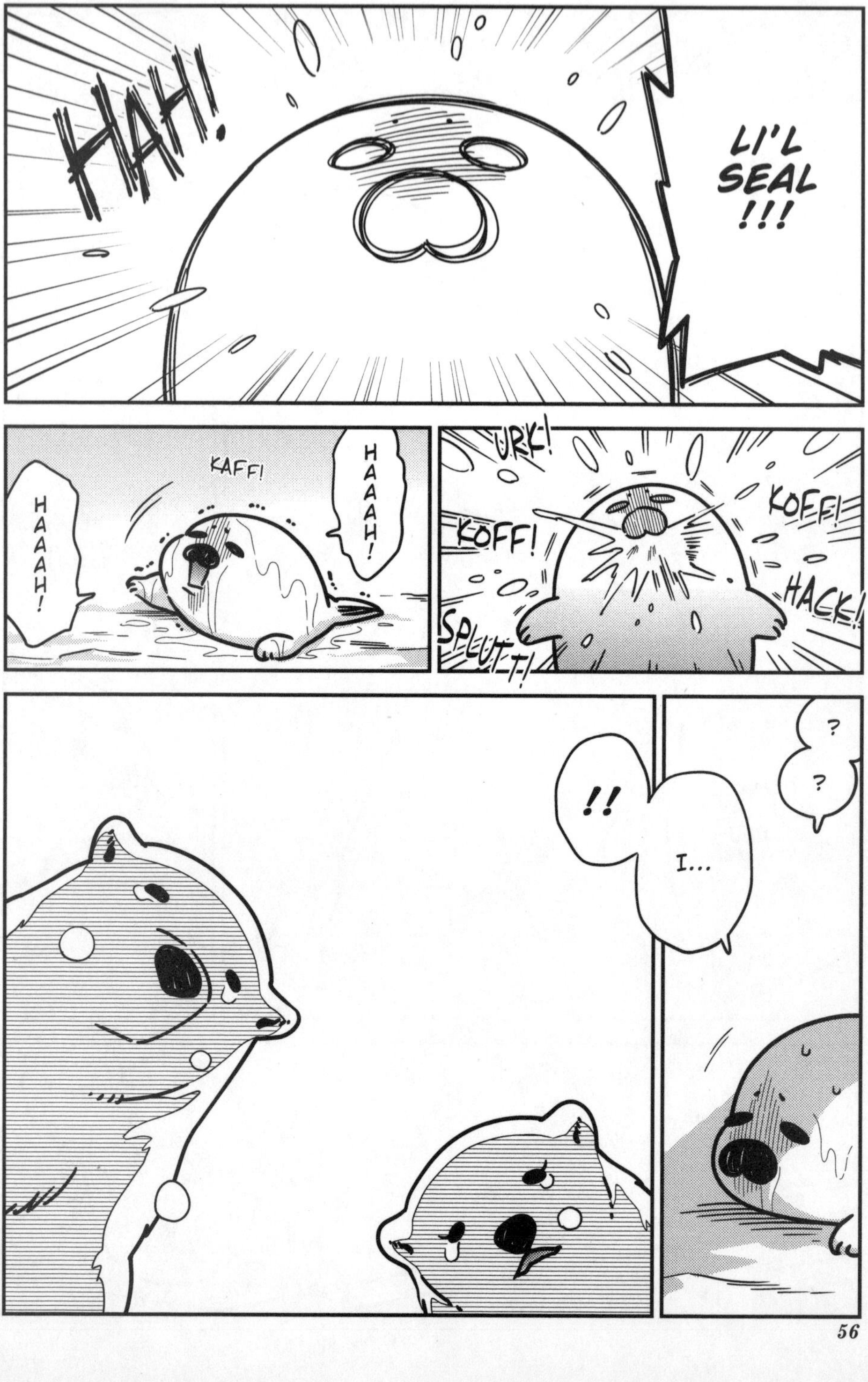
LI'L SEAL!!!
HAH!
URK!
KOFF!
KOFF!
HACK!
SPLUTT!
HAAAAH!
KAFF!
HAAAAH!
? ?
!!
I...

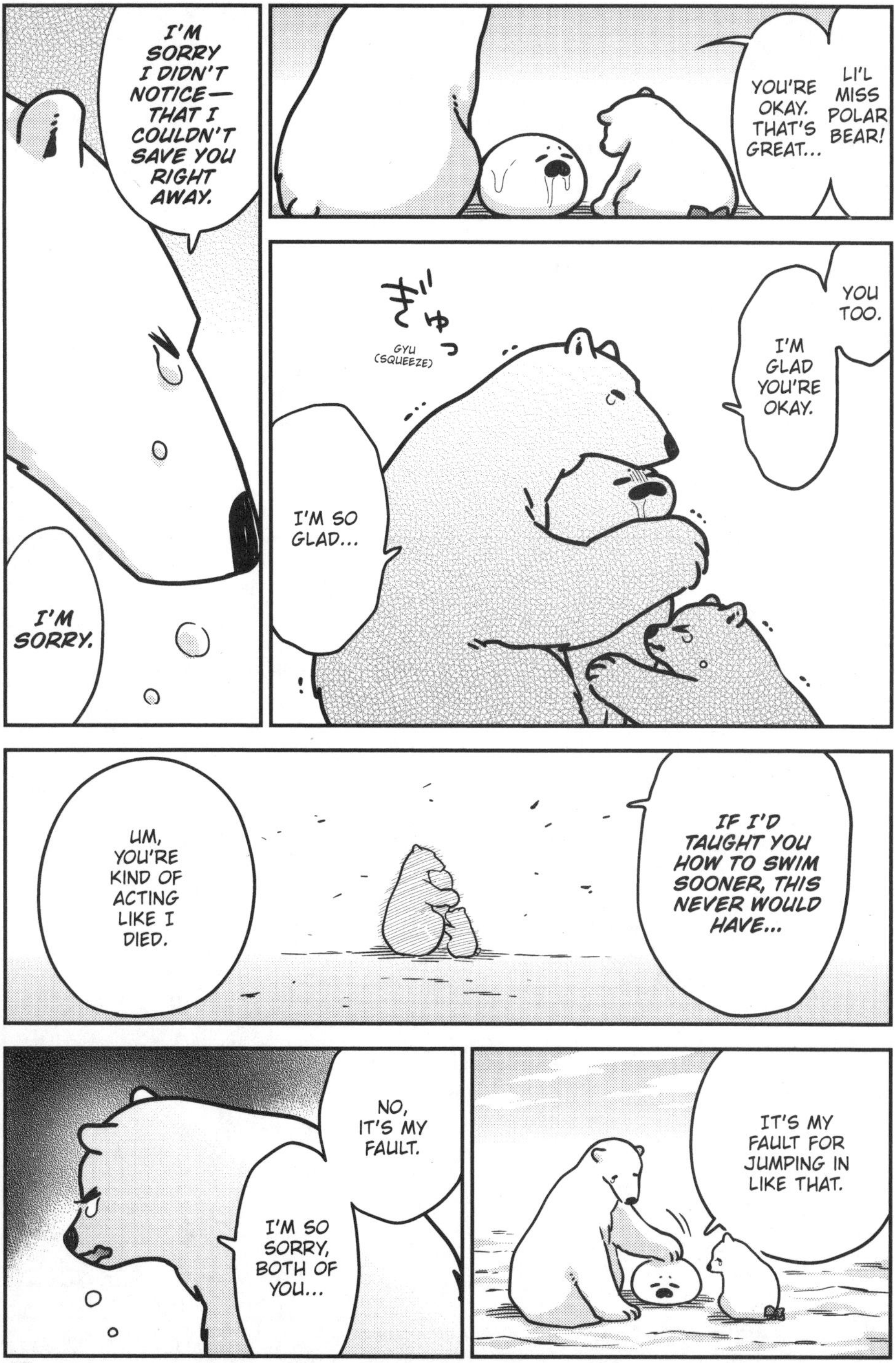
LI'L MISS POLAR BEAR!
YOU'RE OKAY. THAT'S GREAT...
YOU TOO.
I'M GLAD YOU'RE OKAY.
ぎゅっ
GYU (SQUEEZE)
I'M SO GLAD...
I'M SORRY I DIDN'T NOTICE—THAT I COULDN'T SAVE YOU RIGHT AWAY.
I'M SORRY.
IF I'D TAUGHT YOU HOW TO SWIM SOONER, THIS NEVER WOULD HAVE...
UM, YOU'RE KIND OF ACTING LIKE I DIED.
IT'S MY FAULT FOR JUMPING IN LIKE THAT.
NO, IT'S MY FAULT.
I'M SO SORRY, BOTH OF YOU...

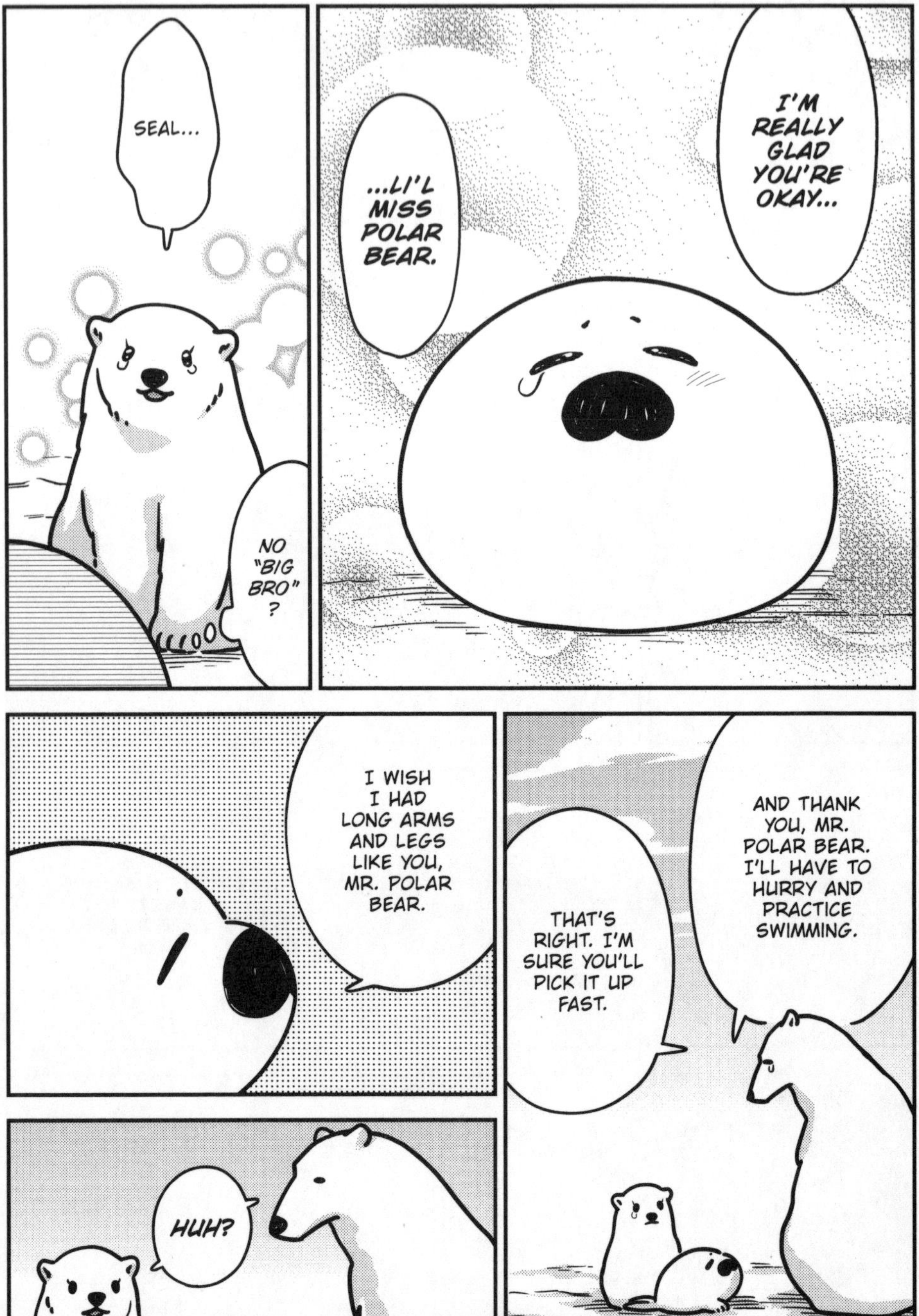
I'M REALLY GLAD YOU'RE OKAY...
...LI'L MISS POLAR BEAR.
SEAL...
NO "BIG BRO"?
AND THANK YOU, MR. POLAR BEAR. I'LL HAVE TO HURRY AND PRACTICE SWIMMING.
THAT'S RIGHT. I'M SURE YOU'LL PICK IT UP FAST.
I WISH I HAD LONG ARMS AND LEGS LIKE YOU, MR. POLAR BEAR.
HUH?

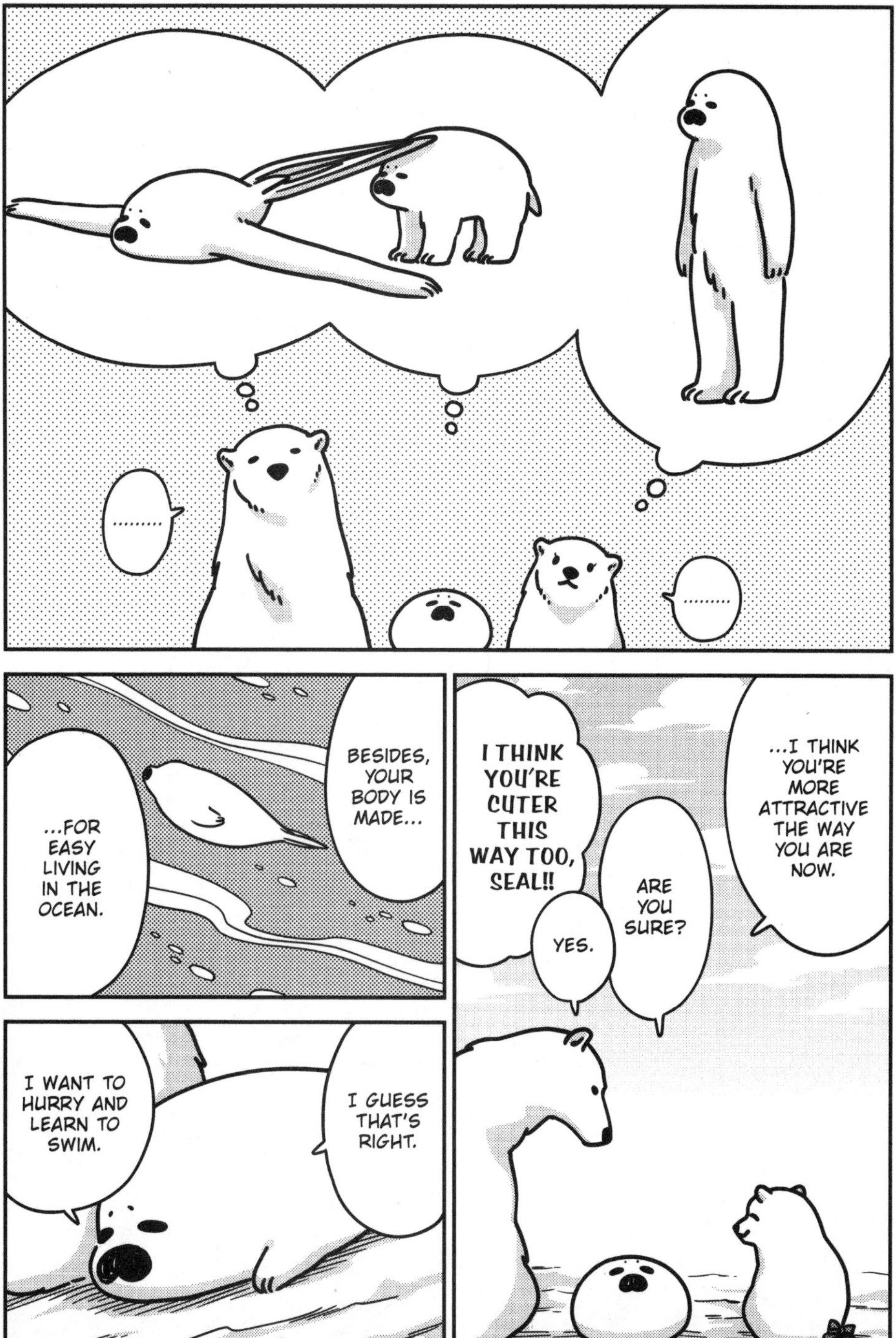

....
....
...I THINK YOU'RE MORE ATTRACTIVE THE WAY YOU ARE NOW.
I THINK YOU'RE CUTER THIS WAY TOO, SEAL!!
ARE YOU SURE?
YES.
BESIDES, YOUR BODY IS MADE...
...FOR EASY LIVING IN THE OCEAN.
I GUESS THAT'S RIGHT.
I WANT TO HURRY AND LEARN TO SWIM.

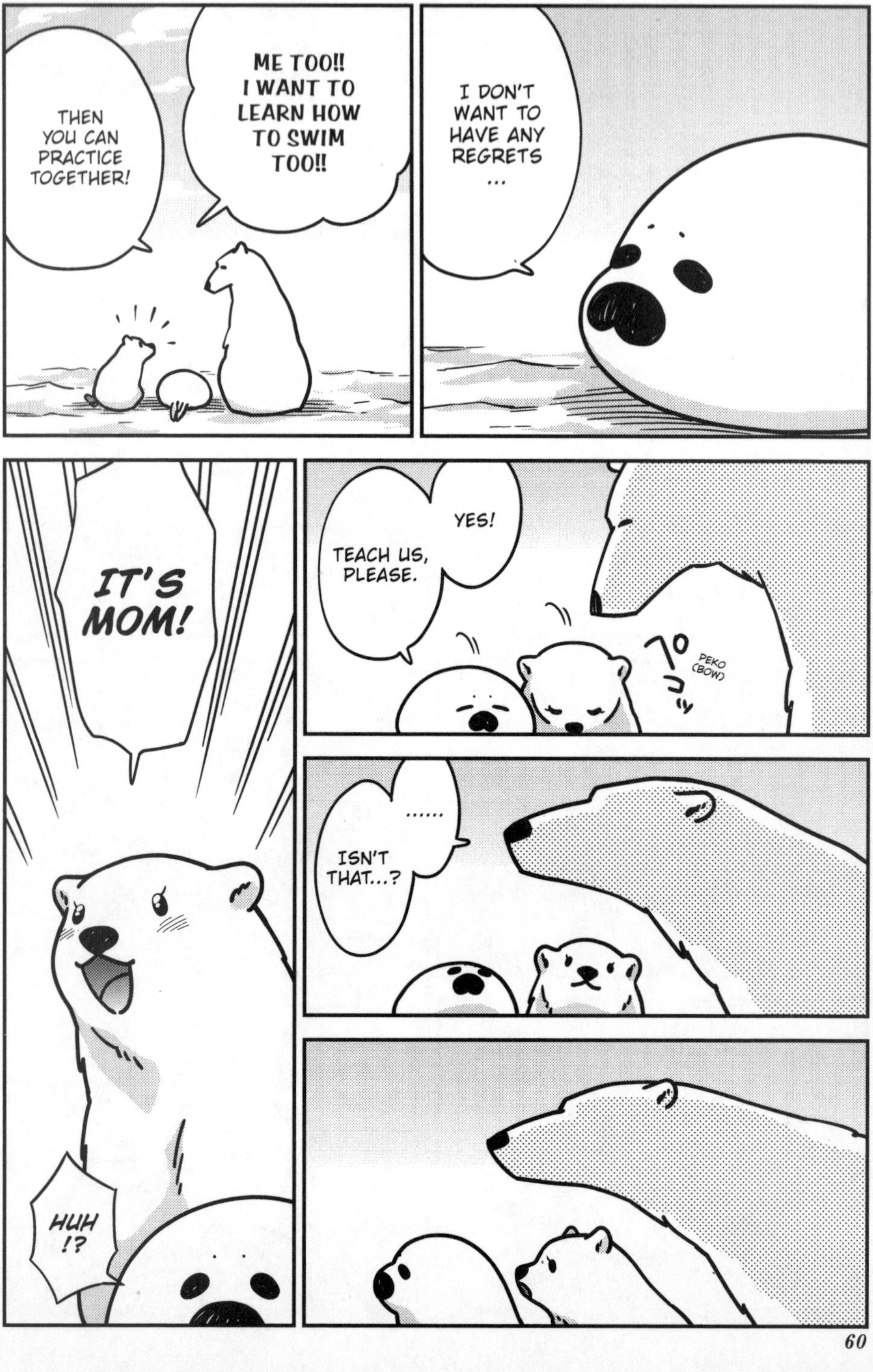
I DON'T WANT TO HAVE ANY REGRETS ...
ME TOO!! I WANT TO LEARN HOW TO SWIM TOO!!
THEN YOU CAN PRACTICE TOGETHER!
YES!
TEACH US, PLEASE.
ペコッ
PEKO (BOW)
......
ISN'T THAT...?
IT'S MOM!
HUH !?

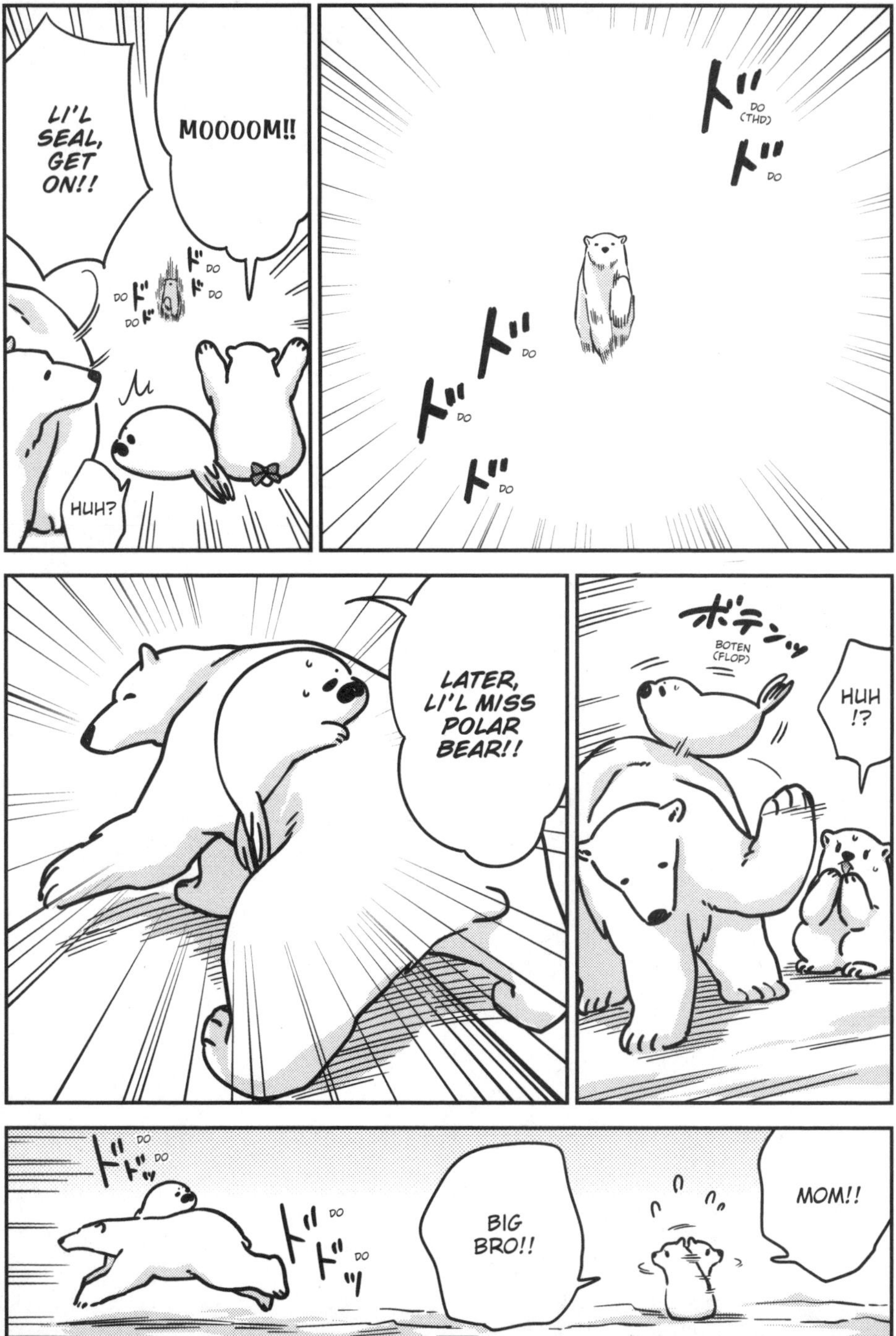
ド DO (THD)
ド DO
ド DO
ド DO
ド DO
MOOOOM!!
LI'L SEAL, GET ON!!
ド DO
ド DO
ド DO
ド DO
HUH?
ボテンッ
BOTEN (FLOP)
HUH !?
LATER, LI'L MISS POLAR BEAR!!
MOM!!
BIG BRO!!
ドドッ DO DO
ドドッ DO DO

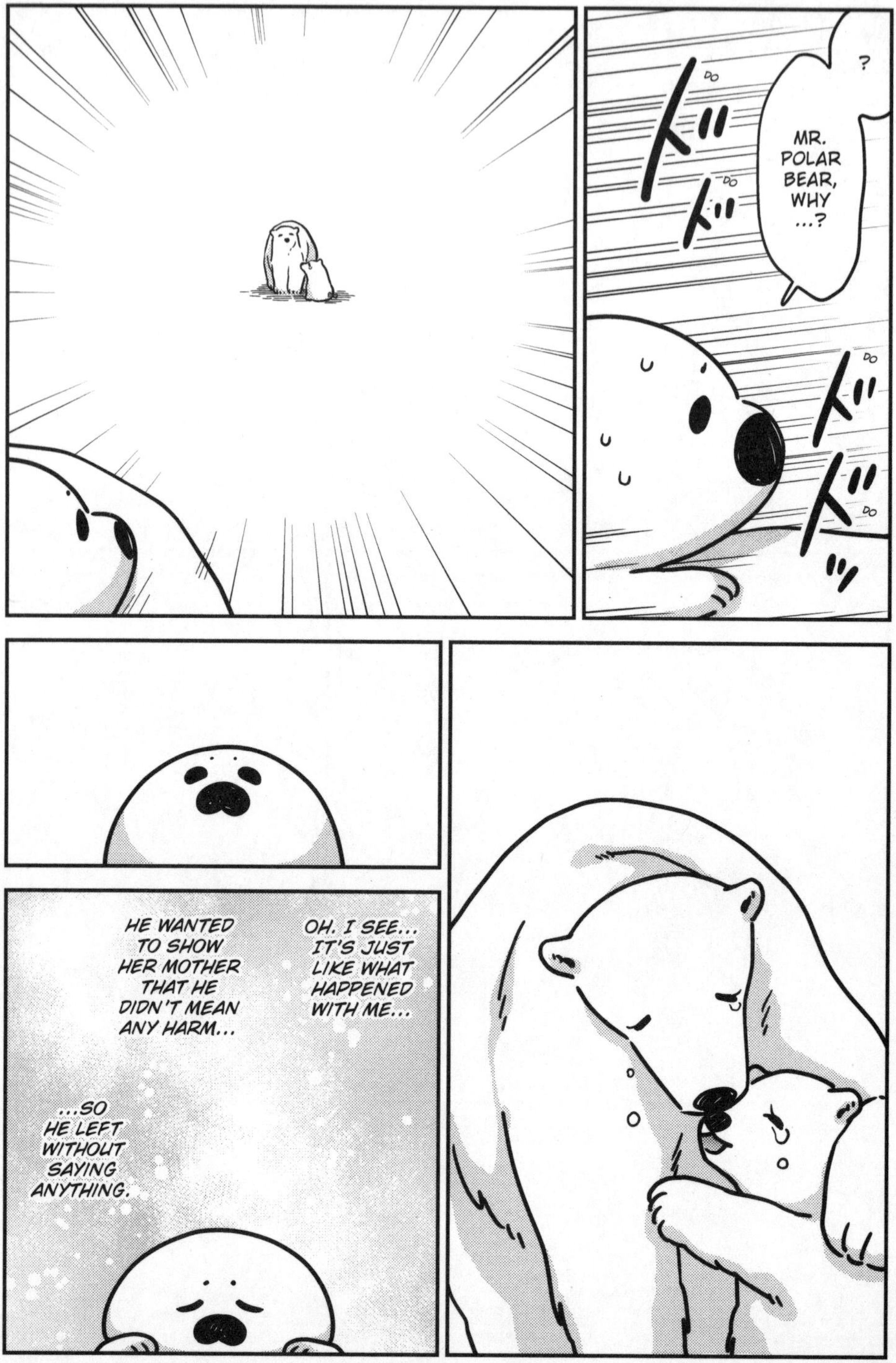
?
MR. POLAR BEAR, WHY ...?
ドド DO DO
ドドッ DO DO
OH. I SEE... IT'S JUST LIKE WHAT HAPPENED WITH ME...
HE WANTED TO SHOW HER MOTHER THAT HE DIDN'T MEAN ANY HARM...
...SO HE LEFT WITHOUT SAYING ANYTHING.

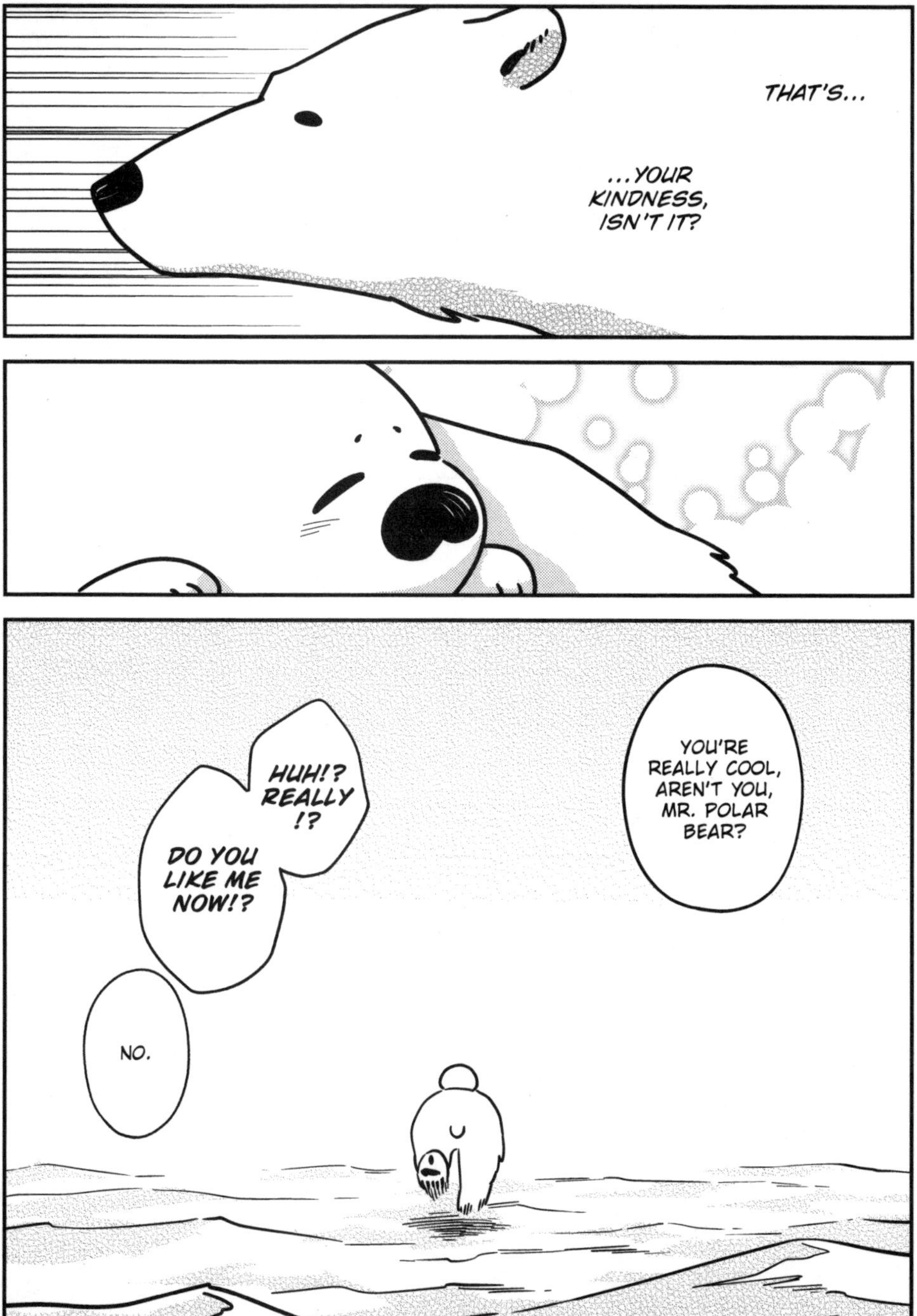
THAT'S...
...YOUR KINDNESS, ISN'T IT?
YOU'RE REALLY COOL, AREN'T YOU, MR. POLAR BEAR?
HUH!? REALLY!?
DO YOU LIKE ME NOW!?
NO.

SOMEDAY, ONCE AGAIN

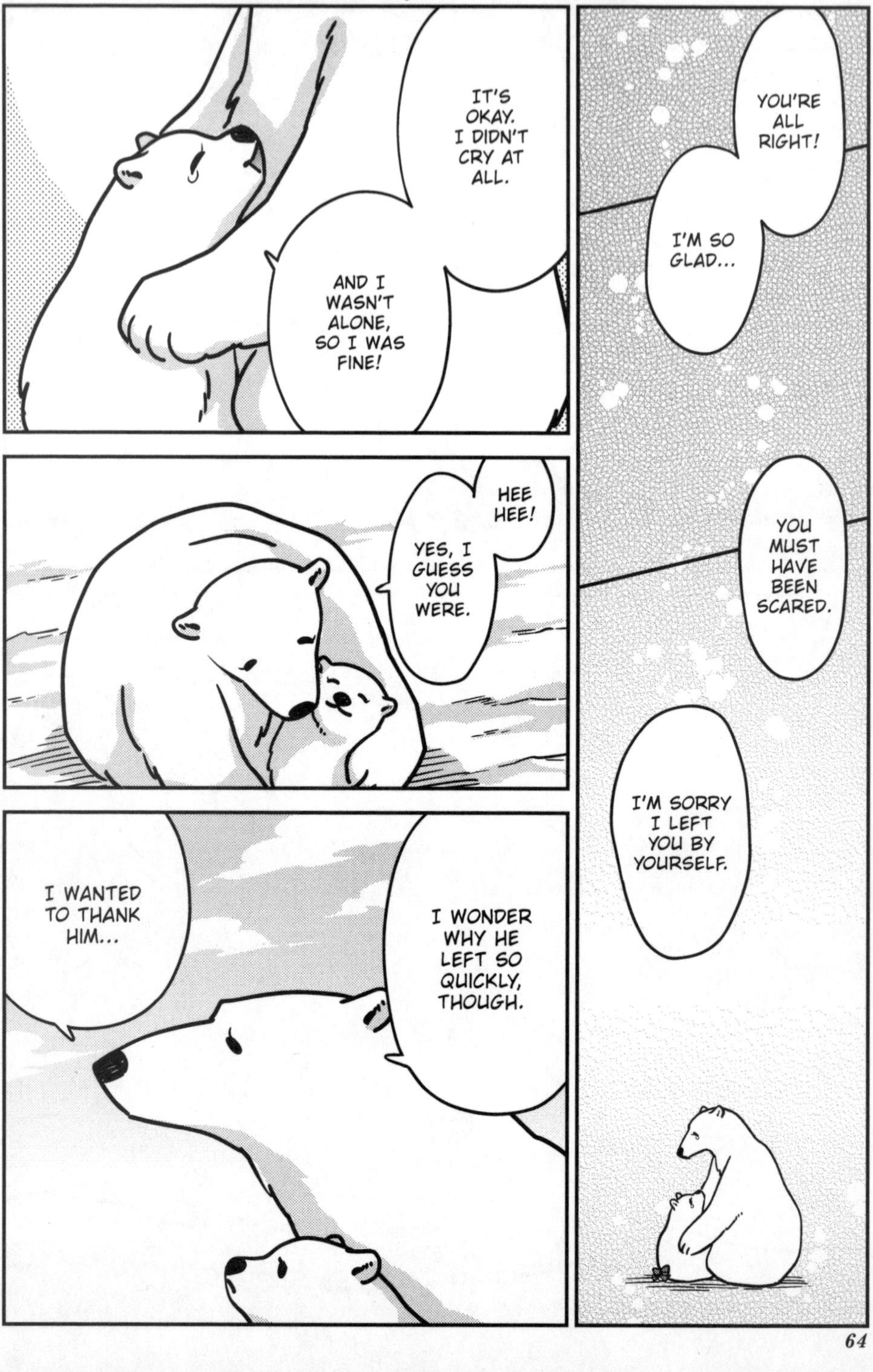

YOU'RE ALL RIGHT!
I'M SO GLAD...
YOU MUST HAVE BEEN SCARED.
I'M SORRY I LEFT YOU BY YOURSELF.
IT'S OKAY. I DIDN'T CRY AT ALL.
AND I WASN'T ALONE, SO I WAS FINE!
HEE HEE!
YES, I GUESS YOU WERE.
I WONDER WHY HE LEFT SO QUICKLY, THOUGH.
I WANTED TO THANK HIM...

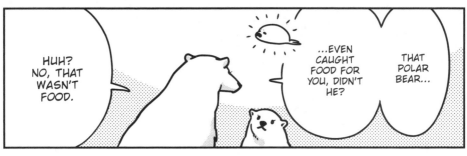

THAT POLAR BEAR...
...EVEN CAUGHT FOOD FOR YOU, DIDN'T HE?
HUH? NO, THAT WASN'T FOOD.
THAT SEAL IS...
...BIG BRO'S SPECIAL SOME-ONE!
HOW ODD.
BUT LISTEN! I LOVE THEM BOTH TOO!

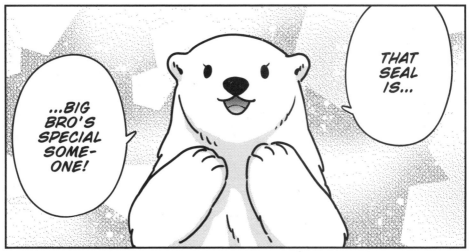

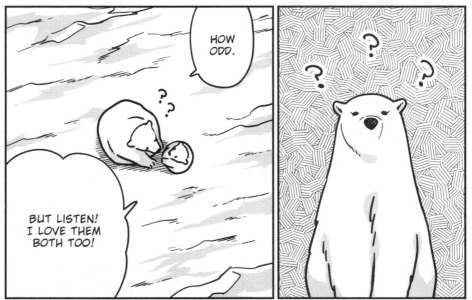

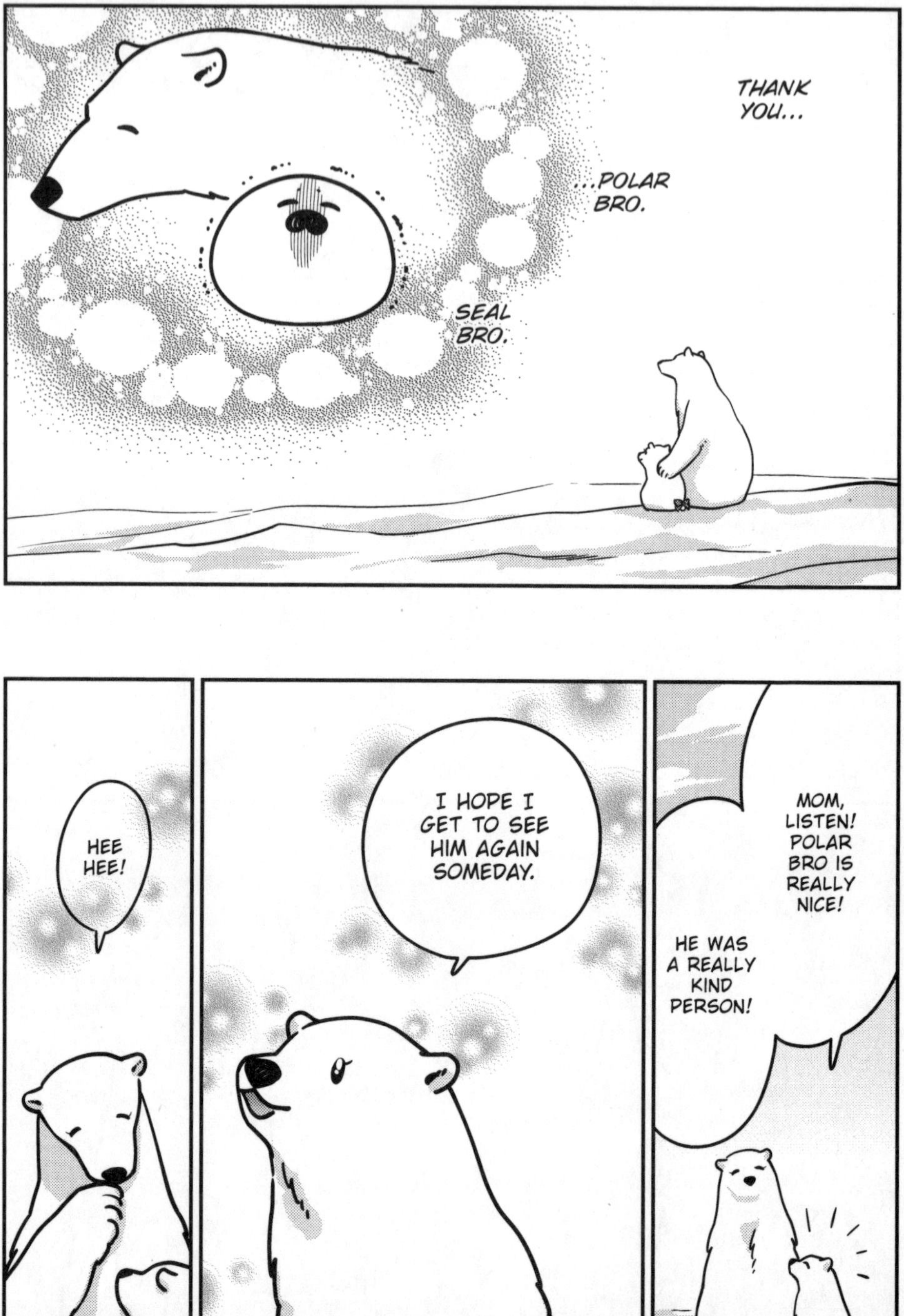
THANK YOU...
...POLAR BRO.
SEAL BRO.
MOM, LISTEN! POLAR BRO IS REALLY NICE!
HE WAS A REALLY KIND PERSON!
I HOPE I GET TO SEE HIM AGAIN SOMEDAY.
HEE HEE!

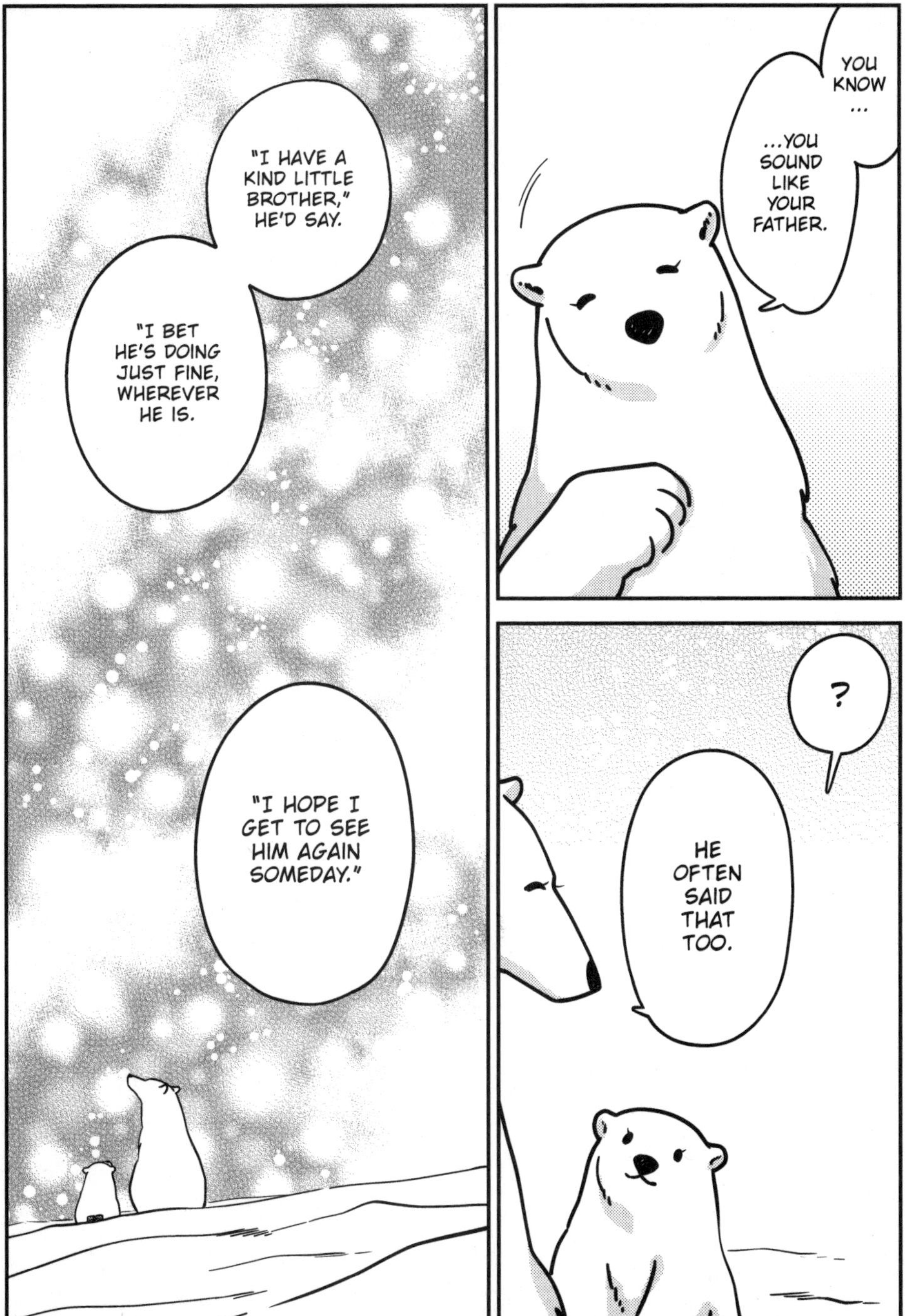
YOU KNOW ...
...YOU SOUND LIKE YOUR FATHER.
?
HE OFTEN SAID THAT TOO.
"I HAVE A KIND LITTLE BROTHER," HE'D SAY.
"I BET HE'S DOING JUST FINE, WHEREVER HE IS.
"I HOPE I GET TO SEE HIM AGAIN SOMEDAY."

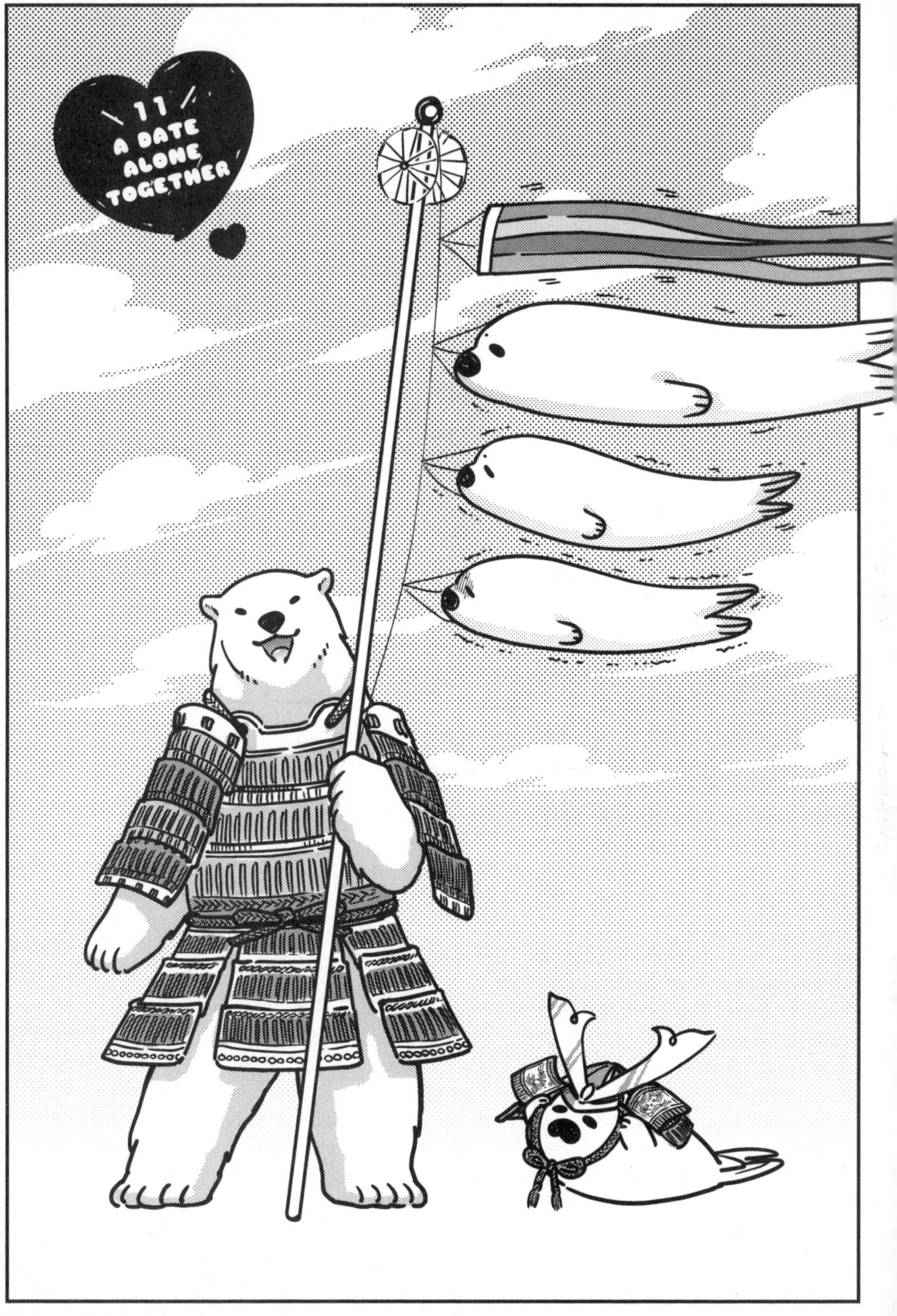
11
A DATE ALONE TOGETHER

WARMTH

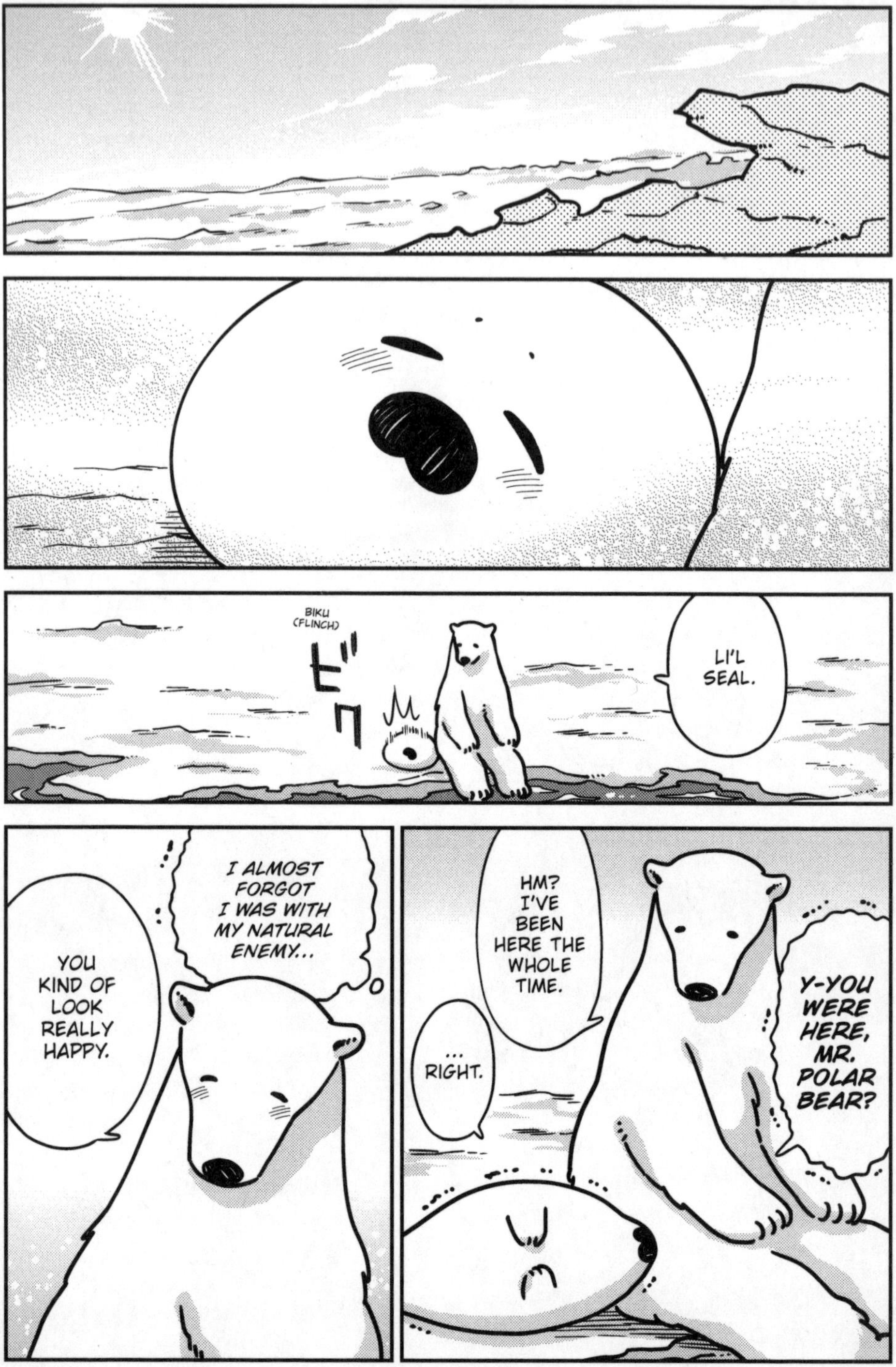
LI'L SEAL.
BIKU (FLINCH)
ビク
Y-YOU WERE HERE, MR. POLAR BEAR?
HM? I'VE BEEN HERE THE WHOLE TIME.
... RIGHT.
I ALMOST FORGOT I WAS WITH MY NATURAL ENEMY...
YOU KIND OF LOOK REALLY HAPPY.

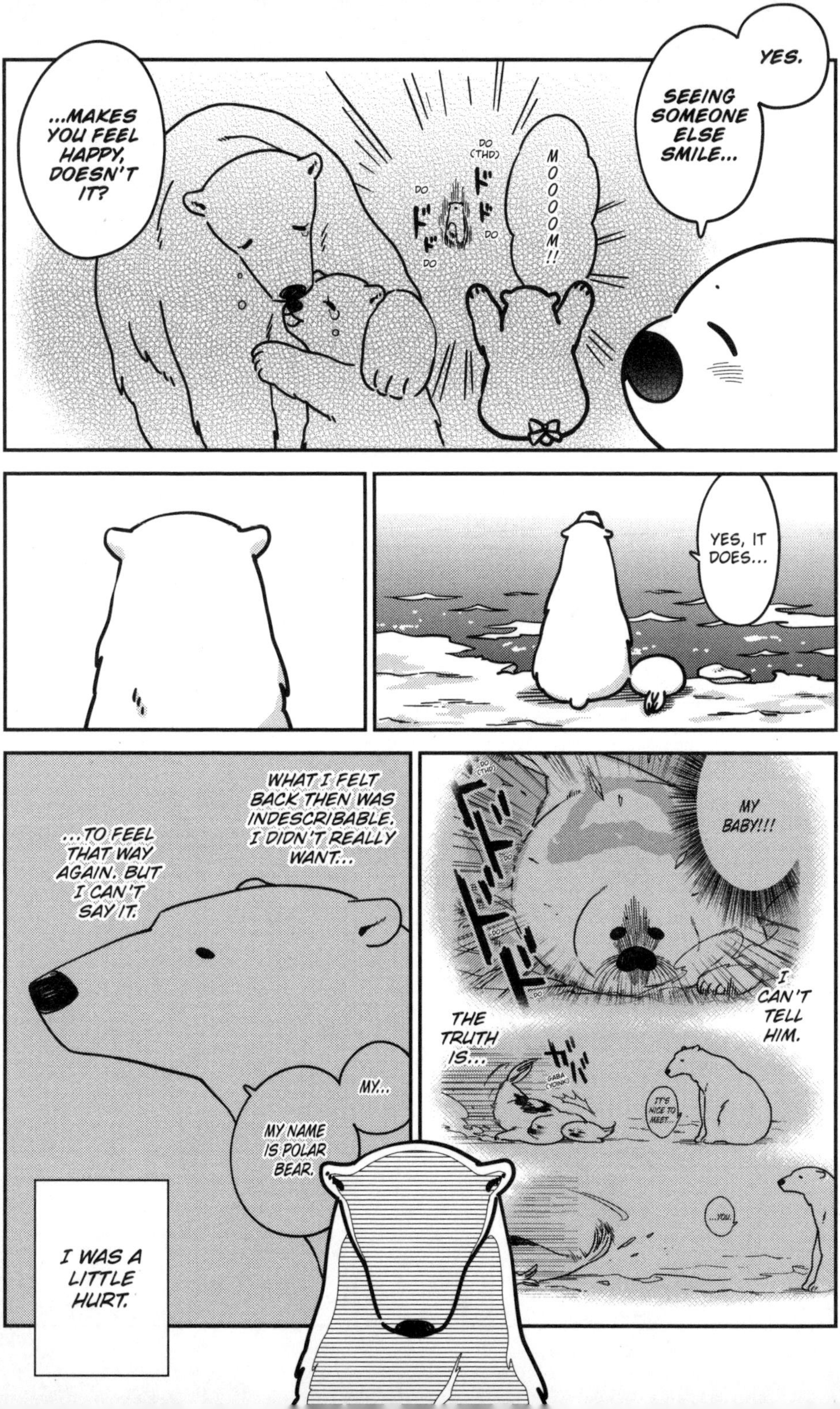
YES.
SEEING SOMEONE ELSE SMILE...
MOOOOOM!!
DO (THD)
DO
DO
DO
...MAKES YOU FEEL HAPPY, DOESN'T IT?
YES, IT DOES...
DO (THD)
DO
DO
DO
MY BABY!!!
I CAN'T TELL HIM.
THE TRUTH IS...
GABA (YOINK)
IT'S NICE TO MEET...
...YOU.
WHAT I FELT BACK THEN WAS INDESCRIBABLE. I DIDN'T REALLY WANT...
...TO FEEL THAT WAY AGAIN. BUT I CAN'T SAY IT.
MY...
MY NAME IS POLAR BEAR.
I WAS A LITTLE HURT.

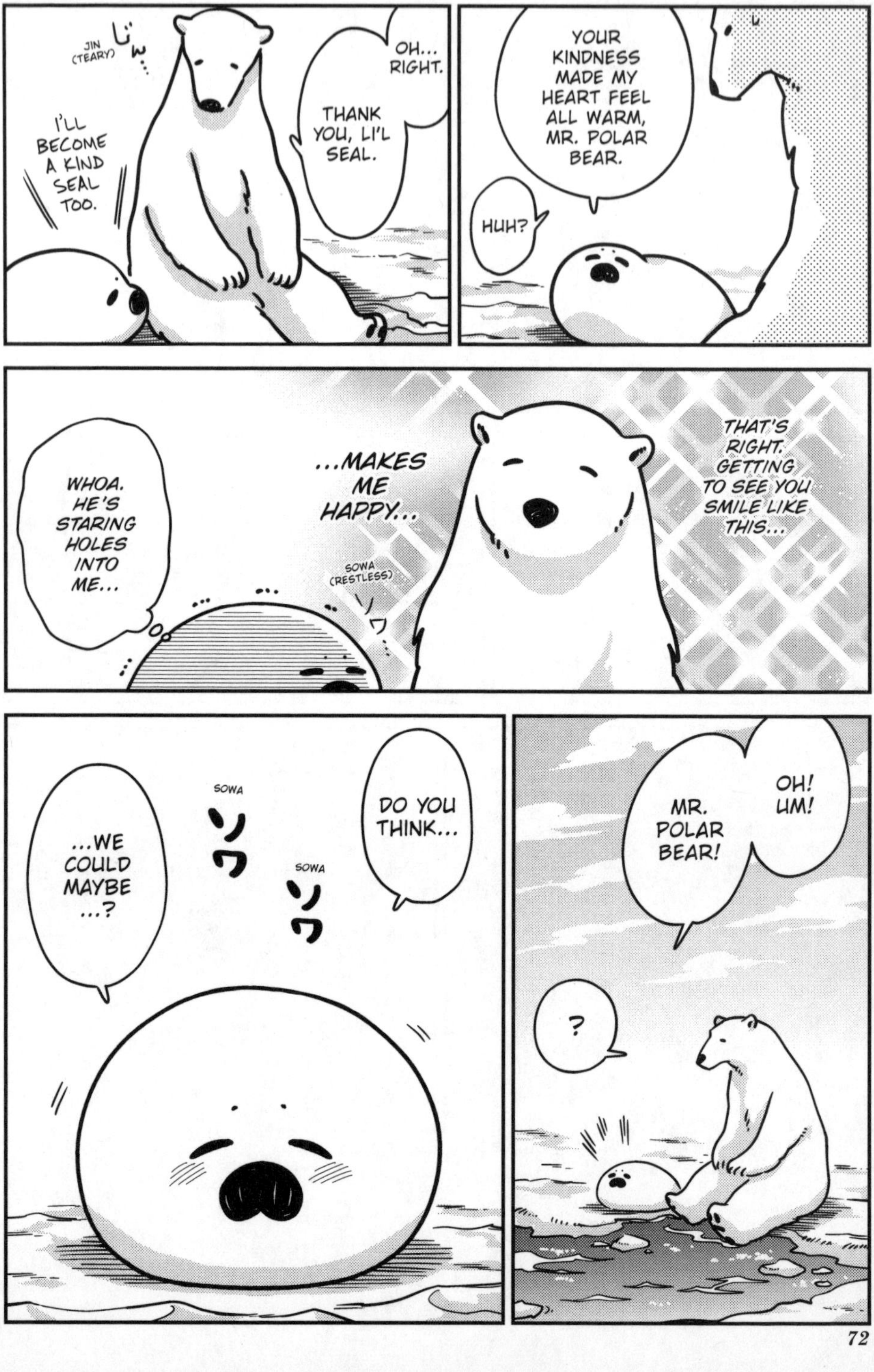
YOUR KINDNESS MADE MY HEART FEEL ALL WARM, MR. POLAR BEAR.
HUH?
OH... RIGHT.
THANK YOU, LI'L SEAL.
JIN (TEARY)
じん…
I'LL BECOME A KIND SEAL TOO.
THAT'S RIGHT. GETTING TO SEE YOU SMILE LIKE THIS...
...MAKES ME HAPPY...
SOWA (RESTLESS)
ソワ…
WHOA. HE'S STARING HOLES INTO ME...
OH! UM!
MR. POLAR BEAR!
?
DO YOU THINK...
SOWA
ソワ
SOWA
ソワ
...WE COULD MAYBE ...?

LOOK OF ANTICIPATION

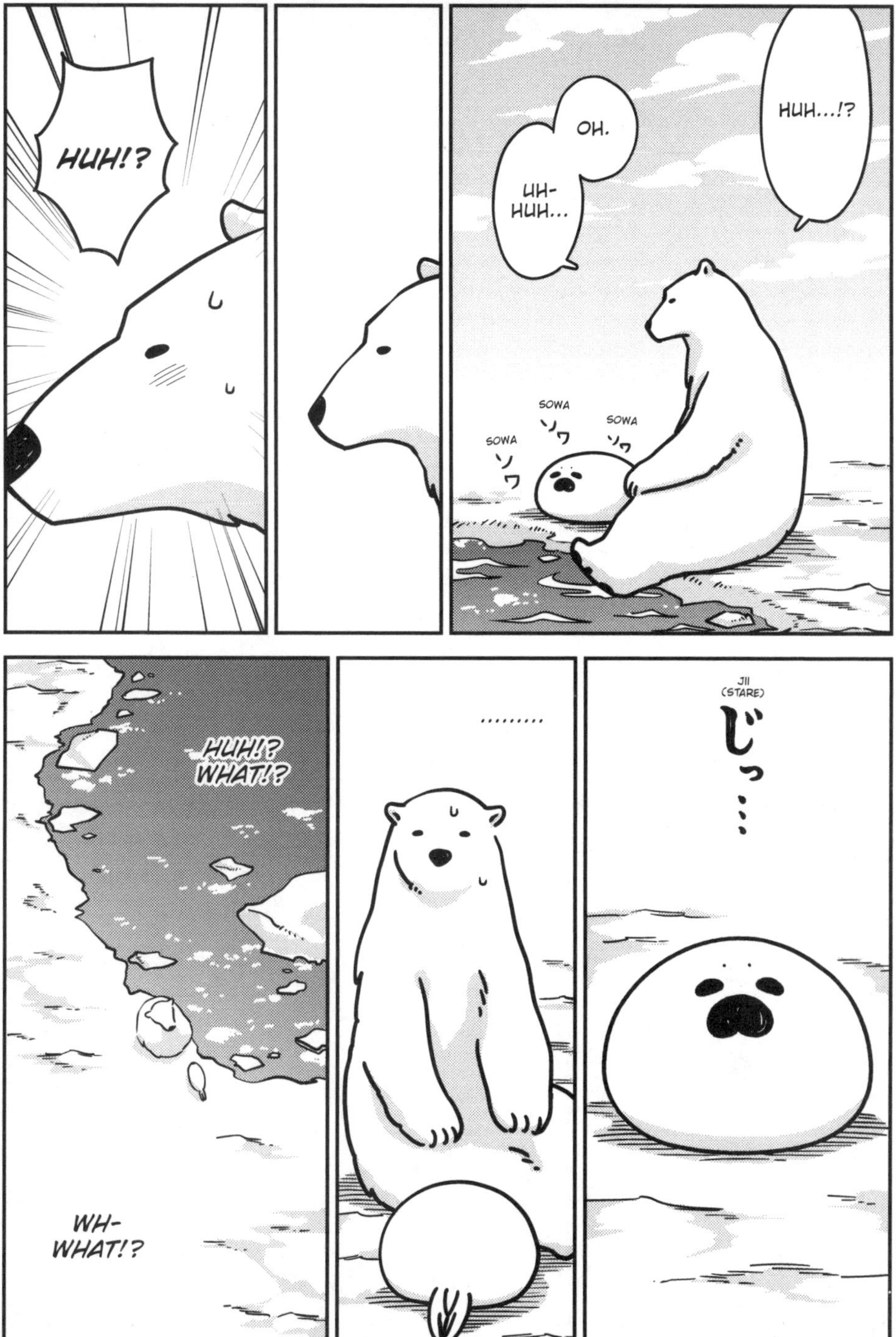
HUH...!?
OH.
UH-HUH...
SOWA ソワ
SOWA ソワ
SOWA ソワ
HUH!?
JII (STARE)
じっ…
....
HUH!? WHAT!?
WH-WHAT!?

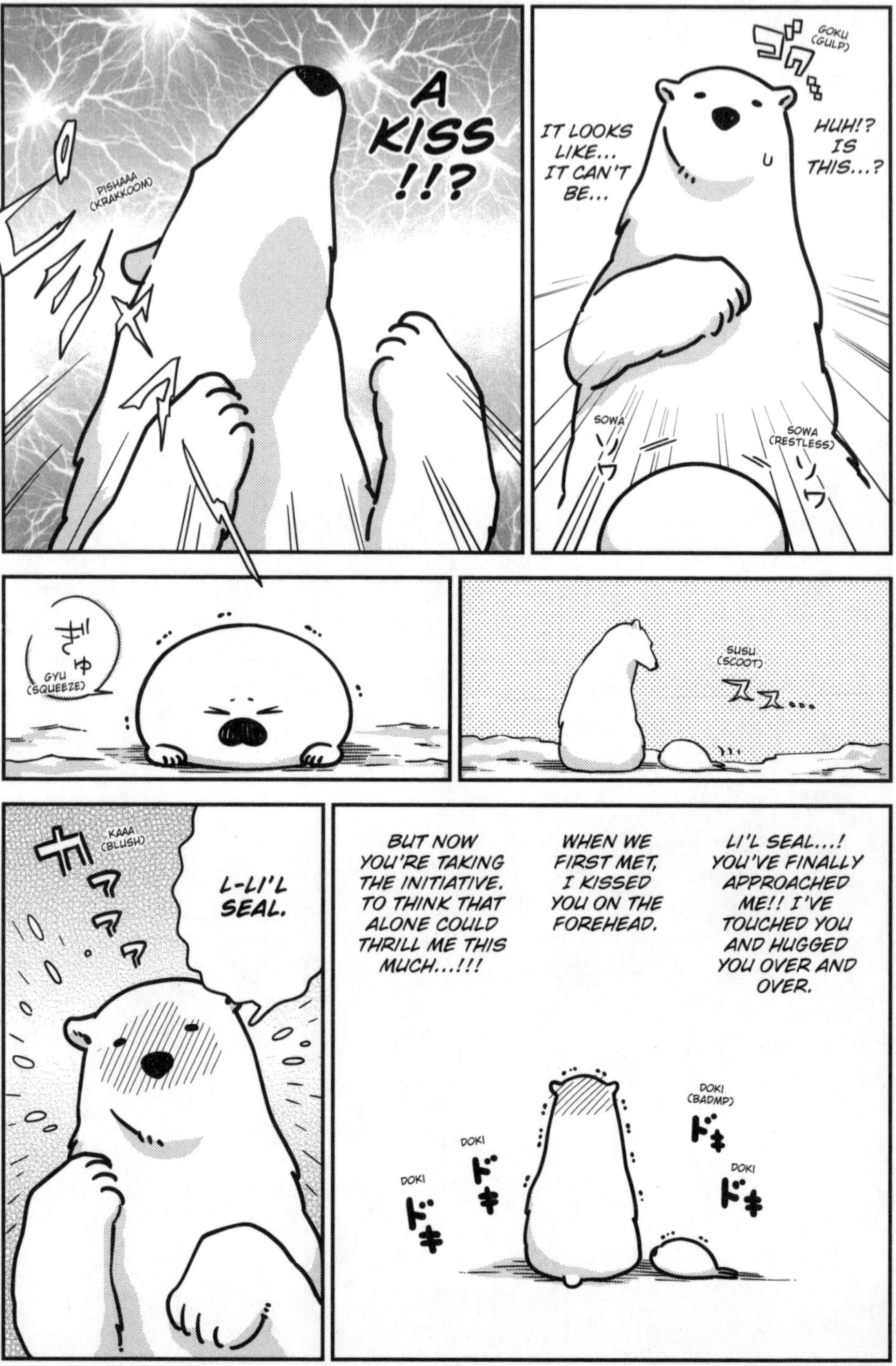
GOKU (GULP)
HUH!? IS THIS...?
IT LOOKS LIKE... IT CAN'T BE...
SOWA (RESTLESS)
SOWA
A KISS!!?
PISHAAA (KRAKKOOM)
SUSU (SCOOT)
GYU (SQUEEZE)
LI'L SEAL...! YOU'VE FINALLY APPROACHED ME!! I'VE TOUCHED YOU AND HUGGED YOU OVER AND OVER.
WHEN WE FIRST MET, I KISSED YOU ON THE FOREHEAD.
BUT NOW YOU'RE TAKING THE INITIATIVE. TO THINK THAT ALONE COULD THRILL ME THIS MUCH...!!!
DOKI (BADMP)
DOKI
DOKI
DOKI
KAAA (BLUSH)
L-LI'L SEAL.

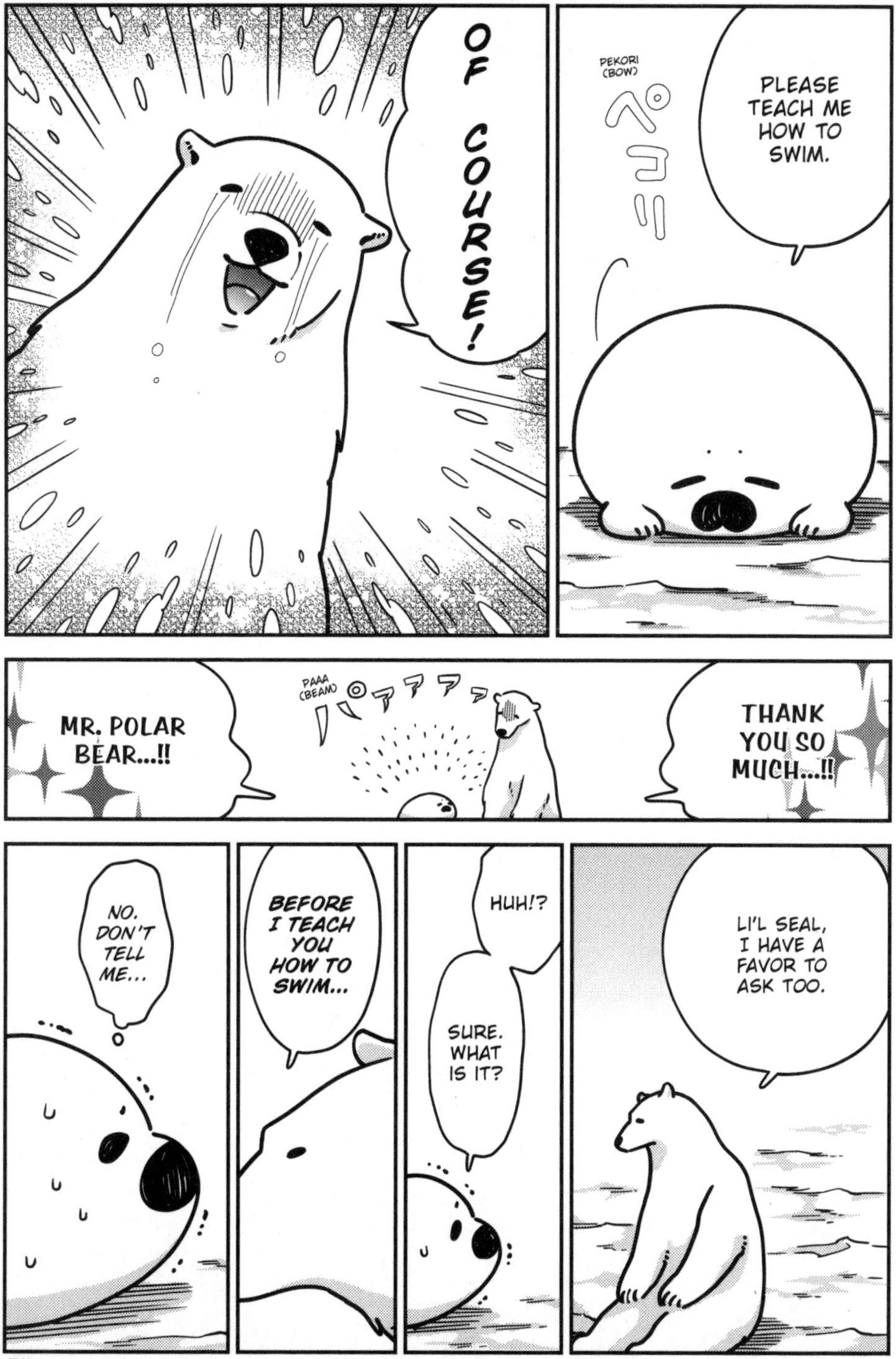
PLEASE TEACH ME HOW TO SWIM.
PEKORI (BOW)
ペコリ
OF COURSE!
THANK YOU SO MUCH...!!
PAAA (BEAM)
パァァァァ
MR. POLAR BEAR...!!
LI'L SEAL, I HAVE A FAVOR TO ASK TOO.
HUH!?
SURE. WHAT IS IT?
BEFORE I TEACH YOU HOW TO SWIM...
NO. DON'T TELL ME...

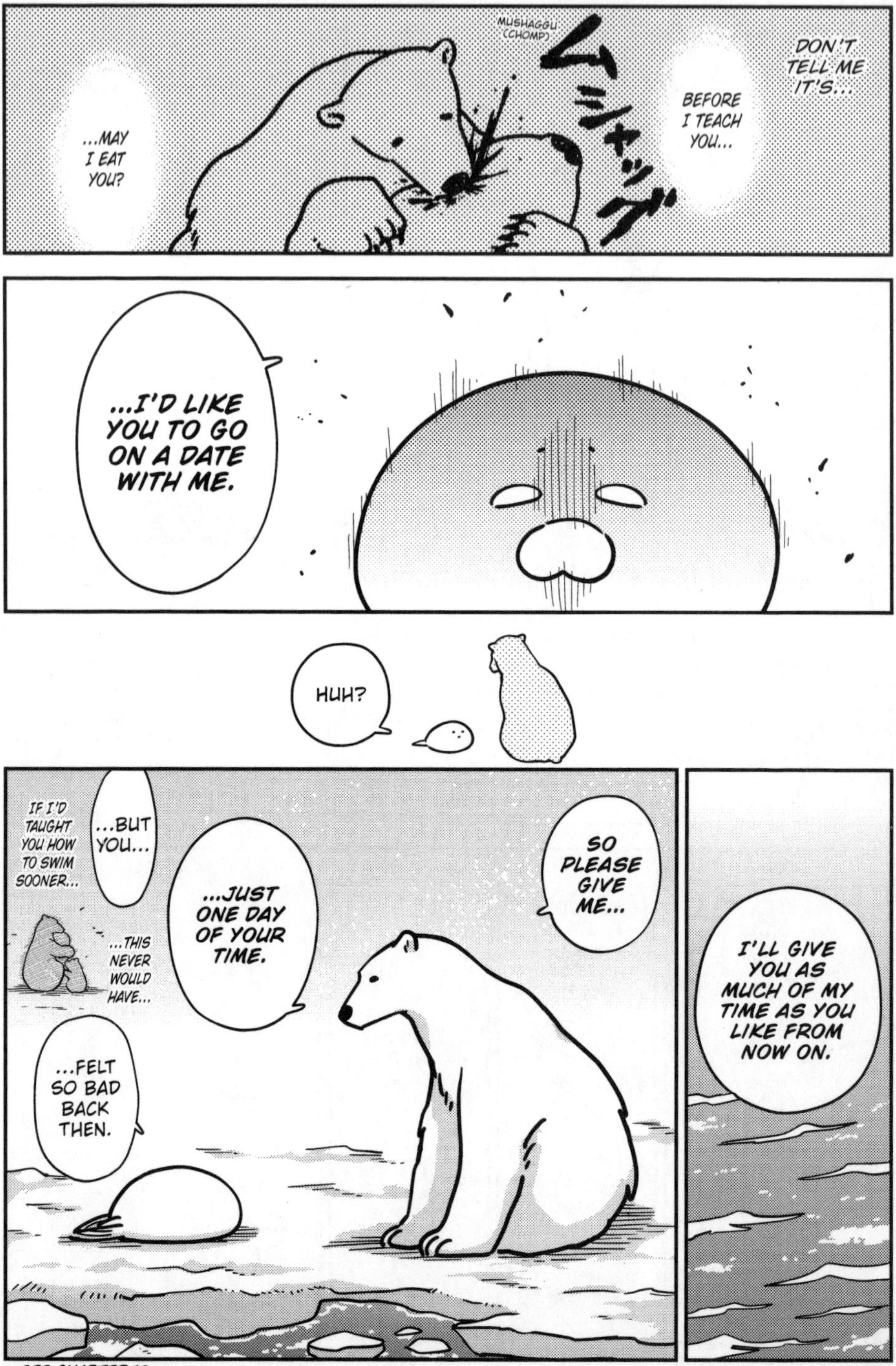
DON'T TELL ME IT'S...
BEFORE I TEACH YOU...
MUSHAGGU (CHOMP)
...MAY I EAT YOU?
...I'D LIKE YOU TO GO ON A DATE WITH ME.
HUH?
I'LL GIVE YOU AS MUCH OF MY TIME AS YOU LIKE FROM NOW ON.
SO PLEASE GIVE ME...
...JUST ONE DAY OF YOUR TIME.
...BUT YOU...
IF I'D TAUGHT YOU HOW TO SWIM SOONER...
...THIS NEVER WOULD HAVE...
...FELT SO BAD BACK THEN.

※SEE CHAPTER 10.

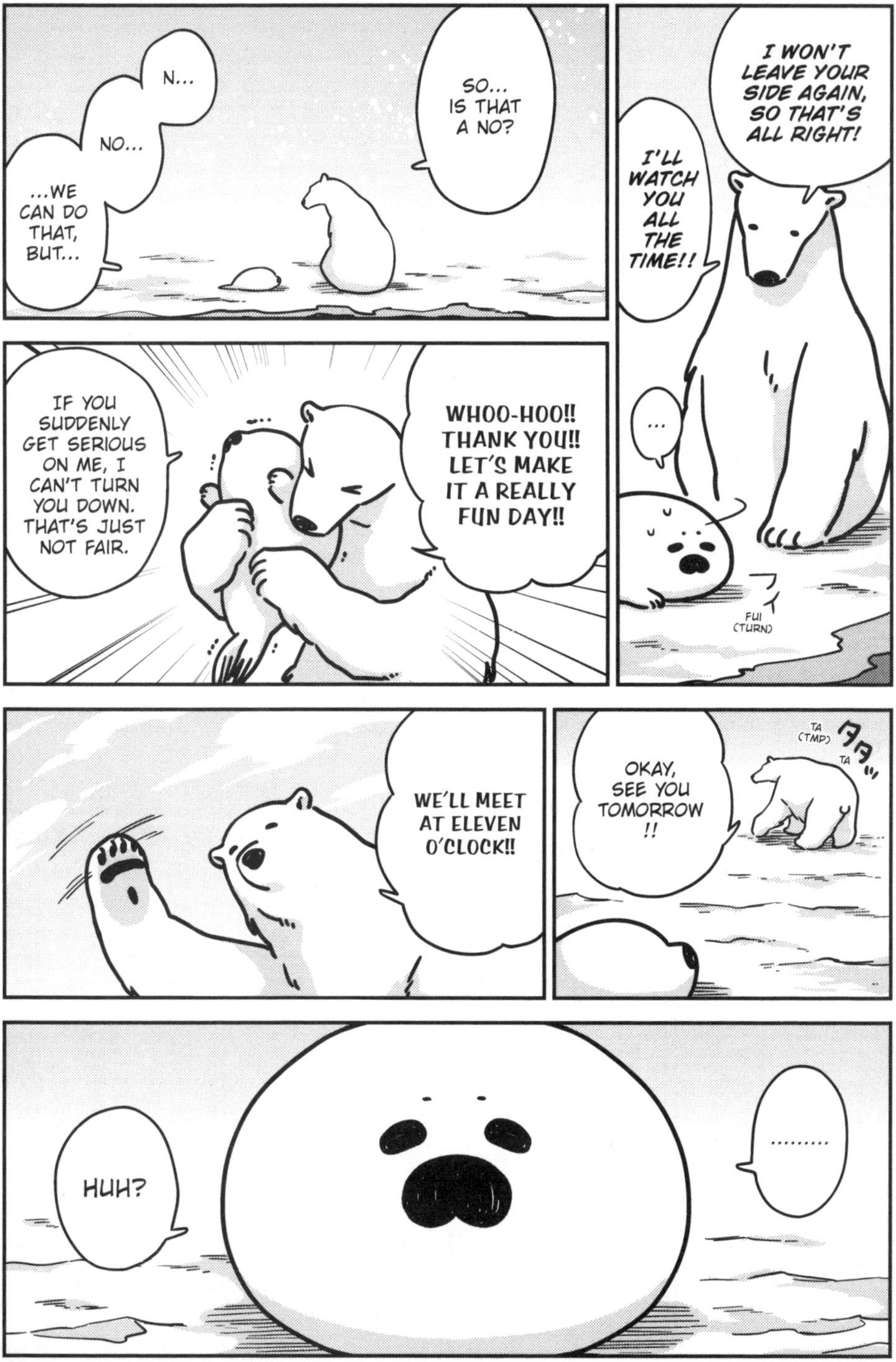
I WON'T LEAVE YOUR SIDE AGAIN, SO THAT'S ALL RIGHT!
I'LL WATCH YOU ALL THE TIME!!
...
FUI (TURN)
SO... IS THAT A NO?
N...
NO...
...WE CAN DO THAT, BUT...
WHOO-HOO!! THANK YOU!! LET'S MAKE IT A REALLY FUN DAY!!
IF YOU SUDDENLY GET SERIOUS ON ME, I CAN'T TURN YOU DOWN. THAT'S JUST NOT FAIR.
TA (TMP) TA
OKAY, SEE YOU TOMORROW !!
WE'LL MEET AT ELEVEN O'CLOCK!!
....
HUH?

A DATE FOR JUST THE TWO OF US

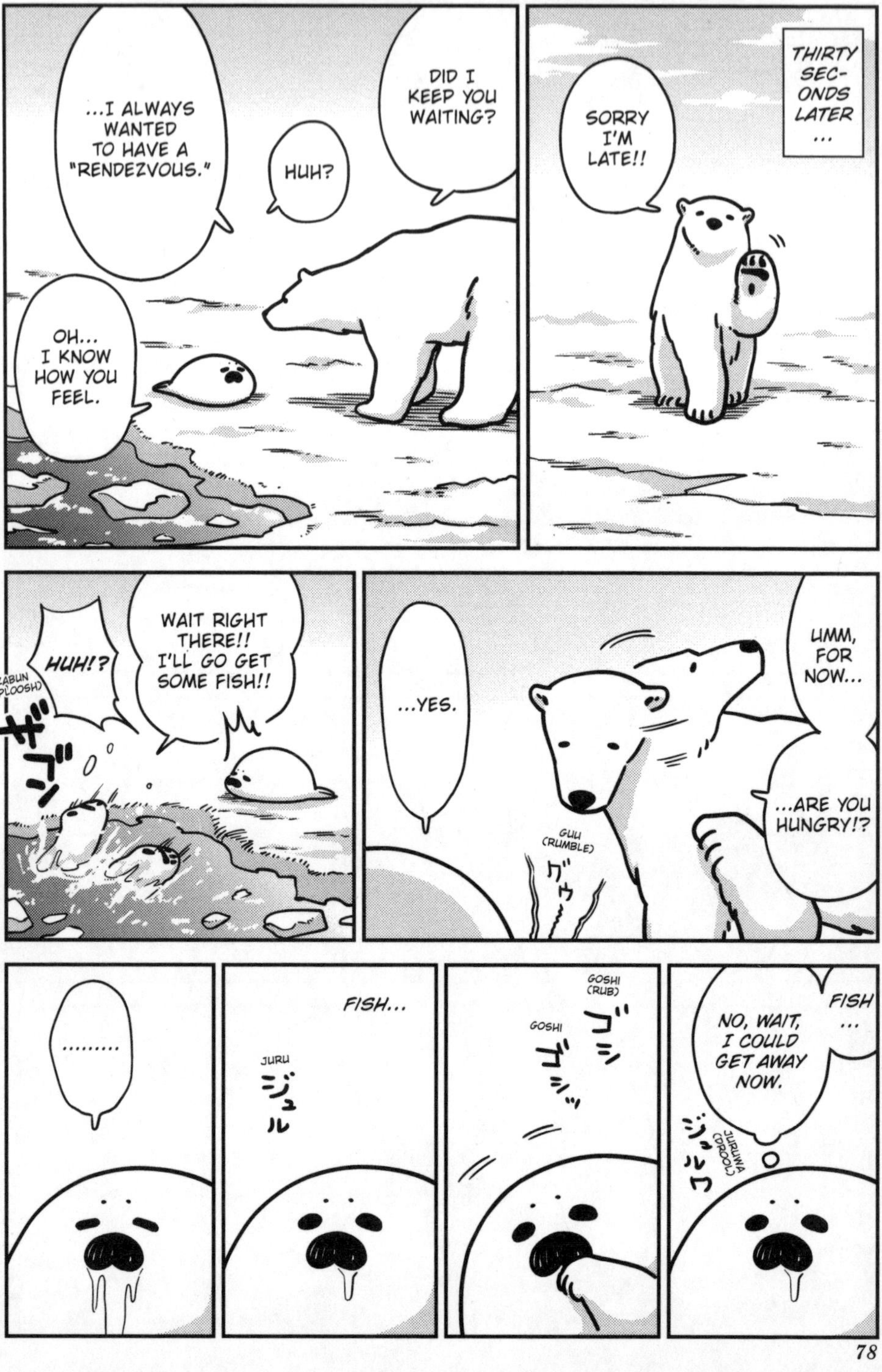
THIRTY SEC-ONDS LATER...
SORRY I'M LATE!!
DID I KEEP YOU WAITING?
HUH?
...I ALWAYS WANTED TO HAVE A "RENDEZVOUS."
OH... I KNOW HOW YOU FEEL.
UMM, FOR NOW...
...ARE YOU HUNGRY!?
GUU (RUMBLE)
...YES.
WAIT RIGHT THERE!! I'LL GO GET SOME FISH!!
HUH!?
ZABUN (SPLOOSH)
FISH...
NO, WAIT, I COULD GET AWAY NOW.
JURUWA (DROOL)
GOSHI (RUB)
GOSHI
FISH...
JURU
....

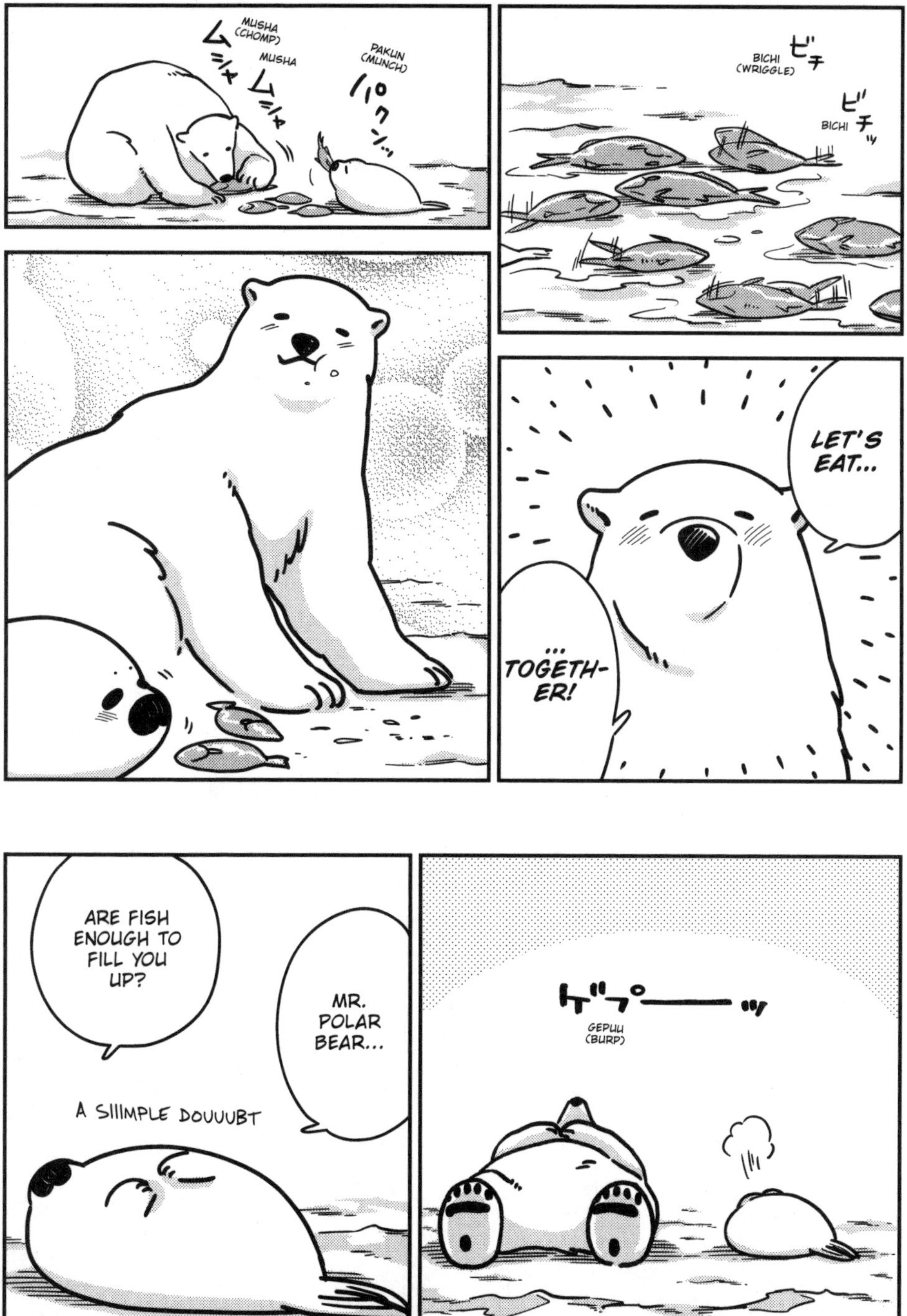

ビチ
BICHI (WRIGGLE)
ビチッ
BICHI
パクンッ
PAKUN (MUNCH)
ムシャ
MUSHA (CHOMP)
ムシャ
MUSHA
LET'S EAT...
...TOGETH-ER!
ゲプーーッ
GEPUU (BURP)
MR. POLAR BEAR...
ARE FISH ENOUGH TO FILL YOU UP?
A SIIIMPLE DOUUUBT

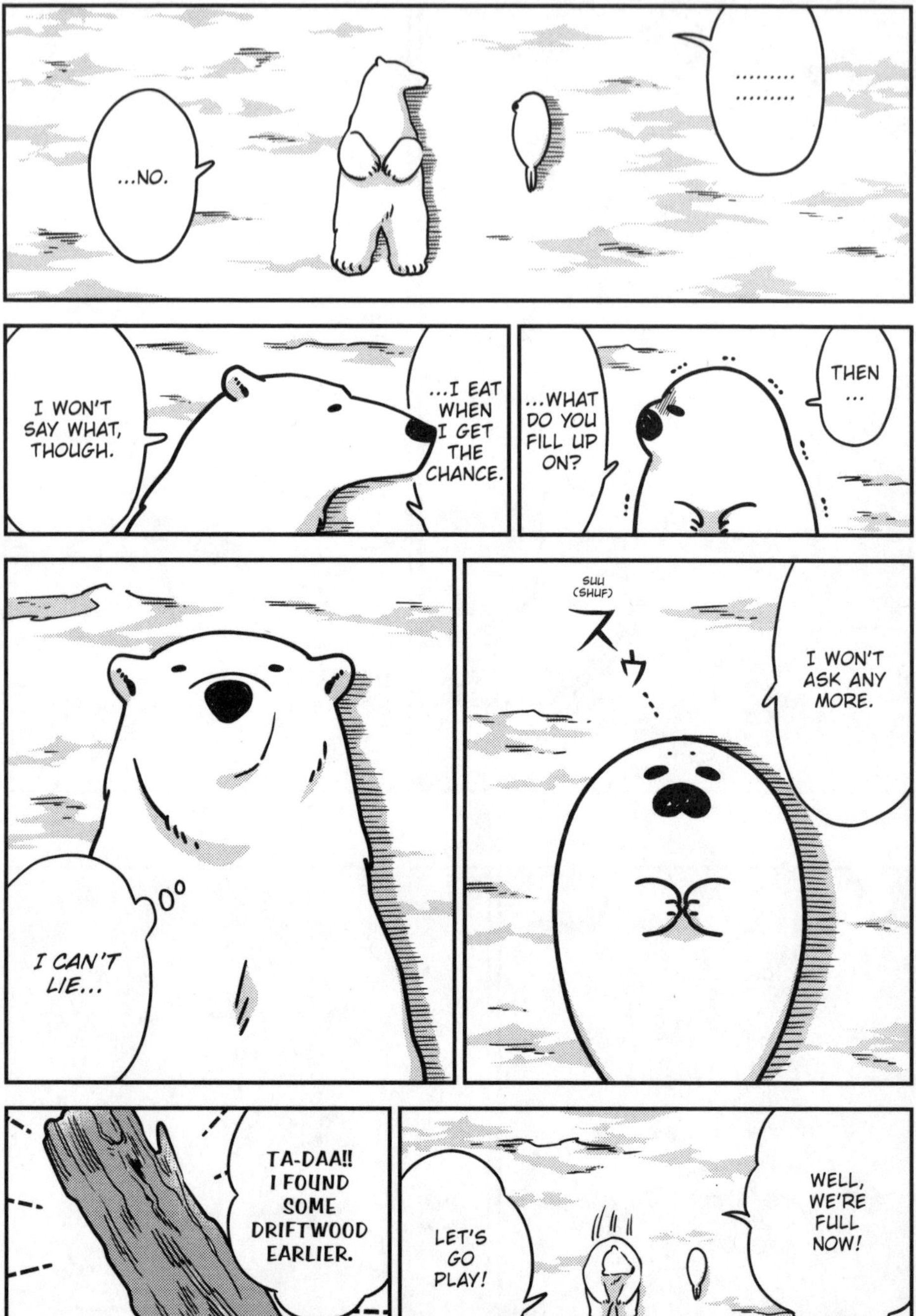
....
....
...NO.
THEN ...
...WHAT DO YOU FILL UP ON?
...I EAT WHEN I GET THE CHANCE.
I WON'T SAY WHAT, THOUGH.
I WON'T ASK ANY MORE.
SUU (SHUF)
スゥ…
I CAN'T LIE...
WELL, WE'RE FULL NOW!
LET'S GO PLAY!
TA-DAA!! I FOUND SOME DRIFTWOOD EARLIER.

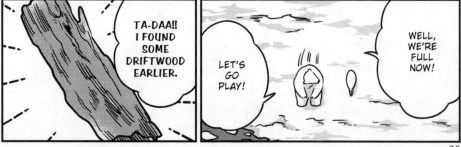

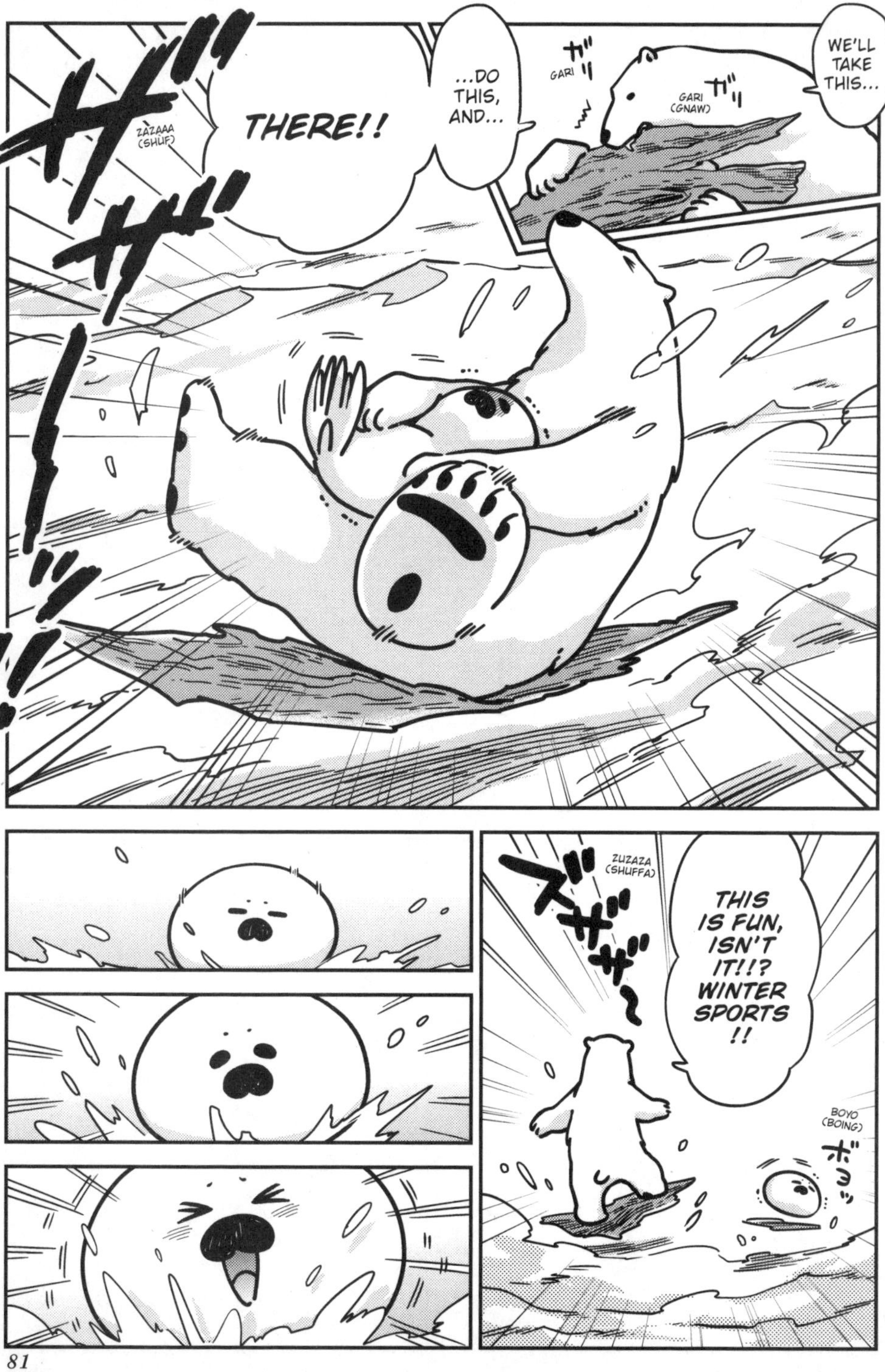
WE'LL TAKE THIS...
GARI (GNAW)
GARI
...DO THIS, AND...
THERE!!
ZAZAAA (SHUF)
ZUZAZA (SHUFFA)
THIS IS FUN, ISN'T IT!!? WINTER SPORTS!!
BOYO (BOING)

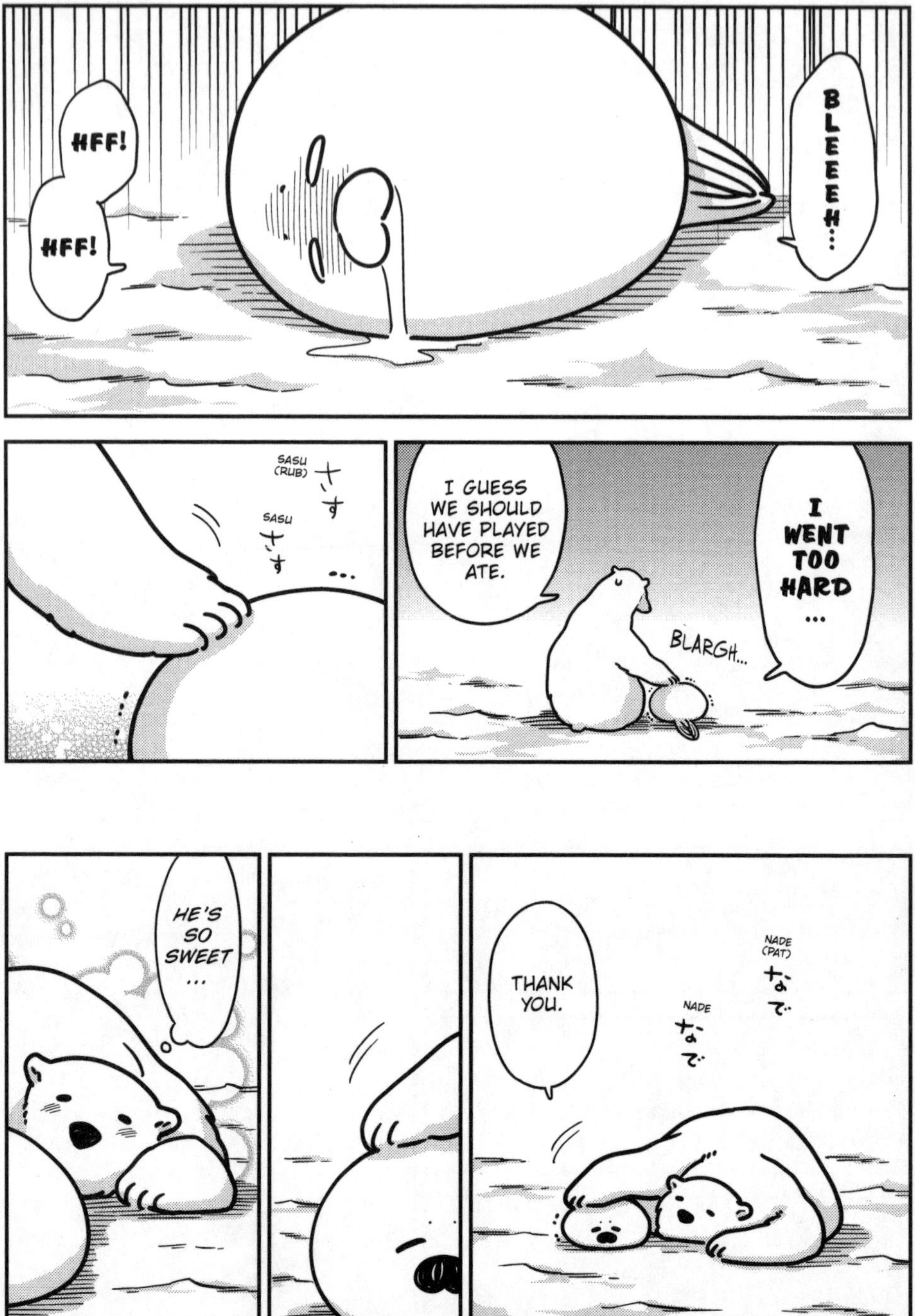
BLEEEEH...
HFF!
HFF!
I WENT TOO HARD...
I GUESS WE SHOULD HAVE PLAYED BEFORE WE ATE.
BLARGH...
SASU (RUB)
さす
SASU
さす
...
...
NADE (PAT)
なで
NADE
なで
THANK YOU.
HE'S SO SWEET...

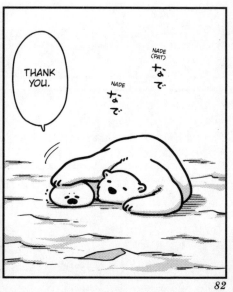

SKEWER

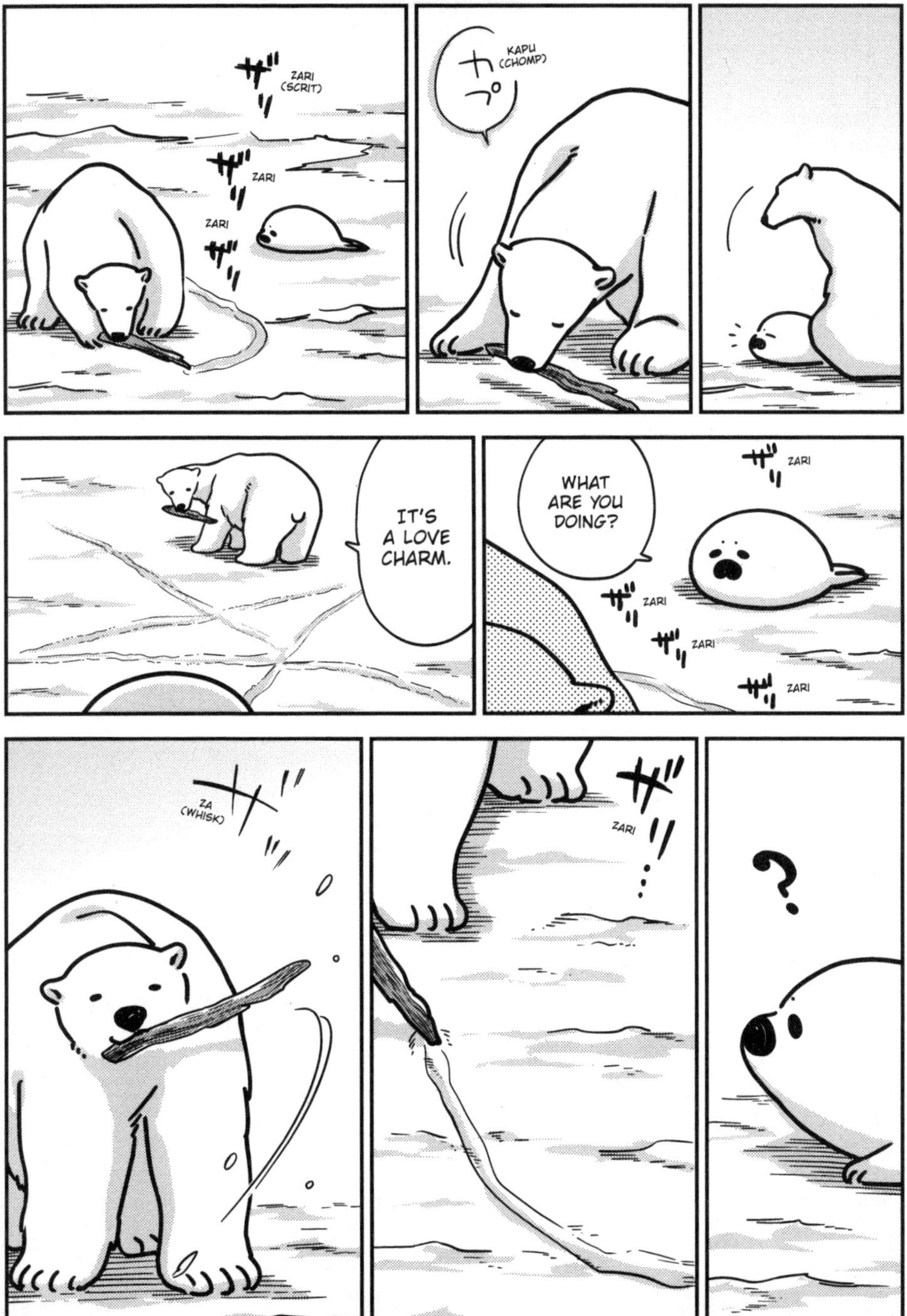
KAPU (CHOMP)
ZARI (SCRIT)
ZARI
ZARI
ZARI
WHAT ARE YOU DOING?
ZARI
ZARI
ZARI
IT'S A LOVE CHARM.
?
ZARI
ZA (WHISK)

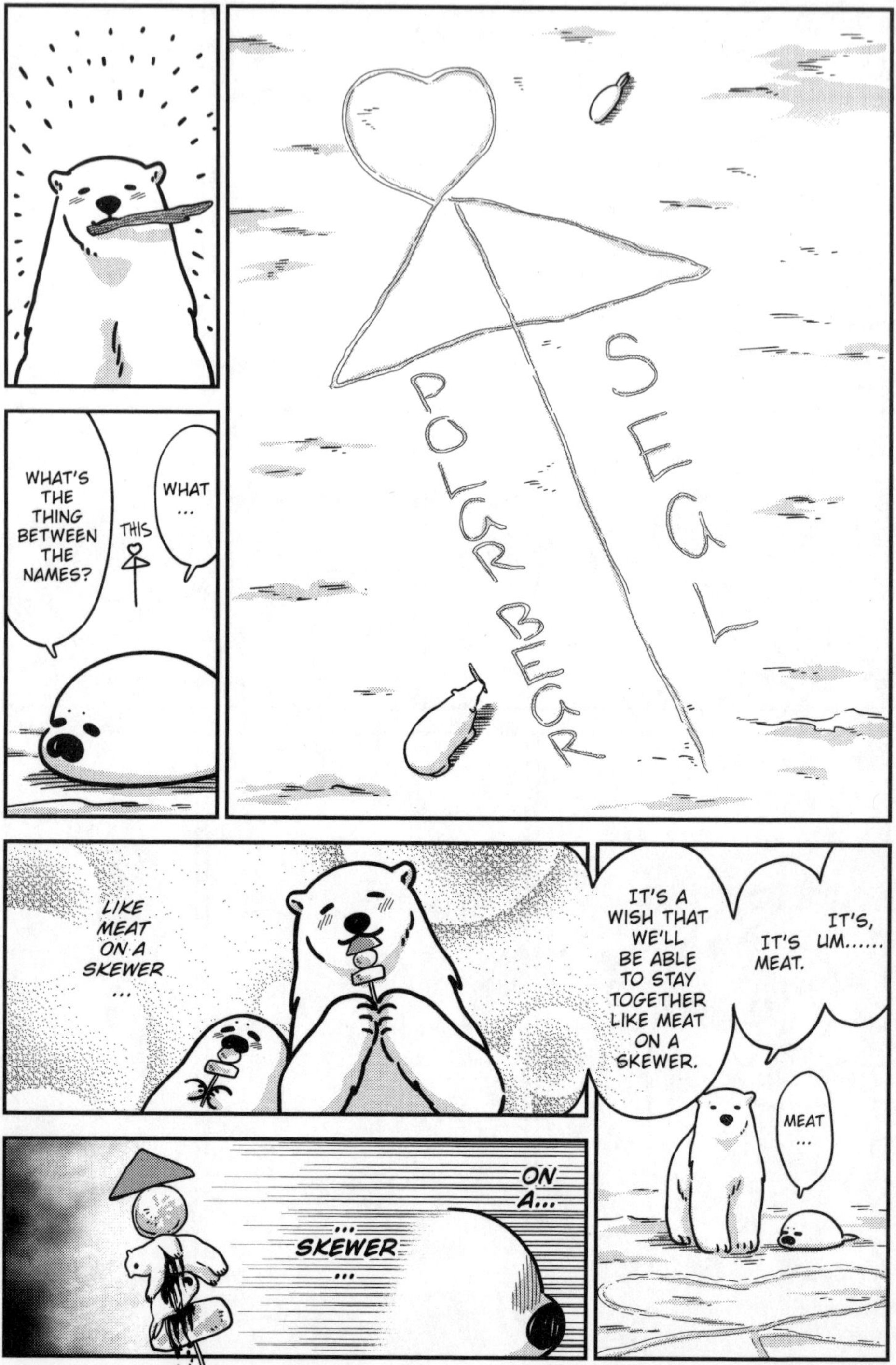
SEGL
POLGR BEGR
WHAT ...
WHAT'S THE THING BETWEEN THE NAMES?
THIS
IT'S, UM......
IT'S MEAT.
IT'S A WISH THAT WE'LL BE ABLE TO STAY TOGETHER LIKE MEAT ON A SKEWER.
MEAT ...
LIKE MEAT ON A SKEWER ...
ON A...
... SKEWER ...

ALEX AND JULIE

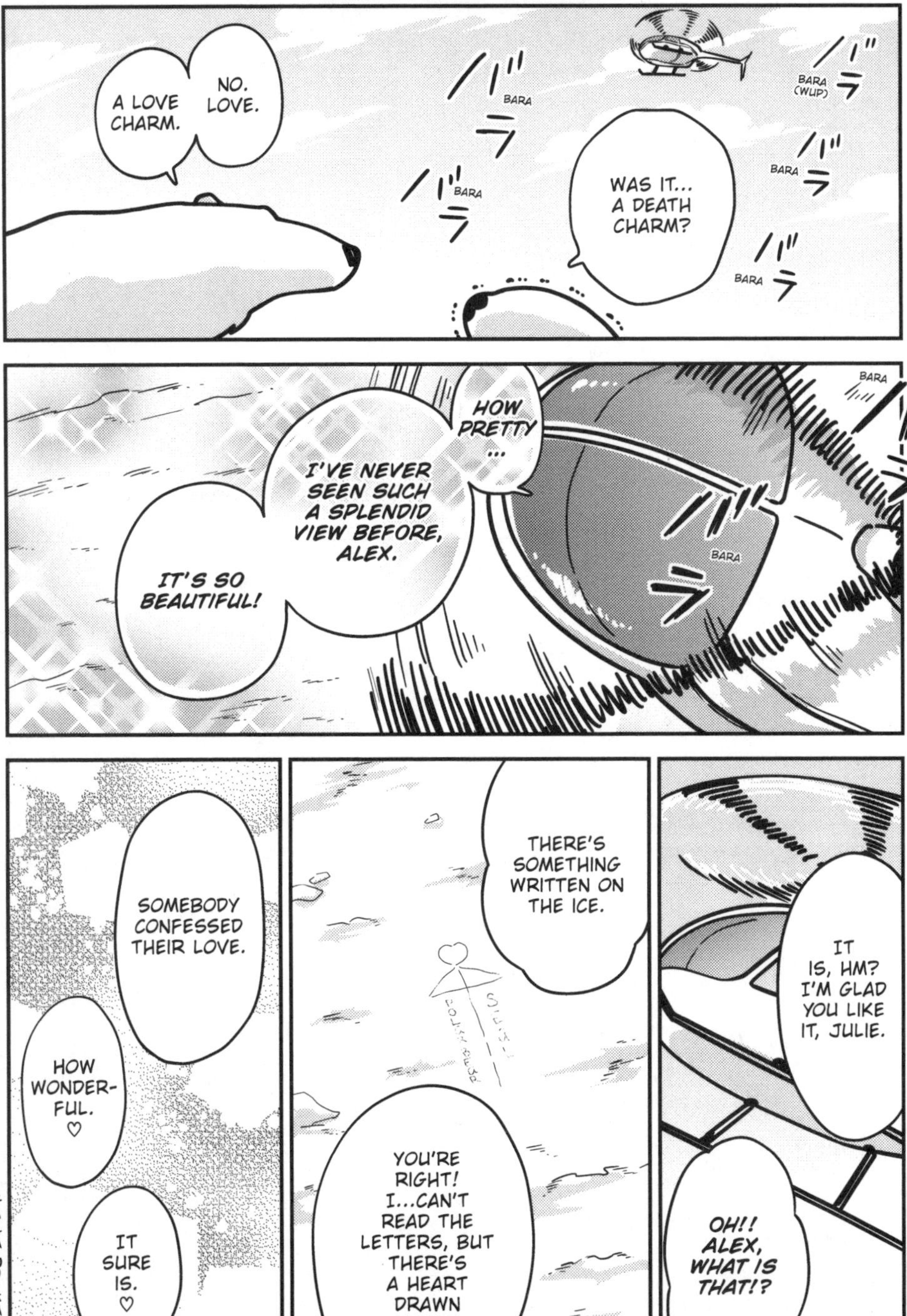
BARA (WUP)
BARA
WAS IT... A DEATH CHARM?
BARA
BARA
BARA
NO. LOVE.
A LOVE CHARM.
BARA
BARA
HOW PRETTY...
I'VE NEVER SEEN SUCH A SPLENDID VIEW BEFORE, ALEX.
IT'S SO BEAUTIFUL!
IT IS, HM? I'M GLAD YOU LIKE IT, JULIE.
OH!! ALEX, WHAT IS THAT!?
THERE'S SOMETHING WRITTEN ON THE ICE.
YOU'RE RIGHT! I...CAN'T READ THE LETTERS, BUT THERE'S A HEART DRAWN THERE.
SOMEBODY CONFESSED THEIR LOVE.
HOW WONDERFUL. ♡
IT SURE IS. ♡

※SHE BROKE UP WITH KENNY.

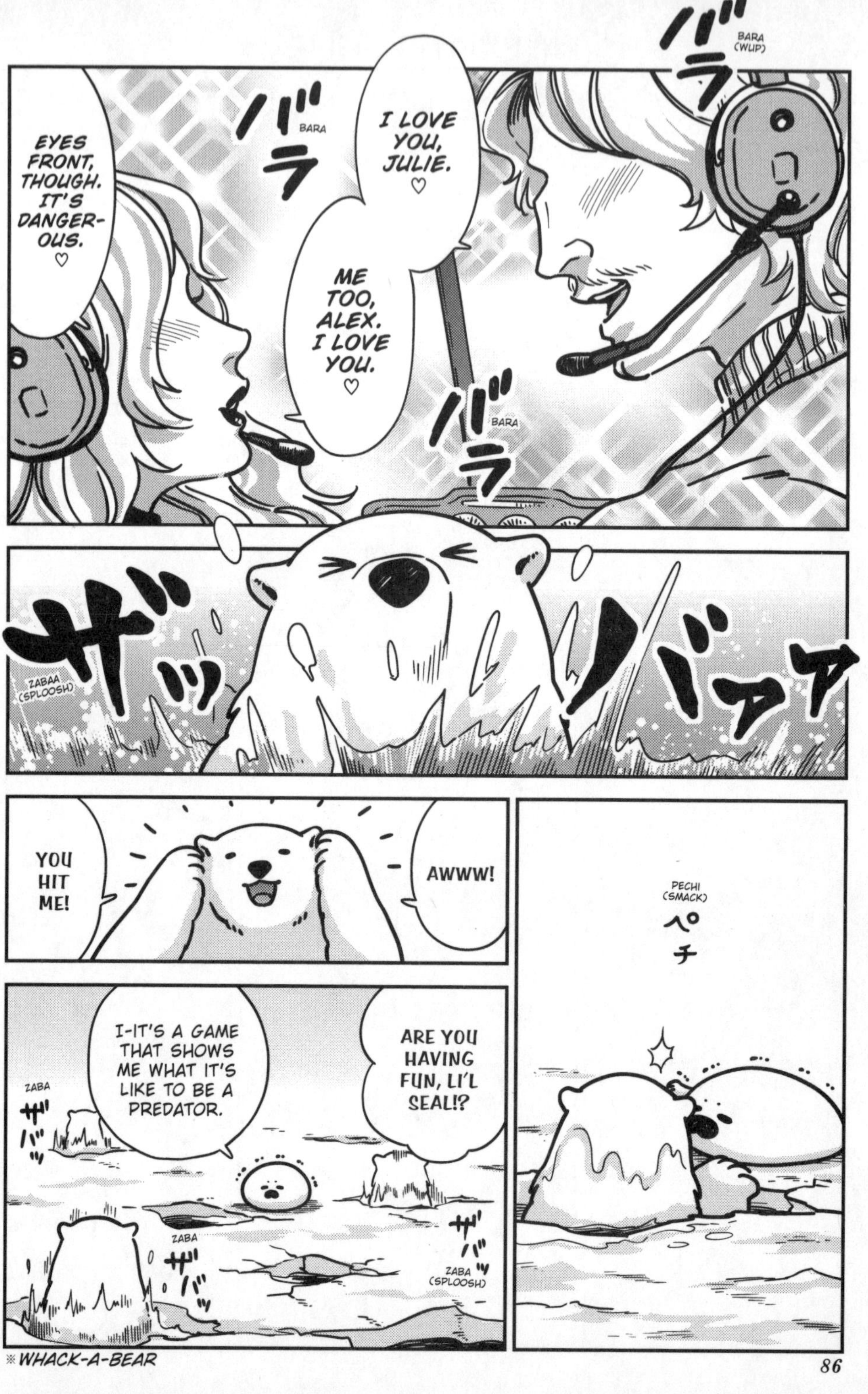
バラ
BARA (WUP)
I LOVE YOU, JULIE. ♡
バラ
BARA
EYES FRONT, THOUGH. IT'S DANGER-OUS. ♡
ME TOO, ALEX. I LOVE YOU. ♡
バラ
BARA
ザッバァ
ZABAA (SPLOOSH)
PECHI (SMACK)
ペチ
AWWW!
YOU HIT ME!
ARE YOU HAVING FUN, LI'L SEAL!?
I-IT'S A GAME THAT SHOWS ME WHAT IT'S LIKE TO BE A PREDATOR.
ザバッ
ZABA (SPLOOSH)
ザバ
ZABA
ザバッ
ZABA

※WHACK-A-BEAR

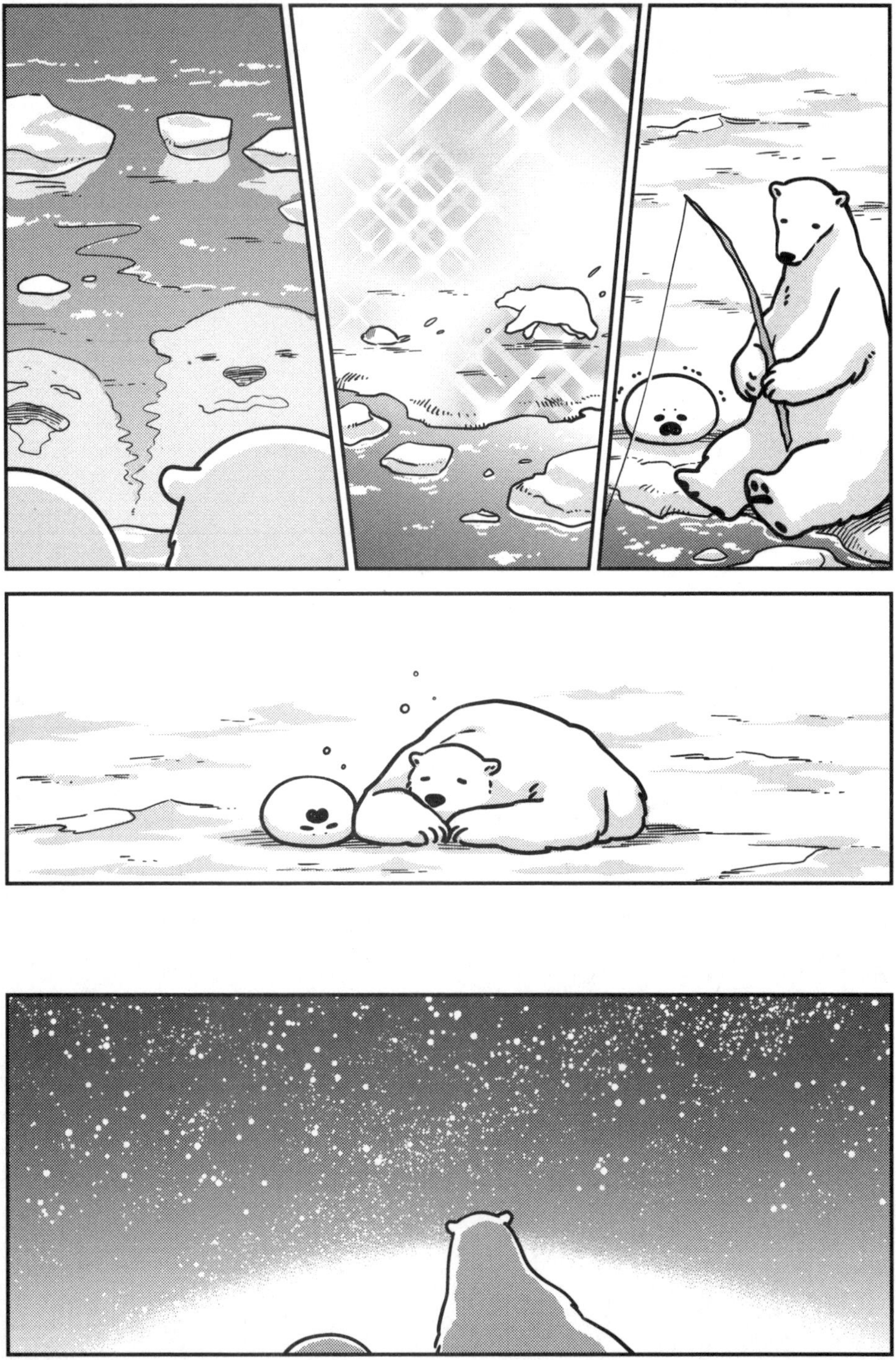

TWINKLING IN THE STARRY SKY

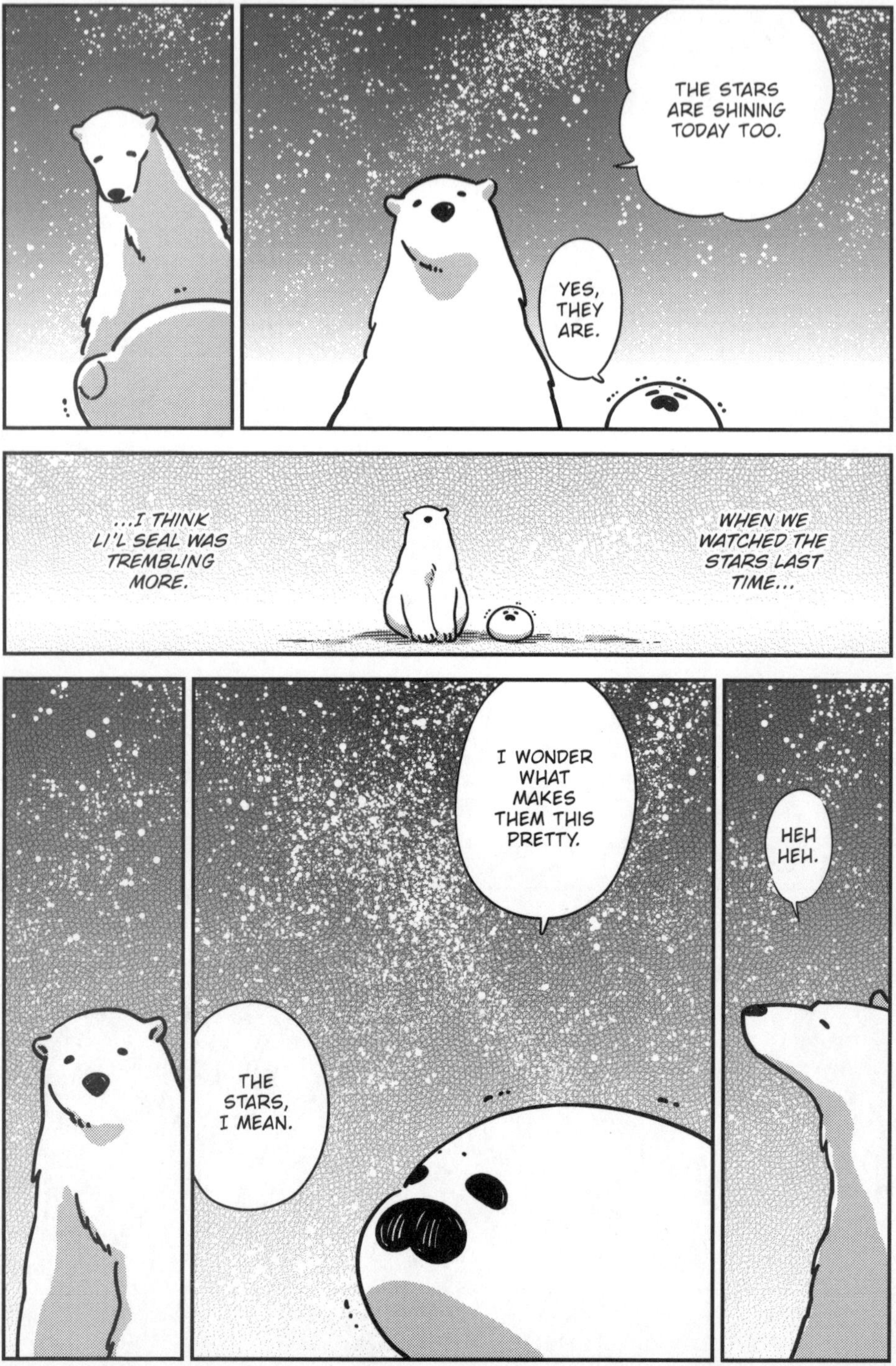
THE STARS ARE SHINING TODAY TOO.
YES, THEY ARE.
WHEN WE WATCHED THE STARS LAST TIME...
...I THINK LI'L SEAL WAS TREMBLING MORE.
HEH HEH.
I WONDER WHAT MAKES THEM THIS PRETTY.
THE STARS, I MEAN.

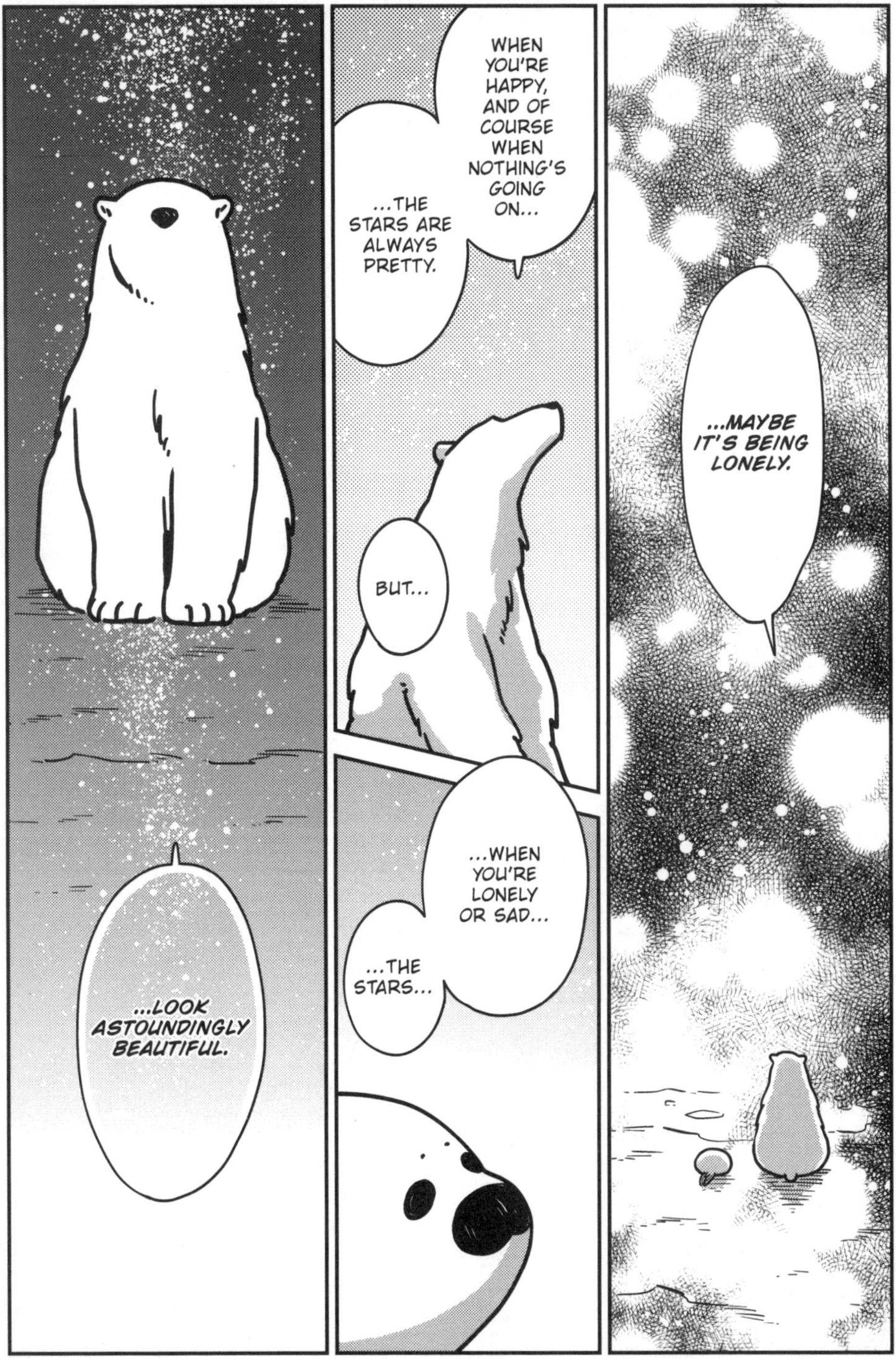
...MAYBE IT'S BEING LONELY.
WHEN YOU'RE HAPPY, AND OF COURSE WHEN NOTHING'S GOING ON...
...THE STARS ARE ALWAYS PRETTY.
BUT...
...WHEN YOU'RE LONELY OR SAD...
...THE STARS...
...LOOK ASTOUNDINGLY BEAUTIFUL.

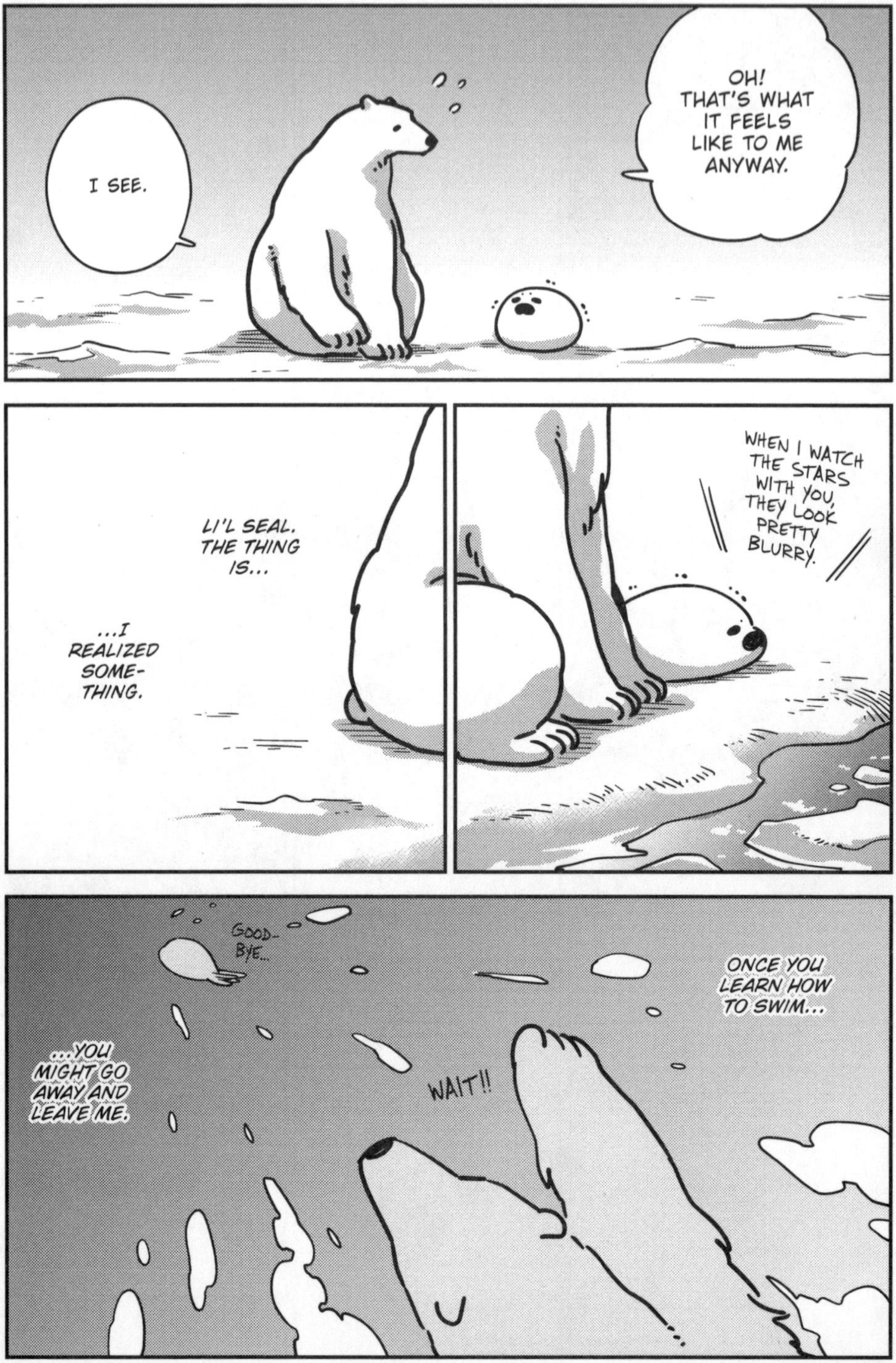
OH! THAT'S WHAT IT FEELS LIKE TO ME ANYWAY.
I SEE.
WHEN I WATCH THE STARS WITH YOU, THEY LOOK PRETTY BLURRY.
LI'L SEAL. THE THING IS...
...I REALIZED SOME-THING.
ONCE YOU LEARN HOW TO SWIM...
...YOU MIGHT GO AWAY AND LEAVE ME.
GOOD-BYE...
WAIT!!

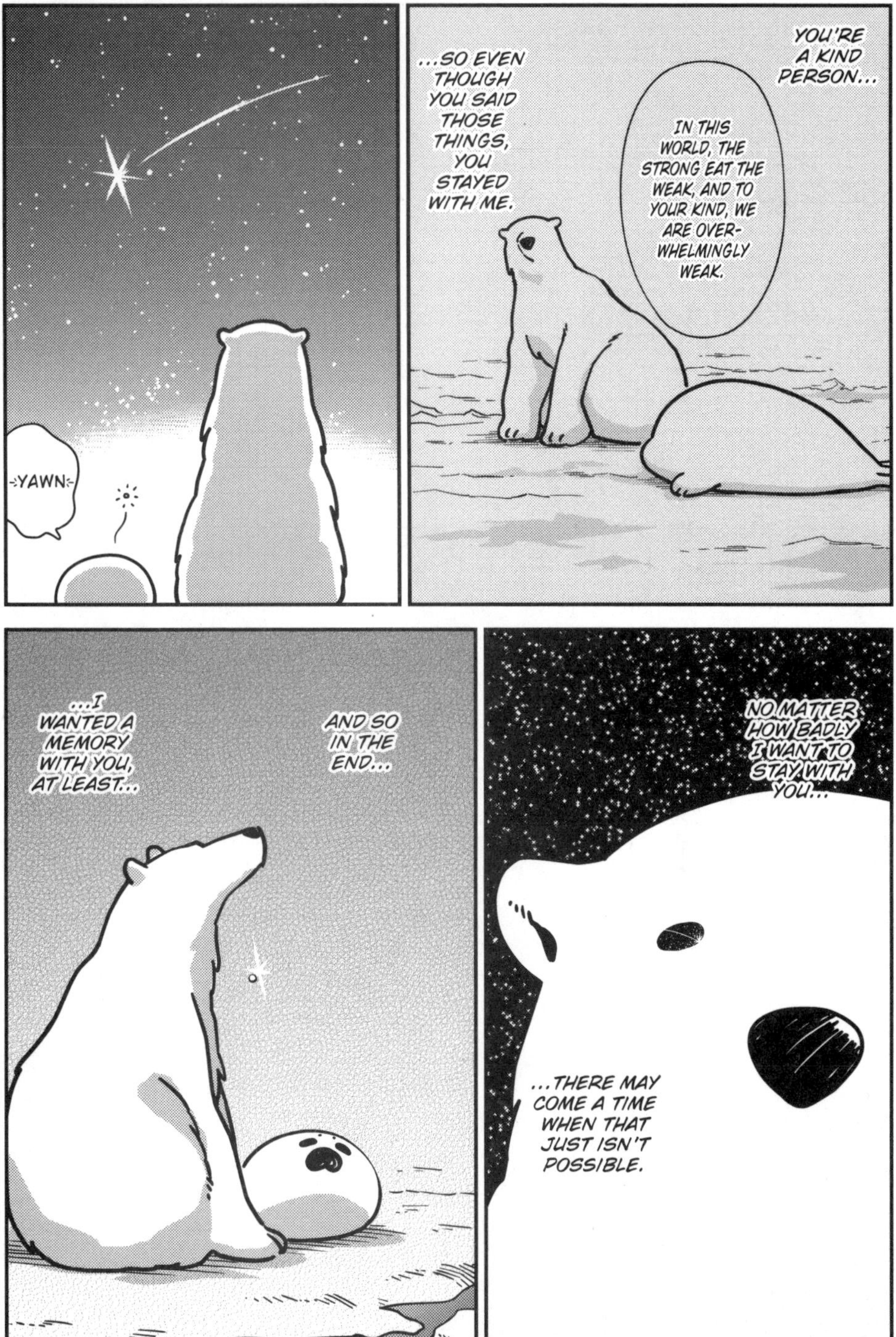
YOU'RE A KIND PERSON...
IN THIS WORLD, THE STRONG EAT THE WEAK, AND TO YOUR KIND, WE ARE OVER-WHELMINGLY WEAK.
...SO EVEN THOUGH YOU SAID THOSE THINGS, YOU STAYED WITH ME.
YAWN
NO MATTER HOW BADLY I WANT TO STAY WITH YOU...
...THERE MAY COME A TIME WHEN THAT JUST ISN'T POSSIBLE.
AND SO IN THE END...
...I WANTED A MEMORY WITH YOU, AT LEAST...

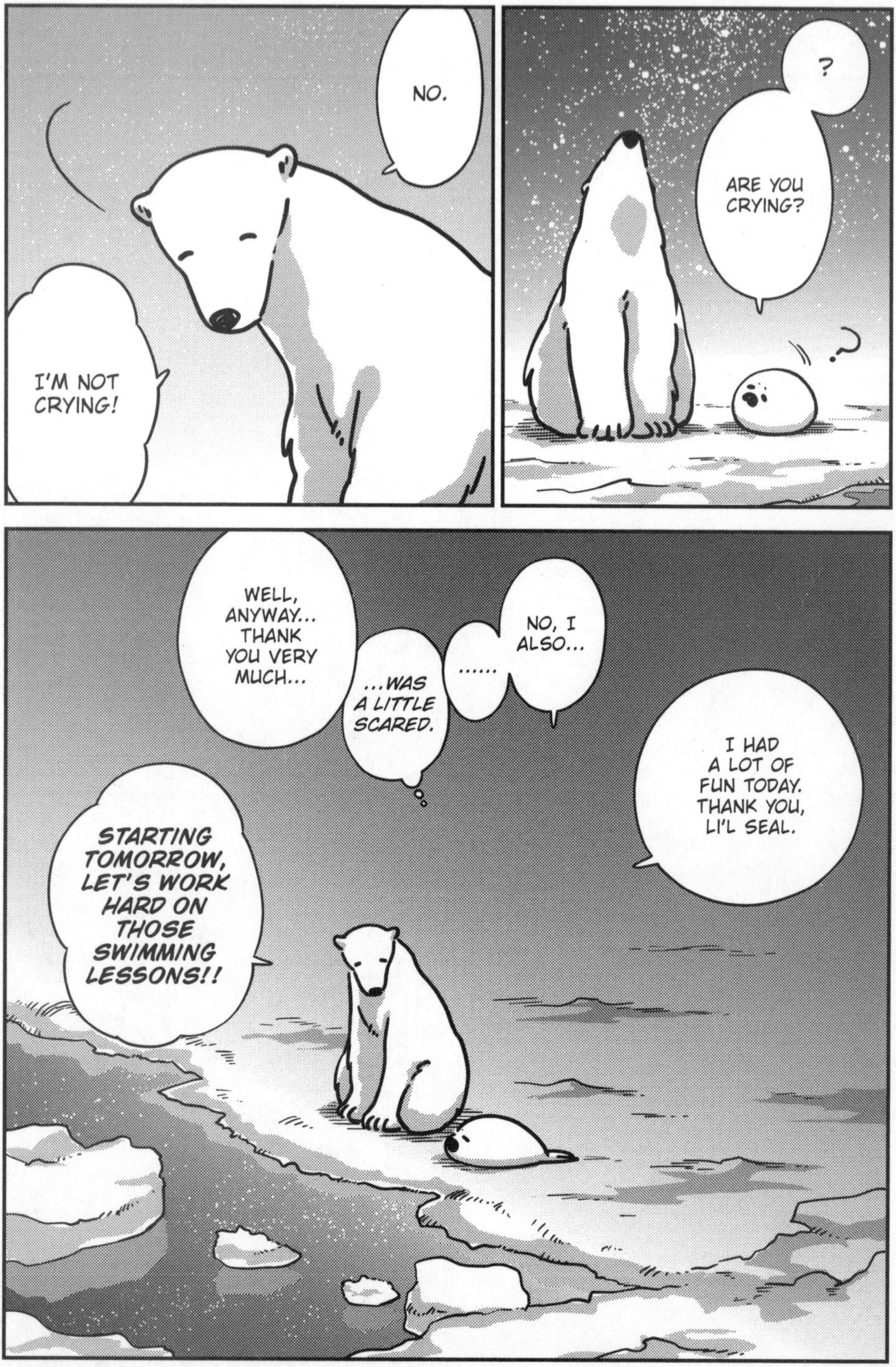
?
ARE YOU CRYING?
NO.
I'M NOT CRYING!
NO, I ALSO...
......
...WAS A LITTLE SCARED.
WELL, ANYWAY... THANK YOU VERY MUCH...
I HAD A LOT OF FUN TODAY. THANK YOU, LI'L SEAL.
STARTING TOMORROW, LET'S WORK HARD ON THOSE SWIMMING LESSONS!!

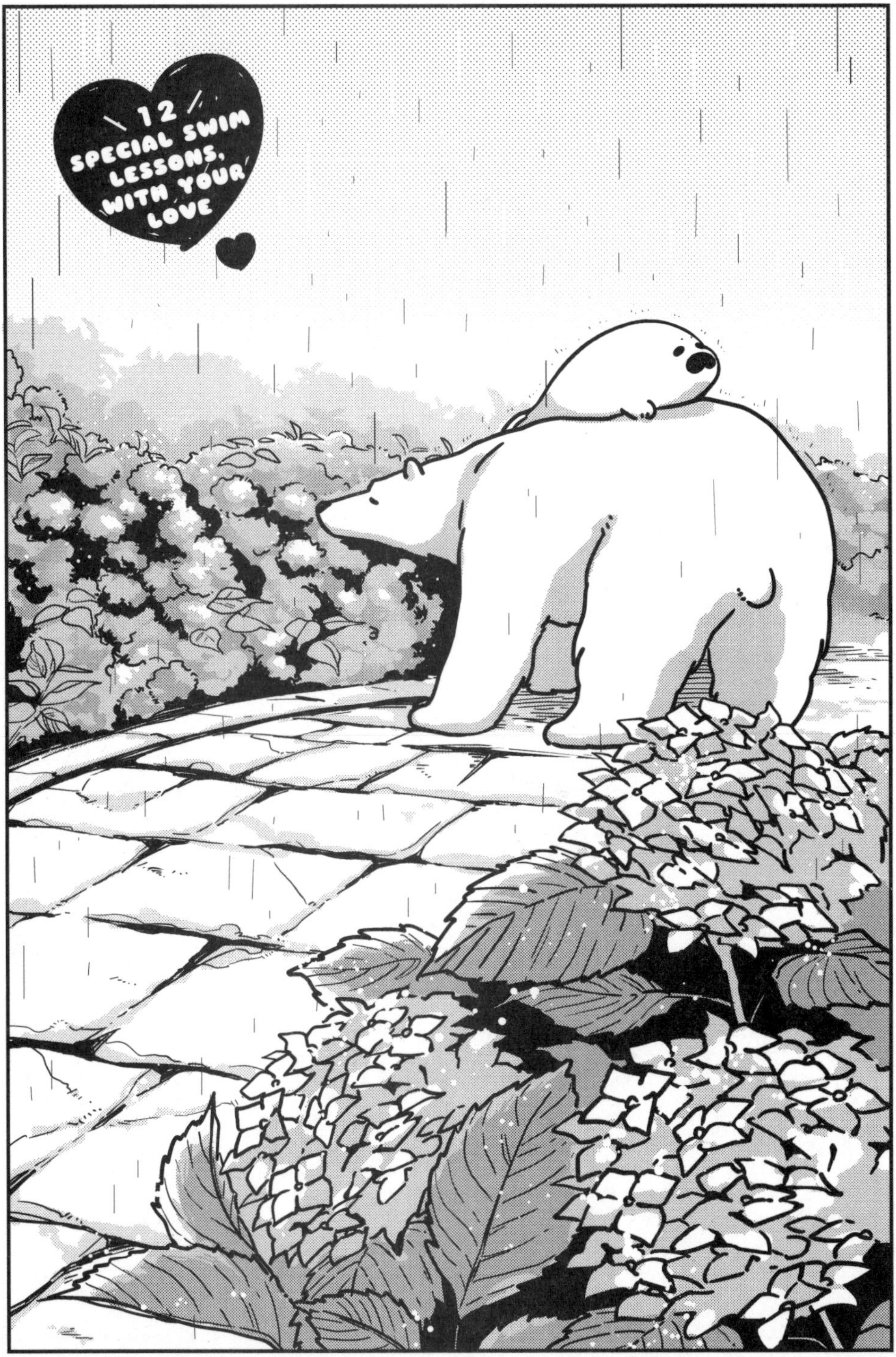
12
SPECIAL SWIM LESSONS, WITH YOUR LOVE

LOVE THE OCEAN!

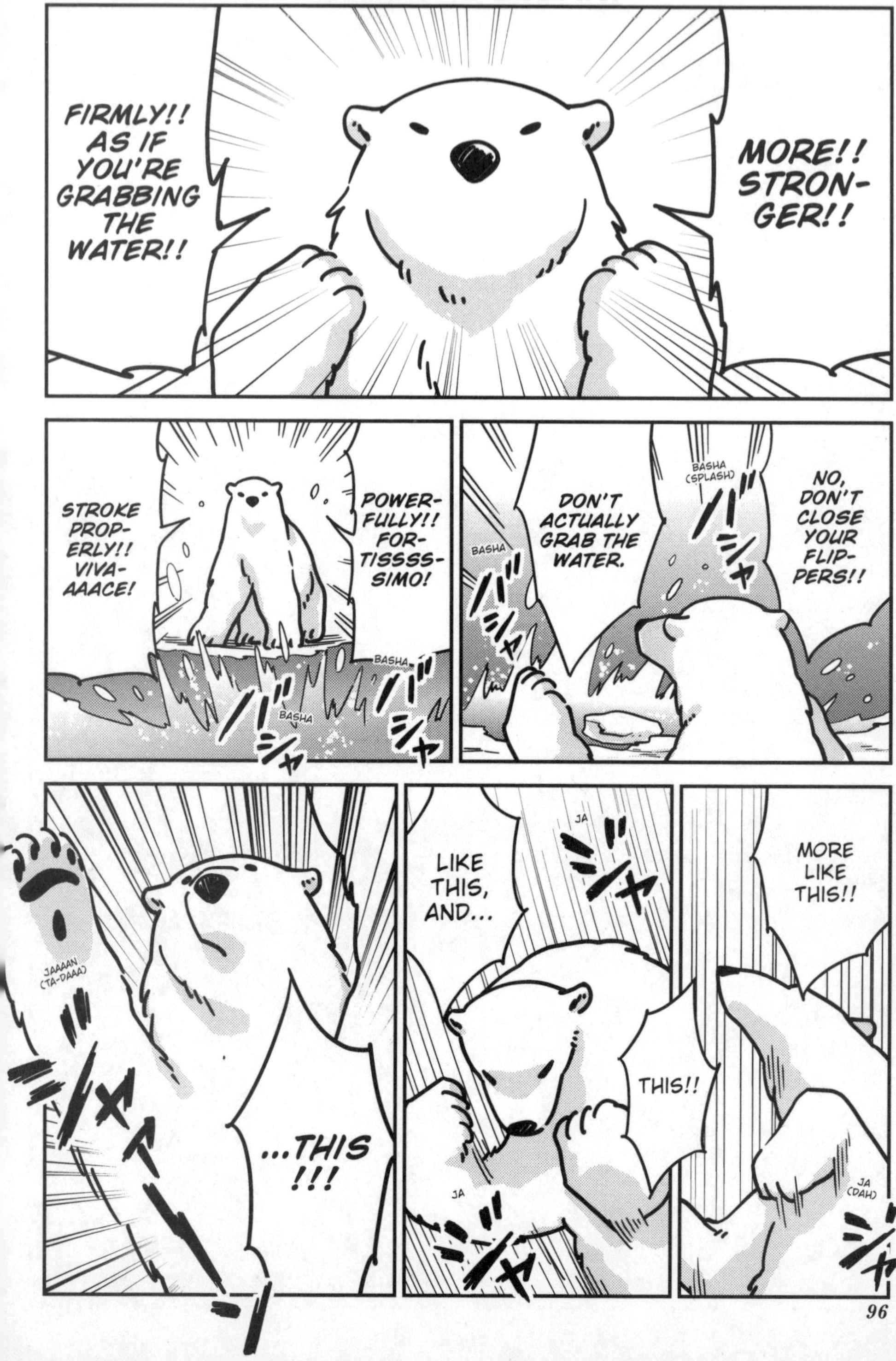
MORE!! STRON-GER!!
FIRMLY!! AS IF YOU'RE GRABBING THE WATER!!
NO, DON'T CLOSE YOUR FLIP-PERS!!
BASHA (SPLASH)
バシャ
DON'T ACTUALLY GRAB THE WATER.
BASHA
バシャ
POWER-FULLY!! FOR-TISSSS-SIMO!
STROKE PROP-ERLY!! VIVA-AAACE!
BASHA
バシャ
BASHA
バシャ
MORE LIKE THIS!!
JA (DAH)
ジャ
JA
ジャ
LIKE THIS, AND...
THIS!!
JA
ジャ
JAAAAN (TA-DAAA)
ジャーン
...THIS !!!

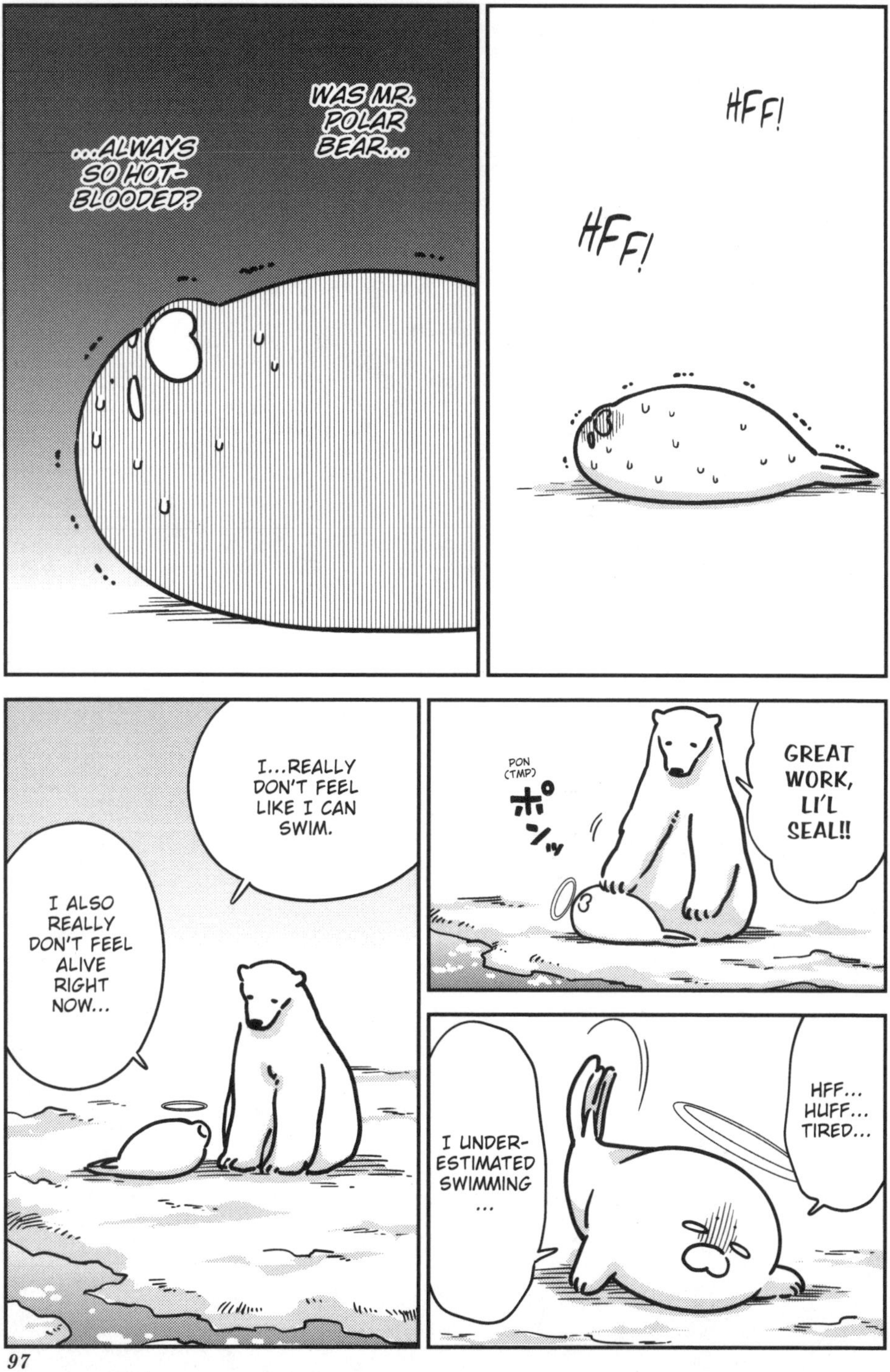
HFF!
HFF!
WAS MR. POLAR BEAR...
...ALWAYS SO HOT-BLOODED?
GREAT WORK, LI'L SEAL!!
PON (TMP)
ポンッ
HFF... HUFF... TIRED...
I UNDER-ESTIMATED SWIMMING ...
I...REALLY DON'T FEEL LIKE I CAN SWIM.
I ALSO REALLY DON'T FEEL ALIVE RIGHT NOW...

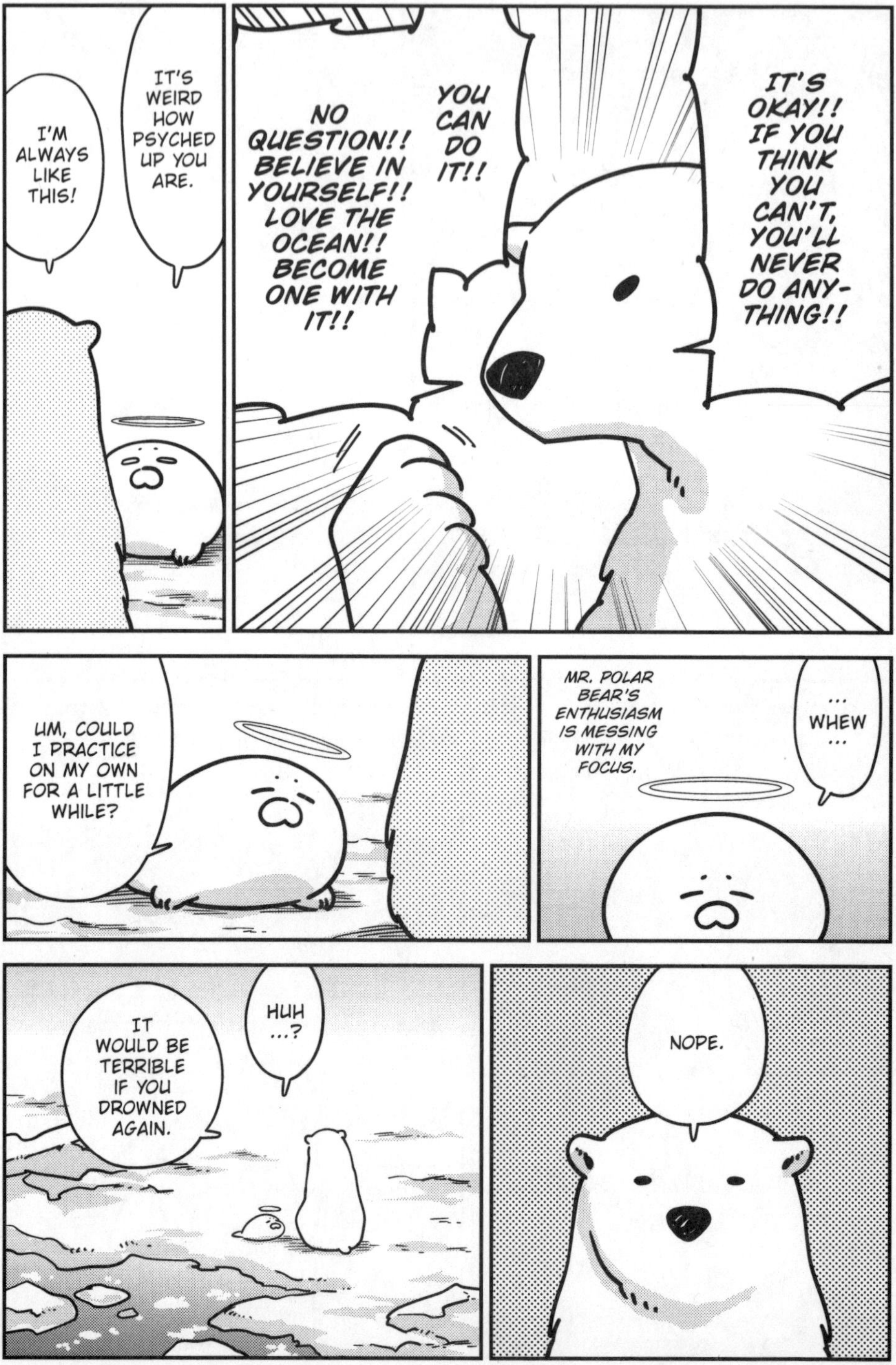
IT'S OKAY!! IF YOU THINK YOU CAN'T, YOU'LL NEVER DO ANY-THING!!
YOU CAN DO IT!!
NO QUESTION!! BELIEVE IN YOURSELF!! LOVE THE OCEAN!! BECOME ONE WITH IT!!
IT'S WEIRD HOW PSYCHED UP YOU ARE.
I'M ALWAYS LIKE THIS!
...WHEW...
MR. POLAR BEAR'S ENTHUSIASM IS MESSING WITH MY FOCUS.
UM, COULD I PRACTICE ON MY OWN FOR A LITTLE WHILE?
NOPE.
HUH...?
IT WOULD BE TERRIBLE IF YOU DROWNED AGAIN.

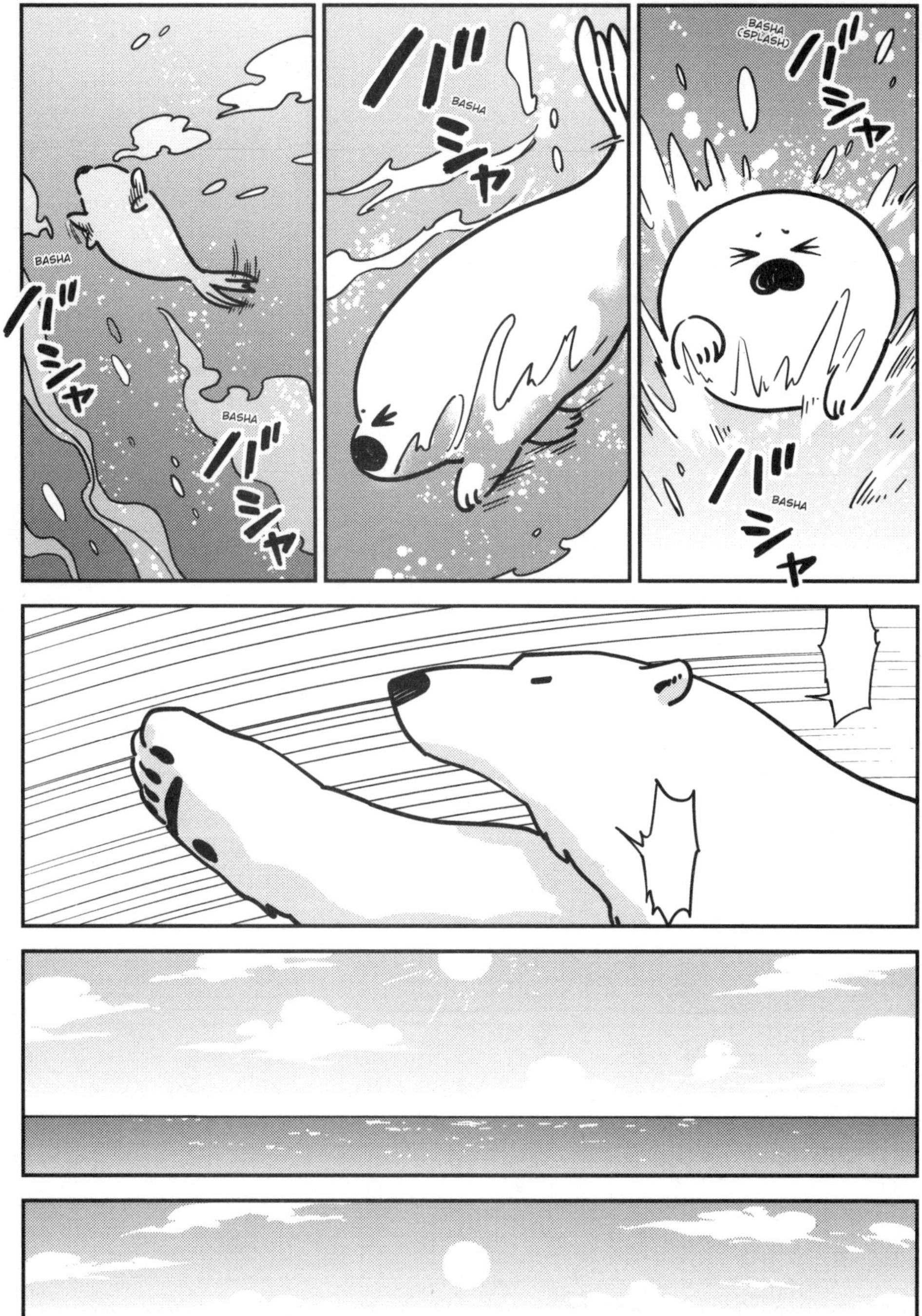
BASHA (SPLASH)
バシャ
バシャ
BASHA
バシャ
BASHA
BASHA
バシャ
BASHA
バシャ

THANK YOU VERY MUCH FOR...HELPING ME ALL DAY...

ZABA (SPLOOSH)

HEH HEH...

I'LL WORK HARD AGAIN TOMORROW.

SUYA
SUYA

SUYA (SNOOZE)

!

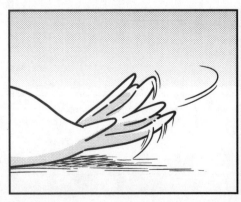

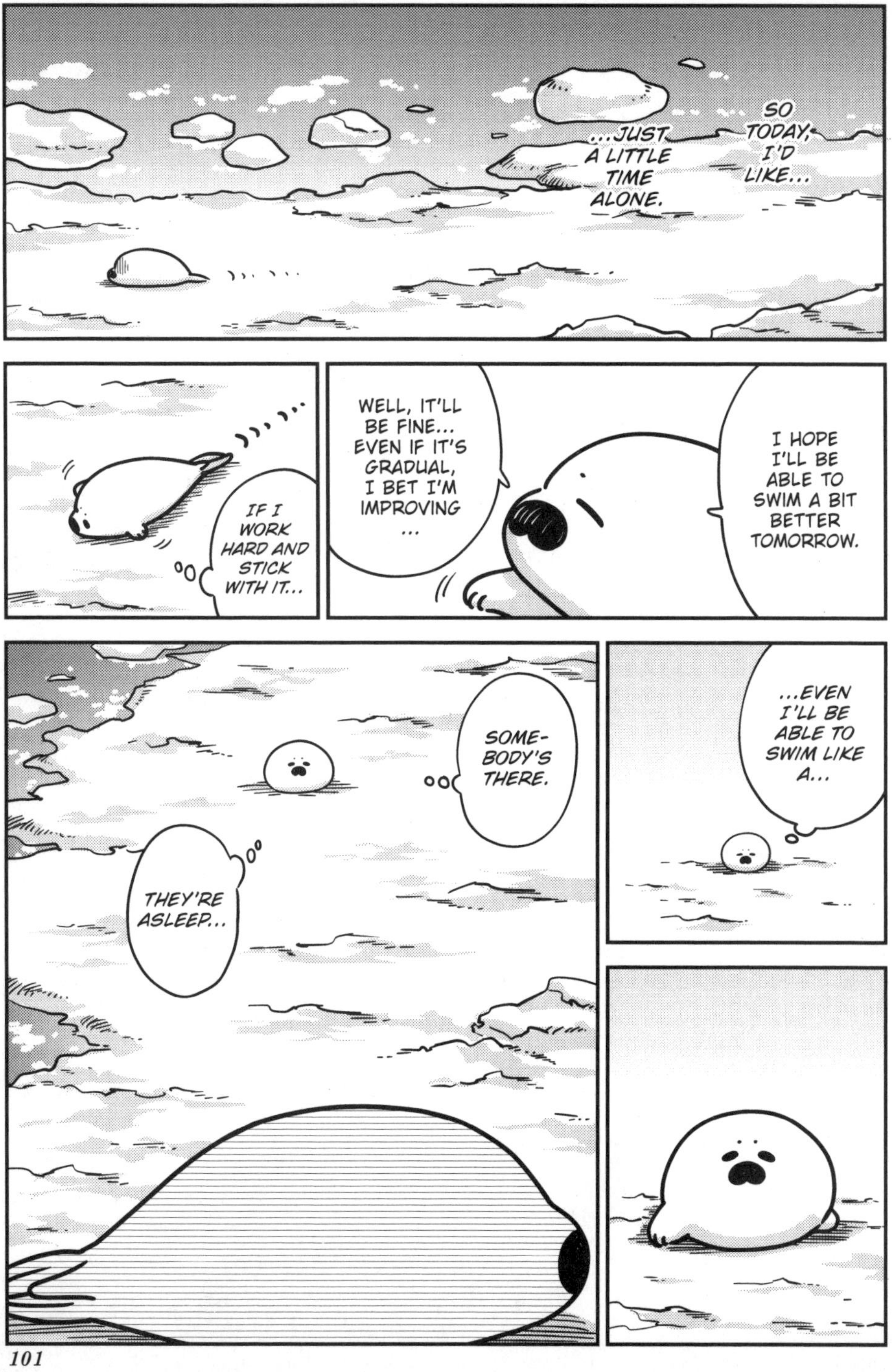
SO TODAY, I'D LIKE...
...JUST A LITTLE TIME ALONE.
I HOPE I'LL BE ABLE TO SWIM A BIT BETTER TOMORROW.
WELL, IT'LL BE FINE... EVEN IF IT'S GRADUAL, I BET I'M IMPROVING ...
IF I WORK HARD AND STICK WITH IT...
...EVEN I'LL BE ABLE TO SWIM LIKE A...
SOME-BODY'S THERE.
THEY'RE ASLEEP...

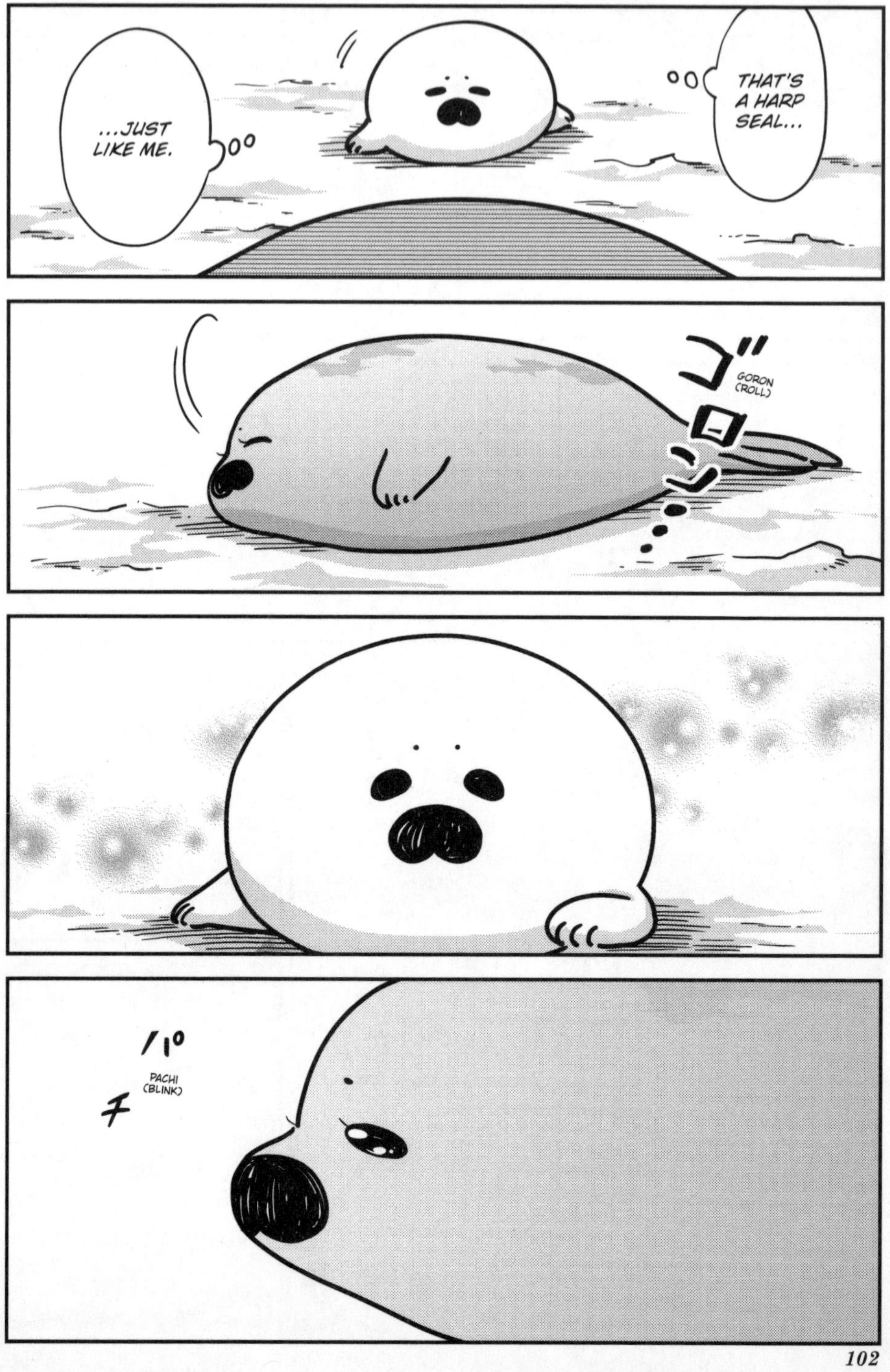
THAT'S A HARP SEAL...
...JUST LIKE ME.
ゴロン
GORON (ROLL)
パチ
PACHI (BLINK)

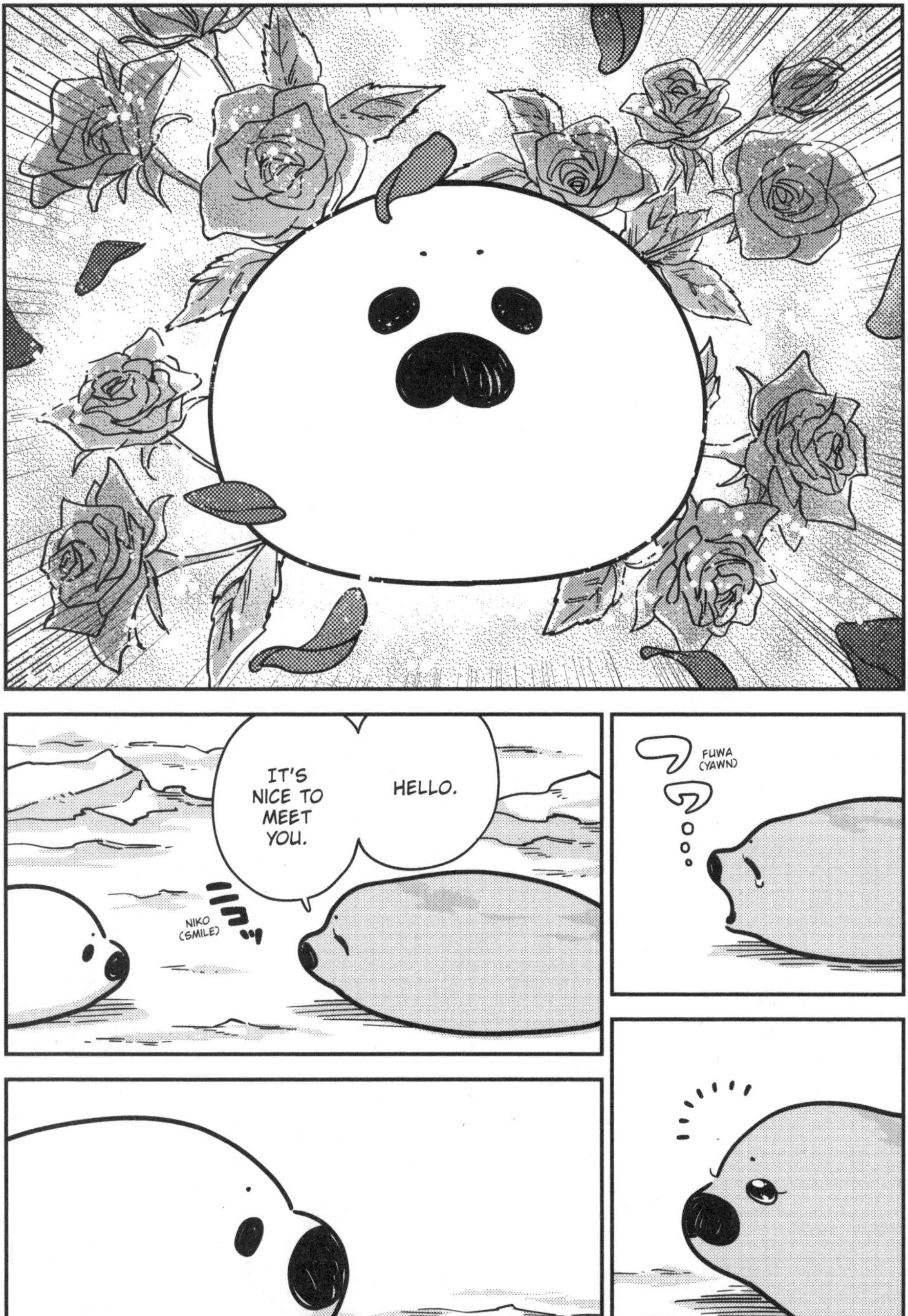
FUWA (YAWN)
HELLO.
IT'S NICE TO MEET YOU.
NIKO (SMILE)

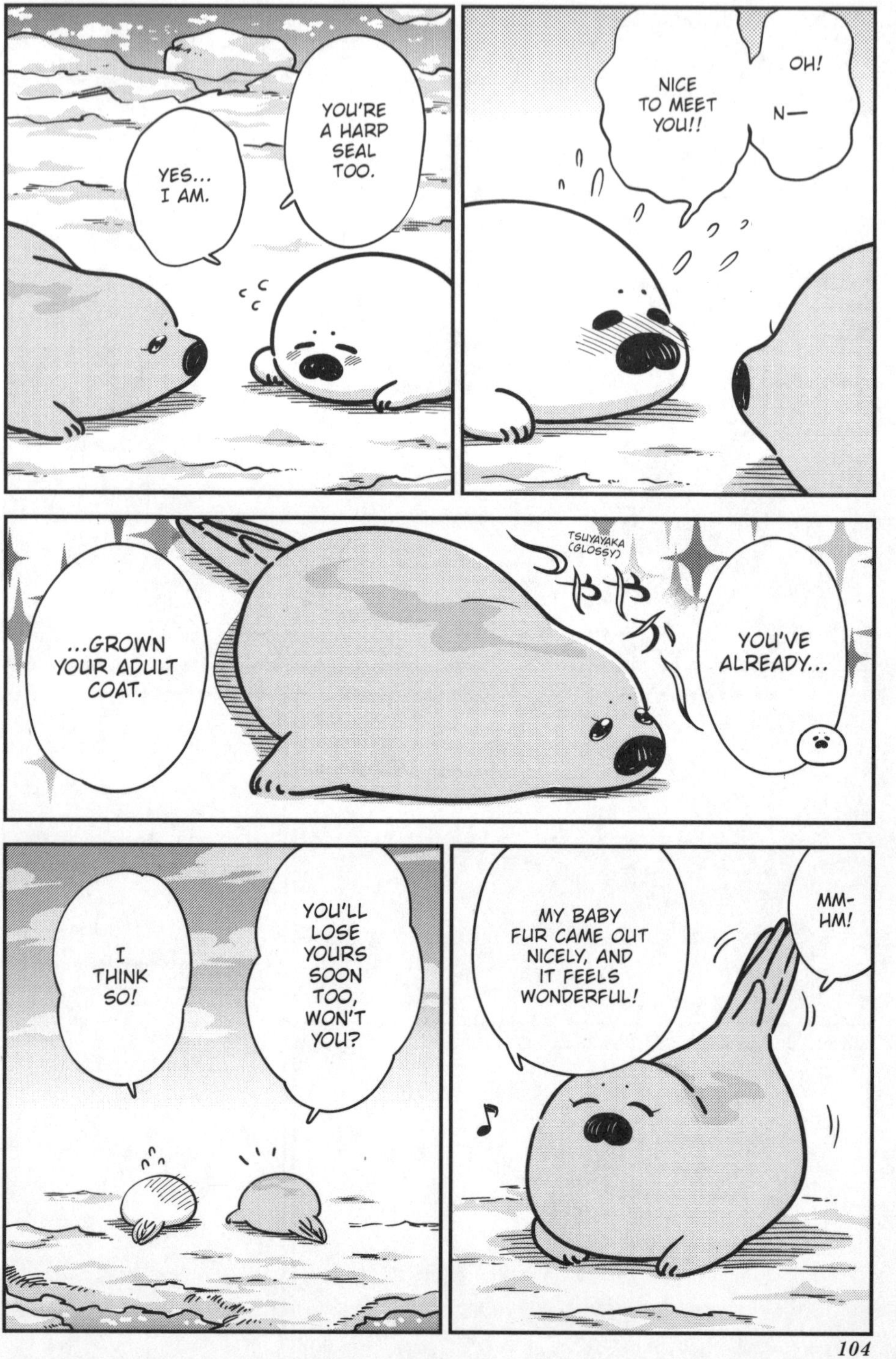
OH!
N—
NICE TO MEET YOU!!
YOU'RE A HARP SEAL TOO.
YES... I AM.
YOU'VE ALREADY...
TSUYAYAKA (GLOSSY)
...GROWN YOUR ADULT COAT.
MM-HM!
MY BABY FUR CAME OUT NICELY, AND IT FEELS WONDERFUL!
YOU'LL LOSE YOURS SOON TOO, WON'T YOU?
I THINK SO!

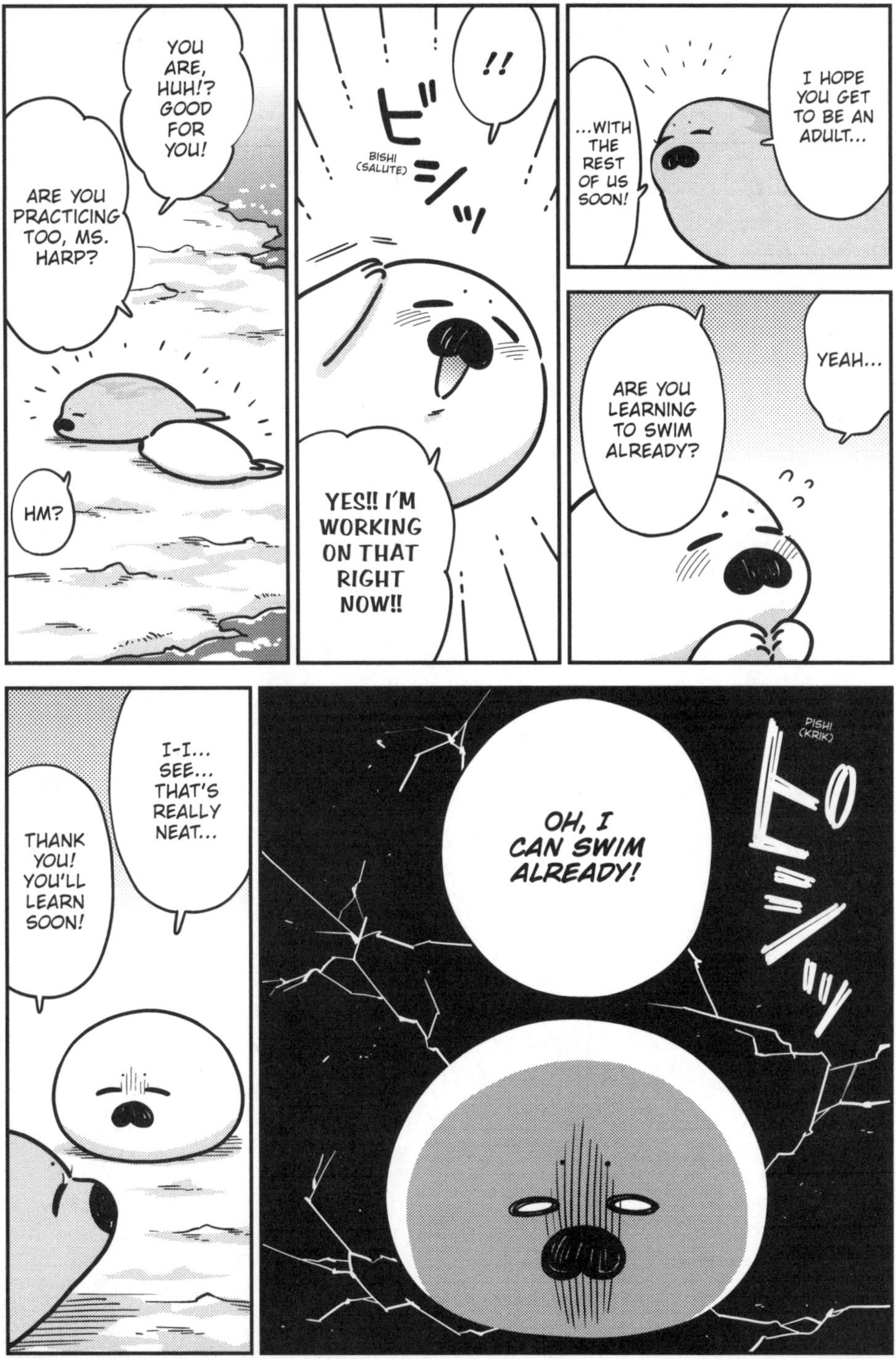
I HOPE YOU GET TO BE AN ADULT...
...WITH THE REST OF US SOON!
YEAH...
ARE YOU LEARNING TO SWIM ALREADY?
!!
ビシッ
BISHI (SALUTE)
YES!! I'M WORKING ON THAT RIGHT NOW!!
YOU ARE, HUH!? GOOD FOR YOU!
ARE YOU PRACTICING TOO, MS. HARP?
HM?
ピシッ
PISHI (KRIK)
OH, I CAN SWIM ALREADY!
I-I... SEE... THAT'S REALLY NEAT...
THANK YOU! YOU'LL LEARN SOON!

I'LL BE CHEERING FOR YOU, ALL RIGHT?

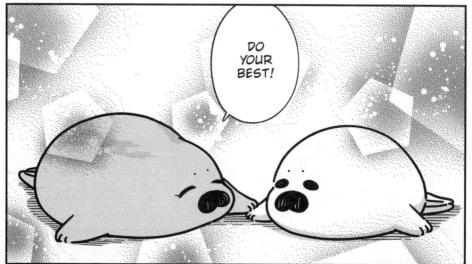

DO YOUR BEST!

I...I-I-I, I WILL!!!

IT'S A STEAMED MEAT BUN.

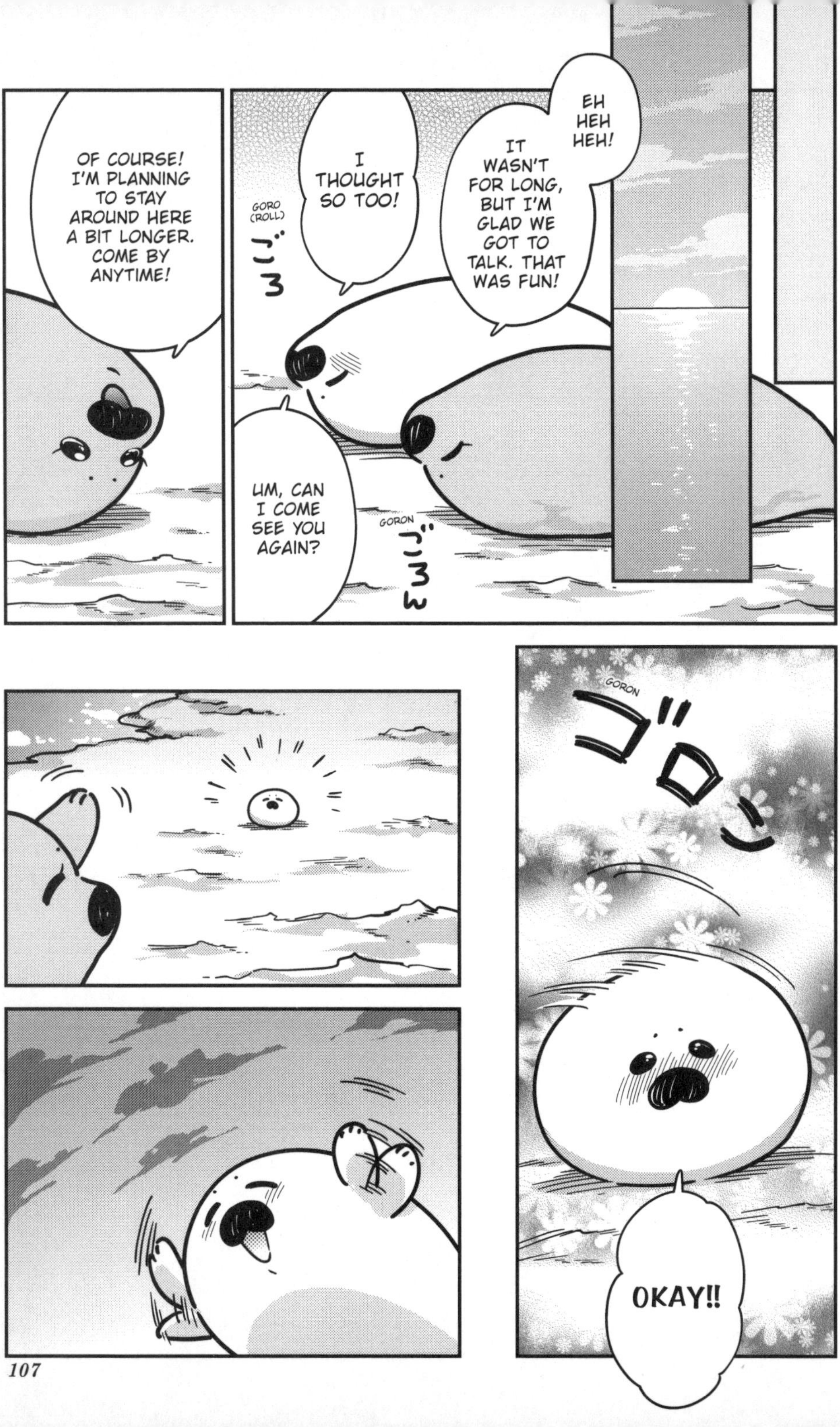
EH HEH HEH!
IT WASN'T FOR LONG, BUT I'M GLAD WE GOT TO TALK. THAT WAS FUN!
I THOUGHT SO TOO!
GORO (ROLL)
UM, CAN I COME SEE YOU AGAIN?
GORON
OF COURSE! I'M PLANNING TO STAY AROUND HERE A BIT LONGER. COME BY ANYTIME!
GORON
OKAY!!

YOU FELL IN LOVE, DIDN'T YOU?

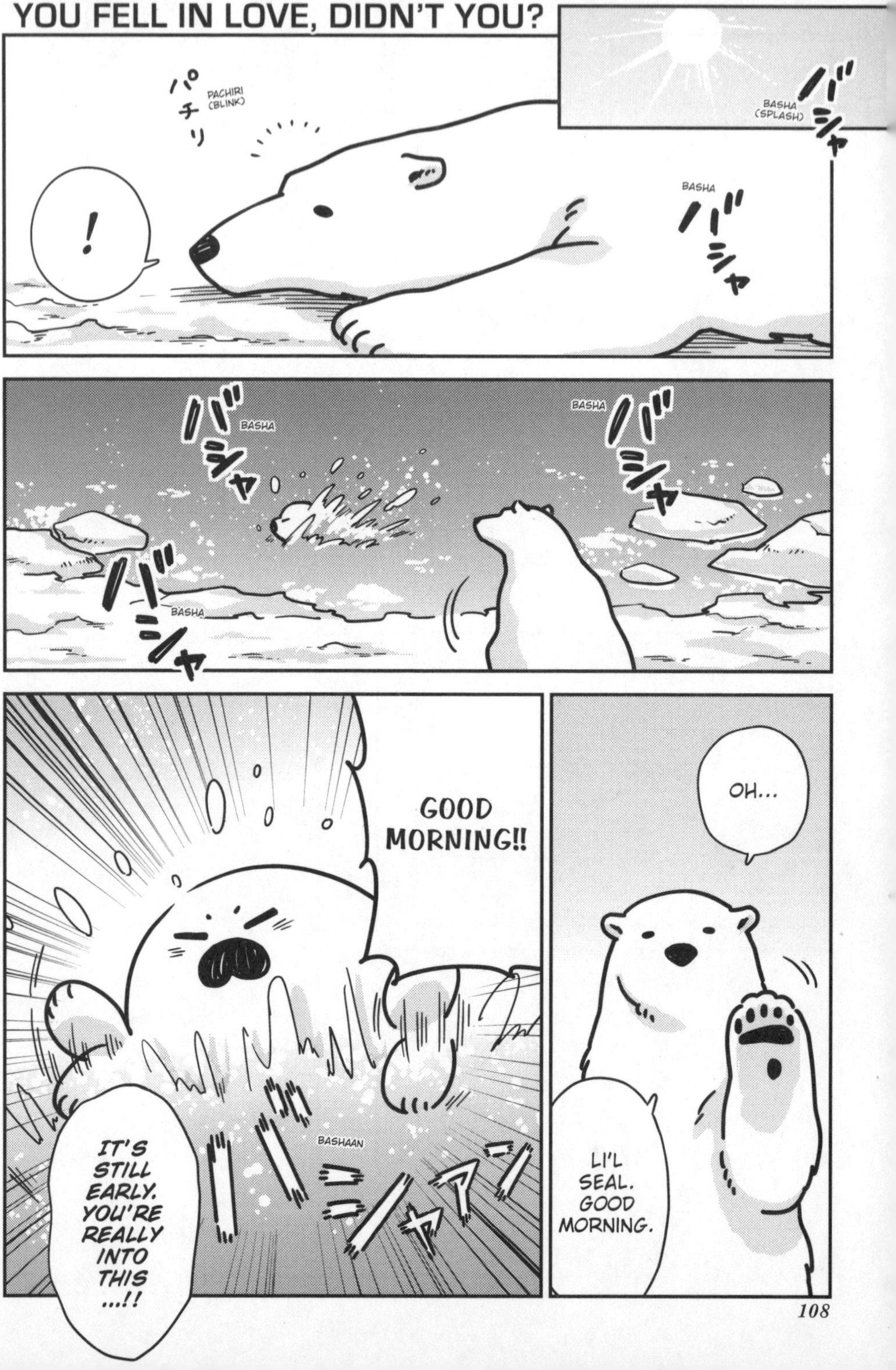
BASHA (SPLASH)
バシャ
BASHA
バシャ
PACHIRI (BLINK)
パチリ
!
BASHA
バシャ
BASHA
バシャ
BASHA
バシャ
OH...
LI'L SEAL. GOOD MORNING.
GOOD MORNING!!
IT'S STILL EARLY. YOU'RE REALLY INTO THIS ...!!
BASHAAN

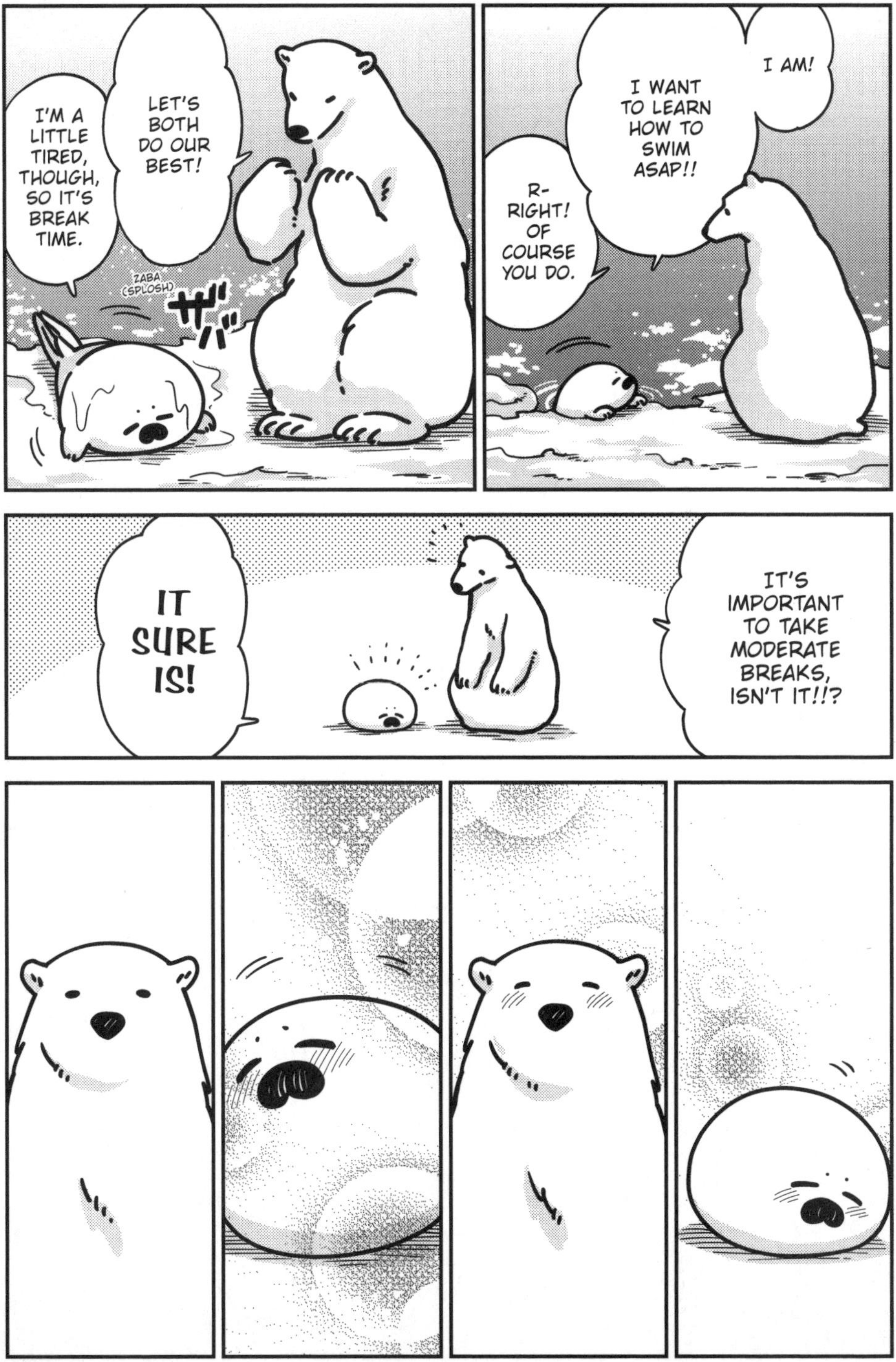
I AM!
I WANT TO LEARN HOW TO SWIM ASAP!!
R-RIGHT! OF COURSE YOU DO.
LET'S BOTH DO OUR BEST!
I'M A LITTLE TIRED, THOUGH, SO IT'S BREAK TIME.
ZABA (SPLOSH)
IT'S IMPORTANT TO TAKE MODERATE BREAKS, ISN'T IT!!?
IT SURE IS!

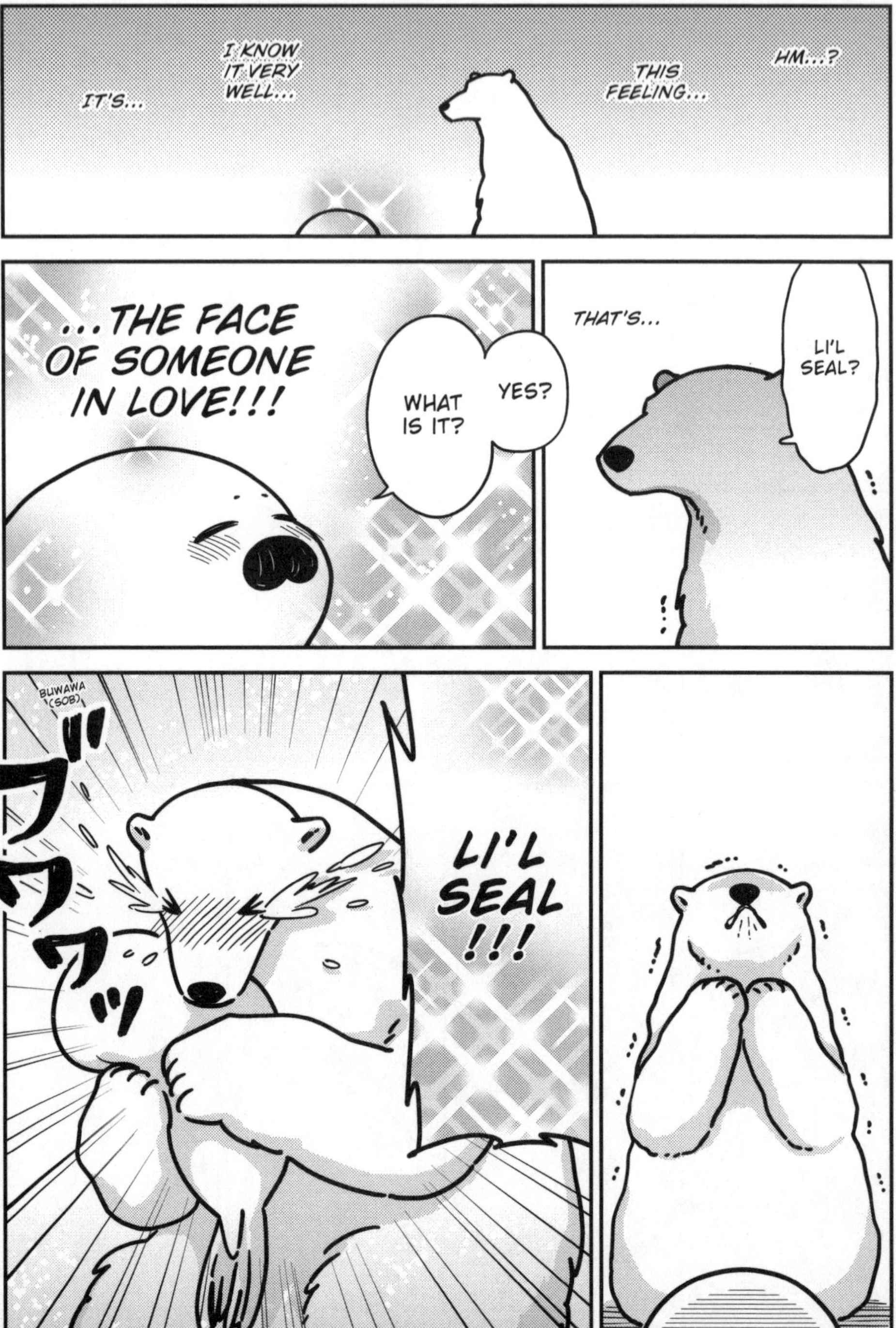
HM...?
THIS FEELING...
I KNOW IT VERY WELL...
IT'S...
LI'L SEAL?
THAT'S...
YES?
WHAT IS IT?
...THE FACE OF SOMEONE IN LOVE!!!
LI'L SEAL!!!
ブワワッ
BUWAWA (SOB)

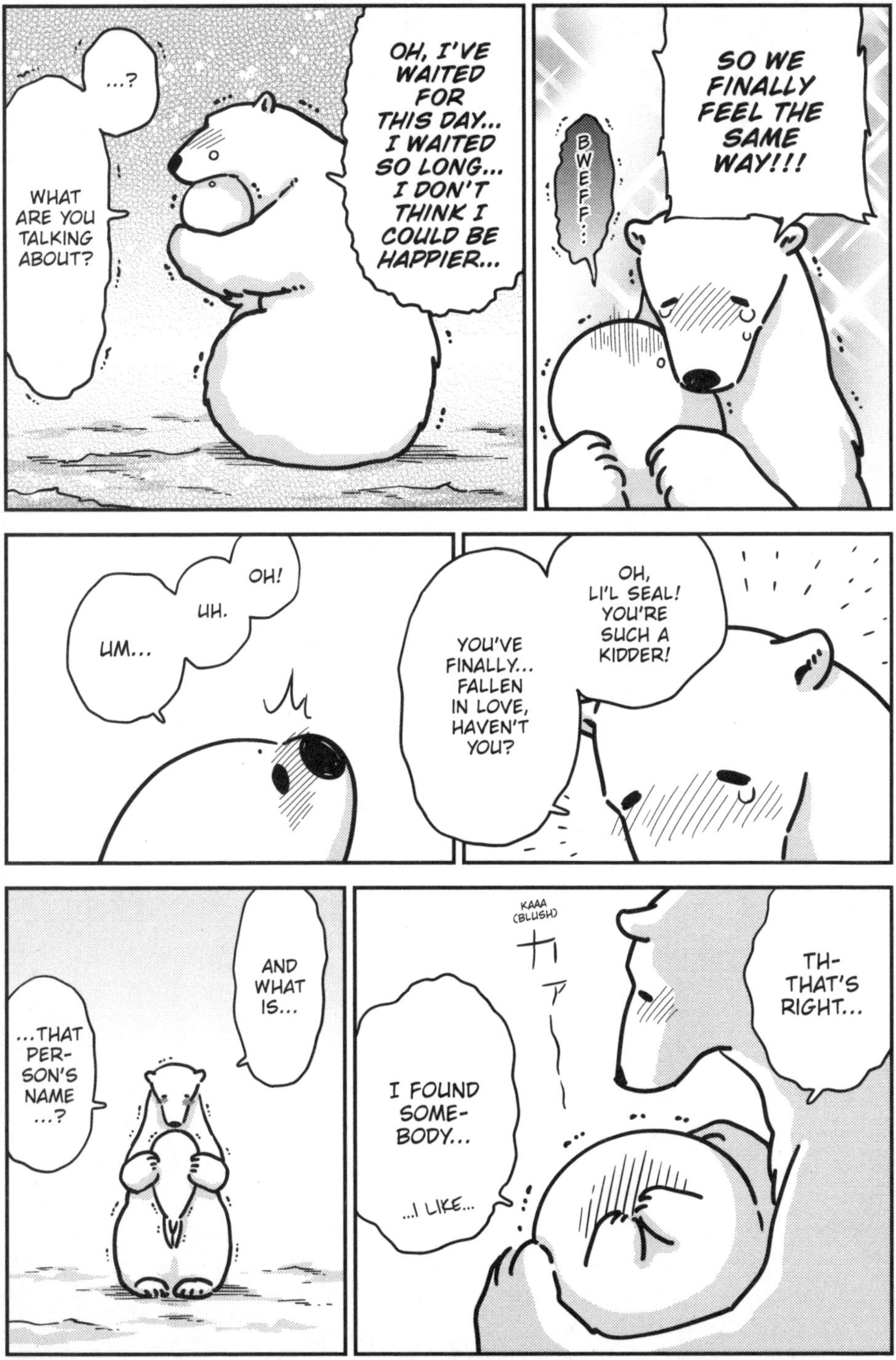
SO WE FINALLY FEEL THE SAME WAY!!!
BWEFF...
OH, I'VE WAITED FOR THIS DAY... I WAITED SO LONG... I DON'T THINK I COULD BE HAPPIER...
...?
WHAT ARE YOU TALKING ABOUT?
OH, LI'L SEAL! YOU'RE SUCH A KIDDER!
YOU'VE FINALLY... FALLEN IN LOVE, HAVEN'T YOU?
OH!
UH.
UM...
KAAA (BLUSH)
TH-THAT'S RIGHT...
I FOUND SOMEBODY...
...I LIKE...
AND WHAT IS...
...THAT PERSON'S NAME...?

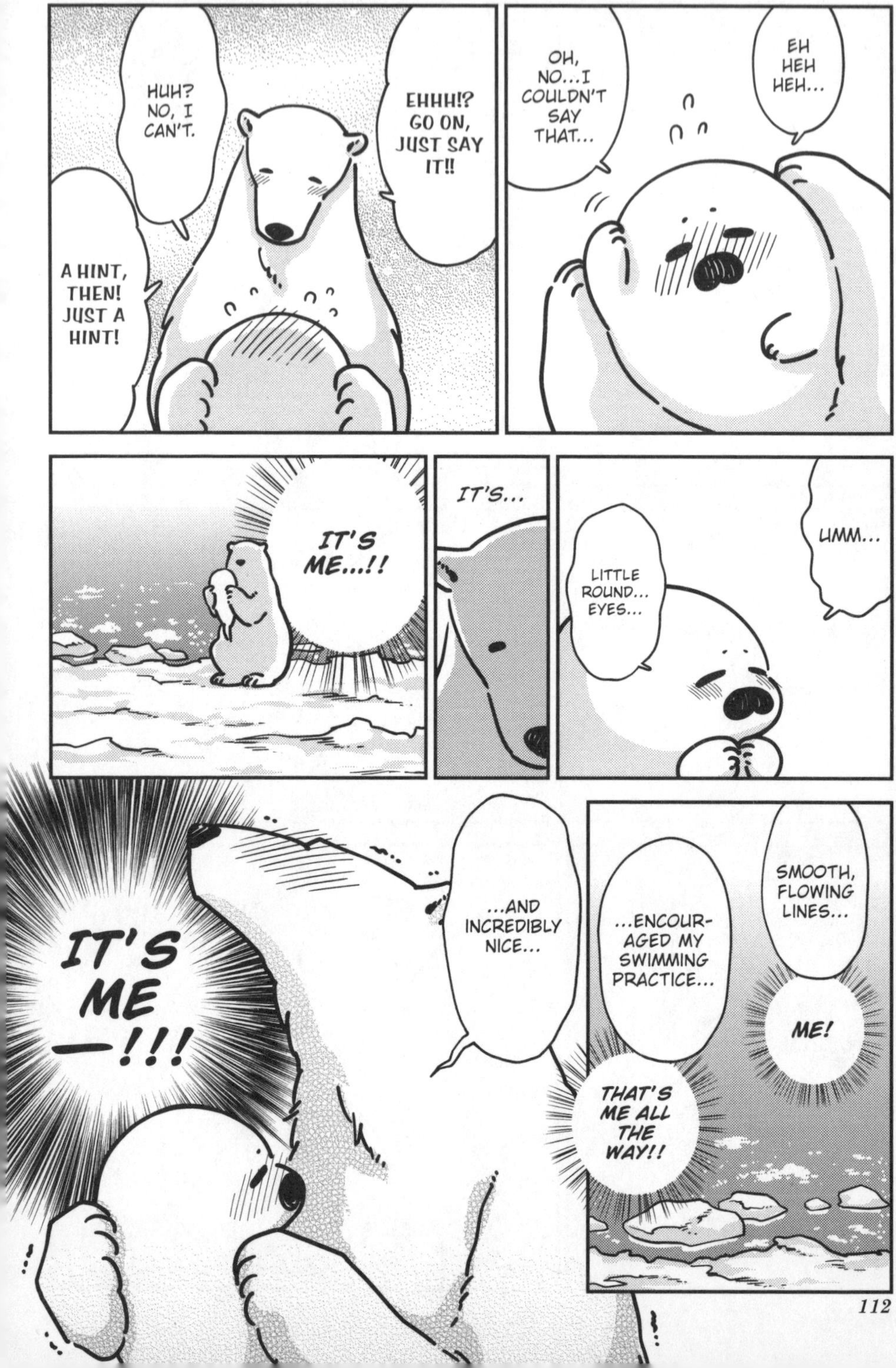
EH HEH HEH...
OH, NO...I COULDN'T SAY THAT...
EHHH!? GO ON, JUST SAY IT!!
HUH? NO, I CAN'T.
A HINT, THEN! JUST A HINT!
UMM...
LITTLE ROUND... EYES...
IT'S...
IT'S ME...!!
SMOOTH, FLOWING LINES...
...ENCOURAGED MY SWIMMING PRACTICE...
ME!
THAT'S ME ALL THE WAY!!
...AND INCREDIBLY NICE...
IT'S ME—!!!

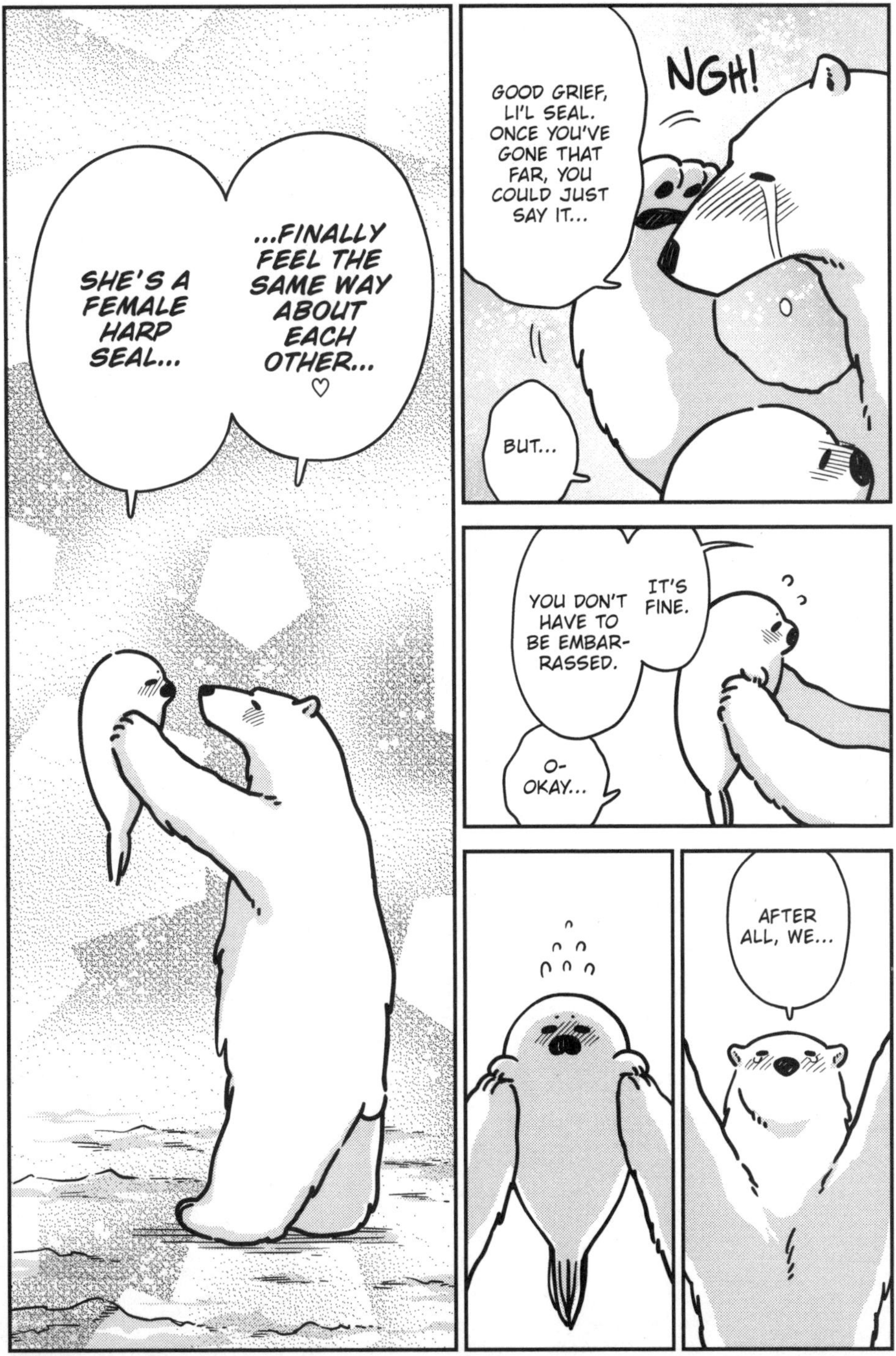
NGH!
GOOD GRIEF, LI'L SEAL. ONCE YOU'VE GONE THAT FAR, YOU COULD JUST SAY IT...
BUT...
IT'S FINE.
YOU DON'T HAVE TO BE EMBAR-RASSED.
O-OKAY...
AFTER ALL, WE...
...FINALLY FEEL THE SAME WAY ABOUT EACH OTHER... ♡
SHE'S A FEMALE HARP SEAL...

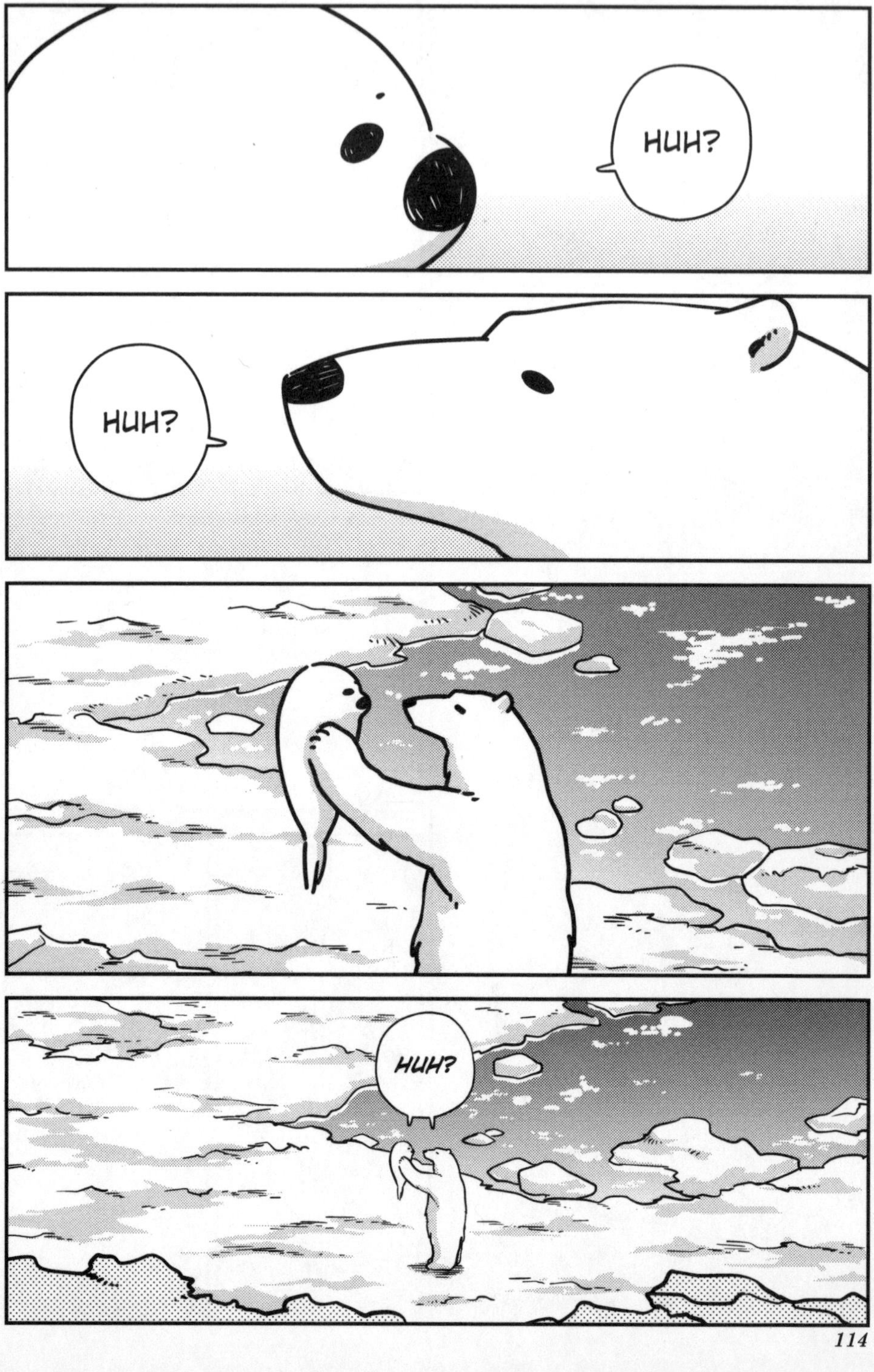
HUH?
HUH?
HUH?

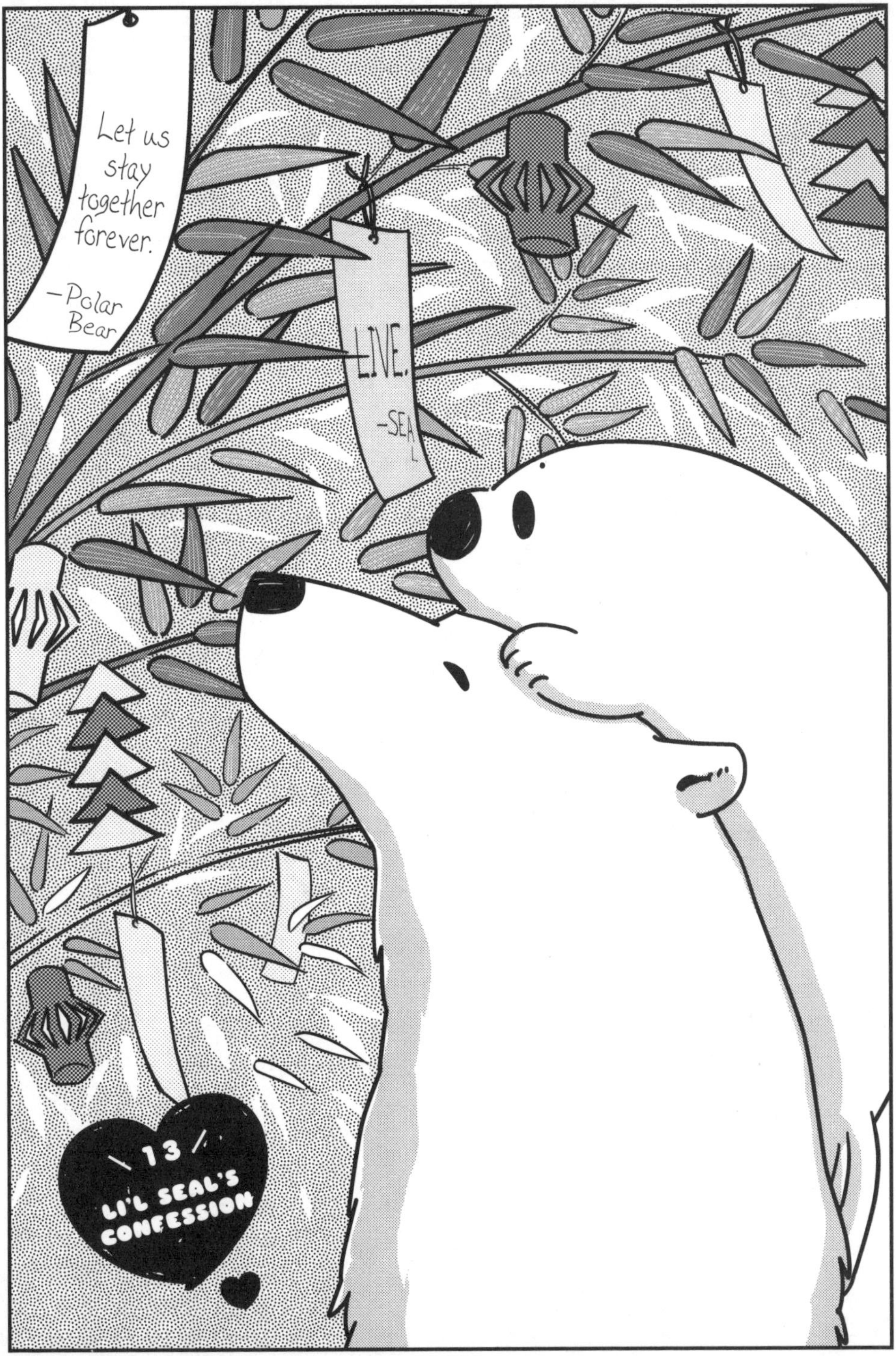
Let us stay together forever. —Polar Bear
LIVE. —SEAL
13
LI'L SEAL'S CONFESSION

THE POWER OF LOVE

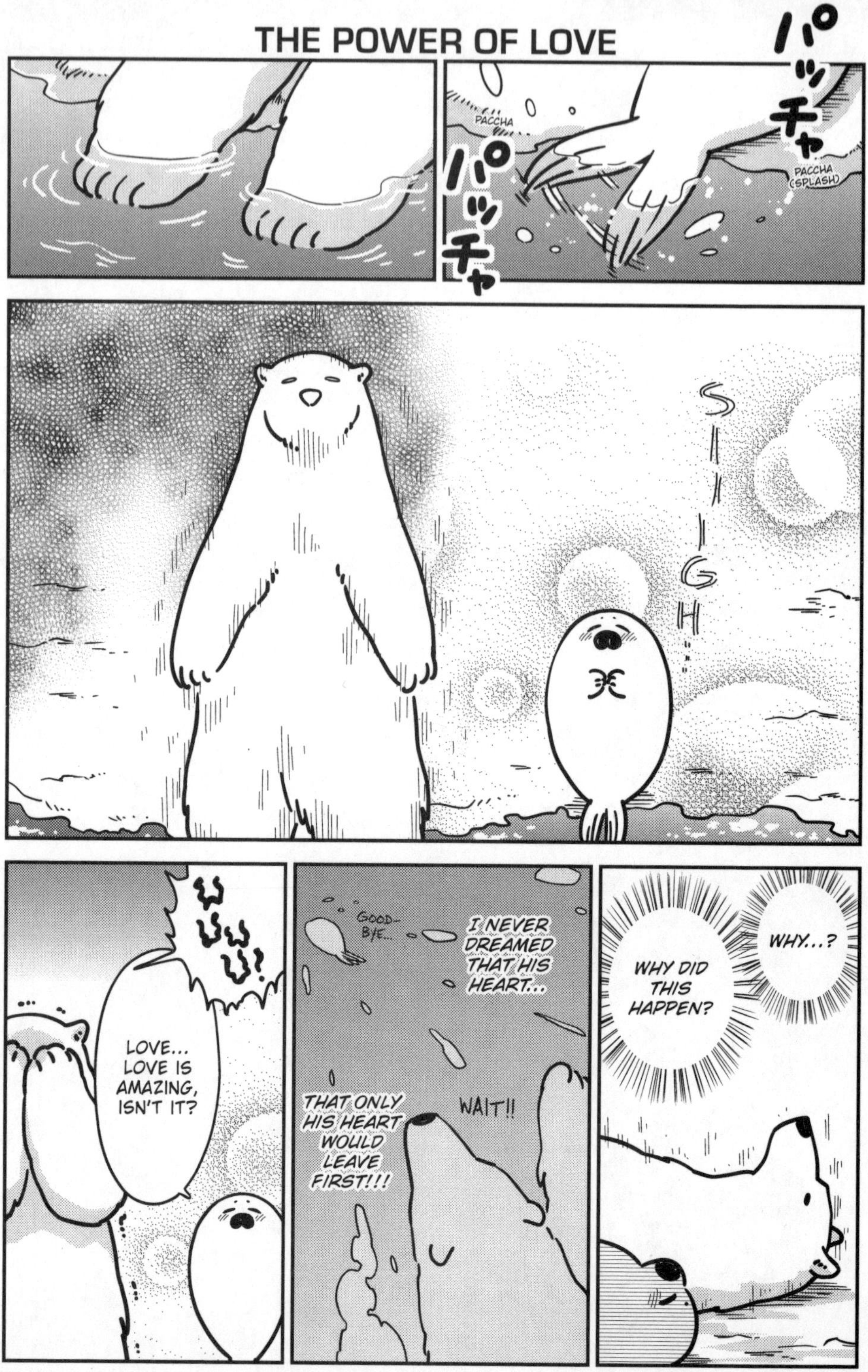

パッチャ
PACCHA (SPLASH)
パッチャ
PACCHA
SIGH...
WHY...?
WHY DID THIS HAPPEN?
I NEVER DREAMED THAT HIS HEART...
GOOD-BYE...
WAIT!!
THAT ONLY HIS HEART WOULD LEAVE FIRST!!!
LOVE... LOVE IS AMAZING, ISN'T IT?
...

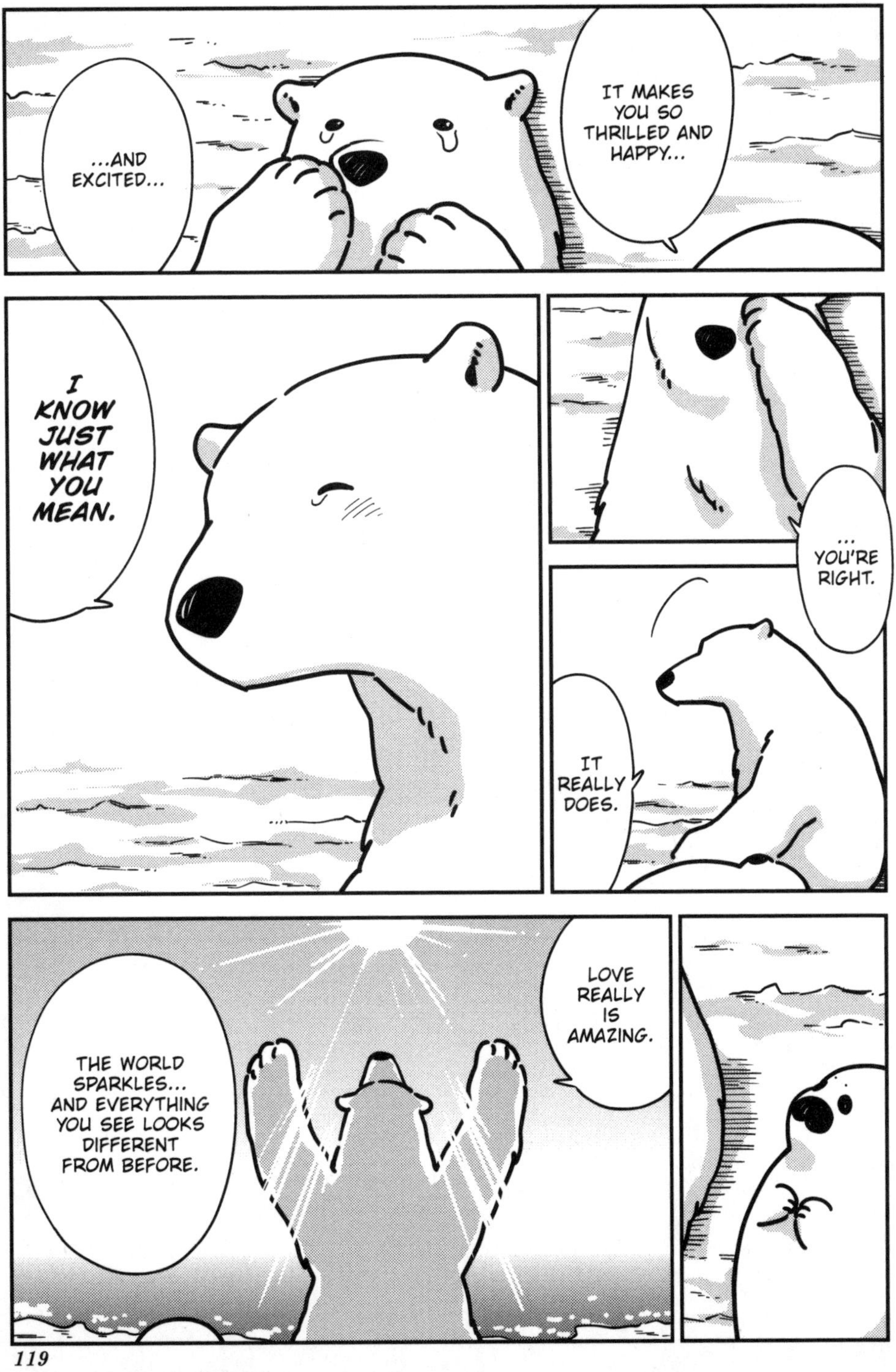
IT MAKES YOU SO THRILLED AND HAPPY...
...AND EXCITED...
... YOU'RE RIGHT.
IT REALLY DOES.
I KNOW JUST WHAT YOU MEAN.
LOVE REALLY IS AMAZING.
THE WORLD SPARKLES... AND EVERYTHING YOU SEE LOOKS DIFFERENT FROM BEFORE.

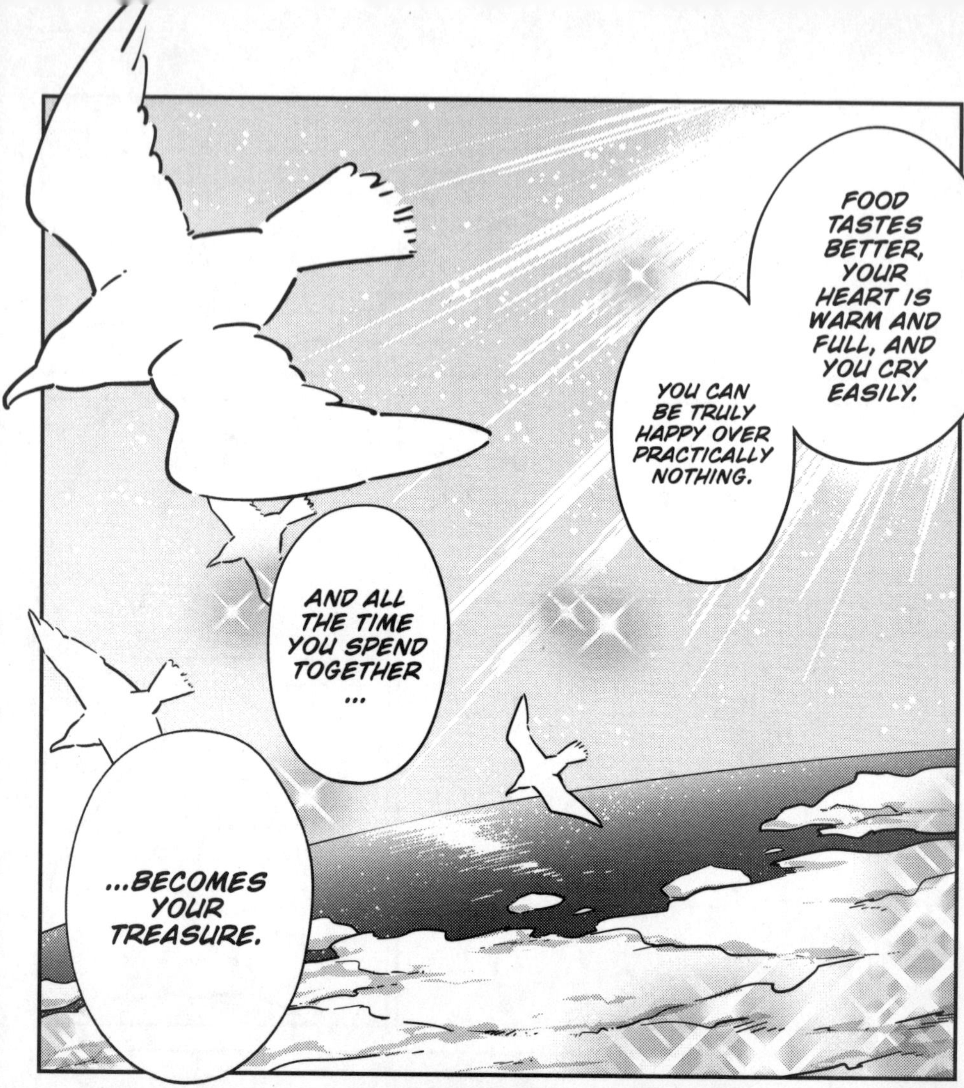
FOOD TASTES BETTER, YOUR HEART IS WARM AND FULL, AND YOU CRY EASILY.
YOU CAN BE TRULY HAPPY OVER PRACTICALLY NOTHING.
AND ALL THE TIME YOU SPEND TOGETHER ...
...BECOMES YOUR TREASURE.

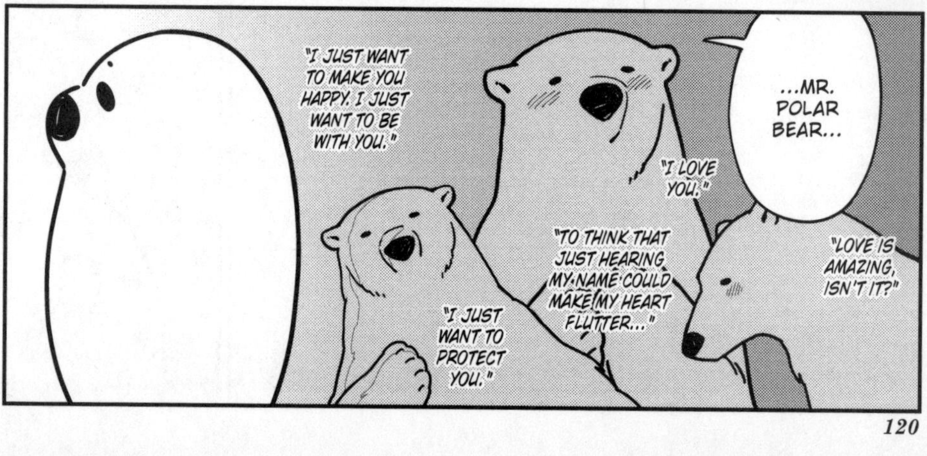
...MR. POLAR BEAR...
"LOVE IS AMAZING, ISN'T IT?"
"I LOVE YOU."
"I JUST WANT TO MAKE YOU HAPPY. I JUST WANT TO BE WITH YOU."
"TO THINK THAT JUST HEARING MY NAME COULD MAKE MY HEART FLUTTER..."
"I JUST WANT TO PROTECT YOU."

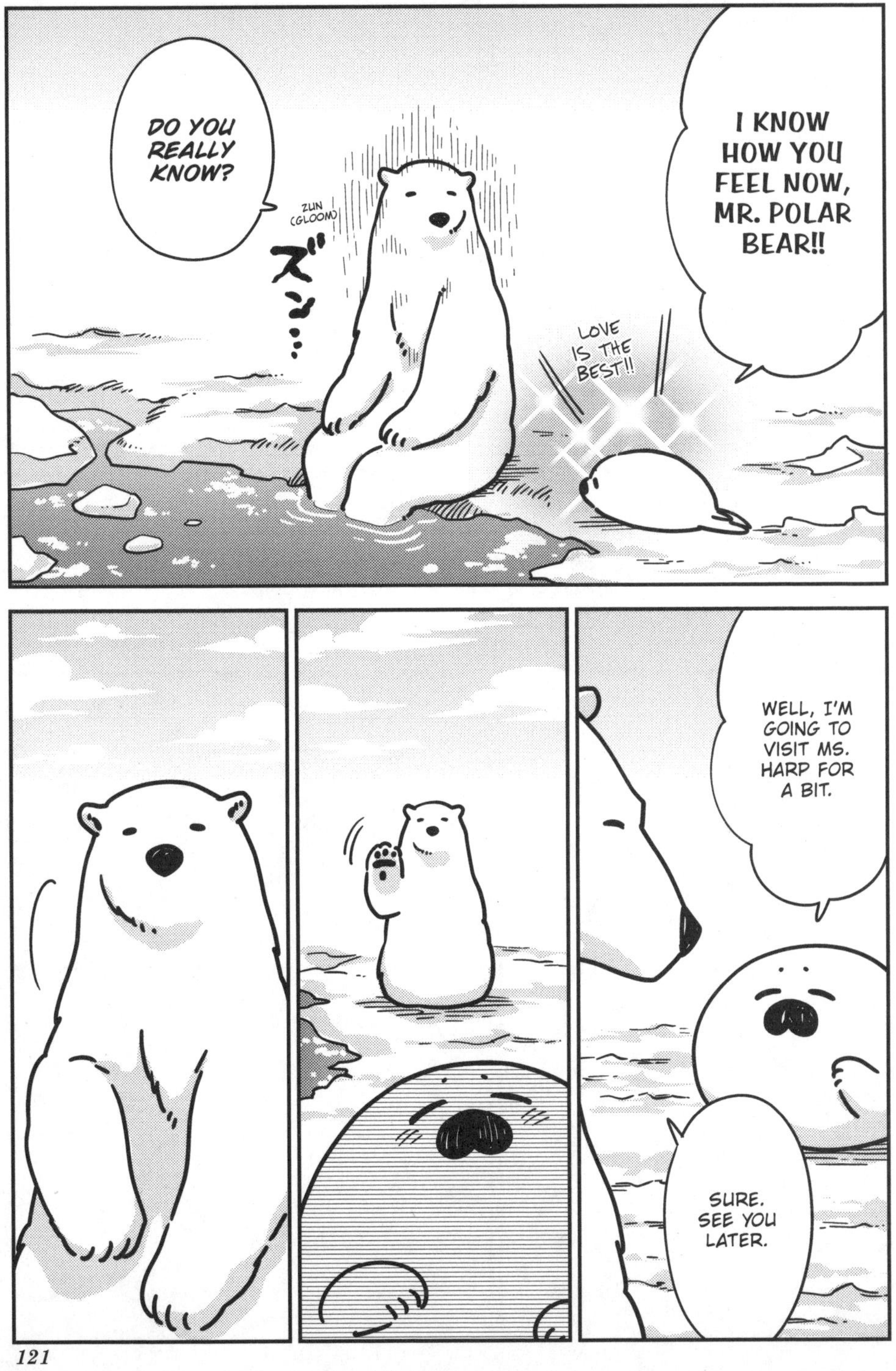
I KNOW HOW YOU FEEL NOW, MR. POLAR BEAR!!
LOVE IS THE BEST!!
ZUN (GLOOM)
ズン…
DO YOU REALLY KNOW?
WELL, I'M GOING TO VISIT MS. HARP FOR A BIT.
SURE. SEE YOU LATER.

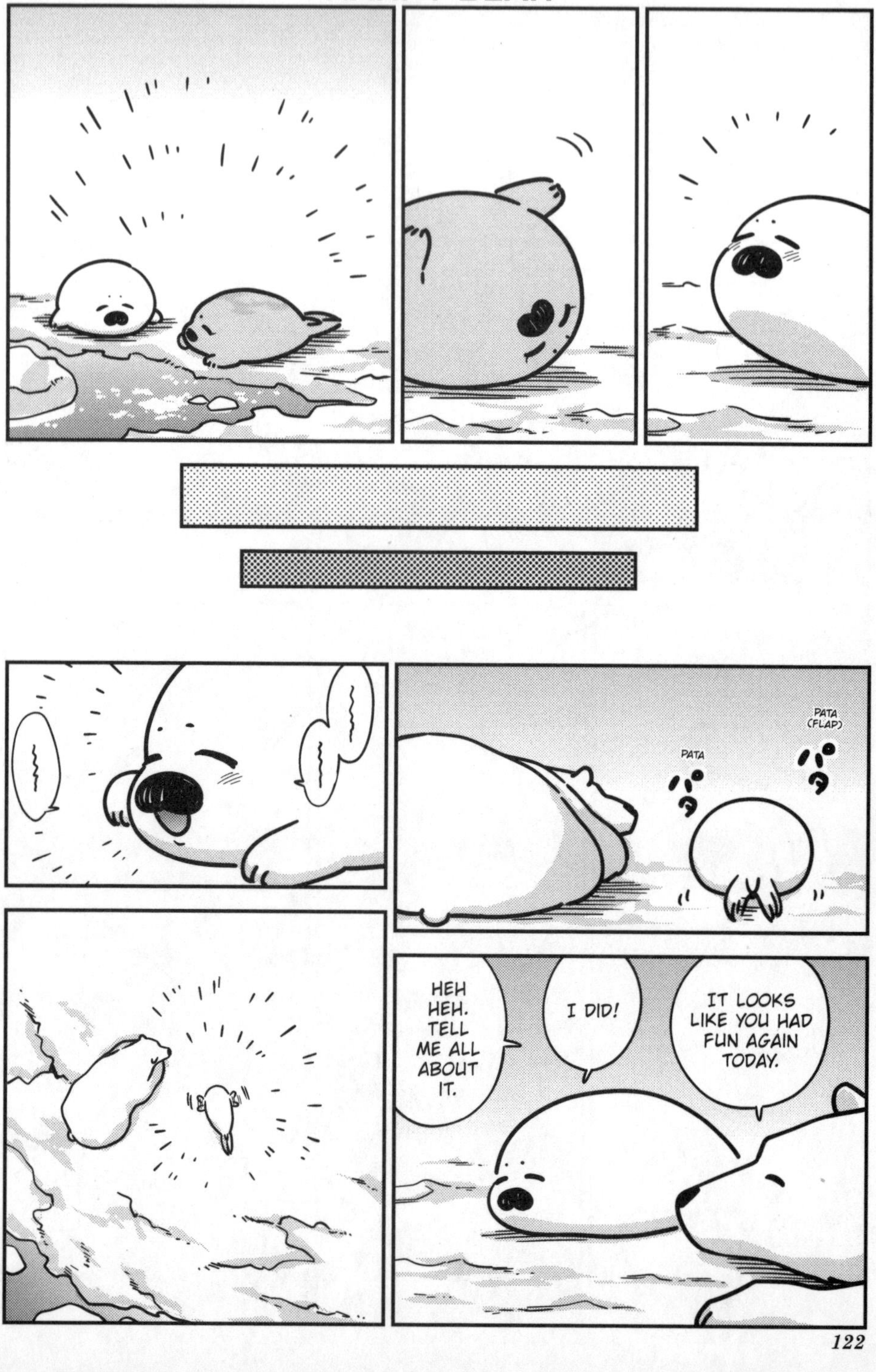
PATA (FLAP)
パタ
PATA
パタ
IT LOOKS LIKE YOU HAD FUN AGAIN TODAY.
I DID!
HEH HEH. TELL ME ALL ABOUT IT.

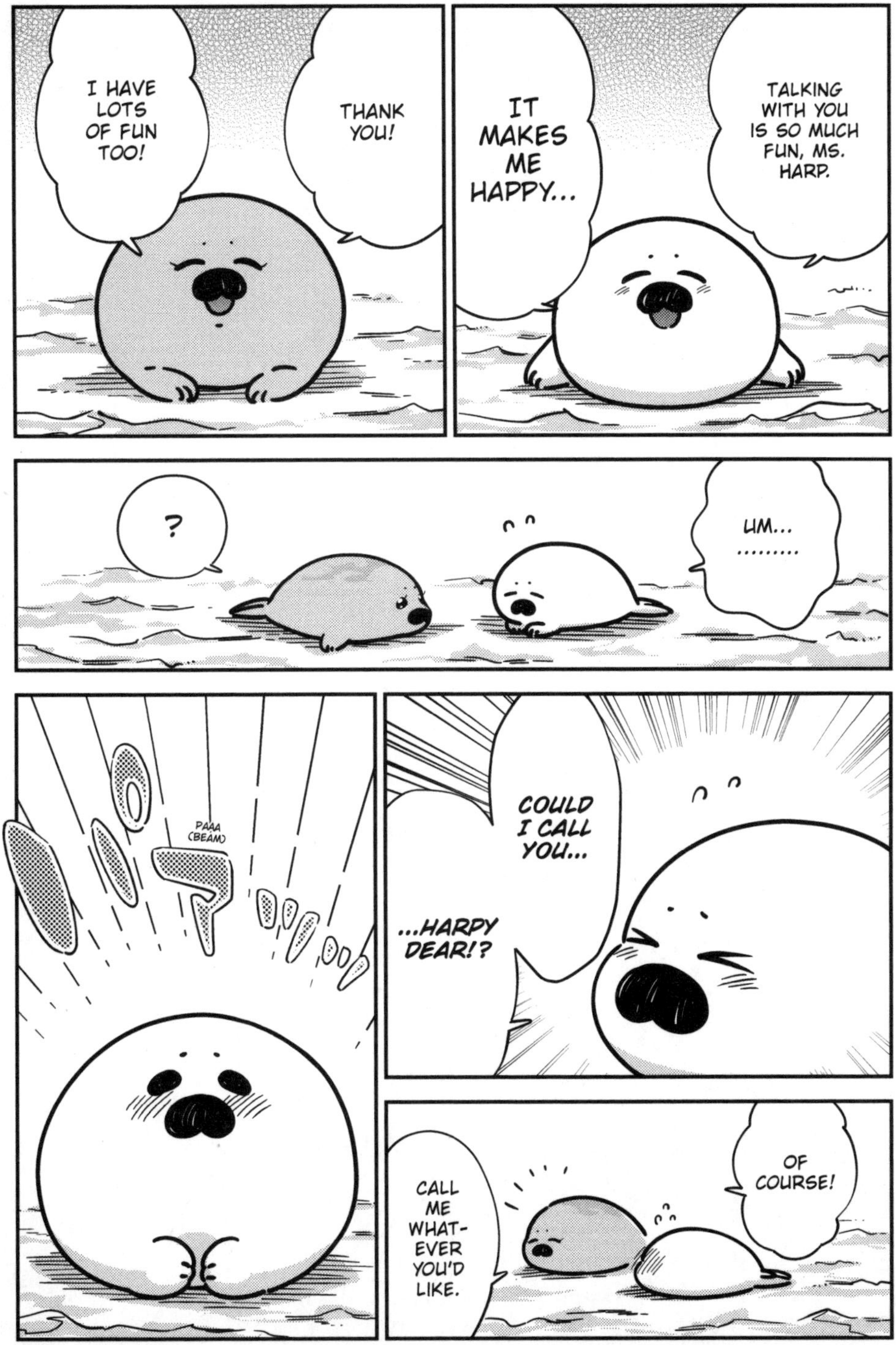
TALKING WITH YOU IS SO MUCH FUN, MS. HARP.
IT MAKES ME HAPPY...
THANK YOU!
I HAVE LOTS OF FUN TOO!
UM... ....
?
COULD I CALL YOU...
...HARPY DEAR!?
OF COURSE!
CALL ME WHATEVER YOU'D LIKE.
PAAA (BEAM)

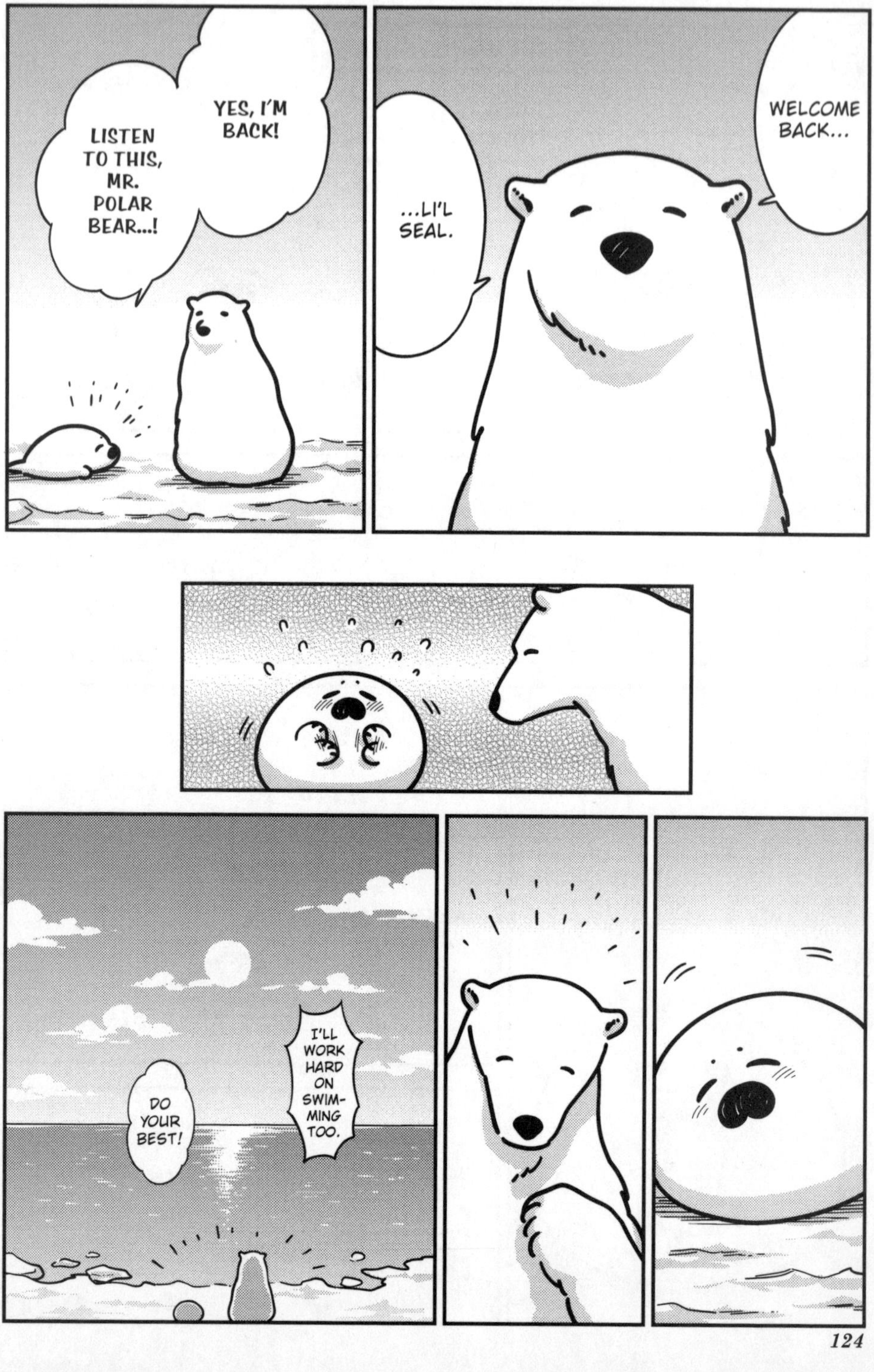
WELCOME BACK...
...LI'L SEAL.
YES, I'M BACK!
LISTEN TO THIS, MR. POLAR BEAR...!
I'LL WORK HARD ON SWIMMING TOO.
DO YOUR BEST!

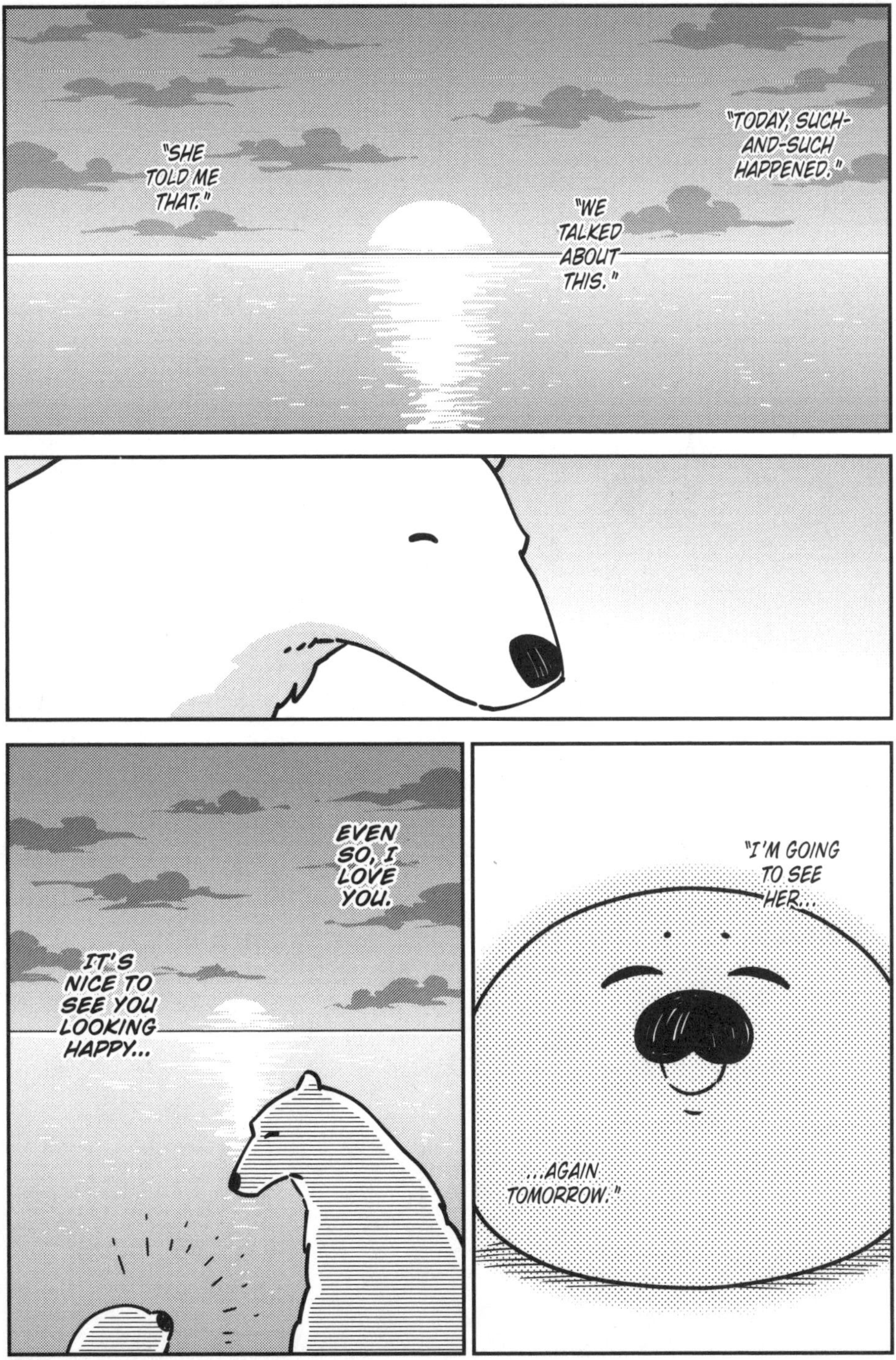
"TODAY, SUCH-AND-SUCH HAPPENED."
"WE TALKED ABOUT THIS."
"SHE TOLD ME THAT."
"I'M GOING TO SEE HER...
...AGAIN TOMORROW."
EVEN SO, I LOVE YOU.
IT'S NICE TO SEE YOU LOOKING HAPPY...

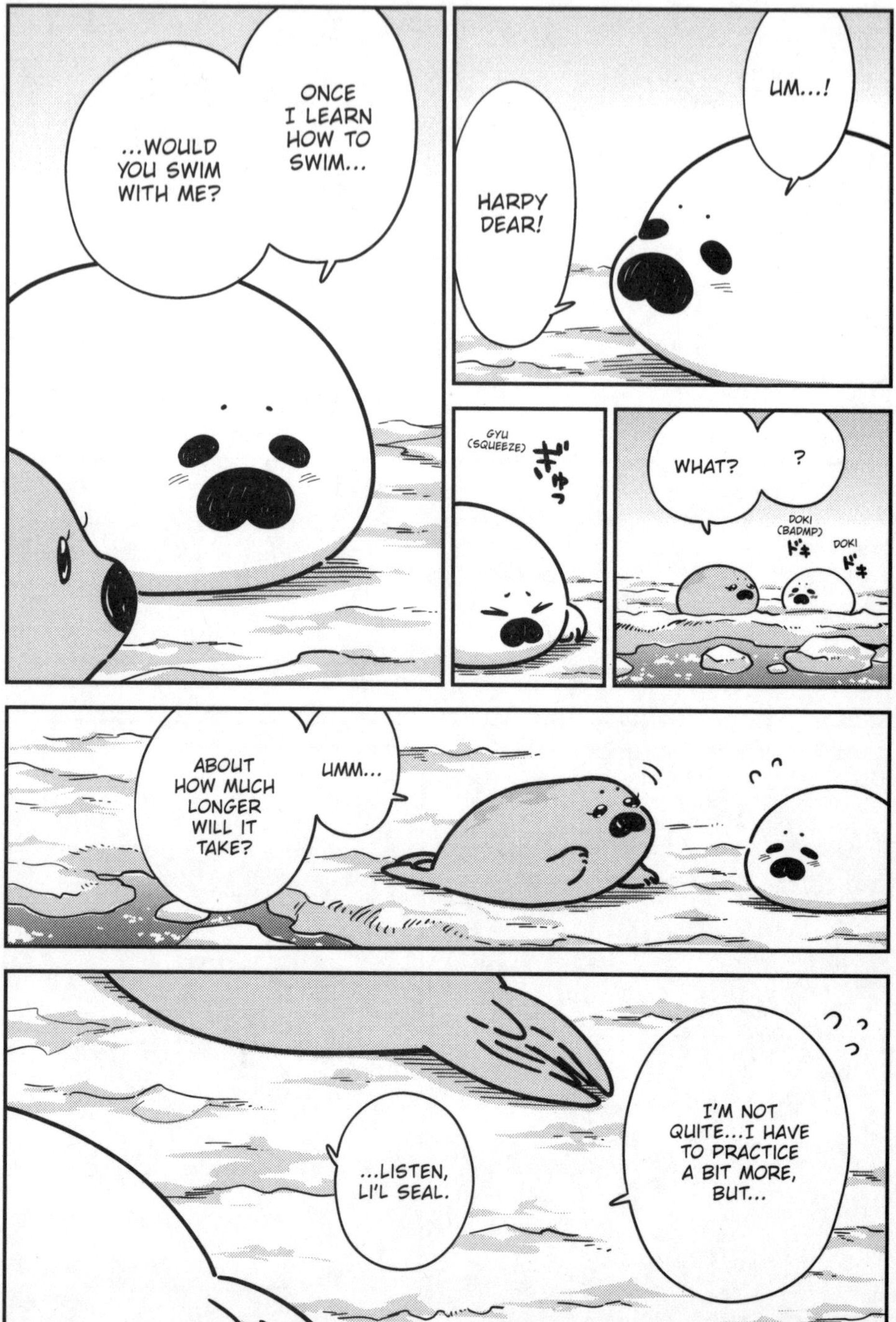
UM...!
HARPY DEAR!
WHAT? ?
DOKI (BADMP) DOKI
GYU (SQUEEZE)
ONCE I LEARN HOW TO SWIM...
...WOULD YOU SWIM WITH ME?
UMM...
ABOUT HOW MUCH LONGER WILL IT TAKE?
I'M NOT QUITE...I HAVE TO PRACTICE A BIT MORE, BUT...
...LISTEN, LI'L SEAL.

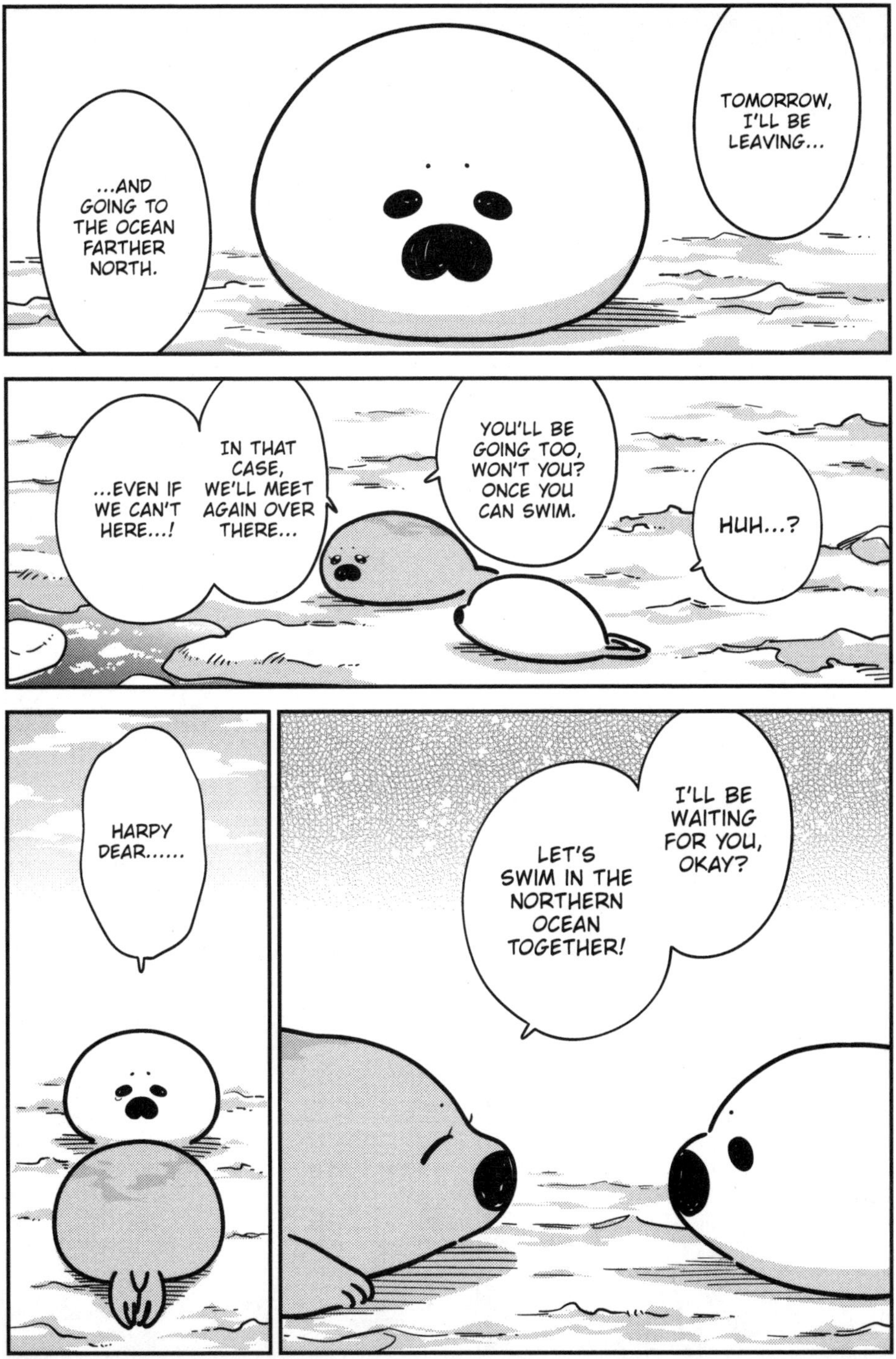
TOMORROW, I'LL BE LEAVING...
...AND GOING TO THE OCEAN FARTHER NORTH.
HUH...?
YOU'LL BE GOING TOO, WON'T YOU? ONCE YOU CAN SWIM.
IN THAT CASE, WE'LL MEET AGAIN OVER THERE...
...EVEN IF WE CAN'T HERE...!
I'LL BE WAITING FOR YOU, OKAY?
LET'S SWIM IN THE NORTHERN OCEAN TOGETHER!
HARPY DEAR......

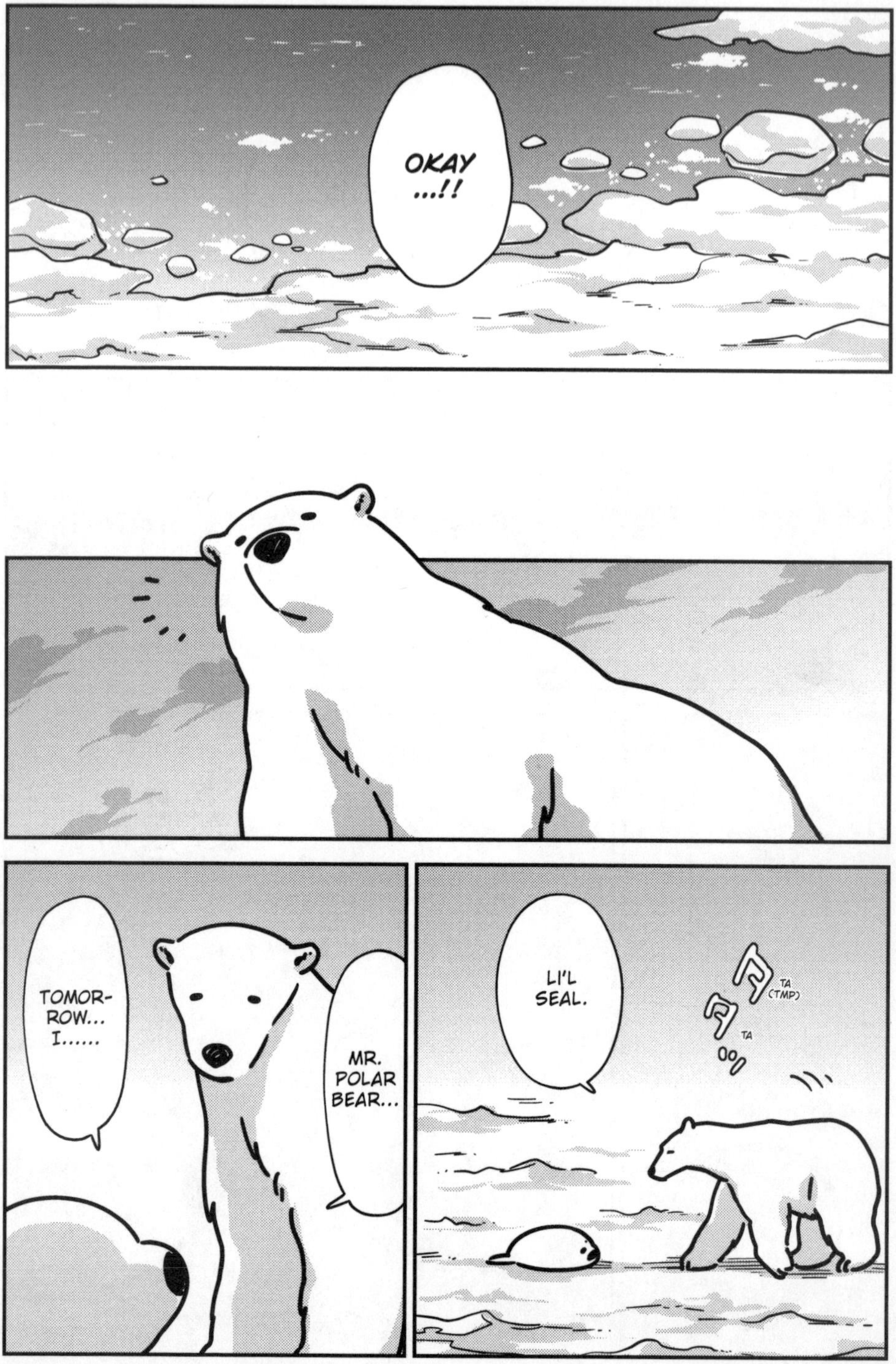
OKAY ...!!
LI'L SEAL.
TA (TMP) TA
MR. POLAR BEAR...
TOMOR-ROW... I......

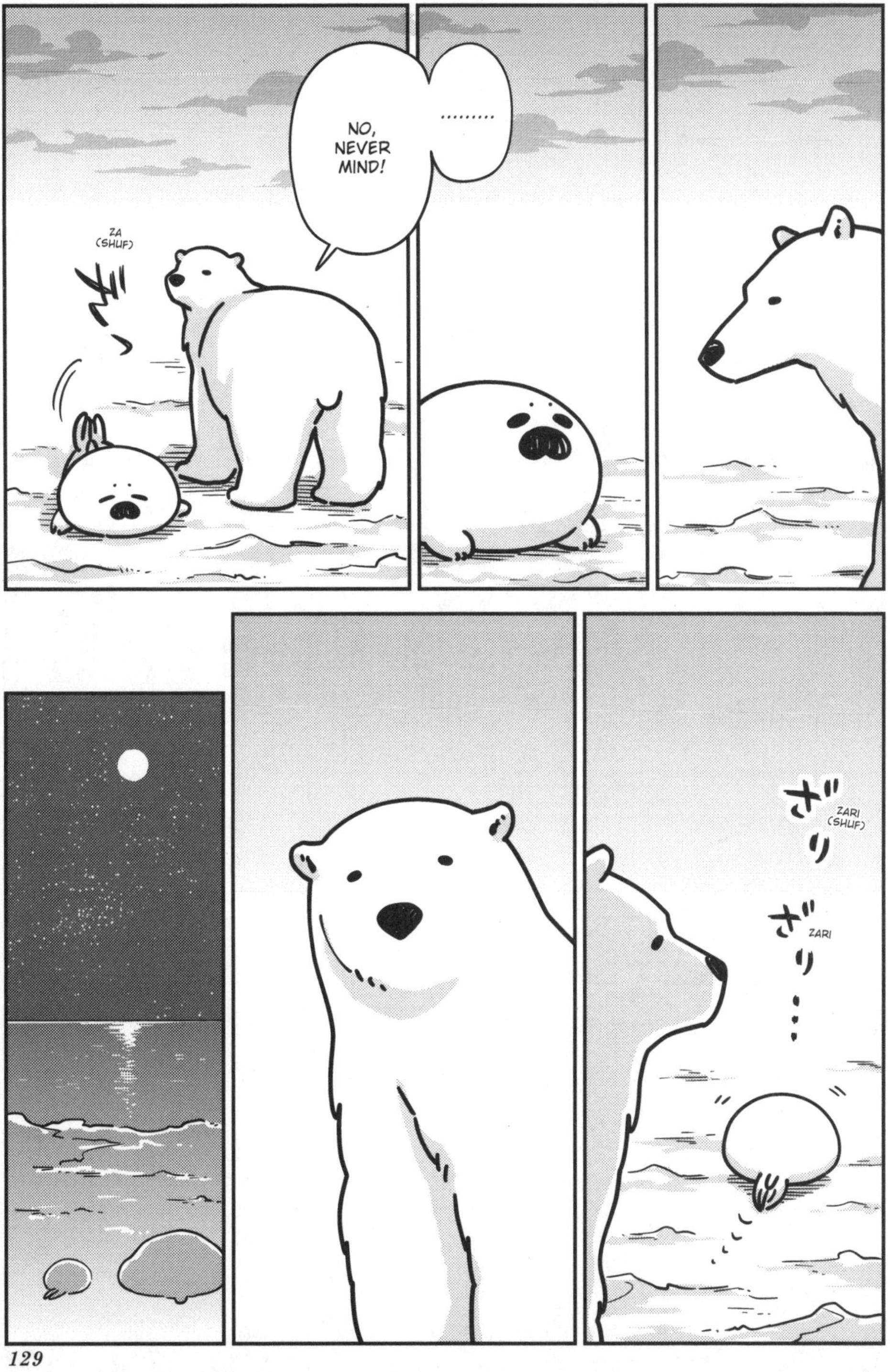

....
NO, NEVER MIND!
ZA (SHUF)
ざり
ZARI (SHUF)
ざり…
ZARI

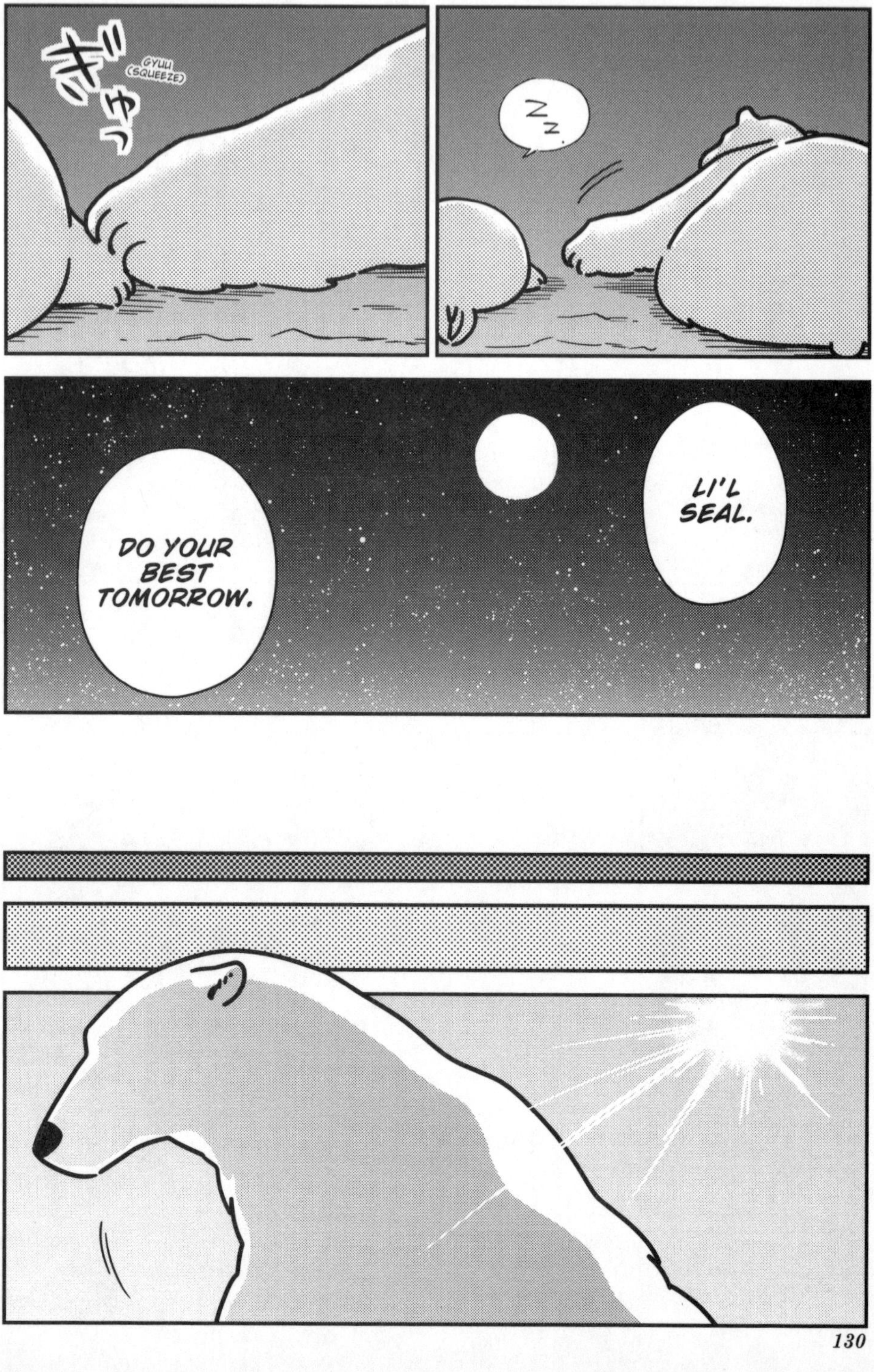
Zz
ぎゅっ
GYUU (SQUEEZE)
LI'L SEAL.
DO YOUR BEST TOMORROW.

THE FEELING OF LIKING SOMEBODY

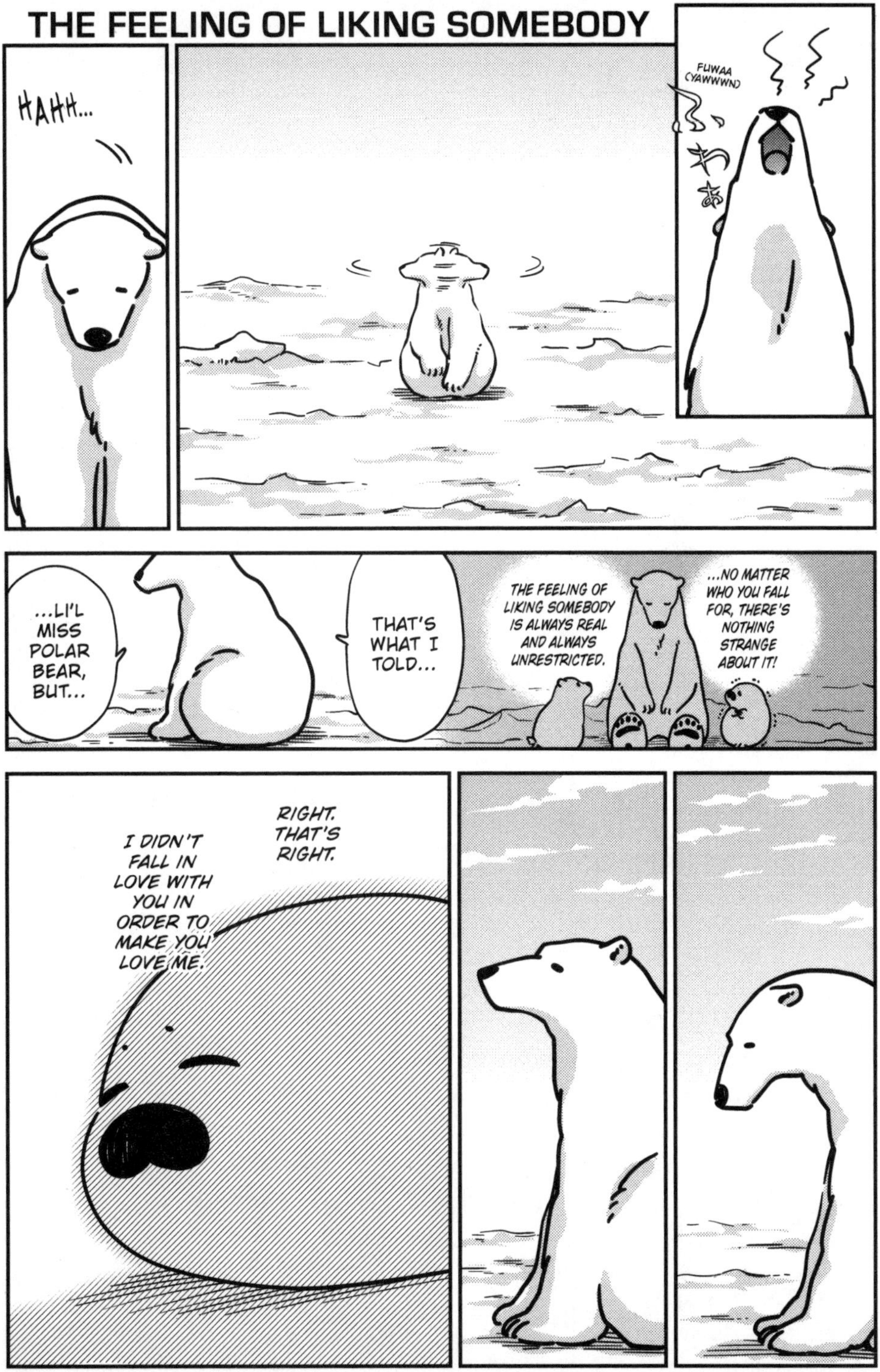
FUWAA (YAWWWN)
HAHH...
...NO MATTER WHO YOU FALL FOR, THERE'S NOTHING STRANGE ABOUT IT!
THE FEELING OF LIKING SOMEBODY IS ALWAYS REAL AND ALWAYS UNRESTRICTED.
THAT'S WHAT I TOLD...
...LI'L MISS POLAR BEAR, BUT...
RIGHT. THAT'S RIGHT.
I DIDN'T FALL IN LOVE WITH YOU IN ORDER TO MAKE YOU LOVE ME.

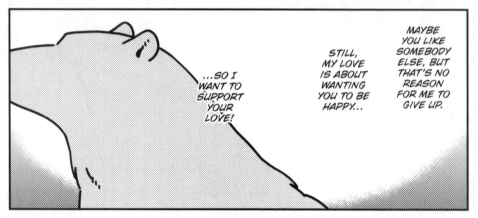

MAYBE YOU LIKE SOMEBODY ELSE, BUT THAT'S NO REASON FOR ME TO GIVE UP.
STILL, MY LOVE IS ABOUT WANTING YOU TO BE HAPPY...
...SO I WANT TO SUPPORT YOUR LOVE!
I WANT ...
...TO SUPPORT IT.
GOSHI (RUB) ゴシ
GOSHI ゴシ
....
......
...I LIED.
ZA (WSH)
ZA
I DON'T LIKE BEING GLOOMY, SO LET'S SAY GOOD-BYE WITH A SMILE.
WE'LL MEET AGAIN ANYWAY!

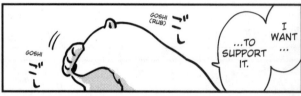

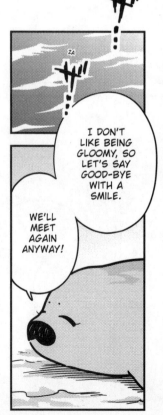

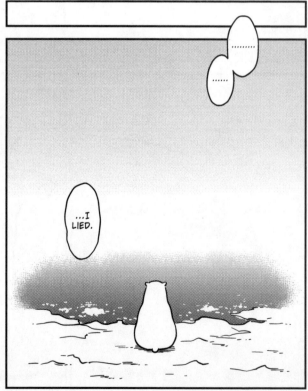

....
HARPY DEAR.
HARPY DEAR, I LOVE YOU.
HUH ...!?
I'VE LOVED YOU SINCE I FIRST MET YOU.
THE DAY WAS SO MUCH FUN AND SO THRILLING, AND IT WENT BY SO FAST...
HOW CAN ONE DAY...
GATA
(SHIVER)
...FEEL THIS LONG?
I'VE NEVER FELT THAT BEFORE.

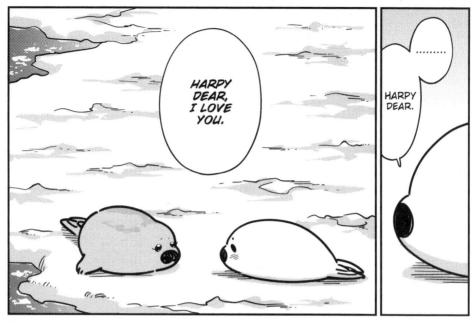

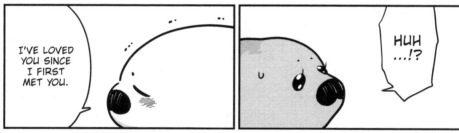

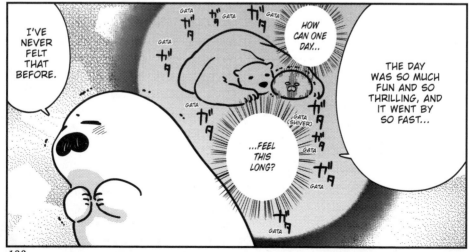

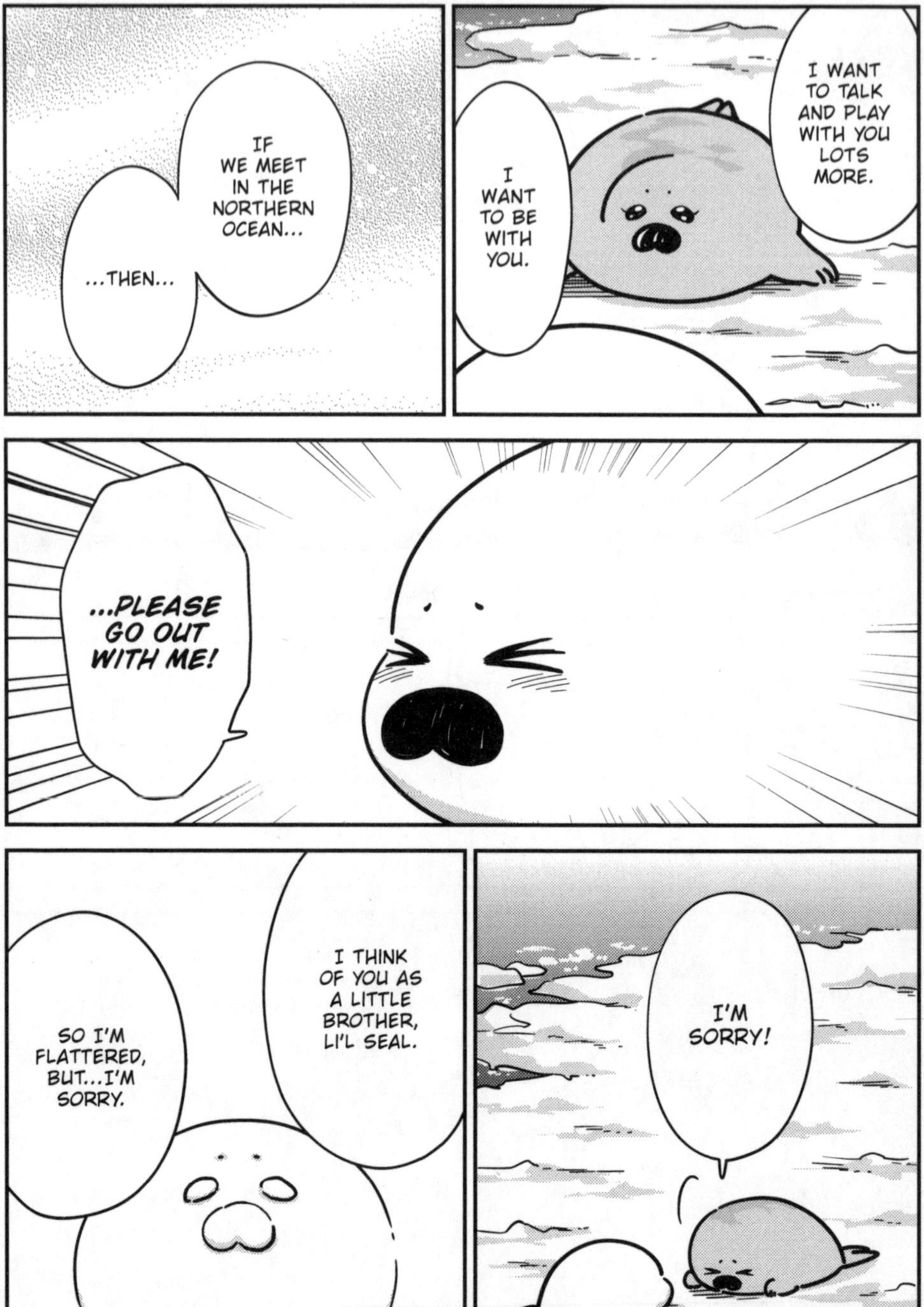
I WANT TO TALK AND PLAY WITH YOU LOTS MORE.
I WANT TO BE WITH YOU.
IF WE MEET IN THE NORTHERN OCEAN...
...THEN...
...PLEASE GO OUT WITH ME!
I'M SORRY!
I THINK OF YOU AS A LITTLE BROTHER, LI'L SEAL.
SO I'M FLATTERED, BUT...I'M SORRY.

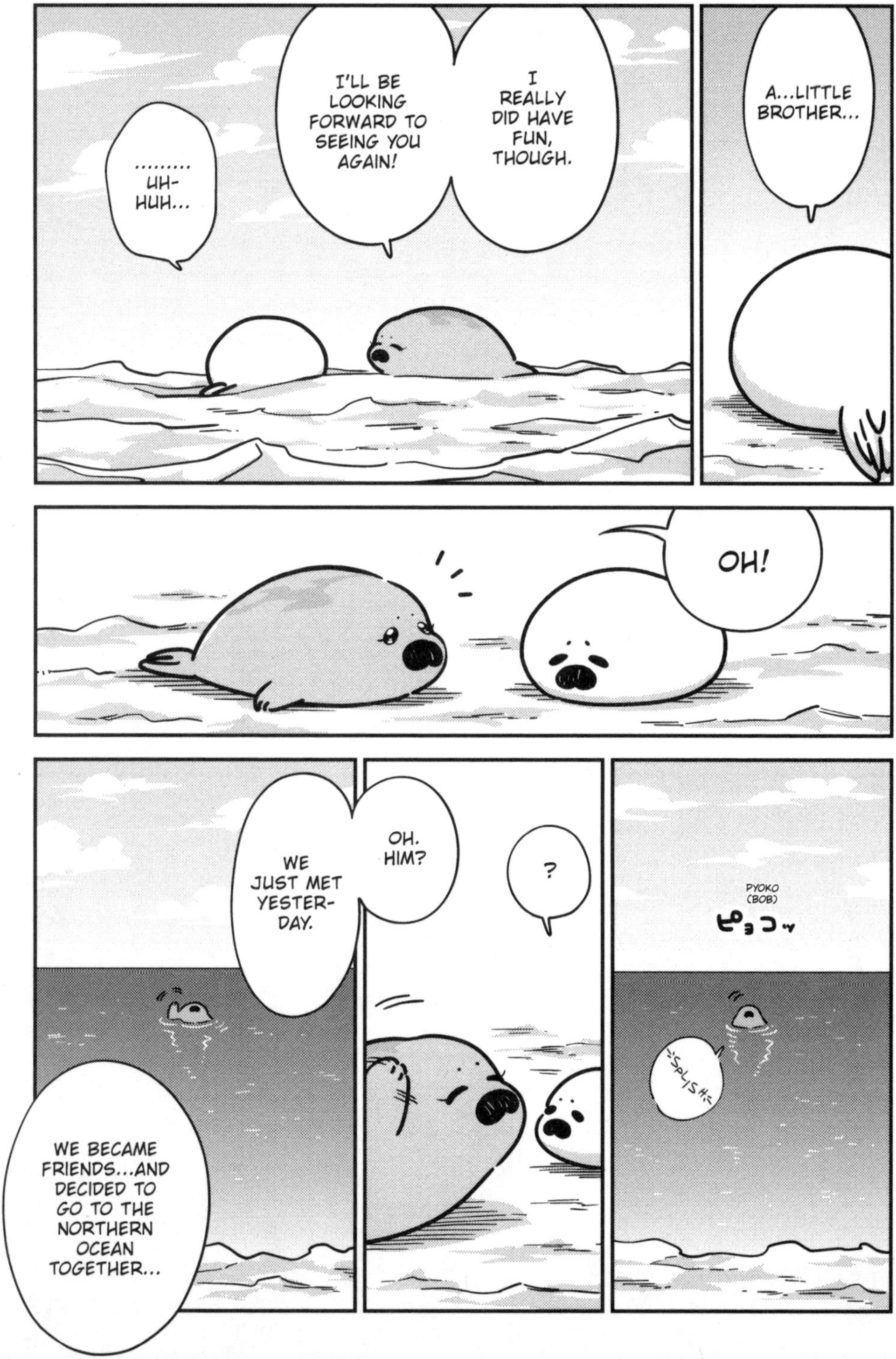
A...LITTLE BROTHER...
I REALLY DID HAVE FUN, THOUGH.
I'LL BE LOOKING FORWARD TO SEEING YOU AGAIN!
.........UH-HUH...
OH!
PYOKO (BOB)
ピョコッ
SPLISH
?
OH. HIM?
WE JUST MET YESTER-DAY.
WE BECAME FRIENDS...AND DECIDED TO GO TO THE NORTHERN OCEAN TOGETHER...

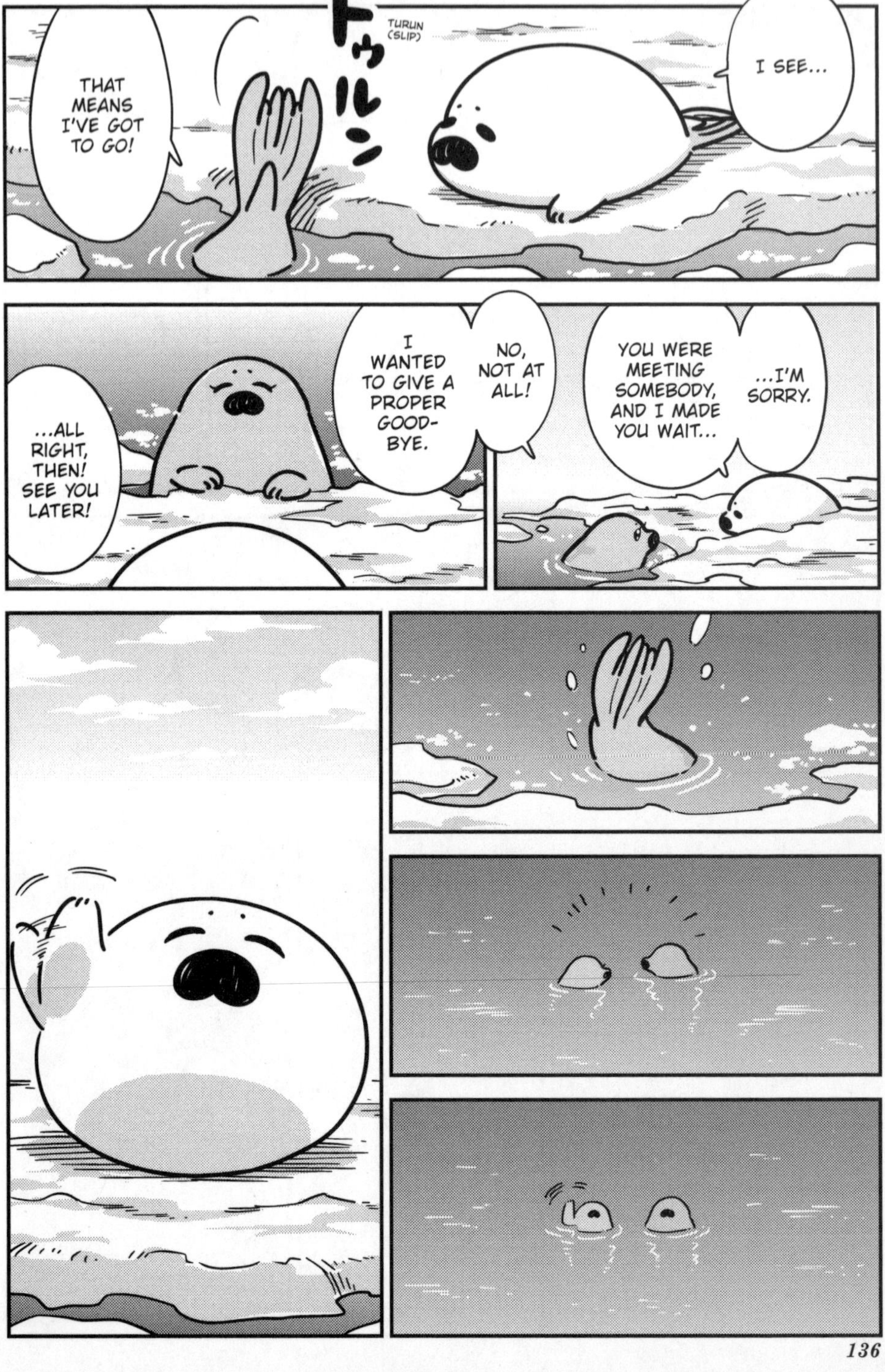
I SEE...
トゥルン
TURUN (SLIP)
THAT MEANS I'VE GOT TO GO!
...I'M SORRY.
YOU WERE MEETING SOMEBODY, AND I MADE YOU WAIT...
NO, NOT AT ALL!
I WANTED TO GIVE A PROPER GOOD-BYE.
...ALL RIGHT, THEN! SEE YOU LATER!

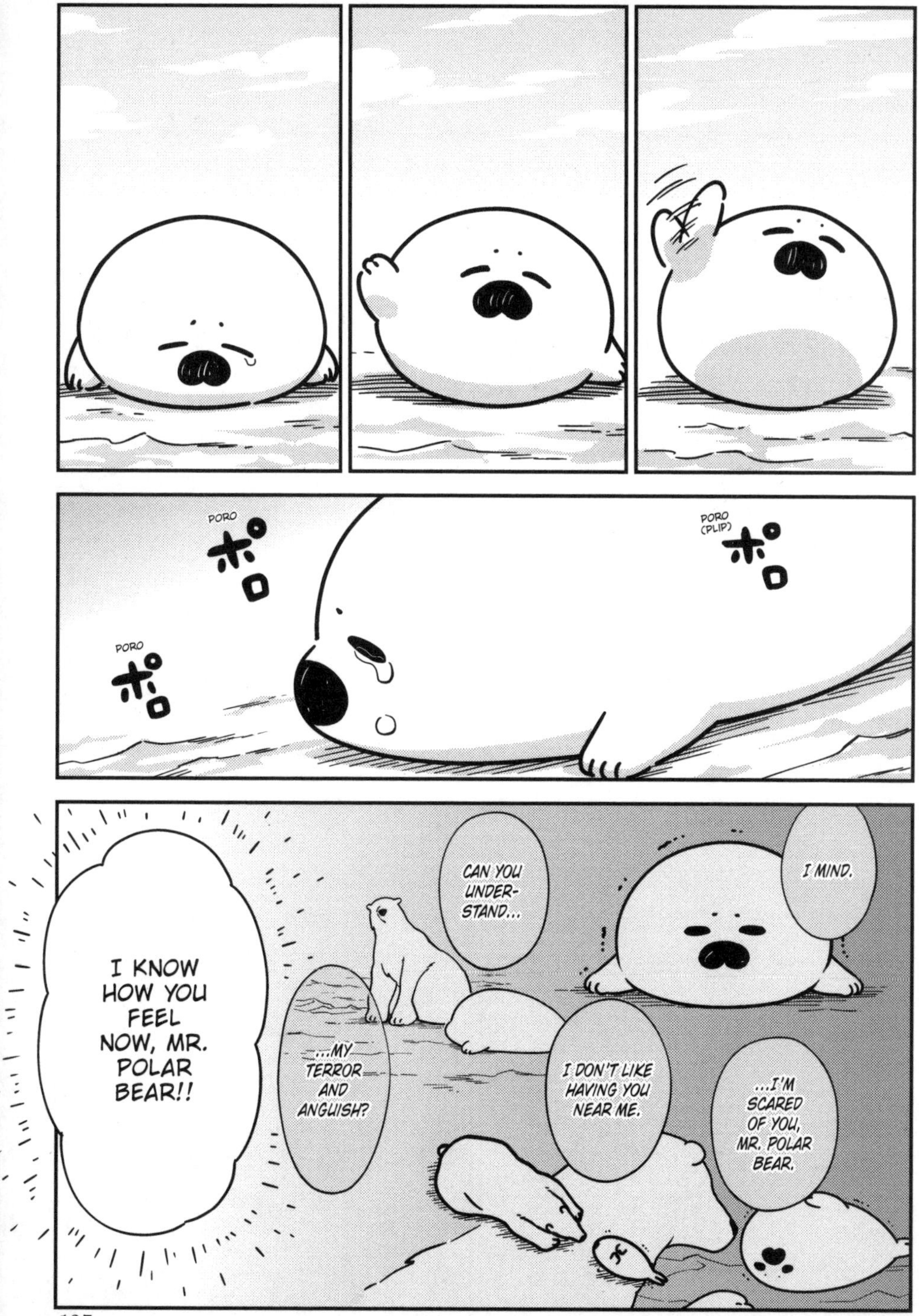
PORO (PLIP)
ポロ
PORO
ポロ
PORO
ポロ
I MIND.
CAN YOU UNDER-STAND...
...I'M SCARED OF YOU, MR. POLAR BEAR.
I DON'T LIKE HAVING YOU NEAR ME.
...MY TERROR AND ANGUISH?
I KNOW HOW YOU FEEL NOW, MR. POLAR BEAR!!

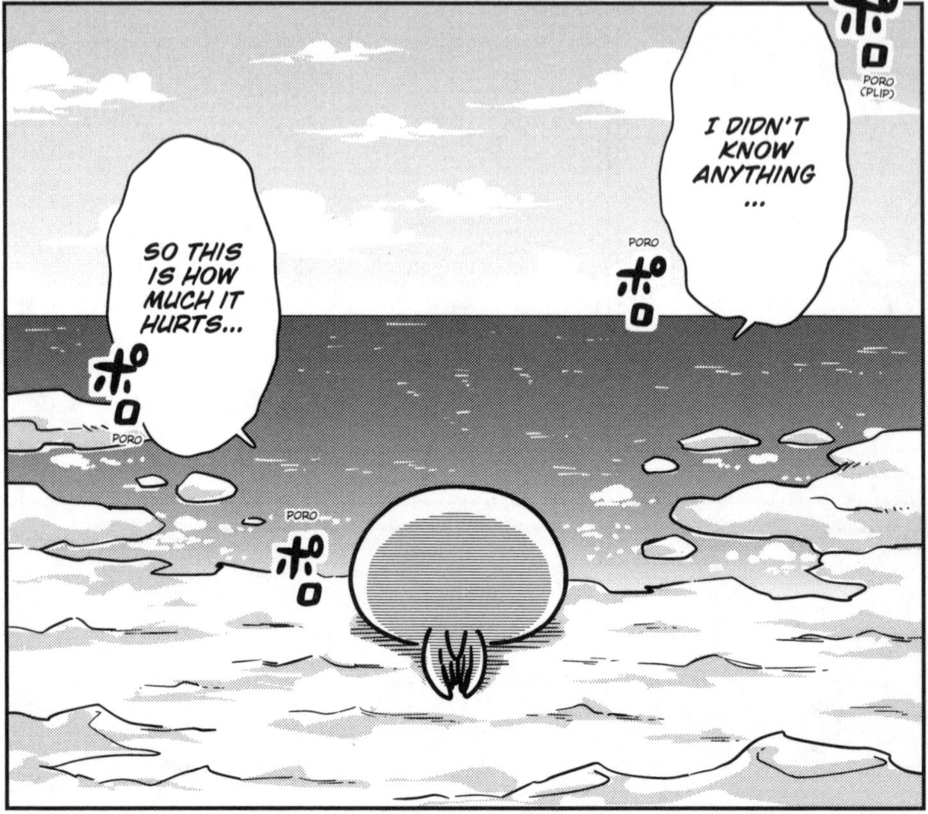
ポロ
PORO (PLIP)
I DIDN'T KNOW ANYTHING ...
PORO
ポロ
SO THIS IS HOW MUCH IT HURTS...
ポロ
PORO
PORO
ポロ

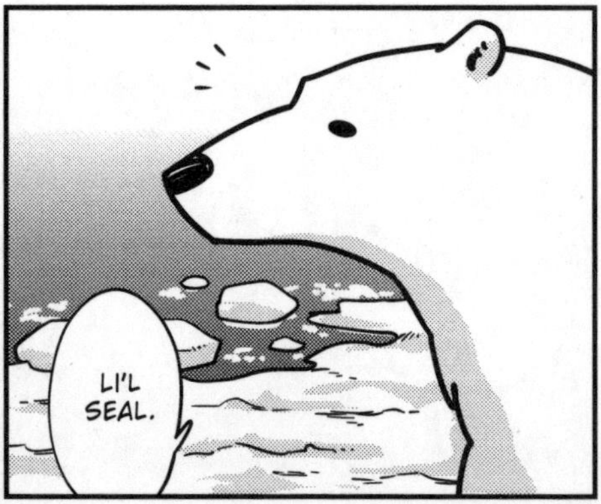
LI'L SEAL.

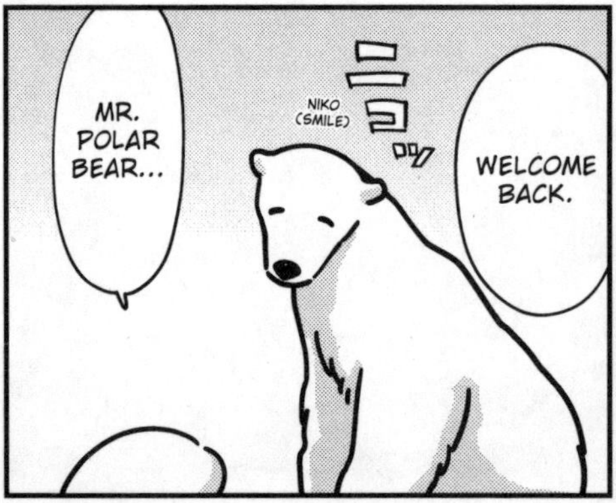
WELCOME BACK.
ニコッ
NIKO (SMILE)
MR. POLAR BEAR...

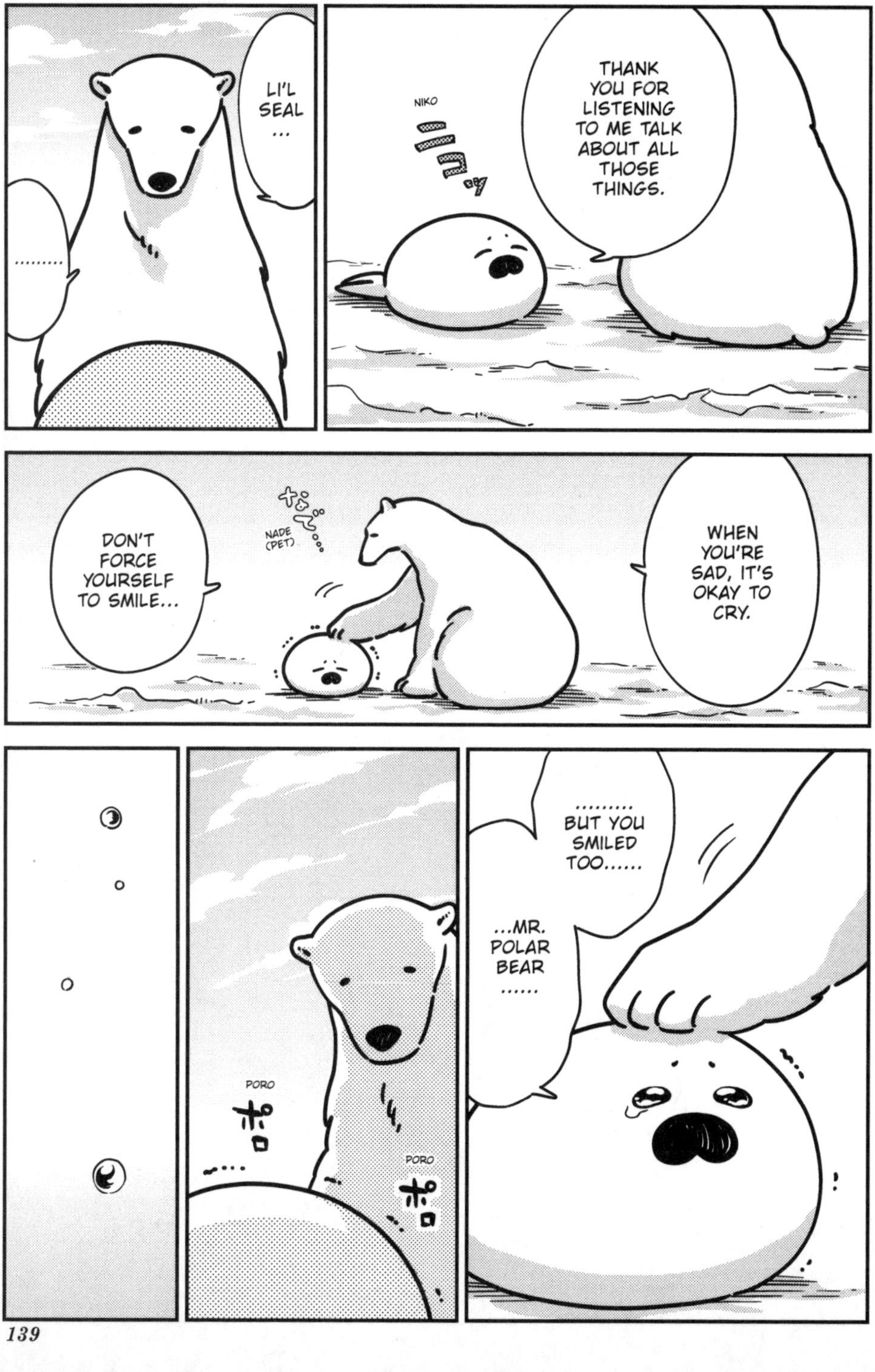

NIKO
ニコッ
THANK YOU FOR LISTENING TO ME TALK ABOUT ALL THOSE THINGS.
LI'L SEAL ...
....
WHEN YOU'RE SAD, IT'S OKAY TO CRY.
なで
NADE (PET)
DON'T FORCE YOURSELF TO SMILE...
.... BUT YOU SMILED TOO......
...MR. POLAR BEAR ......
PORO
ポロ
PORO
ポロ

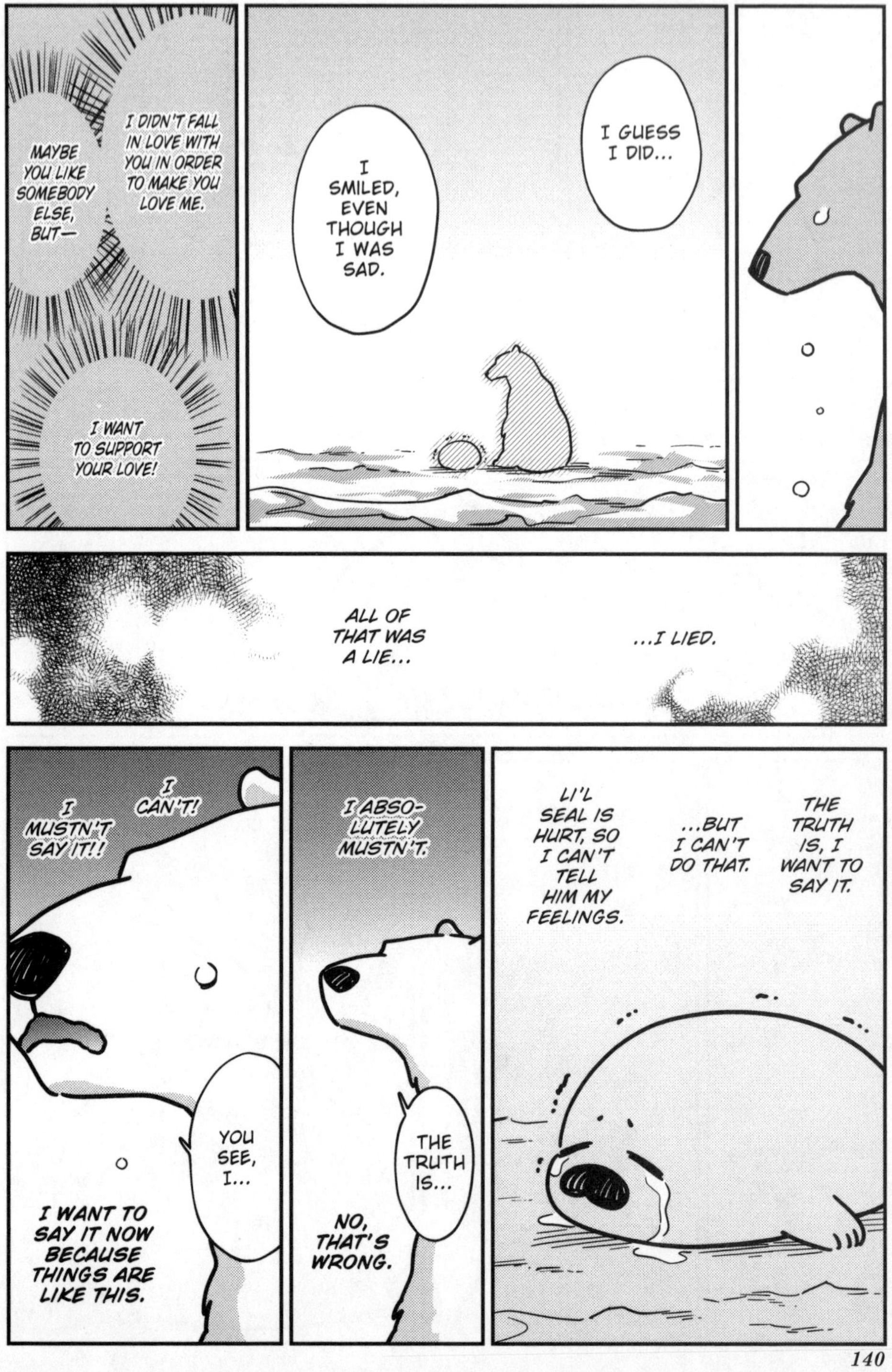
I GUESS I DID...
I SMILED, EVEN THOUGH I WAS SAD.
I DIDN'T FALL IN LOVE WITH YOU IN ORDER TO MAKE YOU LOVE ME.
MAYBE YOU LIKE SOMEBODY ELSE, BUT—
I WANT TO SUPPORT YOUR LOVE!
...I LIED.
ALL OF THAT WAS A LIE...
THE TRUTH IS, I WANT TO SAY IT.
...BUT I CAN'T DO THAT.
LI'L SEAL IS HURT, SO I CAN'T TELL HIM MY FEELINGS.
I ABSOLUTELY MUSTN'T.
THE TRUTH IS...
NO, THAT'S WRONG.
I CAN'T!
I MUSTN'T SAY IT!!
YOU SEE, I...
I WANT TO SAY IT NOW BECAUSE THINGS ARE LIKE THIS.

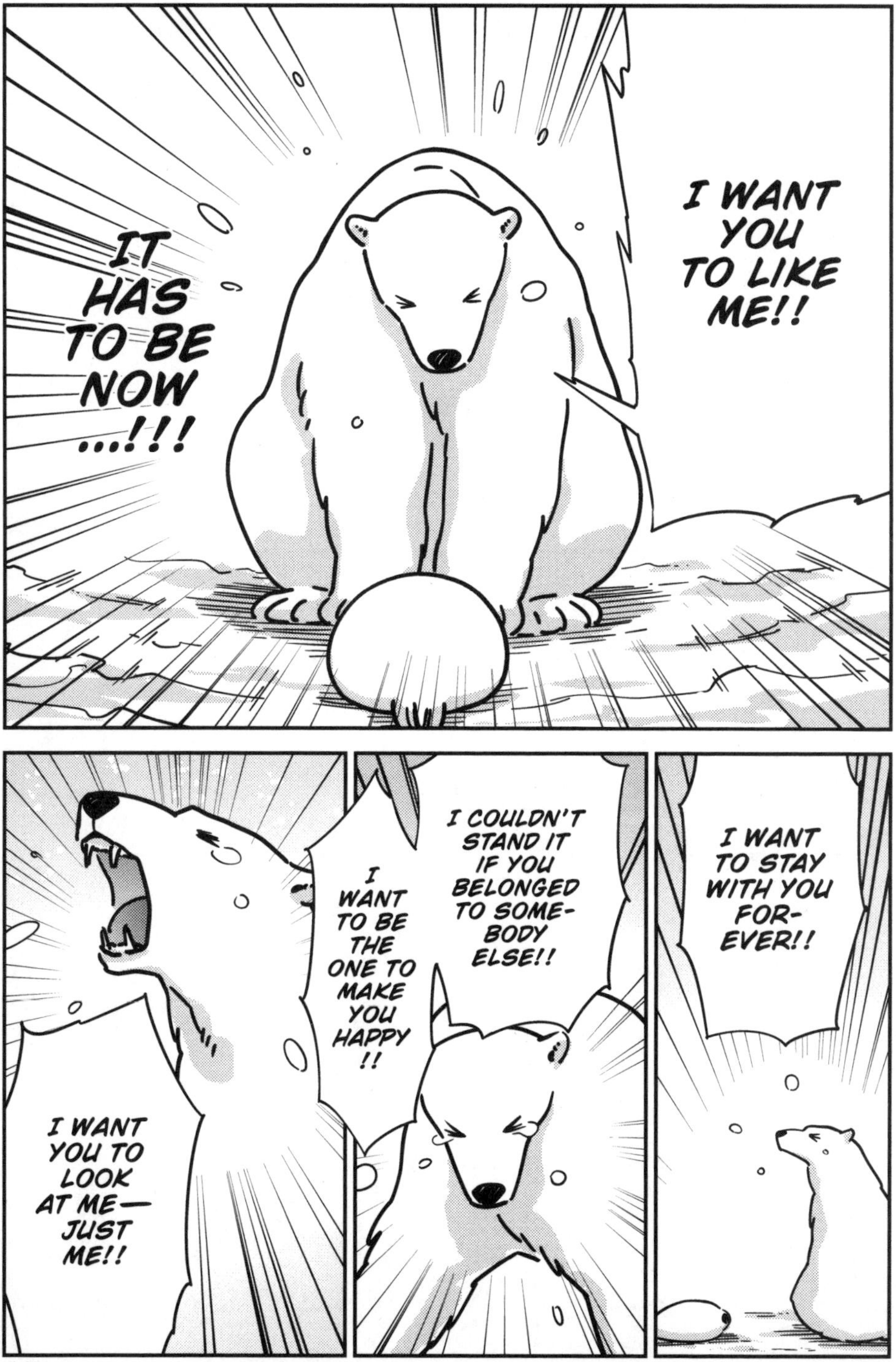
I WANT YOU TO LIKE ME!!
IT HAS TO BE NOW...!!!
I WANT TO STAY WITH YOU FOR-EVER!!
I COULDN'T STAND IT IF YOU BELONGED TO SOME-BODY ELSE!!
I WANT TO BE THE ONE TO MAKE YOU HAPPY!!
I WANT YOU TO LOOK AT ME—JUST ME!!

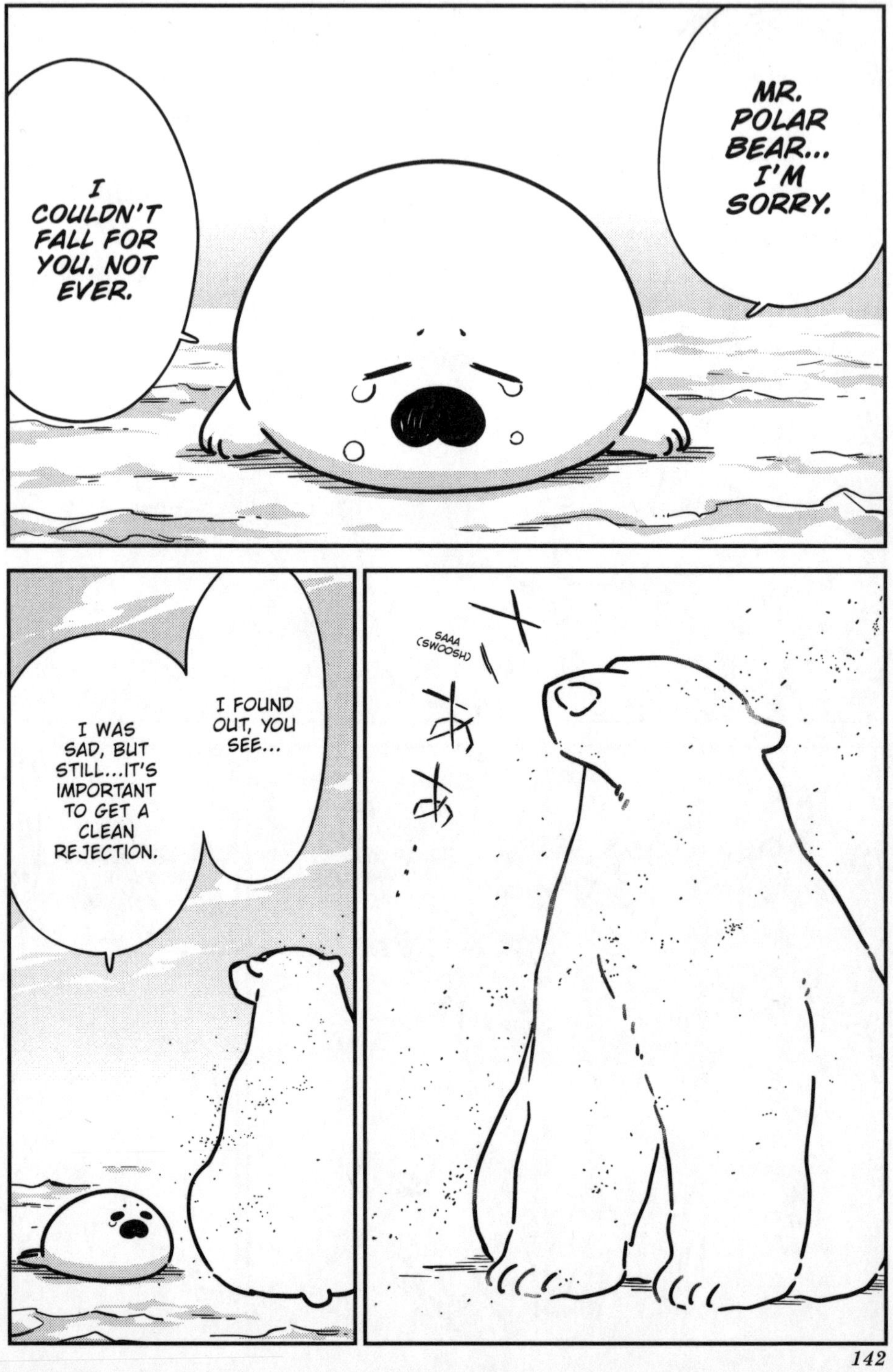
MR. POLAR BEAR... I'M SORRY.
I COULDN'T FALL FOR YOU. NOT EVER.
SAAA (SWOOSH)
I FOUND OUT, YOU SEE...
I WAS SAD, BUT STILL...IT'S IMPORTANT TO GET A CLEAN REJECTION.

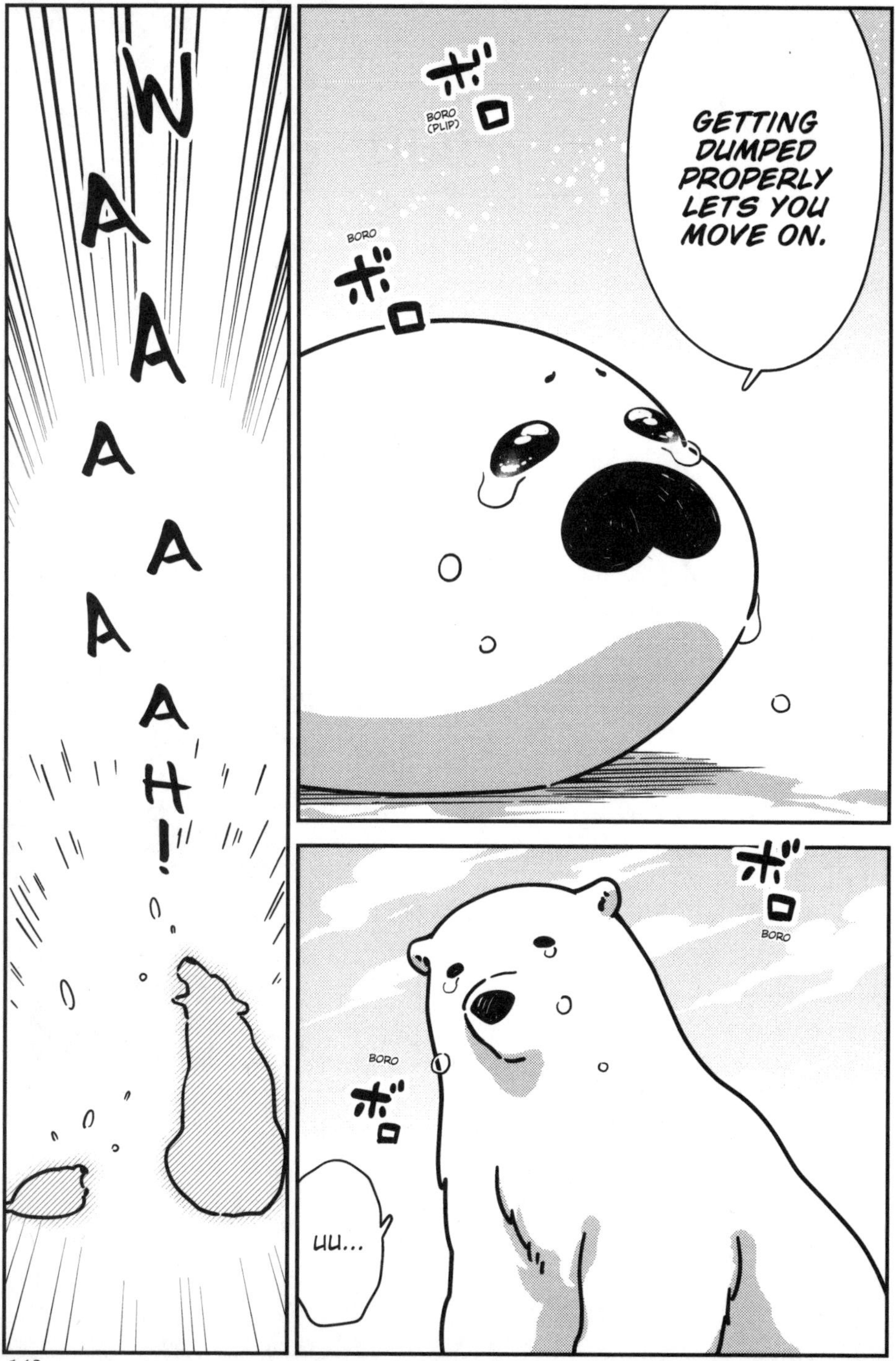
GETTING DUMPED PROPERLY LETS YOU MOVE ON.
ボロ
BORO (PLIP)
BORO
ボロ
ボロ
BORO
BORO
ボロ
UU...
WAAAAAAH!

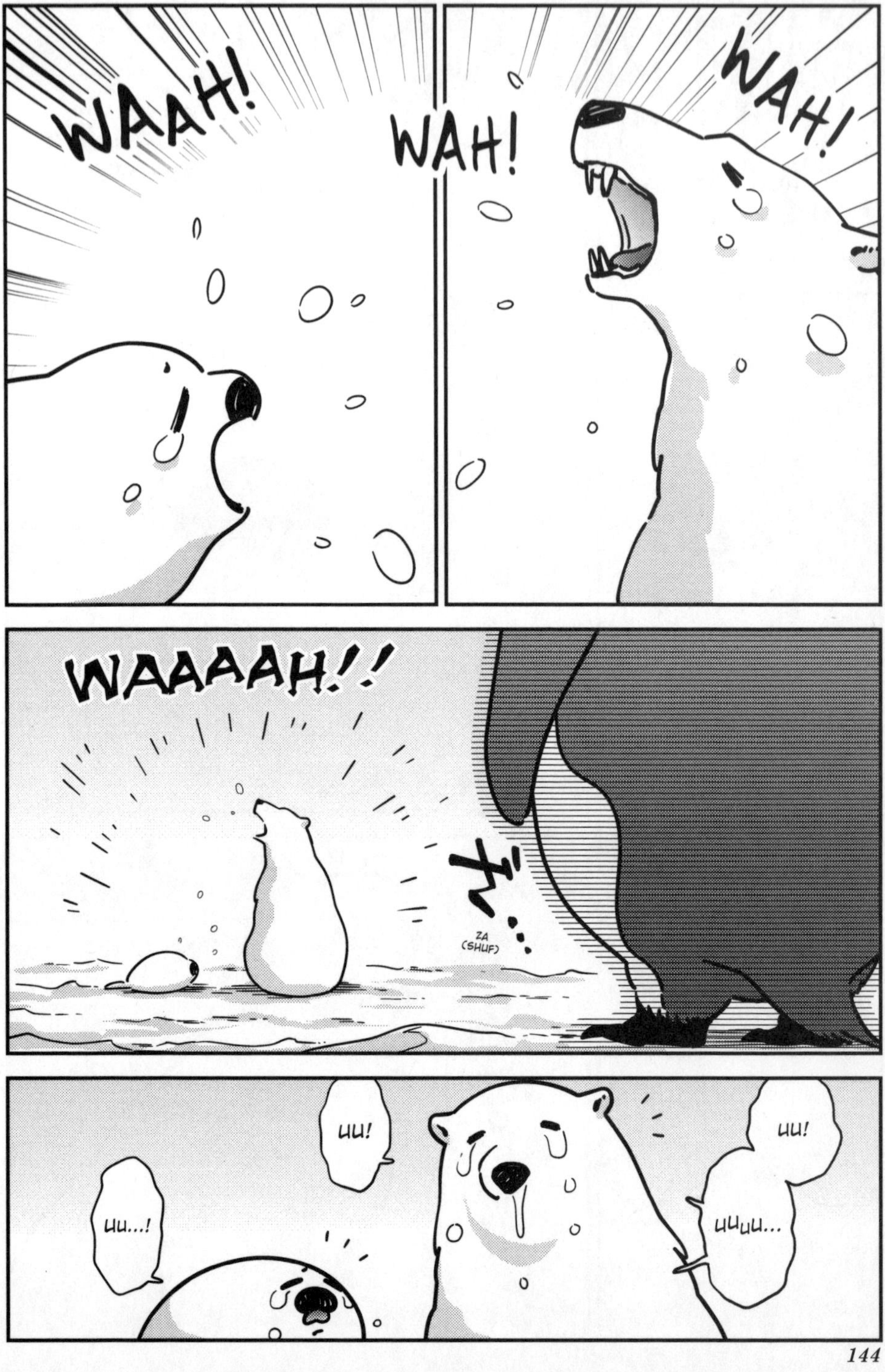
WAH!
WAH!
WAAH!
WAAAAH!!
ZA (SHUF)
UU!
UUUU...
UU!
UU...!

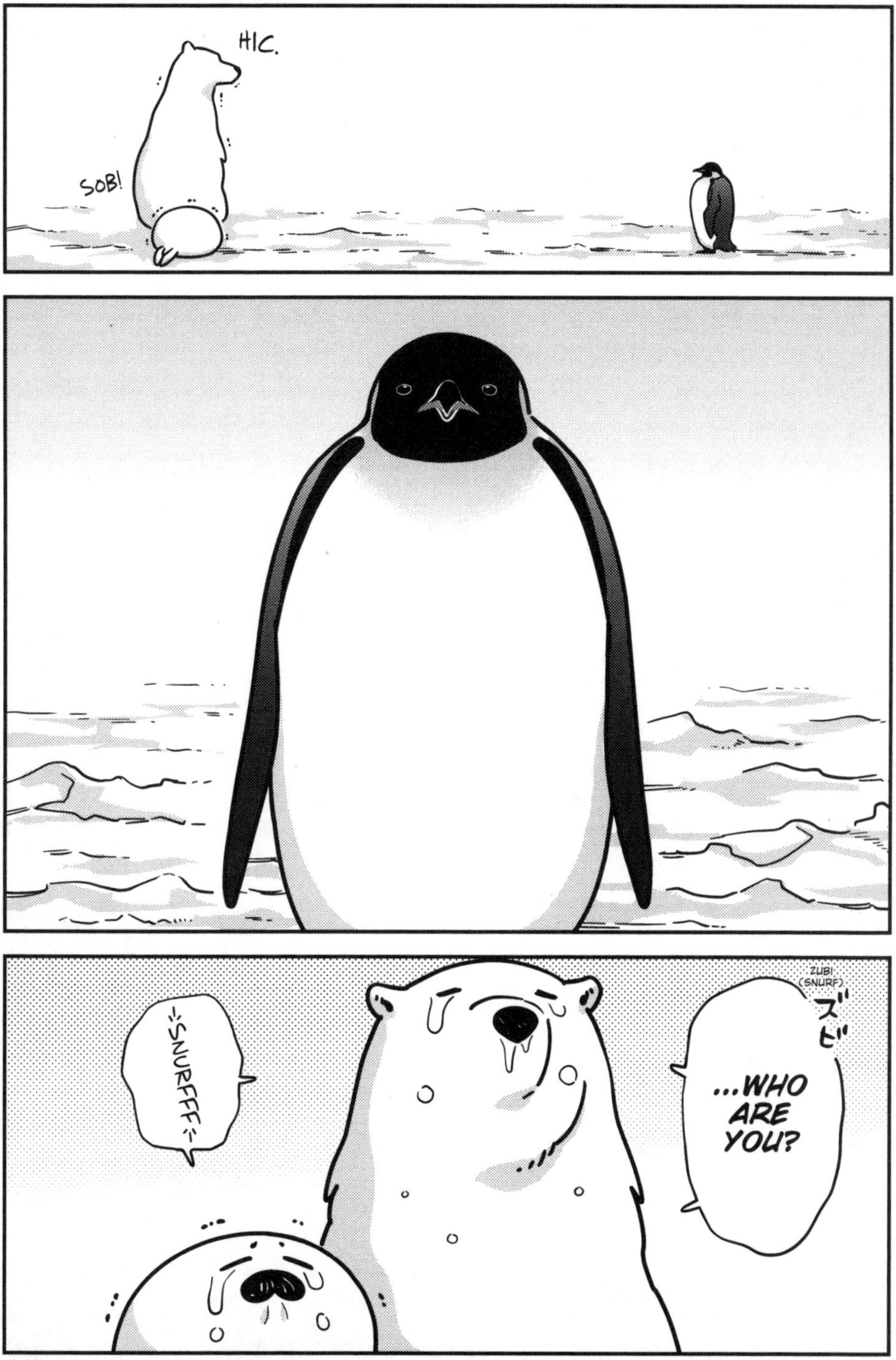
HIC.
SOB!
ZUBI (SNURF) ズビ
...WHO ARE YOU?
SNURFFF

TO BE CONTINUED IN VOLUME 3 ♥

BACKGROUND MANGA FOR THE CHAPTER SPLASH PAGES

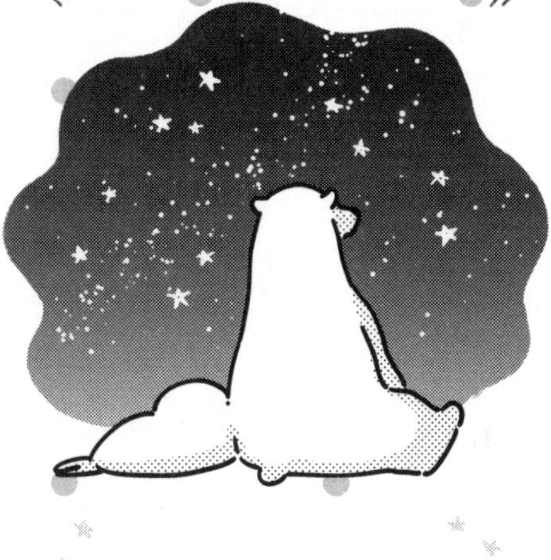

THE DOLL FESTIVAL

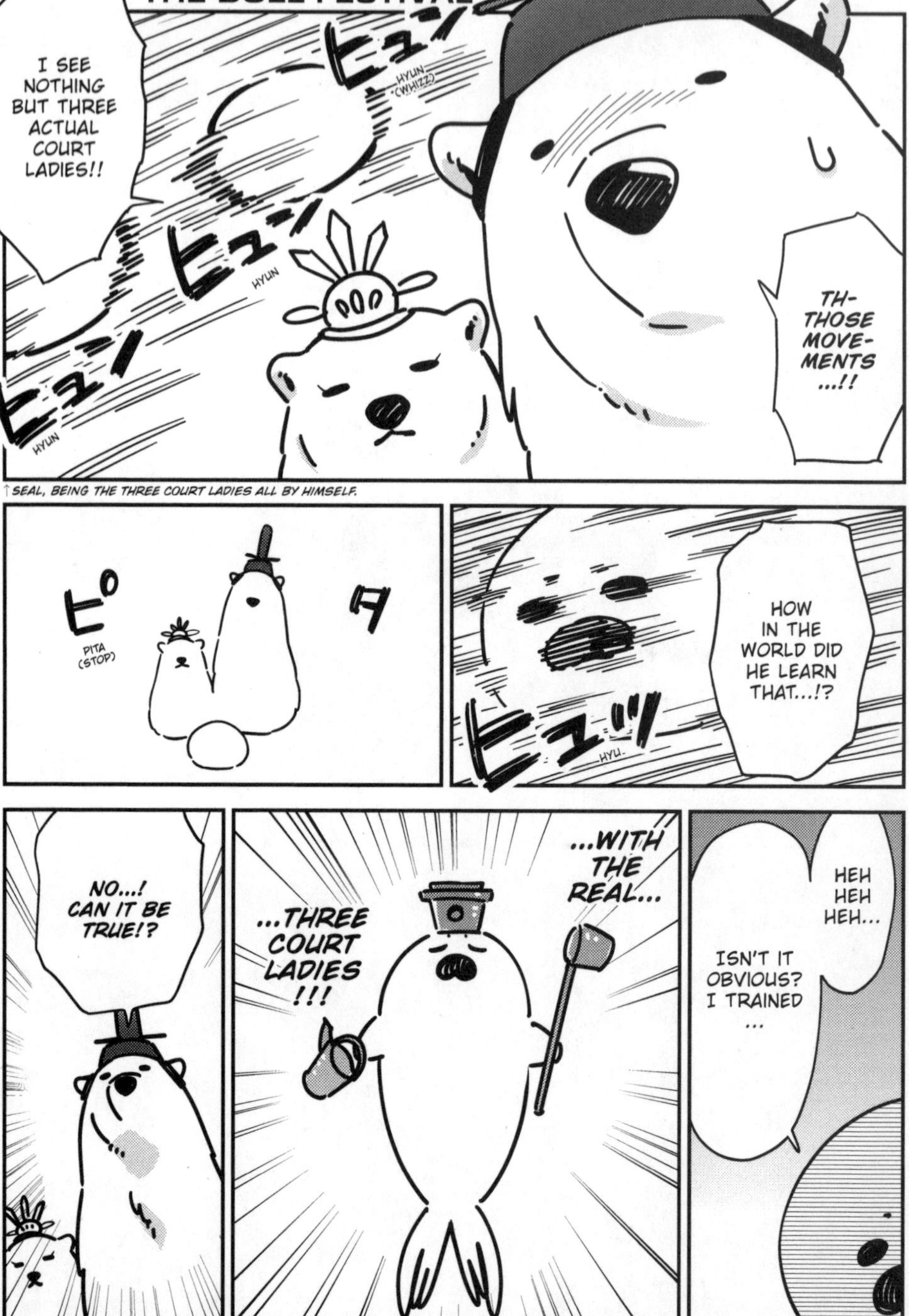
TH-THOSE MOVEMENTS...!!
ヒュン
HYUN (WHIZZ)
ヒュン
HYUN
ヒュン
HYUN
I SEE NOTHING BUT THREE ACTUAL COURT LADIES!!
↑SEAL, BEING THE THREE COURT LADIES ALL BY HIMSELF.
HOW IN THE WORLD DID HE LEARN THAT...!?
ヒュッ
HYU
ピタ
PITA (STOP)
HEH HEH HEH...
ISN'T IT OBVIOUS? I TRAINED ...
...WITH THE REAL...
...THREE COURT LADIES!!!
NO...! CAN IT BE TRUE!?

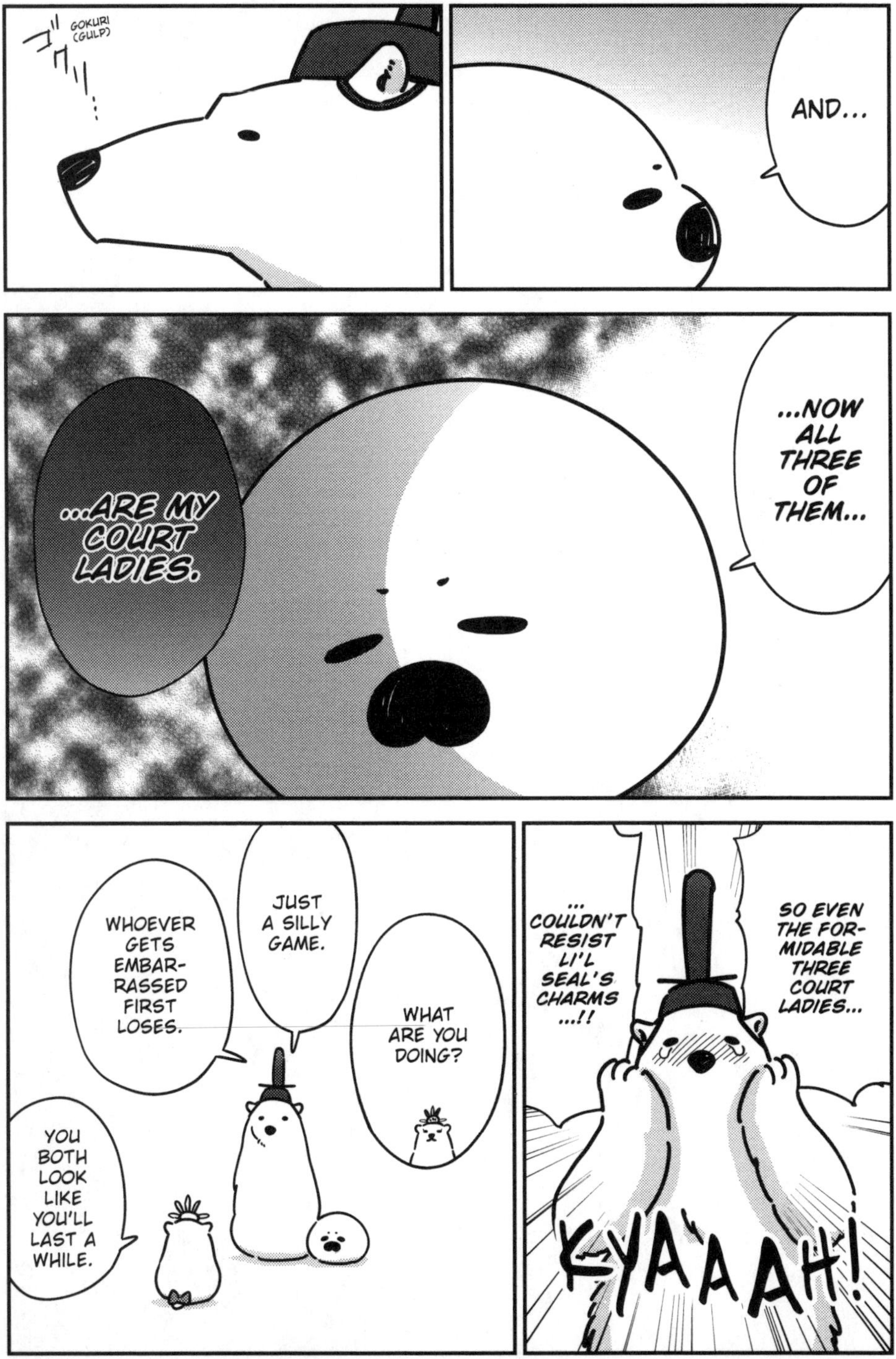

AND...
ゴクリ
GOKURI (GULP)
...NOW ALL THREE OF THEM...
...ARE MY COURT LADIES.
SO EVEN THE FOR-MIDABLE THREE COURT LADIES...
...COULDN'T RESIST LI'L SEAL'S CHARMS...!!
KYAAAH!
WHAT ARE YOU DOING?
JUST A SILLY GAME.
WHOEVER GETS EMBAR-RASSED FIRST LOSES.
YOU BOTH LOOK LIKE YOU'LL LAST A WHILE.

CHERRY BLOSSOMS AT NIGHT

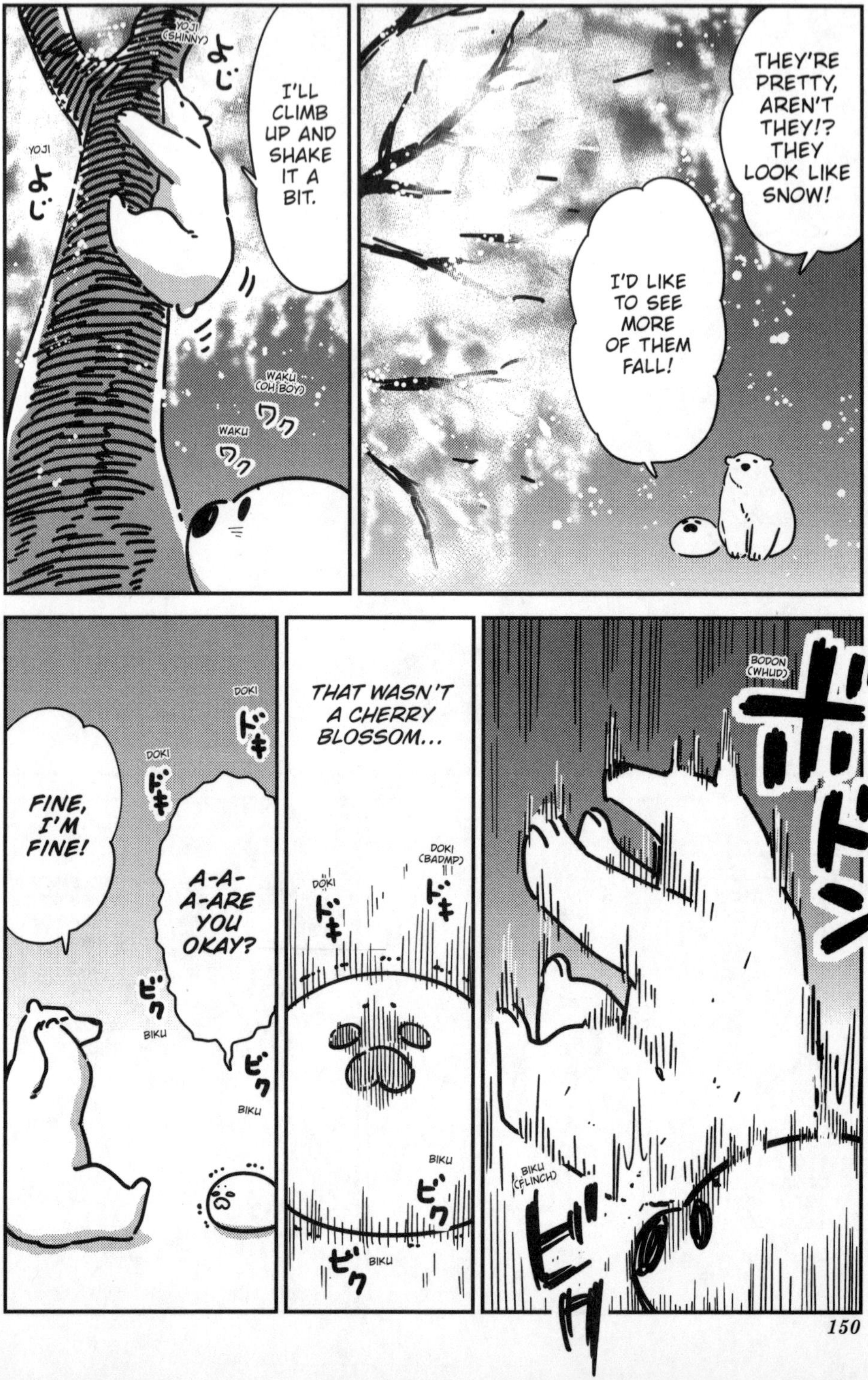
THEY'RE PRETTY, AREN'T THEY!? THEY LOOK LIKE SNOW!
I'D LIKE TO SEE MORE OF THEM FALL!
YOJI (SHINNY) よじ
I'LL CLIMB UP AND SHAKE IT A BIT.
YOJI よじ
WAKU (OH BOY) ワク
WAKU ワク
BODON (WHUD) ボドン
BIKU (FLINCH) ビク
THAT WASN'T A CHERRY BLOSSOM...
DOKI (BADMP) ドキ
DOKI ドキ
...
BIKU ビク
BIKU ビク
DOKI ドキ
DOKI ドキ
A-A-A-ARE YOU OKAY?
FINE, I'M FINE!
ビク BIKU
ビク BIKU

~~CARP~~ SEAL STREAMERS

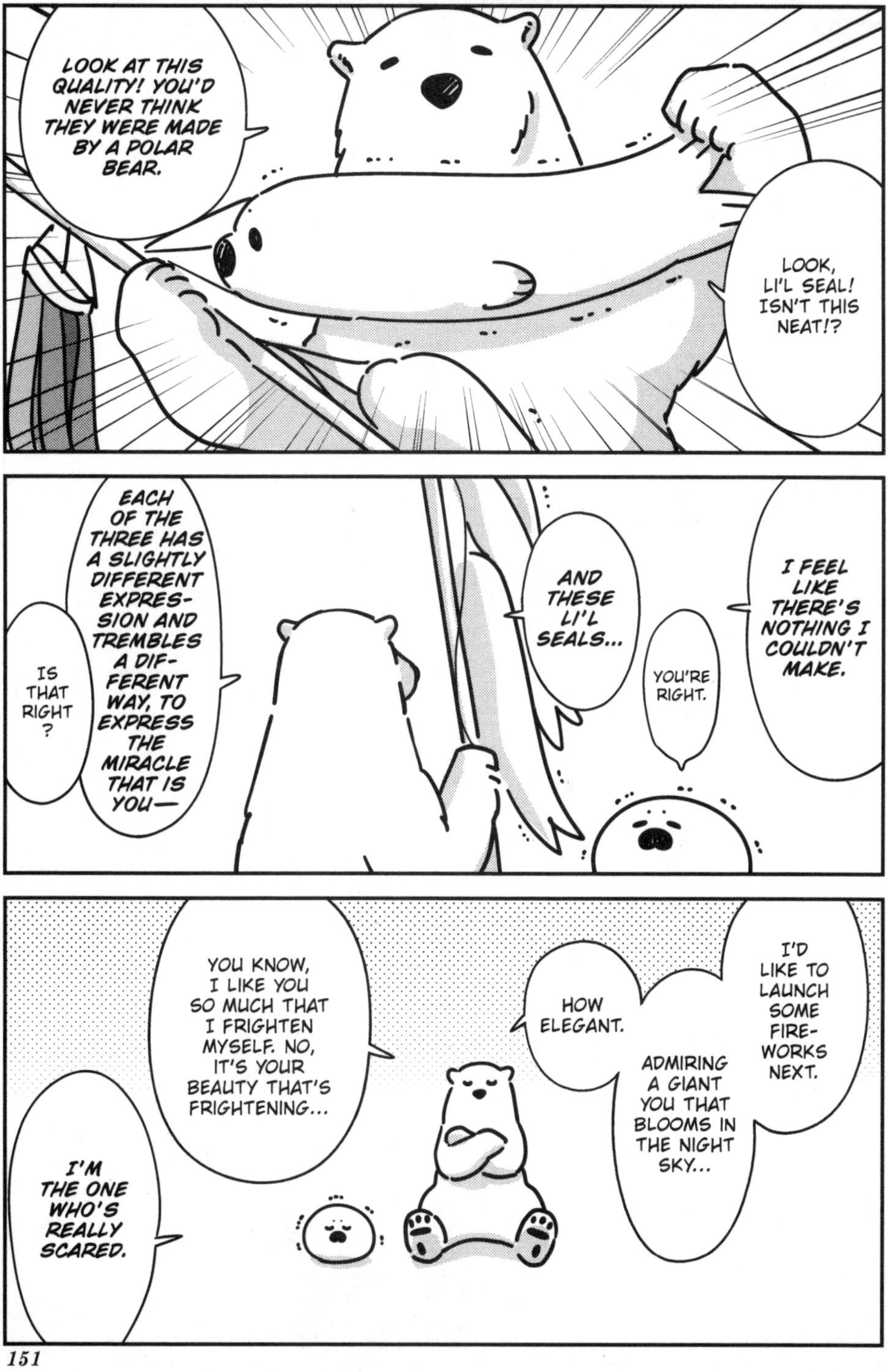
LOOK, LI'L SEAL! ISN'T THIS NEAT!?
LOOK AT THIS QUALITY! YOU'D NEVER THINK THEY WERE MADE BY A POLAR BEAR.
I FEEL LIKE THERE'S NOTHING I COULDN'T MAKE.
YOU'RE RIGHT.
AND THESE LI'L SEALS...
EACH OF THE THREE HAS A SLIGHTLY DIFFERENT EXPRES-SION AND TREMBLES A DIF-FERENT WAY, TO EXPRESS THE MIRACLE THAT IS YOU—
IS THAT RIGHT?
I'D LIKE TO LAUNCH SOME FIRE-WORKS NEXT.
HOW ELEGANT.
ADMIRING A GIANT YOU THAT BLOOMS IN THE NIGHT SKY...
YOU KNOW, I LIKE YOU SO MUCH THAT I FRIGHTEN MYSELF. NO, IT'S YOUR BEAUTY THAT'S FRIGHTENING...
I'M THE ONE WHO'S REALLY SCARED.

HYDRANGEAS

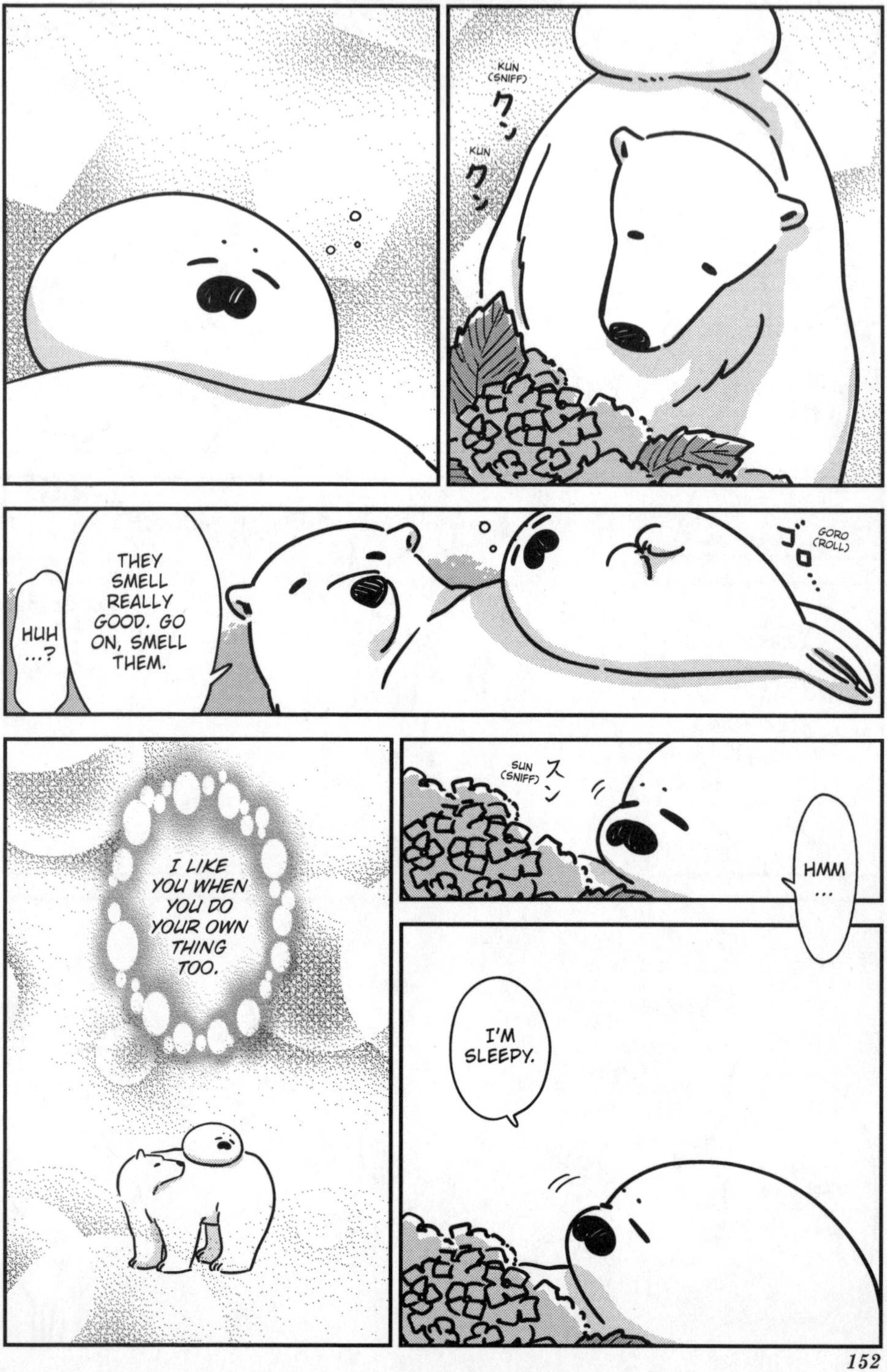
KUN (SNIFF)
クン
KUN
クン
ゴロ
GORO (ROLL)
...
THEY SMELL REALLY GOOD. GO ON, SMELL THEM.
HUH ...?
SUN (SNIFF)
スン
HMM ...
I'M SLEEPY.
I LIKE YOU WHEN YOU DO YOUR OWN THING TOO.

THE STAR FESTIVAL

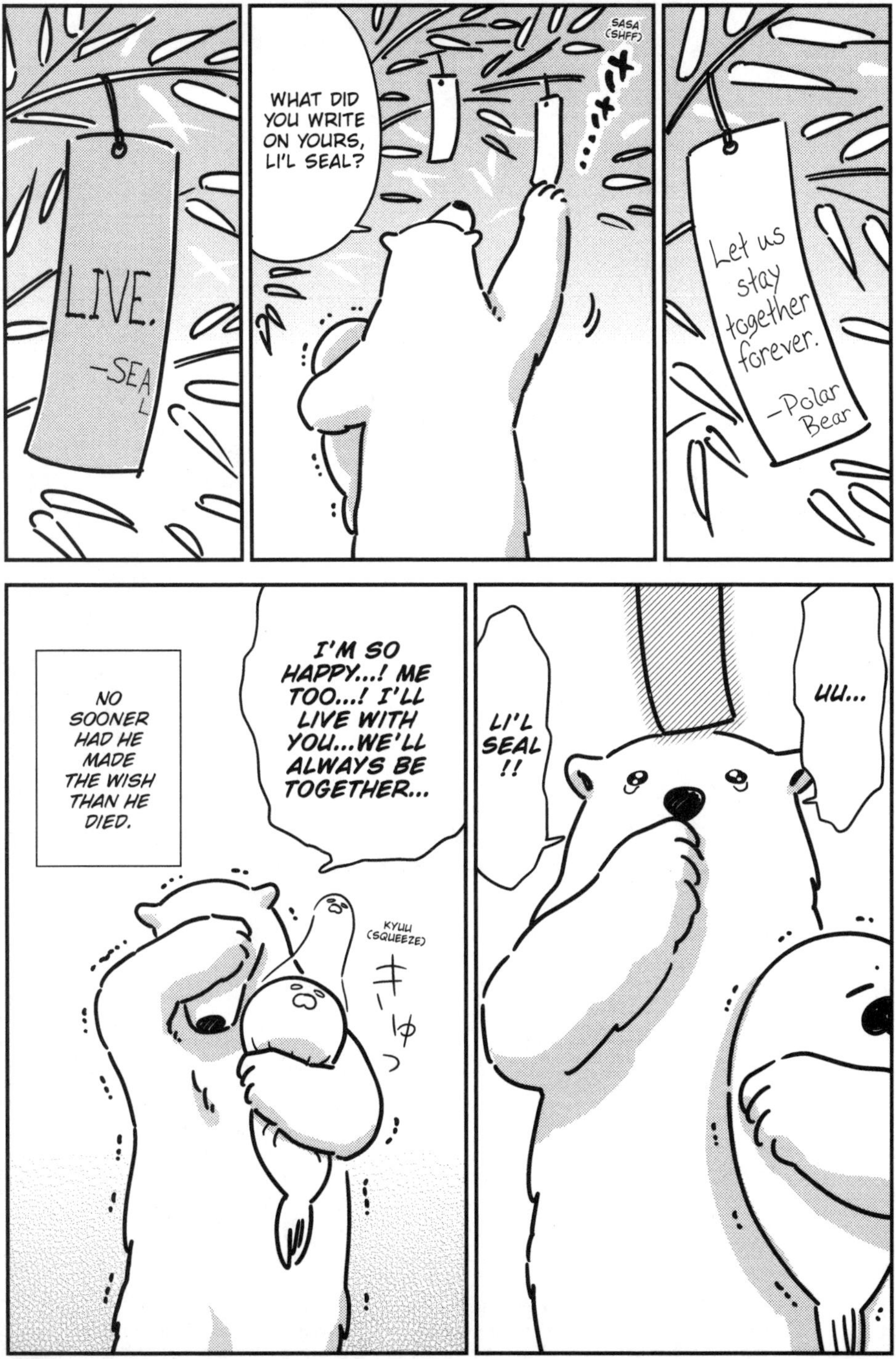
Let us stay together forever.
—Polar Bear
SASA (SHFF)
...!!
WHAT DID YOU WRITE ON YOURS, LI'L SEAL?
LIVE.
—SEAL
UU...
LI'L SEAL !!
I'M SO HAPPY...! ME TOO...! I'LL LIVE WITH YOU...WE'LL ALWAYS BE TOGETHER...
NO SOONER HAD HE MADE THE WISH THAN HE DIED.
KYUU (SQUEEZE)

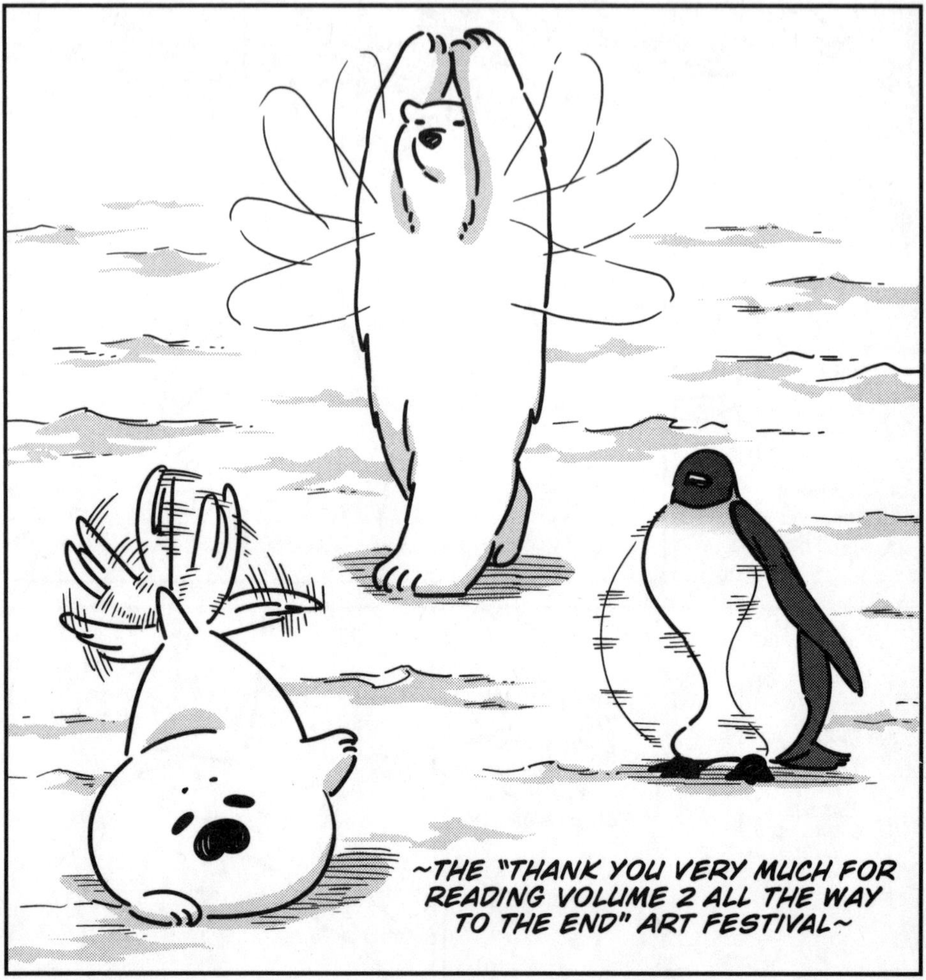
~THE "THANK YOU VERY MUCH FOR READING VOLUME 2 ALL THE WAY TO THE END" ART FESTIVAL~

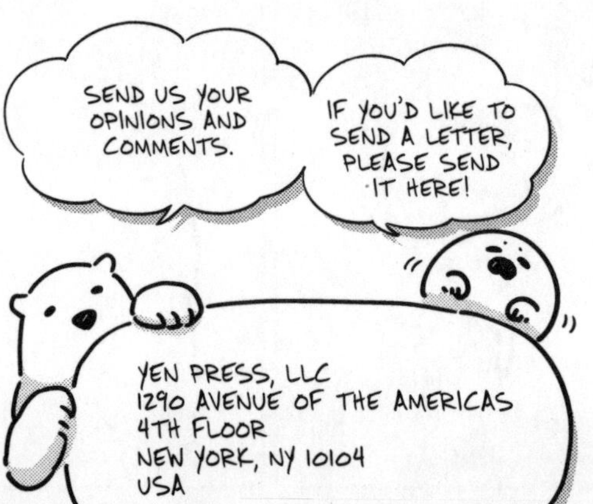
IF YOU'D LIKE TO SEND A LETTER, PLEASE SEND IT HERE!
SEND US YOUR OPINIONS AND COMMENTS.
YEN PRESS, LLC
1290 AVENUE OF THE AMERICAS
4TH FLOOR
NEW YORK, NY 10104
USA

AUTHOR'S NOTE

Koromo

I LIKE THE OCEAN AND
THE THINGS THAT LIVE IN
IT. I DON'T KNOW MUCH
ABOUT THE OCEAN OR ITS
CREATURES, AND I DON'T
SWIM, BUT I LOVE LOOKING
AT IT. IN MY PREVIOUS
LIFE, I MAY HAVE BEEN
SOMETHING...SOMETHING
THAT LIVED IN THE OCEAN...
LIKE PLANKTON MAYBE.

THE FRONT COVER, CONTINUED ①

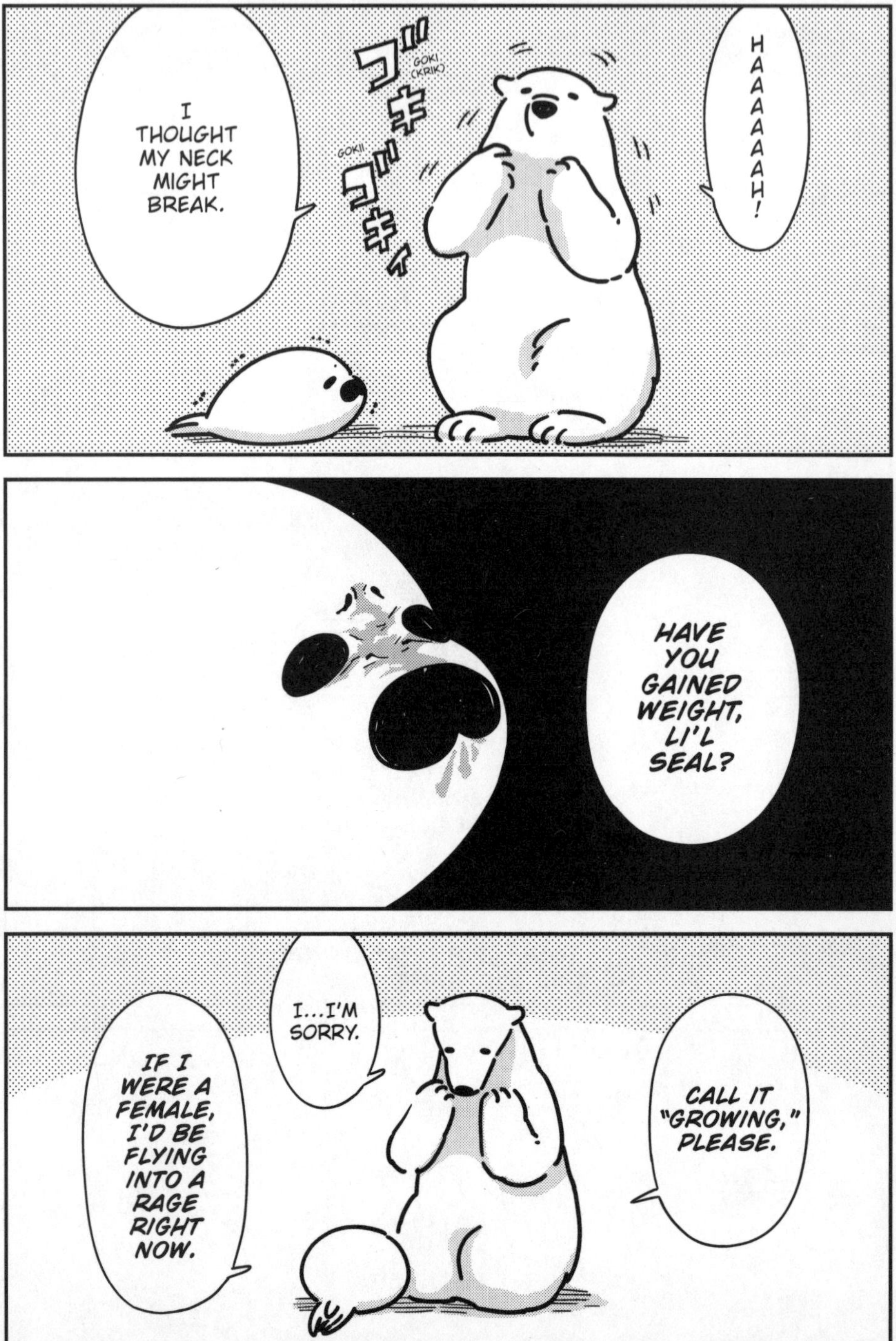
HAAAAAAAH!
ゴキ
GOKI (KRIK)
ゴキィ
GOKI!
I THOUGHT MY NECK MIGHT BREAK.
HAVE YOU GAINED WEIGHT, LI'L SEAL?
CALL IT "GROWING," PLEASE.
I...I'M SORRY.
IF I WERE A FEMALE, I'D BE FLYING INTO A RAGE RIGHT NOW.

THE FRONT COVER, CONTINUED ②

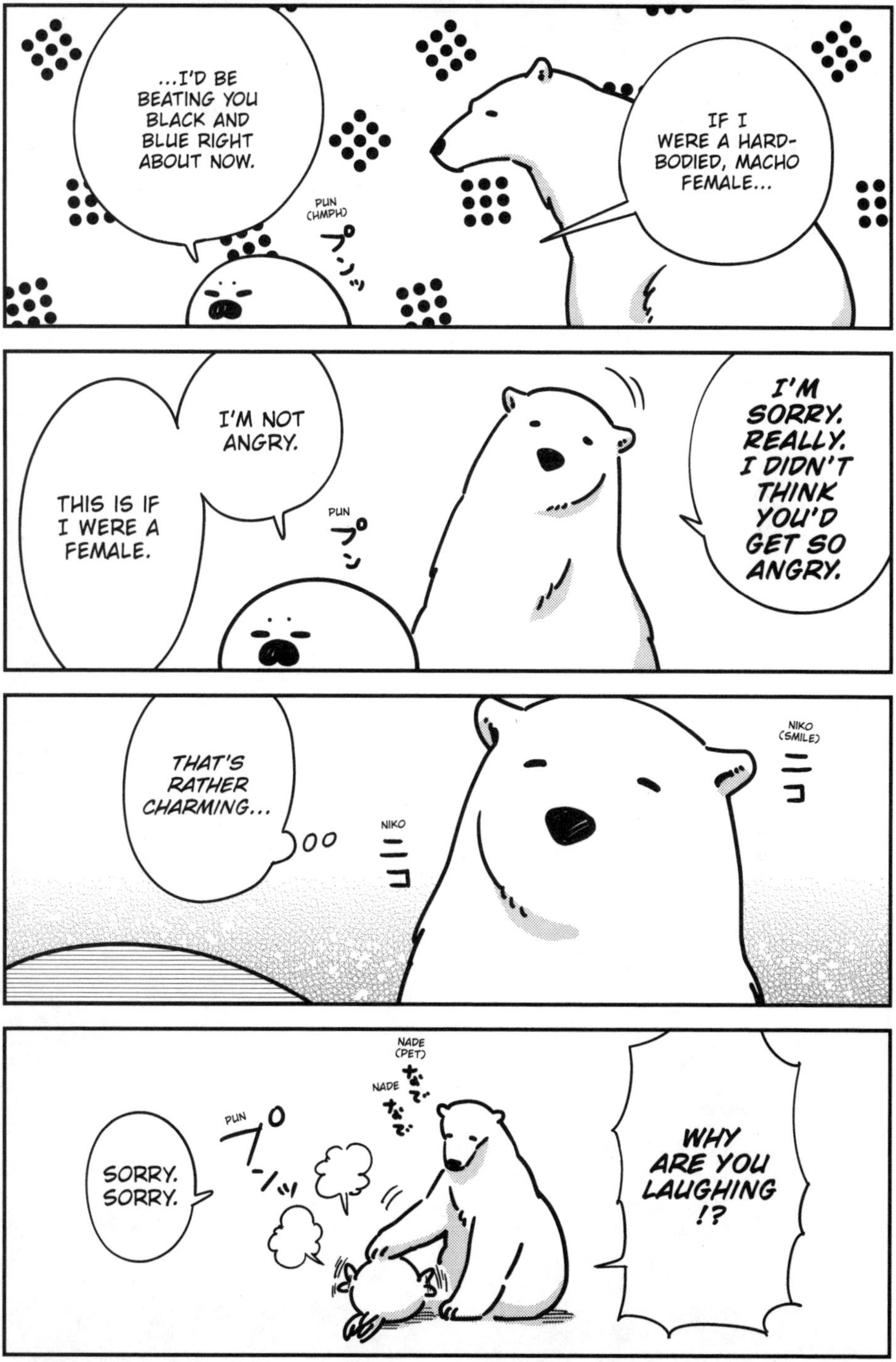
IF I WERE A HARD-BODIED, MACHO FEMALE...
PUN (HMPH)
プンッ
...I'D BE BEATING YOU BLACK AND BLUE RIGHT ABOUT NOW.
I'M SORRY. REALLY. I DIDN'T THINK YOU'D GET SO ANGRY.
PUN
プン
I'M NOT ANGRY.
THIS IS IF I WERE A FEMALE.
NIKO (SMILE)
ニコ
NIKO
ニコ
THAT'S RATHER CHARMING...
WHY ARE YOU LAUGHING !?
NADE (PET)
なで
NADE
なで
PUN
SORRY. SORRY.

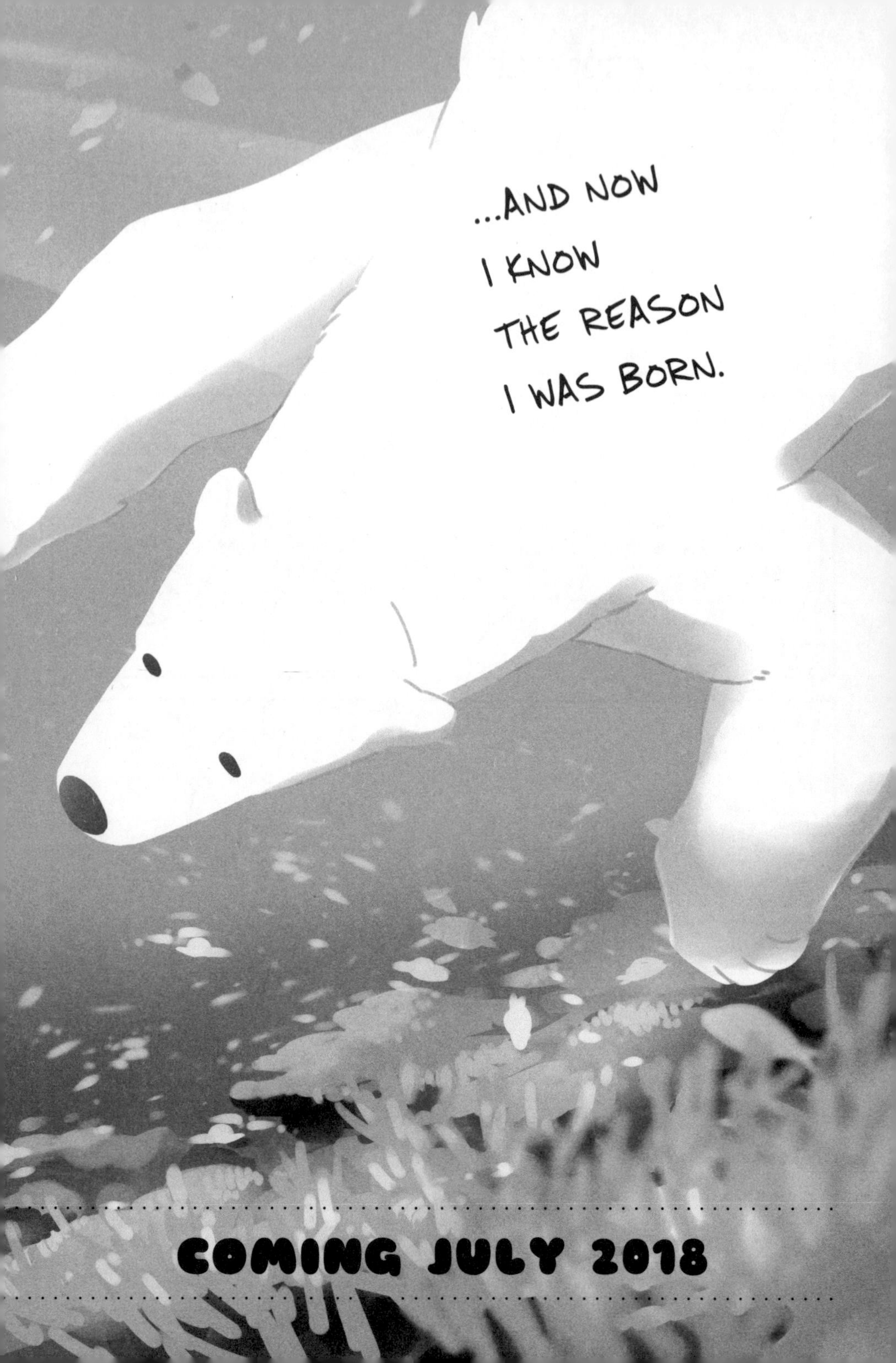
...AND NOW
I KNOW
THE REASON
I WAS BORN.
COMING JULY 2018

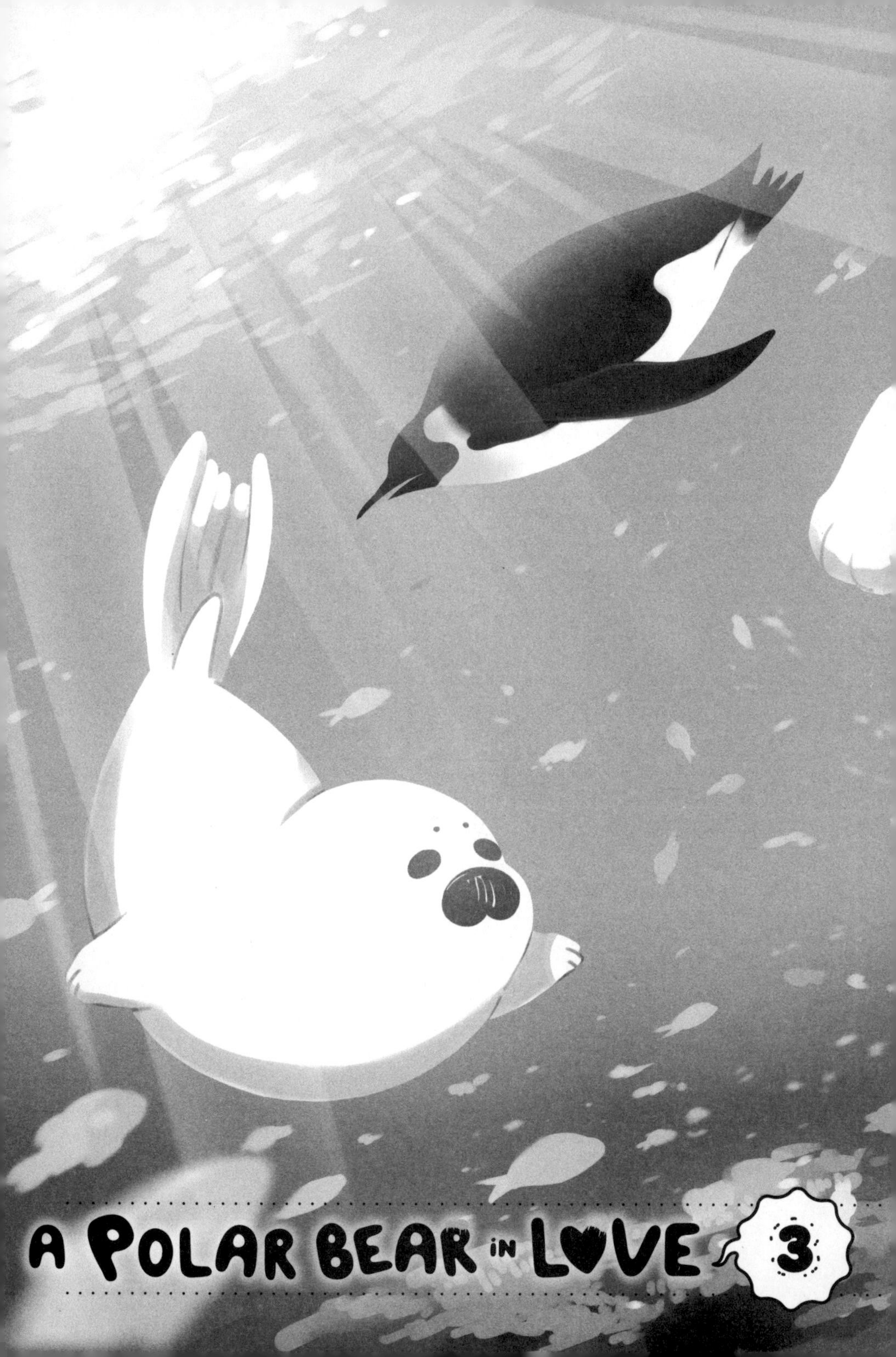
A POLAR BEAR in LOVE
3

TRANSLATION NOTES

PAGE 15
Sweet steamed buns, or *manjuu*, are made with wheat flour and filled with sweetened red bean paste.

PAGE 84
The "meat on a skewer" is actually an umbrella. This is known as an *ai-ai gasa*, or "shared umbrella." It's a very common doodle in Japan, and it's used to show that the named couple is in a relationship (although it's usually written by someone else in order to tease said couple and can also be drawn as a private doodle by people who *wish* they were in a relationship with the other named party).

In the Japanese version, the meat on a skewer was "*oden* on a stick," with oden being a kind of soy sauce–based hot pot.

PAGE 148
The Doll Festival, also known as "Girls' Day," is celebrated on March 3. Families with daughters set up very elaborate sets of dolls at some point in February and take them down on March 4. The characters are dressed as the dolls: Mr. Polar Bear is the emperor, Li'l Miss Polar Bear is the empress, and Seal is the three court ladies.

PAGE 153
The Star Festival, or *Tanabata*, is on July 7. Legend has it that the stars Vega (Orihime) and Altair (Hikoboshi) are lovers, and they're allowed to meet each other just once every year, on this day. People write wishes on slips of paper and tie them to bamboo branches in the hope that the stars will grant them.

Hello! This is YOTSUBA!

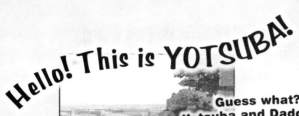

Guess what? Guess what? Yotsuba and Daddy just moved here from waaaay over there!

And Yotsuba met these nice people next door and made new friends to play with!

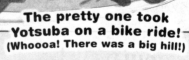

The pretty one took Yotsuba on a bike ride!
(Whoooa! There was a big hill!)

And Ena's a good drawer!
(Almost as good as Yotsuba!)

And their mom always gives Yotsuba ice cream!
(Yummy!)

And...
And...
OHHHH!

A POLAR BEAR in LOVE 2

Koromo

TRANSLATION: **Taylor Engel** ❤ LETTERING: **Lys Blakeslee**

KOI SURU SHIROKUMA Vol.2
©Koromo 2016
First published in Japan in 2016 by KADOKAWA CORPORATION, Tokyo. English translation rights arranged with KADOKAWA CORPORATION, Tokyo through TUTTLE-MORI AGENCY, INC., Tokyo.

English translation © 2018 by Yen Press, LLC

Yen Press
1290 Avenue of the Americas
New York, NY 10104

Visit us at yenpress.com
facebook.com/yenpress
twitter.com/yenpress
yenpress.tumblr.com
instagram.com/yenpress

First Yen Press Edition: February 2018

Yen Press is an imprint of Yen Press, LLC.
The Yen Press name and logo are trademarks of Yen Press, LLC.

The publisher is not responsible for websites (or their content) that are not owned by the publisher.

Library of Congress Control Number: 2017949438

ISBNs: 978-0-316-44173-5 (paperback)
978-0-316-44174-2 (ebook)

10 9 8 7 6 5 4 3

WOR

Printed in the United States of America